Paris
Spring

JAMES NAUGHTIE, who presented *Today*
on BBC Radio 4 for twenty-one years,
is a special correspondent for BBC News.
He has written books on politics and
music and published his first novel,
The Madness of July, in 2014. He lives
in Edinburgh and London.

Also by James Naughtie:

The Madness of July

JAMES NAUGHTIE

Paris Spring

HEAD OF ZEUS

First published in the UK in 2016 by Head of Zeus Ltd

This paperback edition first published in the UK in 2016
by Head of Zeus Ltd

9 7 5 3 1 2 4 6 8

A catalogue record for this book is available from the British Library

Paperback ISBN 9781784080211
Ebook ISBN 9781784080181

Typeset by Adrian McLaughlin

Printed and bound by CPI Group (UK) Ltd, Croydon, CR0 4YY

MIX
Paper from
responsible sources
FSC® C020471

Head of Zeus Ltd
Clerkenwell House
45–47 Clerkenwell Green
London EC1R OHT

WWW.HEADOFZEUS.COM

For everyone on the Today programme

The early months of 1968 were a time of conflict and protest around the world. The Vietnam war was dividing the United States, which had half a million men under arms in south-east Asia, and it destroyed a presidency. Lyndon B. Johnson spoke from the White House on 31 March to announce that he was standing down as a candidate for re-election. Five days later, the civil rights leader Martin Luther King was assassinated in Memphis, Tennessee, and violent anger swept through the black ghettoes of America. In eastern Europe, challenges to Communist orthodoxy were alarming the Soviet Union. Throughout the spring, the Soviet-led Warsaw Pact threatened the reforming government in Prague, demanding loyalty to Moscow and reminding the Czechs of the military might that could crush them. West of the Iron Curtain, France was a cauldron of youthful anti-establishment unrest, for which the government of the ageing President Charles de Gaulle was quite unprepared. In the week after Easter, which fell on 14 April, Paris was a city on the brink of an eruption.

ONE

'I've seen you somewhere before.'

Will Flemyng turned his head a little to the left to look at him. 'Who knows?' he said. 'Paris may not be as big as it seems.'

He had watched the man come into the carriage at Solférino metro station and move directly to a place beside him, taking a moment or two to settle. It was Flemyng's usual hour, and he recognized that his companion, who hadn't turned towards him to follow his own question, was not a regular. He could be certain, because the man was memorable. His left shoe seemed to have been built up, he wore old man's trousers and an unlit pipe was pushed into his breast pocket, stem outwards so that it spewed unlit tobacco over his clothes. His navy blazer glistened with age, completing the picture of someone who might be expected to have a decade or two on Flemyng, and he seemed stiff with weariness. Yet his face was that of a youngish man, despite his greying hair, and a signet ring on the little finger of his left hand was incongruous, a fleck of gold in the dust. The effect was unsettling, a portrait split in two.

It produced pleasure in Flemyng. He waited for the follow-up, which came as the train slowed down for the next station, the man having turned to face him.

'It may have been at the Salle Pleyel last month. Did you attend the concert with the Gewandhaus? And perhaps the reception afterwards?' His English was accented but accurate and flowing, the words delivered at a practised pace, and his gaze was direct. Flemyng shook his head.

At the next stop the carriage thinned out quickly. The National Assembly was somewhere above. 'So many civil servants,' Flemyng said, and smiled. No reply.

They reached Concorde, and Flemyng rose. 'Someone else, I'm afraid,' he said. 'But, who knows, we may see each other again on the metro. It's like that, don't you find?' The man nodded as Flemyng stepped on to the platform, and he gently tipped a hand from his knee to say goodbye.

On most mornings, Flemyng stopped for a coffee at a corner café on rue du Faubourg St-Honoré but today he walked directly to his office. The last days of April held the promise of summer and a stirring breeze with the dampness of coming rain seemed to brighten the streets. The sweepers had left pavements clean, and the trickle of water in the roadside gutters was a clear stream. Flemyng savoured the natural smells and sounds of the city. Bread from the café, the faint scent of blossom drifting from the trees over the wall, long trails of cigarette smoke from the workmen outside the apartments across the way and always the horns blaring down the street. Paris appeared content. But as the high wooden gate opened for him and he turned from the pavement into the embassy courtyard, he could see the security barricades being hauled into place at the Élysée Palace, a hundred yards away. The guard had been doubled at every entrance.

May Day promised thunderstorms.

Within five minutes he had reached his eyrie on the third floor, and before going to his desk he pushed open Craven's door, giving a light knock as he stuck his head inside. 'Freddy – can I see you, in ten minutes or so?'

The room was filled with smoke, with yellowing curls on the ceiling, and through the fog a warm and gravelly voice welcomed him. It was quiet, and musical. 'Be my guest, but give me a hint. A little clue, my boy?'

Flemyng leaned forward through the doorway. 'Well, I've just been picked up.'

*

Wilfred Craven ran a merry ship. Although his office reeked and the walls were drab, the one painting hanging askew, he contrived to give it spirit. A place for confessions and stories, a centre of operations that was also a hidey-hole from the world. A boys' room. Freddy was a joker who rationed the high seriousness in his life, and made a stand against office tedium in the hope of keeping the flame of good humour burning. As an emblem of his regime he'd placed in one corner of his small room a mechanical wooden doll, half life-size – a grinning black figure with lurid painted lips, striped trousers and a patchwork jacket of many colours, who raised his bowler hat with one jerky hand when a glass was removed from the other, in Freddy's case usually filled with Scotch and soda.

His last ambassador, in Vienna, had ordered it out of the embassy, and for a while Craven secreted it in the garage with the rest of his fabled collection of ephemera. There were Victorian theatre bills, shiny boxing gloves from long-gone title fights, a model of HMS *Victory* made from matchsticks because he was a navy man, and the silk stockings of a music-hall star. Even a black ballot box he'd bought in a backstreet in Chicago to remind him of shenanigans, and the doll fitted in. He had brought it out of retirement for the entertainment of his boys in Paris, because they understood his need for the absurd.

Taste didn't come into it. Freddy Craven never wanted to forget the ludicrous things he'd known, sometimes the ones he'd done. He had spotted the doll in a small-town auction in North Carolina and knew that some day it would be a grotesque antique. So he took it home, and it still made him smile.

Flemyng had been picked up. The young man, whom Craven had steered through his first secret forays in the streets of Berlin, had a quick eye and, precociously, the tender touch of a veteran. He would handle the contact delicately. Craven made a rough pile of the books scattered across his desk, crumpled yesterday's newspaper into the bin and split the foil on a new packet of cigarettes. He lay back in his chair, grey waterspout hair flopping behind him and a country-check shirt tight over his belly, which was starting to shrink like the rest of him. With an effort, he put his feet on his desk and stretched out. Flemyng.

The good-looking boy had arrived in Vienna green and eager, and with an advantage. Craven came of West Country farming stock and preferred the few youngsters who knew something of rural ways, taking them under his wing. Flemyng's family was a little different, having an estate in Perthshire that covered forest and hill, but there was still a bond. Even as he felt the shadow of illness coming on, Craven found in Flemyng a listener and an outlet for old enthusiasms lived out on the front line, and often in the darkness beyond. They would talk for long nights, Flemyng drinking from the well of stories that Freddy wanted to pass on before they disappeared with him and became folklore. And it was on the orders of Freddy in Vienna that Flemyng had taken to the lanes behind St Stephen's Cathedral on a November night five years before and crawled back to the embassy slashed from neck to right breast with a knife wound that nearly killed him.

Craven was coughing when Flemyng knocked on his door a few minutes later, and took a moment to recover.

'Apologies, my boy. One of my bad days, I can tell.' He smiled.

'I'm sorry, Freddy. Water?'

He shook his head. 'I want to hear it all.'

Flemyng sat between him and the window. He was dark-haired and slim, dressed without ostentation and with natural style. His shoes were polished but his hair cut longer than anyone in the embassy except Craven, who was past all that. On this morning his shirt was white, and his tie was a soft green. The jacket of his grey suit hung over the chair, and he put his hands behind his head.

'I was spoken to, on the metro.'

'Did you get on at your usual station?'

'Yes. Rue du Bac, at my regular time.'

'A man?'

Flemyng said, 'East German, pretty sure. Not Russian anyway. We spoke in English. He mentioned the Leipzig orchestra and wondered if we'd encountered each other before, maybe at a party after a concert. I said no, which was true, and that was all.'

But more than enough, said Craven, who promised to get an up-to-date book of photographs from the library so that they could look for a match. 'Did you get the feeling that he wanted a meeting?'

'No doubt of it,' Flemyng said. 'There was hardly any pretence.'

Craven was making circles with both hands on the desk, tracing patterns on the leather. 'Let's consider, just for the sake of it, the possibility that it was a genuine inquiry, that came to him from a chance collision – that he did think he'd seen you somewhere before.'

'Come on,' said Flemyng. 'He knew what he was doing, and I felt it. He was staring straight ahead when he started the conversation, and he'll have known that I understood his purpose.'

Freddy Craven smiled. 'So?'

'I'll make sure I meet him again. I said we might bump into each other on the metro, and he'll know what I meant. I wanted to put it to you so that we play by the rules without misunderstandings. Advice?'

It took Craven some effort to stand up, and he edged round the desk, leaning on one hand for support. 'The timing's interesting, wouldn't you say?'

He looked through the window, with a hand on the back of Flemyng's chair. 'We know this place is heading for trouble. Wemyss was murmuring at the ambassador's last night about revolution, although I'm not sure I believe in that any more. The Movement of 22 March – come on. Sounds like some South American fandango, and I've seen many a flop in my time. But you tell me the Sorbonne's boiling. The unions can get everybody on the streets in May if they want to, as we know. They think the old man will panic.' He waved towards the gardens of the Élysée beyond the walls, the high trees dipping in the wind. 'I don't, but they probably think it's worth a try. Do you?'

'There's stirring,' Flemyng said. 'They think that if students can do it in Poland, they can do it here. Warsaw, Prague, why not Paris? They're terribly serious, and I think there's something else. The London demonstration. They think they're more anti-war than we are, and it embarrassed them. They hadn't thought they'd see police horses charging in London. They think they can do better.'

'Maybe they will, maybe they will,' Freddy Craven said.

He put a hand on Flemyng's shoulder and spoke quietly. 'So why is now a good moment to make a play at you?'

Flemyng said, 'It depends on whether or not I'm a target. Is he a buyer or a seller?'

'Exactly,' said Craven. 'And there's only one way to find out.'

Flemyng said he still lived by one of Freddy's first pieces of advice in Vienna – 'never rush, unless you're on the run'.

So he would do nothing on the next day, and come to work by a different route. The following day, a repeat performance by another way. But on the third day, he'd catch the metro at his usual time at rue du Bac and sit in the same carriage, as near as possible to the seat he'd occupied that morning. 'And we'll let things take their course.'

Craven said he'd have the photographs called down from the attic archive for the afternoon, so they should rendezvous for tea. 'I have a little lunch lined up in the 7th and I'll take a stroll through the Sorbonne afterwards.'

Flemyng watched him struggle to the desk, putting all his weight on one hand as he swivelled round, and a gust of sadness swept over him. Freddy should have been in retirement by now, and the Paris posting was an indulgence all round. A long-service medal, with wine list attached. He was loved, could still run a sure-footed operation from his desk, and represented a story that Flemyng's masters wanted to keep alive, against the odds. Because Craven was dying, and everyone knew it. He concealed as many of the signs as he could, but the decline had been obvious since illness had taken hold in Vienna. First his complexion had darkened to a deeper red, sounding the first alarm bell, and then, in the course of a few months, he'd whitened and started to wither. He still mounted displays of his old, irreverent style – he'd worn sandals at a reception for a parliamentary delegation the previous week, and been the happy talk of the embassy for three days – but these moments were throwbacks, no longer the real thing. His days were on the wane.

'I can see the old reaper getting his hood on,' he'd told Flemyng the previous week. 'He's wondering when to come for me.' Like so many of his jokes, it was half true.

But when they sat together that afternoon to look at the picture books, Craven was sparkling. There was a game on. 'Let's forget the Soviets. You say he was German, so I've got them here. Lined up in all their grey glory.'

It took Flemyng only five minutes to trawl through the gallery of faces, some from the mugshots squirrelled out of the East German trade mission in a shared operation with the Americans the year before, and others snatched by Craven's own favourite photographer at public events and gatherings of the diplomatic corps where the expressions were more cheerful, thanks to drink. But none of them reminded Flemyng in any way of the strange young man on the train, his youthful face imprisoned in the body and the garb of a much older man. 'He's not here.'

They looked at the pages of Czechs and Poles, and Craven insisted they checked the Russians. A run through the West Germans in case Flemyng had misunderstood. Nothing.

'He's new,' said Craven. 'Which gives us another interesting question. Has he been sent here with you in mind?'

They couldn't know, he said, and it would be a waste of time to theorize. So why didn't they have a drink? They did, Craven playing his trick with the dumb waiter and Flemyng reminding himself that there was no chance of the bowler-hatted doll surviving Freddy, because no one else would take it on. Might he need to save the thing, and have it for his own? He could hide it at home in Scotland, and no one would know.

The thought had a hallucinatory effect. Flemyng found himself drifting away.

'I'll be here all day on Friday.' Craven was talking. 'I'll wait as long as it takes, but come to me as soon as you can.' He was smiling, a glass in his hand and the light back in his eyes. 'My last game, Will, who knows?'

When Flemyng had left the room, and he was alone, the old man slapped his desk with delight.

*

On the platform for Line 12 at rue du Bac, Flemyng recognized a number of regulars who took the metro just before nine o'clock each day, and stood in his usual place. He took a seat in the third carriage from the front, as he had three days earlier. When the train slowed down for Solférino, Flemyng became aware of his nerves for the first time. He felt his stomach muscles twitch and he was surprised at the way his grip tightened on the briefcase on his lap, which he had emptied for the journey to work. Inside himself he was aware of a hollowness like the rush of vertigo in his legs on the edge of a drop.

The train stopped, and the fourth man to enter the train was the German.

He took a seat next to a window, diagonally across from Flemyng in a set of four, and their knees touched for a moment as he eased into his place and put his black felt hat on his lap. The carriage was full, and smoky. Flemyng smiled, aware that the other man's nerves were likely to be in the same state as his own. He lived for such moments, and knew the tension they brought with them.

The man read his newspaper and his expression showed nothing. He didn't speak. As they approached Concorde, he glanced up at Flemyng and held his eye for the first time. Stay on the train.

For the next ten minutes, Flemyng watched him closely. He wore the same clothes, he'd stretched the foot in front of him as far as he could and, once again, he'd stuck his pipe upside down in his pocket. Strands of tobacco poked out and there were streaks of soot on his blazer. His trousers were grey and baggy, and too long, with deep turn-ups that seemed to have picked up litter along the way. He was now looking away again. Flemyng knew the inspection would come later.

They sat silently until the train reached Pigalle and, without fuss, the man stood and took three steps towards the sliding doors, revealing the hint of a limp. Flemyng stood behind him and they left the train in step. He slowed down to let a gap open up between them and followed him along Boulevard de Clichy, checking as he walked that no one else was in their wake. Nothing. Two young women, roughly painted and bored, got up from an iron bench as they passed and one of them spread her arms in a fake stretch, but they were alert enough to know that there was no business on offer. Flemyng nodded easily at them, as if to suggest that on another day it might have been different, and the younger of the two waved cheerfully over her shoulder as they turned away. The German entered a café on the next corner without looking back, and Flemyng followed, ducking under a ragged parasol at the door and approaching his table against the far wall with no word of explanation, pulling back a chair and sitting down. He slipped his jacket off.

'Good morning,' he said. 'We meet again.'

For the first time, the man smiled. 'As I knew we would. I am pleased to see you, Mr Flemyng. My name is Kristof.'

As they shook hands, Flemyng thought how Freddy would enjoy the absurdity of their politeness.

'Which of us asked for this meeting?' said Kristof, smiling. 'An interesting question.'

'Let me take responsibility.' He laughed. His face lightened and his eyes were bright. For the first time, he seemed in charge. His head was up, his hands high in a gesture of welcome. The years fell away.

Flemyng said, 'Why?' Once again he felt a hollowness in his legs, a tightening in his gut. Fear, his familiar companion and friend.

'That is quite simple,' Kristof said, as he prepared his thunderbolt. 'I can tell you something very interesting about your brother.'

TWO

Flemyng knew immediately that he would tell Freddy Craven only part of the story when he got back to the embassy. The man called Kristof was leading him on a journey where he understood they were bound to share secrets.

'I assume you mean my younger brother,' he said to Kristof, taking his first step into the conversation and knowing, as a result, that he could no longer turn back.

'Abel, of course,' the German said. 'Yes.'

Kristof leaned against the wall in his first gesture of relaxation. With a few words, they were bound together.

Flemyng had hunched forward on the table, working hard to conceal his astonishment at Kristof's opening play. The German, by contrast, now took on an attitude of confidence, his head touching the shining gilt frame of a mirror behind him that reflected Flemyng's anxiety, the long lines on his face deepened by the low lighting as he tried to find an explanation for the figure in front of him. Kristof removed the pipe from his pocket and produced a pouch. He dug into the black tobacco with a stubby finger, and through his steady preparations for a smoke turned into a picture of normality. Confident and methodical. There was no rush, no obvious nervousness in his movements, and he spoke in the same soft, deliberate way.

Flemyng's shock had settled him.

'To begin at the beginning,' he said, 'I should say that I met your brother here in Paris, in his days with the Americans. In their embassy, as you know. Our encounter was on neutral ground, of course. As people with no embassy – no *identity* you might say – we are always at the mercy of our friends. In my case, my Moscow comrades. So hospitable.' He raised his coffee cup.

'We were introduced, but spoke only a few words. This was almost two years ago, and he will not remember my name. You will understand that it is not one I use any more. Not today, anyway.'

He was playing with a matchbox, and Flemyng noticed his boyishness. His skin was pale without any obvious blemishes and his face narrowed to a pointed chin that gave him an elfin look when he smiled and his mouth turned up. He was certainly the younger of the two, but it was hard to tell by how much. As he packed the rest of the tobacco into his pipe, he brushed the remains of his last smoke from his jacket and smoothed himself down.

'I know his trade,' he said. 'Ours, I should say.'

He put a match to his pipe, sending up an orange flare and then a small cloud of smoke. 'Mr Flemyng, I may be here to help. Who can tell? We must give it time.'

He pulled on his pipe. 'A friend.'

He let the smoke drift over the table. 'And if we do become friends, you may be able to help me.'

Flemyng used the mirror to check the room. A middle-aged couple sat in one corner engrossed in each other, and only one other table was occupied, by a young man who had his head on the table, his face turned away. One dangling arm almost touched the floor and he seemed to be asleep. The waiter clattered with cups in his little sink, and from the bar he watched a young woman who had taken a table on the pavement outside and sat alone. The café was dark inside, but she was illuminated by the morning sun. 'I'll listen,' Flemyng said quietly. 'But I'm afraid I really have nothing to say.'

Kristof shook his head. 'I understand. Now, you don't have to. I promise. Later, when we meet again.'

There was silence for a moment. Flemyng held his position, arms on the table. He gave no sign, letting Kristof set the pace.

Abel, the kid brother he'd known all his life, was in his mind. He'd seen him soon after Abel left Paris to go home to America, relaxed and dressed in European style, although his black hair was cut unfashionably short, in deference to the rule in his office. The three years that separated the brothers seemed to Flemyng by then to have dwindled to nothing. Their lives, so similar on different continents, had forced them to accept that secrets would always divide them, but on that one happy weekend, when they visited some of their mother's old haunts up the Hudson Valley, they had been able to close the distance between them for a few days. It was exhilarating, because they knew it couldn't last.

'I can't speak for the closeness between you,' said Kristof, and Flemyng was momentarily thrown. The German's eyes were on him and he felt as if he had revealed his thoughts and provided him with an unnecessary opening. Reassuring himself that he need not respond, he gave a smile and raised a hand. Kristof continued. 'That is not my business, but I know enough to be sure that there is trust between you. We're trained to know our friends, are we not?'

Flemyng stayed silent, bringing both hands together on the table for the first time. He looked down.

'It is in that spirit that I took the chance of speaking to you, because I'm afraid there is a risk for me, Mr Flemyng. I am not acting under orders, nor on behalf of anyone else.'

His voice had dropped nearly to a whisper, and he leaned in. 'You do believe me?'

Flemyng said, 'I'm listening,' and no more.

'Perhaps you imagine that my people know more than they do,' Kristof said. 'Mostly, we are working in the dark. As you might put it, keeping up appearances.

'However, we have taken some trouble with you. You were noticed in Berlin – very young and, as we soon learned, quite active. You brought a dash of colour to the city. The same in Vienna afterwards. Two short years there, but full of such adventure. It must have been tedious to return to London, and your desk. Which means, Mr Flemyng, that Paris is bursting with promise for you. Life on the street again. *La vie en rose.* And what a time to be here.'

The first question for Flemyng was whether the speech had been rehearsed. Kristof's English was strongly accented, but his grammar was disciplined enough to hint at pedantry, and he had a natural flow that suggested time in London. With that skill, in the library and on the street, his people would prize him. He concluded that Kristof had confidence: he knew what he wanted to say, but it was not a performance that any longer felt manufactured and practised, but mature. He was comfortable with his own voice. The shabby uniform that he wore was still a mystery – why try to conceal a bright personality? – but this was a man of purpose. He saw that Kristof, though he spoke of risk, had shown no flicker of nerves.

'You may be wondering why I am proceeding in this roundabout way,' he said.

Flemyng chose not to answer. He smiled for the first time, as if to say that Kristof's tactics were his own affair. But he knew that the explanation was coming, and that the first light might break on their strange encounter.

Kristof said he wanted Flemyng to know that he recognized in him a spirit like his own. 'The difference is that yours can flower. You will savour this city, let it sweep you up. The parties and the wine. The ladies. Mine is a life that is altogether duller.'

Flemyng had been trained to listen. 'Give 'em time,' old Tyson used to say to his boys when they were at the Fort, 'always give 'em time.' The training stuck with him. He wouldn't break the flow.

With Kristof bending forward, waiting for a question or a protest, he did nothing. Waited.

'I was right about you,' the German said. 'I asked myself first if you would decline my approach. Then, if you allowed me to talk – would you charm me, try to turn the tables from the start. And here you are, saying nothing and ready to give me my chance.'

Although he spoke of time – and Flemyng was determined to wait – the opening exchanges had produced an atmosphere that ensured the pace would quicken. Flemyng had noticed that Kristof was speaking to him as an equal, and, in acknowledging his summons to a meeting without complaint or artificial surprise, Flemyng had declared himself open for business. There might be no deal, but he wanted to listen. So the two professionals prepared to take the next steps, each aware that they were going to move fast.

'I knew of Abel before I met him,' Kristof said, 'and I should say that at that time I knew nothing of you. I was not aware of your existence, wherever you were. I was in Paris, and my people noticed your brother. Of course they did, because he was unusual.'

Flemyng said nothing, but his expression was encouraging. He had every interest in hearing Kristof's story.

'A naturalized American, not home-born, working for them

in our world? Joining in the game? My people hadn't heard of such a thing. Our American friends are so careful. But there he was, tucked up in the fourth floor of their embassy with the others, and as busy as a bee.'

The conversation had entered a different phase, and there was only a brief pause before Flemyng asked, 'Where did you meet?'

The gauntlet picked up, Kristof smiled.

'You must realize that I am with my country's trade mission. It's all we have, as you know. One day, perhaps, an embassy. For now, we shelter with comrades, as you understand. We are hiding in their skirts, you would say, as I might be in London. One of the spies on Highgate Hill, you know.' His face had brightened with enjoyment.

'I was invited to a reception, nothing more exciting than that. Routine. Bastille Day at the Quai d'Orsay. The Americans usually avoid us, you understand, because officially – by the book – we don't exist. But on this occasion I had a handshake and a few words. Of course, I had to report my observations.'

In reconstructing the conversation later, Flemyng was surprised at the calm he had managed to hold when he realized where Kristof's story was leading him, into the private shadows of his family and the secrets it had to keep. He had expected it some day, but had never yet been confronted by Abel's history outside the circle of hard-sworn colleagues with whom it had to be shared. And, looking back at the scene in the café later, he realized he had known in the first few minutes of the conversation that he was being carried towards a crisis, of a kind that he couldn't predict.

There was every reason for panic. Instead, his mind cooled.

In response to Kristof's statement, he asked, 'And what did you say about him in your report?'

'Very little, at first.'

For a few moments, Flemyng considered Kristof's unlaboured language. His style was conversational and not formal, his cadences natural. A thought had stirred in Flemyng's mind soon after he sat down, and it was now fully formed. This man might have learned his English in a laboratory and polished it on the street, but there was something more, and Flemyng was certain of it. I know something about you, he thought: at some time in your life you have lived with someone who spoke English as a native. A woman? A man? Were you lovers? In Berlin? Or London? He felt a surge of confidence, enough to steady him, having glimpsed something behind the veil that he might grasp and keep.

Kristof saw the change in Flemyng, as if a shadow had lifted from his face.

'As time went by, there was more. Sightings here and there. A contact with a friend of ours, working here in Paris. Gradually, I assembled a picture of your brother.'

'And?' said Flemyng.

'And… I discovered something strange.'

Kristof was rubbing the table with one hand, as if there was a stain that wouldn't disappear. His eyes were down.

'That I need not have bothered with my research,' he said.

The room was quiet. The couple in the corner had left, and the student slept on. The waiter was outside, leaning over the back of a chair at the young girl's table. Flemyng caught the flash of a bright green scarf in the mirror and saw that she was laughing. At his own table Kristof stared at him, with hungry eyes.

'Let me state it again, Mr Flemyng. I discovered that I need not have taken the trouble.'

They were both serious, their faces in shadow, drawn

towards each other so that their heads nearly touched, but Flemyng stayed silent.

'A chance remark from a colleague stuck in my mind, and over many months I learned more about your brother. Much more.'

Flemyng had the ability, so prized by Freddy Craven when he first joined his crew, to conceal feelings of alarm. As he listened to Kristof, his expression didn't change. His eyes were warm, and there were no worry lines on his brow: he was a man who seemed to encourage openness. But Kristof's features had tightened.

'You will have to explain what you mean,' Flemyng said. 'Precisely.'

Kristof was showing signs of stress for the first time. There was no one to hear him; the waiter was well away and the café quiet. But he spoke very softly. The smoothness disappeared, and his voice was rough.

'I will, Mr Flemyng.'

He spent a few moments relighting his pipe before he resumed, and whispered through a cloud of smoke. A shower of sparks settled on his lapels.

'I found out that my people – your enemies – knew your brother. Knew him very well indeed.'

Long afterwards, Flemyng would recall the shiver of the moment and the question that pricked him. A revelation, or a trap? There was no reason to join a dance with a street artist, nothing that compelled him to follow the trail that led to the dark. But he couldn't turn back. His day had started with the promise of adventure, and the satisfaction of controlled excitement that he knew so well. The German had turned confidence into alarm.

He leaned back, discipline kicking in against the steady tide of panic that flowed towards him. 'Since you have mentioned my family, perhaps we should think of this as a personal encounter. Why don't we stop talking in riddles?'

'Because that's our style. Our language,' Kristof said. 'You know it', and he slapped a hand like a teacher calling for order. 'Besides, I don't know the answer to the question that you certainly want to ask me.'

He waved away the waiter, who was holding up a cup to offer them more coffee.

'Mr Flemyng, I can only suggest that we go on a journey. Nothing more. The question is whether we go together, or whether you choose to travel alone. It is a decision for you.' Kristof's head bumped the mirror behind him. Until then, they had moved closer together with each exchange so that their heads almost touched. The conversation had reached a turning point, which they both recognized. For a few moments, there was silence. Kristof's eyes glistened. They were his most attractive feature, and invited attention.

The table shook when Flemyng brought both his hands down, and he was full-voiced for the first time that morning.

'I don't know who you are, only that you've thrown me a crude line about my brother, which is the stupidest thing I've ever heard. You're waiting for me to react to your suggestion. But why should I go on any kind of journey with you?'

'Because you have no choice, Mr Flemyng.'

Kristof rose and pushed the table forward a little to allow himself to ease out. As he slid past Flemyng he leaned down. 'Shall we say in the next week? I'll get a message to you.'

He placed a hand on Flemyng's shoulder, and pressed down as he put weight on the weaker foot that he disguised well. Flemyng was reminded of Freddy and his failing strength. Kristof walked to the door without turning back, and Flemyng watched in the mirror as he opened it. The girl had gone from her place outside, and the sleeping student had disappeared. He saw Kristof turn back towards the metro without looking through the window. When he had gone, the waiter was busying himself in the kitchen, and Flemyng was alone.

He took a folded piece of writing paper from one inside pocket of his jacket and found a pencil in the other. As if responding to a request from the man who had left him, he began to draw. He had a gift. The outline of the hair, the long ears, a straight nose that emphasized the pointed chin beneath it. Shoulders that were lopsided. In a few minutes he'd produced a sketch of a face that was alert, perhaps with a hint of fun, but with eyes that were sad, touched by wistfulness.

His inclination was to assume despair, but might there be hope behind the eyes?

Flemyng straightened the paper on the table and took away his hands.

Kristof looked up at him.

THREE

Sitting on a cracked gravestone, her back against a slab of pink granite, Grace Quincy closed her book and pushed it into a canvas tote bag that was bulging with newspapers. She stretched and found a position where she could catch the sun, and slipped a cigarette out of the packet that was crushed into her shirt pocket.

There was rain on the way, but at this hour the sun had broken through and was bringing an interlude of warmth and brightness. The breeze had dropped and the air was still. Quincy struck a match on the stone and drew a slow breath. A spiral of smoke rose above her and she was carried off in the moment of calm. The thin blue plume was like an Indian fakir's rope climbing to the sky, and the overgrown stones and statues around her became a landscape removed from the world, their chaos silenced. She savoured the quiet.

It was broken by voices from the path that led through the cypress trees on the rise that concealed the next layer of the cemetery spreading out below her. A group of students, at least two of them American, took the turning that led to Quincy's resting place and chattered their way towards her, their boots making a marching sound on the gravel.

'Hi there.' She waved, and as they approached they gazed in surprise at the figure before them. Blonde, in pale blue jeans and sandals, with a black shirt and heavy silver bangles jangling on the arm that she held up, she was a picture of dizzy relaxation on a stage set of frozen stones and tangled weeds. They would recognize her as a traveller from somewhere far away, and one with enough confidence to command the rocky mausoleum that stretched for acres around her: a startling mermaid on a tomb.

'Wilde's in the next row,' she said, and waved them towards a tall winged statue a few yards away. 'Left at the angel, then take the second path on the right again. You can't miss him. Give him a kiss from me.'

There was laughter in the air for a moment as they thanked her, and one looked back to her before they turned the corner. Quincy waved. But when they disappeared, she rose and walked briskly the other way. She reached the trees and took a rough short cut to the level below, stepping over the broken pediments of a crowded family plot and through the thickets of reeds that had sprung up between the graves. She touched the iron gates that had swung open on a high tomb that gaped like a cave, pushing them back with a loud squeak, and hurried on. Turning into the broad gravel path that encircled the whole cemetery of Père Lachaise, she looked up the slope and back to the trail she'd followed. There was no one behind her. A little further ahead, a workman was filling a wheelbarrow with branches, and she gave him a polite greeting as she passed. In less than five minutes she had climbed another slope, passed behind a row of towering monuments and, cutting towards the cemetery's edge, found the wall where a plaque commemorated the dead of the Paris Commune. She spent a minute or two at the spot, as a tourist might, then counted her way along the graves stretching southwards.

An old woman was tending the square plot at her family tomb, its fresh earth and polished urns a contrast to the decay around her, and Quincy stopped, as if in admiration. They didn't speak, her presence seeming a little act of respect on its own. The woman worried at the soil with her trowel, tossing weeds into the bucket she'd brought with her, and nodded to Quincy as she moved away.

Fifty yards along the path, having passed eight more plots, a yew tree sheltered the high gravestone where she stopped. Stepping behind it after a few moments, she was invisible to any passer-by and the old woman was out of sight. At head height, she found a loose stone in the boundary wall and it came away with little effort. She dug into her canvas bag and extracted an envelope from the pages of the book she'd been reading. It had no markings. Placing it in the cavity, she made sure that it lay flat, pressing it down with her hand before lifting the stone from the grass at her feet and easing it into the wall.

She dusted away all the traces and made certain that the stone was flush with the wall and the envelope invisible. Then she picked up her bag and walked steadily to the cemetery gates and the metro station beyond. The sun had gone and she felt the first spots of rain.

*

Maria Cooney had been born with the gift of friendship and therefore understood the power of loneliness.

She was one of the gang, but was just as happy to walk alone when the others had gone. The monthly lunch of American correspondents was often a trial, but today promised more. The tumult at home having stolen their thunder in recent days, May Day was close and they had persuaded themselves that they might yet be on a front line. Maria's despatches to her wire service had helped.

She was one of the first to reach Restaurant Lapérouse on the Left Bank near the river, and was able to watch the others arrive, one by one.

The comradeship of her adopted trade sustained her, and she knew how much she needed it. Her toughness was real and so was the softness that lay underneath. When young Jeffrey Hoffman banged through the doors and raised his short arms in greeting, the first of the others to come, his relief was obvious. 'Maria, mother of mine.' He put an arm round her shoulder. 'And, guess what,' he said. 'We have stardust on us.'

Maria smiled. 'Tell all.'

'Grace Quincy, no less. In person.'

Maria laughed. 'Well, we must be in the thick of things after all, Jeffrey.'

'You bet,' he said. He was breathless, and rubbing his hands in nervousness. They took the curved stair together and within a few minutes most of the gang had gathered. Two elderly waiters poured drinks and the chatter rose, Maria moving among them and watching for Quincy's arrival. She would be the last, surely.

Maria herself was a dark and shining presence, her neck seeming to arch forwards, and her black eyes bright against pale skin that was a contrast to the bronzed faces around her. She was tall and slim, wore her hair long, and moved gracefully. Next to Hoffman, who was as restless as a terrier, she was a picture of calm. The waiters advanced and retreated, and bowed in response to her signals.

She watched her nine companions, including the soggy core of the American press cadre in Paris, whose regular lunch was going to be enlivened by the arrival of more muscled travellers despatched by their offices in search of unrest and the mood of the moment. The vultures were mustering.

Max Anderson was holding court with tales of riots in Warsaw and a week in Budapest where he had failed to find satisfying cuisine on all but one evening, Max being a gourmand by inclination, though in appearance a skinny rake of a man whose most prominent feature was a Mr Punch nose.

It was he who had chosen the restaurant, because it was a cut above their usual haunt in a corner of Café de Flore. Here there were mirrors, painted doors to private dining rooms that shut with a heavy click and sealed them in, wall murals and a *trompe l'œil* ceiling, with waiters who played the part. They would tell you stories of the great men who had cavorted behind these doors for long afternoons in the arms of their women, and who cared if they were true?

It was made for Max, a luminous stage. He had a sidekick from his magazine with him, fidgeting in the next chair as if fearful that if he were to leave Max's side he might miss a word of wisdom, and attending to his master's glass like an officer's batman, waving the waiters away. Alone among them, Max had a dry martini in his hand.

Quincy arrived. She had been escorted upstairs by the manager himself, his eyes glistening with recognition, and when she entered the room she simply put her arms out and gave a communal greeting that looked like a blessing. The room arranged itself around her, and Maria watched Max with amusement, aware that Quincy's presence was the cause of his grumpiness, his expected place as leader of the gang having been effortlessly and decisively usurped. And her eyes were drawn back to Quincy herself, a beacon of elegance in a room of men who were uncertain about how to manage her presence. Hoffman had raised his glass in a silent, nervous toast.

Max Anderson rose and, although he didn't smile, he announced, 'We are honoured.'

In the office of the wire service where Maria worked, Quincy's words were a source of envy and, sometimes, inspiration. Her journey down the Mekong in the early months of the war had won her a Pulitzer two years before, and she knew the underbelly of half a dozen cities where even Max had found it hard to eat well. She had made and broken presidential candidates in more than one country, run with rebels in the hills and blazed her way to the places no one else reached. Her style commanded space in magazines at home and in Europe, attracting the hungriest of the wandering photographers to her side, and sometimes to her bed. She drew her own route map to follow her star, and roughed it with gusto.

'Hemingway with tits,' Maria's boss called her. But a better writer, he'd often add by way of apology.

As they sat round the long oval table, the old waiters pulling back the chairs one by one, she allowed the high atmosphere that had accompanied her arrival to subside and the room to settle. The others, lifted by a feeling that events were on the move, were still gossiping hard, in whispers. Maria looked at Quincy across the table. Her natural blonde hair was cut long to her shoulders, and she had put on a white jacket over the black shirt and her light-blue denims. Her bangles reflected the light and she wore a simple necklace, with no earrings.

Quincy was placed beside a nervous reporter from New York whose two years in Europe hadn't lessened his fear of threatening deadlines, nor of cables and calls from head office that might follow him across the city on his daily round, maybe catching him at play when he should have been at his desk. Beyond him, young Hoffman was rotund and uncomfortable, scratching himself, and hadn't exchanged words with Quincy since she'd climbed the stairs to lunch, although he'd admired her since he'd begun to travel in Europe for his paper and had half-consciously followed in her tracks to the Middle East, although five hundred miles behind. On Quincy's other side was the place assigned to the guest of honour at lunch, a late and weak substitute for the gang's regular embassy contact, who was therefore awaited with little enthusiasm.

'Who's this boy?' said Max, hooting at the table.

'Butterfield's his name,' said his junior, picking up his cue.

'I hear he knows nothing,' Max said without acknowledging his friend. 'Roll out the barrel of crap.'

Instinctively leading the way, Grace Quincy rose to greet Butterfield, who had come through the door a moment too late to hear Max's words of welcome. She introduced herself, and the tall young man took his place, putting his spectacles on the table without folding them up. His tie was tight and crooked, and his shirt damp with the sweat of his walk. When he had apologized for his timing and his lack of seniority, the table quickly turned to drink.

Maria leaned across to catch Quincy's eye.

'Grace, this is a pleasure.'

'Sure. Our paths haven't crossed. But they were bound to, weren't they?'

'Always. That's the way.'

They spoke of Paris. West of the city, students were in revolt on the Nanterre campus, and Maria had been talking to them for nearly a month, her stories alerting the world beyond France to the crackle of flames in the universities. Their movement was spreading. The Left Bank was buzzing, political sects starting to colonize their different cafés and settling their territories, a crowd always ready to gather round. Pamphleteers were on the streets. Easter weekend, just gone, had brought on a pause but they knew that May would be different. It was promising enough for Quincy to return. The April chaos at home had taken her to New York for ten days, to write of violence in politics, riots and a president humbled. But Europe called her back. 'I'll try to get into Prague again,' she said to Maria. 'That's the place. For now, here we are.'

'I tell you, we should be in Warsaw,' Max was saying at the end of the table. 'Read me Saturday.'

'I'm glad,' said Maria to Quincy, smiling. Her marble skin and the black sheen in her hair made her a contrast with the other woman, who had softer colours, but her voice had the same gentleness. 'Let's get together, more quietly than this.'

She spoke as if she and Quincy were old friends.

Butterfield was struggling in his first efforts to address the table as the two waiters circled to clear away the soup plates.

'I guess you're aware that it's… ah… real sensitive around this town. Movement of 22 March – weird name, but still trouble. Ugly stuff at Nanterre again last week, and still bubbling up. We hear the… ah… government is concerned. Pretty concerned.'

'The embassy must be reading the *Trib* again,' Max said. He sent a bottle of white burgundy sliding across the table, embarrassing the waiters who sprang back to the table and started to pour again.

'Well,' said Butterfield, 'we don't want to get too dramatic. But trouble comes easily. We know what's happening at home. All the sadness and politics going…' and then, because he felt himself approaching treacherous ground, he said 'zany', dried up and returned to his duck.

'Zany!' said Max. 'What kind of word is that? Death and destruction in America. And there's no city in Europe where they're not marching against us.'

His young man said that Max himself had been threatened in a bar in London.

For a few minutes their minds turned to home, some of them expressing a wish to be called back, where they might understand more. A gloom settled on the company, and Maria took it as a signal to rescue Butterfield by allowing him to eat uninterrupted.

'Grace. Prague?' she said, and they took the conversation to the east, speaking of bubbling food riots, party schisms, jumpy Russians. Another Warsaw Pact summit in the wind. After Quincy had offered a thought, Max found his stride and, stroking his long nose as if it were the tiller of his boat, he took them up the Danube from Budapest to Vienna with his own rehearsed commentary, and then one of Maria's wire service friends offered a titbit from the diplomatic foreplay for the Vietnam peace talks. They might be coming to Paris, which would let them set up camp for months. Years, said Max.

Butterfield had to say that it was a matter beyond his reach, dealt with elsewhere in the embassy.

So, after the silence that followed his confession, lunch ended quickly. Max said he would lead a party towards a bar he knew in the rue Gay-Lussac on the other side of the Luxembourg Gardens where they could play, and they began to disperse. Maria heard him say, 'You'll have other business, Grace, I imagine.'

She put a gentle hand on Butterfield's shoulder. 'Benjamin,' she said quietly, the first time anyone had used his name during lunch, 'a word?'

As the others turned towards the stairs, for a few moments the two stood in a corner of the room, near the open window looking out to the river, the smell of the pavement crowd and the noise of the city carried up to them, and they felt the rain coming on. For the first time since he had arrived, he was smiling, with his back to the others. Maria spoke quietly.

She leaned to one side, her eyes taking in her companions round his shoulder as Butterfield came close.

Alone among the crowd, Quincy was watching them.

'Thank you,' Butterfield said under his breath before turning to leave her. 'I'll do what I can. *À plus tard.*'

Quincy reached the top of the stairs before Maria.

'Grace, let's have a quiet dinner,' she said from behind. 'Without everyone...' She gestured downstairs, where Max was herding them, the mother hen gathering the brood, with his sidekick holding a rolled umbrella high in the air like a tourist guide, then letting it spring outwards, against the rain. 'Would you come?' Quincy nodded. They watched the party fanning out behind Max to cross the street.

'Soon,' said Quincy, still looking down from the window. 'Next few days? Before May Day anyway. I'm at the Meurice. Just call.'

Although Maria's office was close to Quincy's hotel, they parted at the door, and Maria took another route across the city. She cut eastwards first, taking an alleyway off the tiny Place de Furstenberg, where the Paulownia trees were in full flower at the height of their spring boastfulness, and then finding a back route towards the river so that she avoided the busier streets. It took her by a dog-leg passage into the confinement of rue de Nevers. The pavements were narrow and uneven, so that she walked in the street that was hardly wide enough for a car. The drizzle was steady and she quickened her pace. Halfway along, she took a key from her pocket and with a slow and heavy turn of her hand opened the lock of a dark blue door. An old woman in black sat on a stool outside the little courtyard of the next-door apartment building, ignoring the rain, and nodded. Pushing the door back, Maria entered a high lobby with a curving stone stairway to her left. She stood still for a moment, heard nothing, and climbed to the first floor, the clatter of her feet sounding high above her and echoing back down.

The apartment was tiny, two rooms with narrow windows that allowed only a little light to filter in from the street. She had a desk and a phone, two bookcases and an overstuffed sofa. In the other room, through an archway, there was a single bed and, in the corner, a china pitcher and painted basin that had been there when she first saw the place, taken there by a young embassy man long since moved on. Two piles of books peeped above the bottom of the bed. On the walls, she'd stuck a few of the posters that were beginning to appear on the trees along the Left Bank – student slogans, a raised fist, a blackened photograph of a bombed city, Mao. But the rich red rug was from home in Boston, and above the desk she'd hung a garish crucifix that her mother had sent her to keep her safe on her travels. Maria locked the door, heated some coffee on the gas ring and began a round of phone calls.

There were two students at Nanterre whom she had befriended with patience and who expected a call around three in the afternoon each day. For a month they'd been in the boiler room of the movement, and had found a taste for politics. Maria was encouraging them, and living their adventure. One had already visited the apartment.

Usually when she rang they were at their post in the lobby of the student building to answer the phone, pressed together in a glass box against the wall, and if not she would call back at five. They had slipped into a routine without thinking. She took in all their news. The protests over visiting rights for women in men's dormitories were already memories, comic in retrospect. They were now speaking of an assault on an entire system, its apparatchiks, their gates and locked doors, dreaming of an end to all the fusty rules. The regime. Day by day she listened to them, heard names that she noted down, cross-referencing as she went, and compared their stories – one was high on an anarchist's adrenalin, the other a mournful innocent who'd only got involved because he wanted to sleep with his girlfriend – and asked them each day what they expected to happen next. Her wire service had been taking a student story regularly since the Nanterre eruption, and she'd write a few paragraphs later raising the prospect of a widening protest. That would come from her office. For now, in this secret place, there were other calls. It was a rule that she didn't ring Washington from the apartment some distance away where her colleagues knew she lived. From there, she only called her wire service office in New York. Rue de Nevers was for other business.

She made her arrangements. A writer from London who'd spent the previous six months in East Berlin and Warsaw, and had dipped into Prague in early March, had let her know he was on his way to Paris and she wanted to see him. Edward Abbott's suppressed romanticism appealed to her, because she enjoyed watching it burst through, and on the long evenings they'd spent together he'd discovered that she was a natural listener like him. As a result, he had penetrated the defences she'd maintained through the years, and understood a good deal of her. How much, she couldn't be sure.

She left a message in the shabby hotel in Oberkampf that she knew Edward would use when he arrived, and rang her own office to say she'd be back within the hour. All quiet, they told her.

Then, using the international operator, she called a friend in Washington. It took a few minutes for the line to come up and the operator to call back, but when the phone rang they plunged straight into gossip about the news, neither using the other's name. And when Maria turned to the reason for the call she kept her tone steady, giving no indication that the mood had changed.

'You asked about Quincy. She's arrived.'

'Good.' His voice was distorted on the line.

The call ended quickly, and Maria prepared to leave the apartment.

First, after a few moments' thought, she rang the Hotel Meurice.

'Miss Quincy, please. An American guest.'

There was no reply from the room, and Maria left no message.

Wrapping a raincoat around herself, she locked the apartment and the blue door leading to the street, waiting for the old mechanism to crash into place. Rain was falling steadily now and the old woman had gone from the door to the neighbouring building. There was no one else to be seen in rue de Nevers, which was darkening fast. Water was starting to drip from the old street lanterns bolted higgledy-piggledy high up on the walls as Maria reached the archway that led to the riverside and which gave the little street its air of privacy. She crossed the *quai* to the Pont Neuf and in ten minutes she was in her office.

It was a bureau of only three reporters, with reinforcements promised if the temperature rose in May. One of them was working, sitting at a teleprinter keyboard in a glass kiosk in the corner; the other was on NATO business in Brussels, where he spent much of his time. Maria checked the trails of paper from the wire service machines near her own wooden desk, unravelling the rolls that had accumulated on the floor, and found the latest edict from the university authorities.

The gates might be closed to students within a few days. In a few minutes, she'd written four hundred words, which she took into the back room from where Jacques, who managed the bureau, would send them to New York. He thought a few paragraphs might survive. Then she was gone.

Walking along rue de Rivoli, she found a stationery shop and spent a few minutes selecting a box of writing paper, taking care with colour and style. She asked if she might use a table near the counter to write a letter, and borrowed a heavy pen from the proprietor, a Frenchwoman of grand bearing with the air of someone in easy charge of her world, sweet-smelling and impenetrable. She arranged the table for Maria and bowed. 'Madame.'

Taking her time, Maria wrote a short note. She hesitated at the first few words, then found it flowing. Sealing the envelope, she smiled warmly as she handed back the pen and expressed her thanks as she opened the door, the bell jangling above as she closed it behind her.

A few yards away, she entered the lobby of the Hotel Meurice and found the concierge, stiff-backed and solemnly turned out, but with dancing eyes that missed nothing.

Maria spoke in English.

'A letter for Miss Quincy. I'd like her to have it immediately. Thank you.'

'Madame.' He bowed and took the letter. Before she had gone, a boy had been handed the letter and was marching to the lift.

Maria lowered her head as she pushed through the revolving door and felt the rain. Her apartment was only a few minutes away. Feeling happier than she had all day, she plunged into the dank afternoon.

FOUR

When Flemyng arrived in Freddy Craven's office, the stage was set for him. The old man was in his chair, with his back to the wide window and that day's *Le Figaro* across his knees, the morning light bestowing a faint halo, and Bolder had arranged himself beside a small square table at the other side of the room, a yellow pad beside him with a green fountain pen laid alongside. Sandy Bolder, loyal and plausible deputy, with a manner that he never allowed to slip. Flemyng knew how much grind and effort had gone into his rise, especially in landing the prize of a Paris posting that might let him accompany Craven to his resting place, and knew too that Bolder had a reputation on the street for worming into closed corners and then out again. A dancer. They shared fragments of their exploits in their daily dealings, and knew the outlines of their individual histories, but Bolder had carried to Paris the confidence of one who treasured a special line to London that would see him through. 'We all need a little something of our own, don't we?' he'd said to Flemyng more than once since the start of the year. 'It's our pride.'

He was short and trim, and always dressed by the rule. His shirts were white and his two office suits dark, one of them striped. At the weekends he was in brown. The only hint of rebellion was in a shock of auburn hair that he allowed to blossom so that it seemed to redden more, as if he were allowing his garden to flirt with the wild. It made his head seem too big for his spare body, but he had graceful feet and they gave him a physical ease and spring. Shabbiness was increasingly the norm in the embassy, he often said, and he tried to stay ahead. No one doubted that determination. He had, however, a lazy lower lip that dropped whenever he spoke, so that he gave the impression of operating at a tilt. He and Flemyng had exchanged quiet confidences often enough to know that they were bound by a few secrets that would keep them yanked together, wherever they might wander. When Flemyng's irritation spilled over, Craven would say that there was a Bolder in everyone's life – a companion who wasn't always wanted, not vindictive by nature but always drawn to other people's troubles like a moth to the flame. Therefore, usually unhelpful.

Sandy had more than a decade on Flemyng, and his rank gave him unquestioned seniority and privileges of access, but everyone around the embassy knew a strange truth – that he behaved in Flemyng's presence as if he were the younger of the two. Craven had long ago put that down as his most obvious weakness, a quest for reassurance that for Bolder would never end.

Flemyng put a hand on Craven's shoulder before sitting down, but the first words were Bolder's.

'A game, do we think?'

'Can't be sure,' said Flemyng, settling himself. 'I've just come from him, but I still don't know.'

Craven waved an arm. That argument could wait. 'I want to hear it all, Will. Start on the metro.'

Bolder was patting the yellow pad with his pen. Perky.

Flemyng began. The atmosphere in the carriage, the signal to sit tight as far as Pigalle, the simple and apparently safe choreography in the café, then the promise of another meeting. The name – first or last he couldn't tell – and the physical appearance of Kristof. He spent a few minutes on the thoughts he'd had before exchanging any words with the German, taking Craven and Bolder through his preparations: say nothing except that you'll listen, assume there is a watcher in the café, mention no names. By the book. He took the pencil sketch from the inside pocket of his jacket and unfolded it.

'There he is, Freddy. A reasonable likeness, I hope.'

Craven looked down at it, then smiled. 'They always said you had your mother's talent, buried in there.'

Bolder threw a questioning frown at the old man, and rose to come across the room and see the sketch. 'New boy to me,' he said, 'but of course that may not mean very much.' He advanced to the window and stretched out his arms, legs apart. He seemed to be limbering up.

'The conversation,' Craven said.

Flemyng spoke for two or three minutes only. He expressed mystification. Kristof had appeared to want to make the contact and open a door. No more. 'I was surprised. But isn't that how it often begins?'

Craven was pressing, already. 'Come on, boy. What was the hook?'

Flemyng was a picture of calm. 'There wasn't one, Freddy.'

The atmosphere didn't change, despite Flemyng's declaration. He stroked the cleft on his right cheek with a finger, a habit they all recognized, and then with his other hand he rubbed a shoulder as if it was threatening to slip out of joint. His dark eyes were still, and they betrayed no sign of unease.

Craven said, 'There must have been. It hardly matters if it's their operation, which we've got to assume it is, or a gamble on his part to make contact, which I doubt. It would be suicide.

Either way, he couldn't leave without enticing you. I know you, Will. You acknowledge gifts. What did he throw you?'

'A morsel?' Flemyng said.

'Something to chew on.'

'And digest,' said Bolder, who had moved to a chair next to Craven and turned his face from the window back to his writing pad. Flemyng's expression didn't change as the old man spoke. 'Look, Will, this Kristof – let's get to know that name – didn't put on this performance for fun, did he? Wandering the streets with you. Maybe he wasn't very good… but a clue, surely?'

He was speaking gently, a determined persuader who didn't want to appear too demanding.

Taking the offer of an opening, and showing no sign of relief, Flemyng said that they might be underestimating Kristof. 'I think he is good, although my experience doesn't match yours, Sandy.' Bolder nodded at the compliment. 'He didn't miss a step, and there was none of the crudeness we usually see. He was smooth in his way, and his English is top drawer.'

'All that, and he gave you nothing?' said Craven, pulling at his neck.

'Only the promise of another contact,' Flemyng replied.

Craven wouldn't let go. 'Why didn't that surprise you?'

'I've been trained not to be, I suppose.'

Bolder had moved his chair to be at a right angle to Craven, and now had his legs crossed and his hands behind his head. He was slim and symmetrical, so that his thatch of hair seemed to be the only part of him allowed to be free. 'Speaking for myself, I'm astonished all the time. I'm *never* unsurprised. Well, hardly ever.'

My secrets are better than yours, he might as well have said.

'I did hear something along the chancery corridor,' Bolder

said. 'From Pierce Bridger himself.' He paused, and Craven's gaze switched quickly to Flemyng. Aware he was being watched, Flemyng overreacted and gave an unconvincing laugh. 'Pierce. What does he know?'

Bolder said, 'Well, he knows how to pick up whispers on the circuit, the parties and so forth. Who's up, who's down, the comings and goings. Without our special contacts, of course. But still he hears things.'

'Out with it, Sandy,' said Craven. 'Don't tread water.' He was still watching Flemyng.

'Well,' said Bolder, 'he asked me if we'd noticed an influx from the east of late. Worker bees for the Russian hive. Word is the trains coming this way are crowded. So it fits, you see.'

'Not necessarily,' said Craven. 'Bridger might be fishing for gossip, that's all.'

But Bolder had made his point, and it had changed the atmosphere. Craven's own voice had hardened a little. 'Come on. This is odd, Will. Bloody odd. Not a hint whether your man was buying or selling?'

Flemyng had recovered, and smiled. Disarming their anxieties, he wondered aloud if he should apologize for having failed to pick up a signal, or maybe for casting a dud fly. Could they help him explain it? Freddy, after all, had been his first guide in Berlin and Vienna where he'd learned the alluring mechanics of his trade, and he'd always understood that promising encounters came in different shapes and sizes. He'd been taught never to rush, in the manner of those in whose footsteps he followed. 'That's all I can say,' he said. 'I thought it best that he should set the pace, at least for now. That was the way of it.'

He was back in the groove.

'I can't argue with that,' said Craven, 'but he's going about things in a strange way. Be prepared. If he's not offering himself to us, then there is only one way to look at this. A threat.'

Bolder was running his hands through his hair and shaking the thatch. 'We may be talking about nasty stuff here. Pressure, with Mother Russia winding the wheel.' A pause. 'Blackmail? You never know.'

Craven was agitated enough to get up, and he stepped forward to put an arm on Flemyng's shoulder. Their eyes met. 'You're white as the driven snow, my boy, so I know we've got no worries of that kind. But watch your step. No new contacts in the next few days. Keep a watch for anything peculiar.'

'Especially if it's wearing a short skirt,' said Bolder, and clapped his hands together.

Craven waved it away. 'Will has taste in that direction, Sandy,' he said. '*Taste*', putting him down. He took his seat again.

Then he added, 'Sorry', because Flemyng's recent romance – Freddy's own word – had been the talk of the embassy, even among those who weren't envious. Especially when it collapsed. Flemyng had spent four months in the arms of an English pianist who'd settled in Paris to be near her famous teacher, and thanks to her he had waltzed elegantly into the city's artistic life. He'd been persuaded into languid weekends in her apartment in the 16th where they lost whole days together. Isabel teased him for the embassy routines that confined him, but she laughed, too, at the way the musicians of the city were conformists of their own kind, seemingly drawn to each other by magnetic forces they didn't understand, hanging together to remind themselves they weren't alone. A conductor and his harem of visitors lived across the street, there was a diva on the top floor around the corner, looking down from her tiny balcony at the diners swinging into Madame Prunier's in the early evening, and another singer across the street who was watching her in turn to measure her decline. A man through the wall from Isabel's own kitchen practised the bassoon at all hours. She understood that although the intensity of her life often invited panic, companions in the tumult offered the hope of safety.

They clung to each other's notes.

In that apartment, where long tapestries softened the sound in the sitting room and the paintings offered paths of escape for him at the end of long days and nights, Flemyng would read while she played Liszt and Ravel and most of all Scriabin, the Russian whose feeling for mysticism and release she wanted to discover for herself but feared she couldn't. And then he would read aloud, while she curled up for him.

They were days of intensity from the start, Flemyng having experienced a *coup de foudre* at the creaky, moth-eaten Théâtre du Châtelet of all places, where he'd gone with an embassy party to see the traditional pre-Christmas Offenbach. Cheery nonsense, said Bolder as he handed out the invitations – *La Grande-Duchesse de Gérolstein*, otherwise known as a Frogs' Panto, he said – and Flemyng, after a harmless evening of laughter, found her at the party that followed in the ambassador's residence, where the back room of the cellars was raided as a seasonal treat. He didn't leave her side all night, and with a perfect understanding of what had occurred, Bolder bestowed an honorary dukedom on him, and the title of *duchesse* on her, at their station meeting on the third floor the next morning.

Flemyng didn't care.

Isabel had captured him, and for many weeks he was by her side. She set the pattern and he followed happily. Even when she spent nights at his apartment across the Seine, usually twice in a week, Flemyng lost the natural authority that marked him out in the office, and became second in command when he left the embassy. They laughed a good deal, ate well at Allard and nonchalantly in the crowd at Les Deux Magots on the Left Bank, deliberately avoiding the formal embassy circuit and almost never arguing. Sometimes in the early hours they'd decamp to La Poule au Pot in the shadow of the market pavilions of Les Halles, and Isabel would breathe deep in the rough, rich odour of the glistening soups and hearty wines that were succour for the men from the stalls, butchers and cheesemongers who crowded round in the hours before dawn at the dark start of their day. She loved noise as well as peace.

Too good to last, Flemyng told himself through those weeks, as he tried to erect a defence against the coming sadness, and he was right.

By the time winter was waning, his emotions had lost their thunder. Days would go by without contact with Isabel, and he ducked two of her concerts on thin excuses. He moped with guilt as a result, and then began to develop, to his sinking alarm, a resistance to the music that she loved the most. Whose fault, he couldn't tell. He had no explanation, but knew that her mysticism, which had dazzled him, turned into an affectation that disturbed him, and as a result his darkness, a natural gift betrayed by his hair and his eyes, seemed to his colleagues to deepen, even when he told them in answer to every probe that he'd never known such elation.

Bolder spotted it first, with delight. '*Too* intense,' he told Craven. 'It will pass with the season, mark my words.' He spread the word on the third floor and beyond, taking time to express his own regrets.

For Flemyng, whose love life had been conventional and regular but never tumultuous, the experience of loss had a special pain. Freddy, inevitably, was his confessor.

'I've never had a broken heart,' Flemyng told him in early

March, feeling a deep stab of embarrassment. 'Maybe that's my difficulty. I find it hard to understand the idea that something like this can just fade away.'

In the end, Flemyng didn't have to, because, even as he was drawing back in pain, Isabel rang the curtain down with a bump, announcing that she was off to New York and a recording contract that might be the making of her. It was over. The apartment would be let, no doubt to another musician, maybe with another lover in tow, and her Paris days were done. They spent one long and tearful night admitting their failures, and she was kind at the last. She played for him one more time on the rosewood Érard piano that she was going to ship across the sea from its Paris home. 'I want to escape from everything,' she told him. 'That's why I play in the way I do. You don't. You'll always be a servant – loyal and decent, brilliant sometimes, but trapped in the ways of the world. I've loved you, but we'd destroy each other, you and I. I promise you that.'

And, leaving him a volume of Emily Dickinson, she said goodbye.

His bruises had taken weeks to soften, and he still felt the pain when Bolder joked about his attractiveness. He wished all of it gone.

Thrown by Craven's kind but clumsy reference to his life beyond the office walls, he wanted to bring the meeting in the embassy to an end. He said he had to catch up with some reading. He'd spend the afternoon alone in his room. 'I'm going to take the air for a few minutes first. In the garden.'

'Of course,' said Bolder. 'Your usual place.'

There was a bench where everyone knew Flemyng liked to sit under the trees, and on this day he wanted to relish the morning sun that spilled across the lawns. The rain had passed in the night. He'd heard the last run of water from the roof of his top-floor apartment just after three o'clock as he sat in the dark by the window and thought of his brother. There was a maze opening up before him, he was sure, so his first act through those long hours had been to try to recover the strength that he found in family reminiscence, taking him back to a time before he and Abel went their separate ways before finding, as the years went by, that they were treading the same path.

He began an exercise that he'd often used before when he felt himself tumbling into a crisis.

Quite deliberately, he placed himself on the landscape he'd known as a boy. He could smell the air, feel the breeze. Closing his eyes, he assembled a series of pictures that took him far away from Paris, then pictured himself at their heart. He was walking from the loch up the slope, through the woods and along the burn, then on to the hill through the bracken and back to the rambling house that was home. Altnabuie lay in the deep folds of the Perthshire hills where Flemyng knew all the tracks and savoured the vistas that opened up at every turn, the long view down the glen that ran westwards from loch to the high hills and the spiked mountains beyond, or the panorama of crags and moor to the north that hinted at an unending trail into the wild where you might succeed for a while in losing every contact with the here and now. The emptiness excited him, and so did the comforting road home to the house where his mother might be painting in her first-floor room and looking down the glen, or his brothers maybe scampering across the hall, playing with the brass orrery that mimed the movement of the planets and reminded him, in its simplistic depiction of infinity, of the preciousness of solitude. To think about brother Abel meant remembering first of all those golden days on the hill, maybe a rainy dawn by the lochside with rod and line, or a climb to the ridge behind the house and high above, with the undulating plateau spreading out to lift your eyes towards the misty rim of the mountains whose tops were always touched by clouds.

He was trying to rediscover the source of his own happiness as a protection against what might lie ahead. There had been weeks of unease, brought on by the love affair gone sour but now evaporated with the coming of the Paris spring, and Flemyng was restoring his energy, drop by drop. It was needed now, even more. So he slipped into a practised routine to steady himself. Home and family were the start, and brought the required comfort, but then there was Craven.

In Flemyng's first palmy days in Berlin, Freddy had been a jovial master of the revels, turning the weary business of listening and watching, sometimes running, into a game that could bring fun to their rigid routine, reminding them that if they couldn't laugh then they'd soon be devoured by the lives they'd chosen. They had a set of draughty, white rooms in the north-east corner of a building at the old Olympic Stadium, with army intelligence on the floor above and the French below. The iron seats and steps in the arena a short walk away seemed to acknowledge their unhappy history and remained bare and unwelcoming, a few of the terraced levels filling up once a month when the Americans threw together a football game, but that was all. The wooden walls of their offices wobbled, and they came and went from work on bleak walkways, but the dining hall in the old gymnasium became a playground for them all, which Flemyng cherished for its strangeness and the unlikely companionship that it sometimes offered. They drank next door in a purpose-built pub called the Somerset Arms, where they taught the Americans to play darts but the French rarely came. There were formal dealings with the Russians, which Craven said was a game of tin soldiers played out on city streets. He understood the advantages of the bizarre setting, and so upstairs, with his door closed and a couple of innocent squaddies on guard outside, he would gather his boys around him late in the afternoon and walk them through the day, like the teacher he was.

In the freezing winter darkness, his nose was red as an apple and Sam Malachy would say that when he rubbed it a genie came out of the lamp. There were tales from the back rooms, and the street. The Russians were expecting a general from Moscow; a driver passed on a whisper about a convoy coming in from Warsaw; a sapper had got something from a girl; someone had dug up a dead letter box in the Tiergarten, and there was a watch on it. Craven's French counterpart had a dose of the clap. Everything went into the pot. And the cast of characters that he brought out of the shadows was turned into a chorus line of jesters and heroes, all of them in his mind caught between a love of duty and a passion for the dance.

Craven's solemn moments, or his rage at a botched job or a broken promise, were lifted by his need for fun. There was always a party, or a wake.

When Flemyng first faced the death of a friend, a young East German of spirit who had played with fire once too often and whom Craven told him one Friday morning had probably been shot, he had recited his litany of guilt to the old man.

He said he thought he might never laugh again.

'Of course you'll laugh again,' Freddy Craven said. 'It's just that you'll never be young again.'

And now Flemyng had betrayed him.

FIVE

Pierce Bridger was always going to spoil the party. Flemyng had never doubted it. His arrival in the embassy a few weeks before Christmas had brought a storm cloud over the city, one that Flemyng knew would find him some day. Their paths had taken them to different continents but the luck that kept them more or less apart for ten years was bound to run out.

The gloom that Flemyng felt on the day his appointment appeared on the chancery noticeboard – Freddy Craven took him to a boozy lunch to give him the news, and held it back until the end – was born of guilt touched with anger. He tried to reason it away. Why should he resent the man's presence after the years that had passed? He knew that he had tried the harder of the two to heal their breach, and if some of the hurt remained it was hardly his fault. So he told himself to be generous, and remember that it would be Bridger who would be the more uncomfortable as a result. But he didn't quite believe himself.

He had tried again. Weren't they now grown up? Their past was slipping away, and Flemyng's efforts to keep their old friendship alive might yet come good – there had been the persistent invitations from him for an early evening drink when they coincided in London, twice successful; a decent weekend drive into the hills when they were thrown together without warning in Hong Kong at the peak of a stormy, sultry July; a long dinner in Washington when Flemyng had imagined hopelessly for a few precious hours that the flush of their boyhood excitements was coming back to warm him.

He knew it was because of the closeness they once shared that there was pain. If they had been rivals from the very start, it would have been easier.

For two young men on national service, their first expedition into the cold had been thrilling. Quietly steered away from the regiments that their families had expected them to join, they found themselves seated like schoolboys in a former district hospital outside Cambridge where they studied Russian grammar for hours each day with two dozen others, tutored in conversation by an eccentric troupe of White Russians commanded by three old men who wore the scars of civil war like polished cap badges, and a chalk-faced woman they called the Countess, dressed from top to toe in black. She was said to be in permanent mourning for the Romanovs.

Flemyng and Bridger laughed in the evenings, and cycled across the East Anglian plains into the fens. They drank ale together, and once swapped girlfriends without a hard word.

A chill winter passed and the translators were given their orders, one by one. Some straight to Whitehall, so the word went, others home to their mother regiments, a handful to university departments, a couple to the BBC. Flemyng and Bridger were interviewed together, and despatched as a pair to the north. 'Even colder than Cambridge,' they were told, and little more. 'Stay close.' The next night they were picked up from a village station in the dark and driven to a craggy corner of the Fife coast, where they felt their first bite of the wind from the North Sea.

Home was a bleak airfield near the shore where there were more classes, and a taste of action. They clamped Bakelite earphones to their heads and learned to pick up the chatter from Russian freighters and trawlers in the distance, waiting for the crackle and tales of battles with the sea, stories of the girls at home. Both of them had felt a shiver of excitement at each discovery of a listening ship in the fishing fleets, and the knowledge that they were in a game with men of their own age, who played with the same kind of dials that faced them in their prefab huts and lived with the same static hiss through the night. Sometimes they caught a puzzling exchange, a piece of chatter that seemed out of place, and buzzed for Jarvie, their leader, who encouraged excitement among them as a matter of policy, even when there seemed to be no reason. He would whip away their pencilled translations to be passed quickly up the line. For the best part of a year they were drawn into the dark, and they laughed.

As a pair, they looked quite different. Bridger was half Irish but blond, red-cheeked and moon-faced, his features contrasting with Flemyng's dark and slim-drawn face. He was the taller by a full two inches, and carried the bulk of a rugby flanker, which he was. They had been born at opposite ends of the country less than a month apart, which was part of their attraction – Flemyng in the central Highlands on a freezing Bonfire Night and Bridger three weeks later in a Suffolk village near the sea. And in the months when they spoke Russian together, childhood memories brought them close. The coming of war a few weeks before their ninth birthdays, the fall of France and the blitz, then early teenage years that were charged with family talk of soldiers and sailors far away, the ones whom they would never see. Their imaginations were fed on the same story.

It was by chance that they were called to Whitehall together.

In the last days of spring, they left Crail and their bare quarters at the airfield, saying farewell in the smoky snug bar at the back of the Marine Hotel where they'd curl up on cold evenings, and spent a long summer without contact. Flemyng went home, and Bridger travelled without a plan, determined to roam. Then they found themselves without warning side by side in the panelled waiting room behind the doors of the old War Office a few steps from Horse Guards on a bracing autumn Wednesday, summoned for interviews on the same day. They exchanged their new addresses, rattled through family gossip for comfort's sake, and joked about Mr Goodwater, whom they had been asked to see – 'I wonder what he'll call himself tomorrow,' Bridger said. They wished each other well; slapped backs. Each imagined a time when they'd be closer than ever, sharing new secrets.

Flemyng missed him in the afternoon, and after his own second interview three days later in another building a short distance away, where he was given the promise of the career that he wanted, he left a message with Bridger's landlady suggesting that they should meet in a pub off the King's Road in the early evening. He waited an hour, and when Bridger arrived he saw a change that he hadn't expected. His friend's wide shoulders had sagged and the brightness that Flemyng loved in his face had dimmed.

'Well, how did it go?'

Bridger's head was down and he pulled at his cheek. 'Not well.'

Flemyng said, 'Tell me all.'

'There's not much to say, except that they've chosen you.' Only his eyes came up. 'Not me.'

Flemyng signalled to the bar for two pints to be pulled. 'What happened? You're not out. I can't believe that.'

'It depends what you mean by out,' said Bridger. 'I'm going straight. They want me to learn Arabic. Maybe Chinese, bugger it. To be a Foreign Office regular.'

Flemyng said, 'Well done', and raised his glass. There was no response. He waited, then said, 'It wasn't a choice between us, you know. That isn't how they play it.'

It all poured out. Bridger's heart was set on a life behind the lines. He knew he was a clandestine adventurer by nature, and longed for permission to be a man of many names and faces. 'I loved those nights when we listened to Ivan. Wondered who he was, what he was thinking. We picked up his spoor; followed it. I thought it was my life.'

'Me, too,' Flemyng said. 'I know.'

But in his kindness he felt pain. In a few minutes, he had been dragged down by guilt. It was Bridger who was showing energy, though it sprang from his anger. 'They closed the door on me. Just like that.' He slapped a hand on the table, spilling some beer. 'Explain it.'

'I can't, Pierce.' Fleming added gloomily, 'I wasn't there.'

He was trying to contain the anger that was bubbling up, and which was unexpected. His spirits had been high, the prospect of the coming months in training an excitement that had kept him awake for two nights, and now he was accused of a betrayal of friendship. He struggled to conceal a rage that he feared might destroy everything, and said as quietly as he could, 'I'm sorry.'

'D'you know what he said – Goodwater, whoever he is – when I mentioned you? Not to fret. That I should realize that we're now on different paths and I might be an ambassador in the end – probably would be. You never will, in your game. As if I give a damn about rank!'

'Maybe you will, some day,' Flemyng said.

And they found they were played out so quickly. The friends

realized that they shouldn't stay. They'd get drunk and angrier, and where would that leave them?

Understanding that it was better to go, Bridger said, 'Perhaps I'll ring you in a week or two.'

'I'm not sure where I'll be, or if you can,' said Flemyng, which made it worse.

They parted with a handshake that neither wanted and went their miserable ways.

The following day, Flemyng rang the number he had been given in case of second thoughts, and asked if he might speak to Mr Goodwater. They met in a corner of the spies' watering hole in the St Ermin's Hotel, which Flemyng took as an act of kindness on Goodwater's part because it was a sign of welcome to the fold, and he asked if he might put a question that stretched the rules.

'Go ahead.'

'My friend Pierce Bridger. He's upset. Shattered, really. He thinks he's been rejected from the life that was... his calling.'

'I shouldn't talk about anyone who may or may not have been in my room,' Goodwater said. He was a genial man, bald as an egg with a wide smile that revealed a twinkling gold tooth. 'But you're friends. I know of your time together, of course. Let me say what I can.

'My colleagues and I find some men who are right for us, and we think we know them when we see them. We have to decide, and perhaps we get it wrong from time to time. I certainly have mistakes to my name. Also, and quite frequently, we spot those whom we know aren't right. Not because they don't have brains or cunning – maybe promising breeding. Not at all. It's because they want it rather too much. They've fallen in love with the idea in a rush. D'you understand? We're wary of too much emotion.'

'Why?' said Flemyng, feeling like a boy again.

'Because we've learned to be. You'll find out.'

And then, as a pick-me-up for Flemyng, Goodwater told stories. He spoke of his own recruitment in the pandemonium of early days of the war by a deputy chief who liked to strike matches on his wooden leg to light his pipe. He kept a wind-up gramophone in his room to play a shellac recording of one of the legends of the service describing his escape from a Turkish assassin in Istanbul, and his adventures with the Italians in Abyssinia, to get youngsters in the mood. Goodwater remembered some of the girls who came back from France telling stories of the others who hadn't, having disappeared in the fray. The German spy who was caught on a train in Scotland because he'd forgotten about the Reichsmarks still in his trouser pocket.

Of his own travels, he said nothing, showing Flemyng how you could be raconteur and man of mystery at the same time. He also took trouble to plant the idea that Flemyng would spend his life in a study of character.

'Scrapes and ploys. They'll come, and pass away. But you'll always watch people – learning their ways, trying to understand them. The game that never ends. Your friends on our side, as well as the others. A comrade-in-arms, or a passing Russian who looks hungry. You'll learn that the fascination is the same.'

And they were back to Bridger. Deliberately or not, Flemyng couldn't know.

'I don't want to sound like an innocent. Nor scared,' Flemyng said. 'But we're only in our twenties. I can be honest and say that I find it hard to know when I'll be able to forget this trouble, this break-up if that's what it is.'

Goodwater's genial smile was reassuring. He said that they were talking about a turning point in two young lives. 'Time is the great healer,' he said. His gold tooth shone. 'But not always, I'm afraid. Not always.'

*

Bridger's office in Paris was on the other side of the building from Flemyng's and much grander in scale. The high windows on the south side opened on to a balcony over the garden where he could entertain when the summer came, and he had requisitioned paintings from London that re-created a belle époque of his own design. There was a revolving globe on a mahogany stand, and floor-to-ceiling books on one long wall. As a trick, Bridger had them arranged as a map, so that his Greek histories were towards the bottom right, with the Arabic texts further along, leading you to Indo-China where he'd won his spurs. Russia was top right, and France, diplomatically, bang in the middle. Bridger enjoyed giving visitors a tour, showing them precisely where the English Channel ran up the wall, with his collection of nineteenth-century novels on its left side and the Americans hard up against the corner. His desk was old and wide with red leather on the top, and though it was a poor relation of the ambassador's – that had been Wellington's after Waterloo – the room was a statement of confidence. Not only was he head of chancery and chargé, but happily and unmistakably an ambassador-in-waiting.

Flemyng made sure that he was one of Bridger's early callers on his first day, a steel-grey January Monday.

'Will. It had to happen.'

'And where better?' said Flemyng.

For half an hour they laughed together, and pretended.

Bridger had tales from the Far East and his two years in London, just past. They'd been nicely timed, he said, because

55

on the roll of the dice he had managed to jump the queue of men a decade older who were jostling for the top embassies. 'Coming round the bend on the rails in good fettle,' he said. 'The Americans helped, of course, laying on a war on my doorstep. So who knows? I've got every chance of a good outcome.' His new office, for all its splendour, was only a waiting room for better things.

About Flemyng's career he said almost nothing. He asked after Sam Malachy and a few of the other boys, passing on some sour gossip from London's nether world, his name for Flemyng's head office. By his account it was floundering. 'Venice, living on lost glory – the city state that lost an empire. Very sad, of course.' When he poured a drink for them both it was to offer his condolences.

'Sandy keeps me abreast of your world.' Bolder and he had served together in Hong Kong. 'Good man, Sandy. Always on the prowl. But straight, of course, so straight. Good to find him here.'

Flemyng said that Sandy had left his mark everywhere.

After a few minutes, Flemyng, having offered little apart from a friendly character sketch of Freddy Craven, prepared to leave.

He gave no sign of his disappointment, which verged on despair.

Bridger suggested they dine the following week, saying his wife Grizelda would be charmed to have him. They had come together in New York, during Bridger's service at the mission to the UN. 'A short and useful time, Will. And not just because it got me a wife. You may get the chance some day.' Flemyng wondered if Grizelda, her German family split by the Atlantic but always trying to be a good-time girl, would be able to rescue the evening.

Hoping to find some of their old rhythm, he had confronted emptiness instead. In his presence, Bridger had lost the brilliance and the edge that was shaping a spectacular career and assembling admirers in the offices where it mattered, and turned to lofty bluster. Flemyng knew that he was the cause.

Louder and less sure with every boast, Bridger was a man confronted by his own shadow, walking in fear of it.

Flemyng was certain that he could expect no comradeship there, because he was the reminder of a failure that rankled still, the wound that never healed.

'Where's your evidence?' Craven said, when Flemyng confessed his disappointment, and his fear.

'There is none. None at all. But you forget how I once knew him, and I can read him like a book. He dislikes the thought that we're here together, because it reminds him of defeat. I think he may even hate me.'

Craven said he was sceptical, but would watch for the signs. 'Don't let it eat away at you. You've done nothing wrong.'

'I know,' Flemyng said. 'But youthful passions are the most painful. We can't forget. Nor forgive.'

SIX

In the three months since his unhappy reunion with Bridger, Flemyng's mood had darkened often enough to trouble Craven. The lightness he had carried with him in Vienna, even at painful moments, was rarely seen. He often laughed with the old man, and on embassy high days he carried himself with élan, but there were long afternoons when his door stayed closed, or when he took to walking the city with no hint of a purpose. Craven suspected he had nowhere to go. It was easy for his colleagues to pin the distraction on the departure of Isabel, whose picture he kept in the top drawer of his desk, but Craven had concluded even before the arrival of Kristof in their lives, unexpectedly and quietly at the cool end of April, that Flemyng was thinking not of her, but of himself.

As the embassy emptied for the weekend on the Friday of his meeting with Kristof, Craven asked Flemyng at the gate to take a walk with him. They stepped away from the two crowded cafés facing each other at the crossroads near the embassy, and Craven led him to a different bar where, despite the young crowd, he seemed at home. There was music playing from a juke box, and Craven was the oldest man in the room. They alone had hats to hang up. Flemyng thought he could smell a joint through the fug of Gauloise. The only women looked like students, draped in black. 'Not my kind of place, you're thinking,' Craven said, and laughed. 'Perhaps you're wrong.'

They drank a beer together, and Flemyng said, 'Why, Freddy?'

'Because I'm worried about you. Have been for a while.'

'Don't be. I've had a difficult time, that's all.'

But Kristof had given Craven his chance. 'I think we have something to play with, you and I. Your man excites me. You?'

'I suppose so, but I learned my caution from you,' said Flemyng. He gave the old man a smile. 'I'm going to take it slowly.'

So he should, said Craven, but he must remember how the game was played. 'You're a fisherman. You know how to pull him in. Don't give him too much line. I want you to think about that this weekend. I'm going to close myself in with my books and my records. Play some music. And you must relax, too – we may have busy days to come. Any parties?'

'As it happens, yes.' He held out his hands in acknowledgement. 'A good crowd tonight.'

'Do have fun,' Craven said, and they drank up.

*

About a mile away, near the dingy maze of the Marais, Maria Cooney was looking through the window of a restaurant. Peeping across the brass rail above the white lace curtain she saw mirrors and murals, light winking from the squat decanters at the side of the bar and warming the red velvet, a few single men enjoying the concentration of their own tables, three couples, and not one diner who didn't seem to be French. A waiter was polishing a plate with his napkin and stared past her through the window, his face blank. Maria leaned closer, and the window's contours gave the scene a happy distortion as she moved her head to look past him. She heard no sound from within, the bustle behind the bar a silent ritual through the glass, and the rosy room glowed with contentment.

An ordered world without threat. She savoured the evening she had planned.

Pushing open the door, however, she was startled. Grace Quincy was already there, sitting in the most private corner with an open book on the table. Maria had missed her from the window.

'Sorry.' She raised an arm and steadied herself. 'Late.'

'Forget it. I'm early. I wanted to walk through Les Halles. I like it. Nothing changes here.'

'Not yet,' said Maria. 'I love Benoit and the people here. So long as it lasts, this is Paris.'

By the time she sat down, and less than a minute had passed, she had recovered her poise. 'I knew you'd be going to Hoffman's party so I thought we might catch that dinner first. Thanks for your call to the office. I'd hoped you wouldn't mind my note to the hotel. I know we just had lunch, but…'

Quincy was taking her in, her head angled and her expression giving nothing away. She'd pulled her blonde hair back over her high forehead, and wore a light denim shirt that was a perfect match for her honeyed skin. Her smile was easy when it came and she moved her arm across the table in a gesture of reassurance. 'Course not. The party could be a bitch, so dinner's great. Let's enjoy ourselves.'

Maria gave her a quick sketch of Hoffman, his habitual discomfort and his heroine-worship. But he was young, she said, and we all had to grow up. He could write, that was the thing.

'He scratched himself right through that lunch,' Quincy said, and they both laughed. 'We'll see if he can run to a party.'

They were due at his apartment at nine, and Hoffman had promised everyone a mixed crowd. It was the eve of his thirtieth birthday, so Maria said the least they could do was to stay until midnight.

Even while they placed their orders, taking all the advice they were offered, and before their soufflés had arrived, Quincy was piecing together Maria's history. The conversation was fast. 'New York before you got here, but you were filing from Saigon last year.'

Maria had a practised story that papered over some of the gaps in her years of work, in which Washington was never mentioned. She spoke of travels that had taken her off the circuit for months, of an assignment in Africa that had taken most of a year, forays to Indo-China when the war was only a baby, and she counterbalanced the vagueness that necessarily clung to these times with a few diamond-hard stories to establish her presence in certain places at particular moments. Within a few minutes they were exchanging experiences like friends on the road, remembering characters they'd encountered at the ends of the earth, and enjoying the closeness of wanderers who find themselves sharing a tempting path to somewhere new.

'Sometimes I feel I need home, but when I'm there – wham! – I've got to get away again,' said Quincy. 'Even last week, if you can believe it. I like it that I'm usually the only girl on the beat. You, too, I guess.'

'Oh, yeah. Suits me,' Maria said.

She was thinking of the office in Washington that was her real home. Its four floors were intimate, and the last time she had spent a week there she had met no other woman except the secretary to her boss, as formal as a porcelain figurine, whose task was to guard the basement lair from which he came and went by a private entrance that allowed him to use an alleyway at the rear rather than the door through which everyone else entered on L Street, next to a diner where none of them was allowed to eat. Maria's secret celebrity was enhanced by her sex, but the stories they told of her were not of seductions, but silky manoeuvres in the field touched by ruthlessness. Always an object of surprise.

In the boss's team, which demanded a loyalty that all his soldiers understood, they knew that she was the equal of any of them save one or two veterans who had been there from the start, and had shed blood, but whose powers were on the wane. These were confusing times for the old warriors, who remembered simpler days, and the reason a woman found herself treated in that building with a deference that would have surprised any outsider was that there were a few gamblers in the ranks who spread the word that if you were trying to pick the boss's successor, or certainly the one after that, you might do worse than place your pot on Maria Delaney Cooney. One of the few women among them, and a flier.

Without fuss, and very quickly, she turned her mind and the conversation away from herself and on to Quincy and her adventures. Her own mysteries remained unspoiled and intact.

They ate easily and happily, Michel Petit himself bringing them the evening's best offerings from his kitchen, and Maria found that more than an hour and a half sped by like a few passing minutes. Quincy's concentrated gaze, which intimidated many of the men around her, was a thrill, and, far from producing nervousness, encouraged her to take the conversation away from the open road to personal and risky ground: home and college, even parents, the shared experience of never having married. The wandering Irish. Lovers. Maria spun a mysterious wrap for her own shoulders.

Quincy seemed to be open. 'Listen. Things happen on the road, like you know. Good times – a night, a week, sometimes a season with someone who seems special. Then you take off again. I've learned that I'm a gypsy, travelling on.'

Maria's state of intoxication, which had little to do with the one glass of wine inside her, was obvious to the man at the next table, a lone diner who had worked his way through a yeoman's hearty meal and a bottle of burgundy, and who was now subsiding with a giant *ballon* of calvados swirling in his hand. He'd pulled a vast napkin from his neck, and it blanketed his knees as he focused his eyes on Maria. He couldn't look away, because there was obvious drama. Quincy was in charge, smoothly directing the evening and drawing power from the attention of her companion and the ambience of the crowd in the room, and Maria was speeding up in her wake. Benoit had filled up and the noise was rising gradually, but neither woman noticed. They were hooked together.

When they left, just before ten, Maria led the way with confidence to their destination near République, squirming through narrow cut-throughs that she knew well. Hoffman's paper had provided him with an apartment in a corner building where he often seemed lost in the high-ceilinged rooms with their peeling walls and Maria knew that the tiny kitchen was hardly ever used. But the birthday party was an opportunity to fill the long salon with acquaintances who might reconsider him as a result.

'You never know, there may be some women there,' said Quincy. Maria laughed.

She had bought a small present for Hoffman, for whom she had affection. When he needed to explain a bout of misery or ask help in a passage of arms with his editors, it was in Maria that he found a listener.

She realized, as they were shown in by a barman hired for the night, that this was meant to be the end of Hoffman's embarrassment. The night he'd grow up. Quincy, who'd only seen him scratching himself through lunch, understood, too. She glanced at Maria and they exchanged a silent vow. They were both there to help.

'Jeffrey,' said Hoffman to Quincy, holding out his hand. 'We hardly spoke at lunch. Sorry.'

The other hand was in his black curls and he swayed from side to side. But to Maria the flower-patterned shirt told a story, like his new shoes. Hoffman was trying harder than ever before.

'No apology, Jeffrey,' Quincy said. 'Please. We'll make this birthday sing.'

There was already a crowd, with Max Anderson in the corner, occupying a chair that he seemed unlikely to abandon until the end of the party. His junior was managing his drinks, and corralling guests who were to be introduced.

'I knew Max when nobody had heard of him,' Quincy said. 'Nobody.'

Maria laughed and put a hand on her arm, touching her for the first time, and it was an electric moment that made her pause before she spoke. 'But d'you know what? I kind of admire how he's done it. Loads of bullshit, but plenty panache, too. You can't take that away. Those paragraphs still sing.'

Then, suddenly, Maria lost her composure for the second time that evening.

It was brief, and she didn't stumble, but her flow stopped. Quincy felt the hand on her arm tightening before Maria pulled it back, and noticed the puzzlement on her face before the moment passed and Maria laughed again.

'Well, here's a surprise,' she said.

Walking forward, she pulled Quincy with her and stood behind a man who was bending forward to talk to Max. They could hear him talking about Prague. Sensing the women's presence, Max's companion straightened and turned towards them. He smiled warmly.

'My dear Maria.'

She turned to Quincy and then gestured towards him.

'Let me introduce a friend of mine, Grace. You'll like each other. This is Will Flemyng.'

He shook hands, and felt Quincy's grip for the first time. They began to talk and, recollecting the conversation later, Flemyng recalled the speed with which their journey began. Quincy's questions were sharp, and would have seemed abrupt without the softness of her appearance that belied the steel underneath. Or, he thought, if they had come from a man. He kept his own history back, and turned her energy back on herself: what had she seen in Prague? Where was she bound? Could it be true that she had little interest in politics at home, despite the fire and blood? She was confident at every turn. Afterwards, he realized how rare it was to have such a conversation with someone who had not changed position once, nor offered an apology for any view. A fast driver who promised danger.

With midnight not far away, Hoffman's time was coming. He'd filled the room, and the accomplishment had settled him. He'd even been able to spend a little while in Max's chair, holding court in his own tentative way. The waiters, from an Irish bar on the other side of République, dispensed Guinness from a tin barrel and oysters from sheaves of wet newspaper in a basin, as well as Hoffman's favourite whisky, and his plan had turned into a shrewd success. 'You party well, Jeffrey,' said Quincy, and it warmed him.

As she spoke she could see Maria and Will Flemyng together at the tall windows at the end of the room that opened on to a small balcony. They were standing close, shoulder to shoulder, and while Quincy watched something passed between them that caused each of them to turn to face the other. For a moment, she saw them both in outline. A street lamp outside lit them from behind and below, as if on a stage, and they were etched against the night, Flemyng's longish face motionless as Maria spoke. His black hair shone, his shoulders were relaxed, and with his slim, gentle profile he was a picture of easy balance. Maria leaned towards him, the light from the room picking up the gleam in her hair, and her hands were on the move, punctuating the story she was telling. Quincy concluded that they knew each other very well.

Across the room, Max was in conversation with Maria's English journalist friend. Edward Abbott was a picture of gentility, as ever, though a fire burned inside. Impeccably polite, his manners were misleading, particularly to Americans. Moved equally by the cracks appearing in Eastern Europe and the smell of protest in the West, he had passions that outsiders often missed, because they confused elegance with detachment. Quincy watched him give Max more time than she would, listening to his state-of-Europe speech and, she had no doubt, to his take on her. It would be sharp.

But Quincy was happy, because her short conversation earlier with Flemyng had intrigued her. Within a few minutes he'd picked up her trail across Eastern Europe and they exchanged memories of Berlin and Vienna. He knew Warsaw just well enough to follow her story of the student riots she'd watched a few weeks before, and they talked about the panic that had gripped the authorities after the police went on the attack outside the theatre and the kids fought back. He turned to the first upheavals in Prague, and revealed as they spoke that he had the eyes and ears of a natural observer. She recognized a listener when she met one. He knew the price of milk in Warsaw, the history of the party boss in Prague who'd been sacrificed in the first desperate purge in March, and when they began to speak of Paris she realized that he knew the names of the very students at Nanterre who were planning their next madcap advance.

'You could be a correspondent,' she said. 'Writing it through. Ever tried?'

'Don't have the flair,' he said with a laugh, and they both knew he didn't believe it. As for the embassy, she recognized his story as one she'd heard so often: settled routine, tedious bureaucracy, wrestling matches with French ministries on treaties and trade, sorties to Brussels to leap on the roundabout of negotiations that was turning backwards.

'My life,' he said. 'Just that.'

Quincy laughed at him, shaking her head. 'And the band played on.'

Then she said, 'Bullshit.'

She showed the thrill she felt when Flemyng shrugged and gave his broadest smile.

He left her side, and they toured the room. Even Max had succumbed to the fatal charms of Guinness and whisky and Hoffman, round and curly and now graced with a permanent smile, knew that for the first time since he'd settled in Paris he'd pulled it off. Maria squeezed him, and the crowd egged him on, determined to stay in the room until the sound of his birthday boomed out on the stroke of midnight from the church tower across the boulevard. He swung from one side of the room to the other like a champion.

Max, back in a huddle with Edward Abbott, eased him away.

When the hour came, Quincy moved towards Flemyng just as Hoffman was opening the glass doors on the balcony to let in the sound of the bells. When the first boom struck, Max took to the out-of-tune piano at the other end of the room and began to play, so that everyone would sing for Hoffman. As a gift it was perfect, and Max, who had a hidden softness, understood. The boy had made it.

And to finish it off, Max rose, quite unsteadily, and roared out another toast. 'The Movement of 22 March.' They all cheered.

Maria was with Max when he rose from the piano and now she saw Quincy, just as she had watched her with Flemyng half an hour before, silhouetted at the window – Flemyng's head back and a laugh on his face, Quincy alive and sparkling, waving a hand above her head. She was telling a story that entranced him, his excitement as obvious to Maria as Quincy's delight.

She forced herself to turn away and sought out Hoffman, saying goodbye with an arm round his shoulder, and wished him a happy weekend. Then, before she joined the stream of guests moving towards the door, she reached Flemyng's side. Quincy was with him. Maria touched one cheek with his, and he pulled her close, a hand tight on her back. 'We'll talk soon,' he said quietly. 'I meant it when I said I needed help. Have a good weekend.'

Maria was hardly able to reply. She nodded, and waved at Quincy, getting a blown kiss in return. Glancing back at Flemyng, she felt as if a shadow had fallen on his face, and caught a hint of desperation. Before it was too late, she moved forward. In a flood of determination, she pulled Quincy's arm.

If there was hesitation, Maria couldn't feel it.

Turning from Flemyng, she led Quincy downstairs.

SEVEN

The brothers spoke to each other more often by letter than telephone.

Flemyng's weekend was a muddle, and he wanted to talk. After the party, his Saturday dragged. He walked beside the river, followed the sound of a jazz saxophone to a café near Odéon where he tagged on to a student crowd for an hour, then decided to find a cinema where he could sit in the dark. The weather had turned and there was spring warmth, and plenty of light, but he spent the next two hours in happy isolation watching a gloomy film of young love. By the time he got to his apartment, the evening was cooling and the walkers on his boulevard were wrapped up. He realized that in the whole day he had not had a conversation of more than a few words. He brewed some tea, and prepared for his call, thinking of home.

In the family house at Altnabuie, Mungo Flemyng kept a file of light-blue airmail envelopes that held the story of the travels of Will and Abel down the years. And because he was a historian, Mungo's archive was complete and arranged in date order, from the mid-fifties onwards. But any of his students would have found it an unusual correspondence to explain, because the letters among the brothers, although regularly spaced, were usually brief and invariably cryptic.

They hinted at an unseen story in which the boys played different roles as they grew up.

When Mungo himself opened the wooden box in his study where he kept the letters, which he did more frequently as the years went by, he would weave tales of his own, imagining a grey Berlin winter or spring in Vienna. Summers in America, perhaps, with Abel coming and going. Experiences he had never had, but he liked to think the best of his brothers and brought his natural optimism to bear on their adventures. Imagining was perhaps even better than knowing. As the oldest of them, and therefore keeper of Altnabuie and its memories, he treasured the archive as a matter of duty as well as reassurance.

He knew it was only a part of the story, sketched out in the letters that had come home. A set of clues, no more. And of the communications between his brothers when they were both abroad he knew nothing.

But they had never lost of the habit of writing – Abel's scribbled postcards filled another box in Mungo's study – which meant that phone calls from abroad were rare. Never on Sunday, an undisturbed time when he prepared for the students he'd see in Edinburgh the next afternoon, and rarely on Saturday, which was a day for a settled routine.

So at the sound of the first phone call he felt a pinprick of alarm. There was no reason for fear, but Mungo's life was usually free of the unexpected.

He was in the garden, feeling the first brush of spring. Only in the last few days of April had some warmth come. The frosts had persisted long after they should have slackened, leaving the ground bone-hard and frightening the spring flowers that Mungo was trying to encourage. Easter had been hard all round. The south-westerly winds that were funnelled up from the loch had blown strong, leaving clusters of broken branches along the side of the house and piled in a jagged trail towards the hill. There were bare slopes beyond, showing no signs of life, and the birch and sycamore that circled the house weren't in leaf. Only now was there a first, tentative softening in the air and some hope that the season was on the move. Mungo was having a smoke against the old wall at the top of the garden, wrapped up against the evening chill, when he heard the phone ringing inside the front door. He walked slowly to the house, but the bell still rang.

Picking up the black handset, he heard the voice of an American operator – 'person-to-person' – as he gave his own quiet greeting, 'Lochgarry two-two-oh.'

Abel.

'I've got good news,' he said, after Mungo had established that there was nothing wrong, his first impulse. 'I'll be home in a week or two. Don't know the dates yet. Alone, I'm afraid. Hannah has to stay stateside with the baby. Is that all right?'

Mungo, who could see the rounded happiness on his own face in the hall mirror, began to talk about how they'd spend the days – who'd come for a drink, how they'd lay the table full out like the old days, where they'd walk on the high paths and how they could spend the evening by the fire, telling family tales.

'I missed you last week at Easter,' he said. 'It was a little lonely here, to be honest. Especially with it being so bright.'

But they could make up for it in May. Will would be bound to join them, because a coming together was so rare these days, and Mungo had received a letter from Paris two weeks before, suggesting that it was his intention anyway. Everything was falling into place as if it had been planned. Abel's presence would surely make it certain that Will would come. And Abel responded to Mungo's evident excitement with relish, his voice rising. He spoke of the house, his memories and his hopes. Most of all of Will, and how he missed him.

'We'll have an old-fashioned time,' he said. 'Babble on hand from start to finish.'

Arthur Babb, handyman and virtual housekeeper, had arrived in their lives after a chance encounter with Mungo's father in the hills where he was wandering in the empty time before the war. Taken on for summer work, the Cockney teenager had stayed because there was no good reason not to. The boys had known him for most of their lives. Now in his sixties, he would always be Babble to them – Abel's name for him had stuck – and, with their parents gone, he was the physical link to their past. On their landscape, he had been the pioneer. Mornings on the burn trying to spot a fish lying in one of the shallow pools, long walks through the wood and on to the hill in the hope of an eagle sighting, evenings when he'd tell them stories of his family in London – a tribe that the boys found numerous beyond their imagination, driving barges on the Thames and seeming to run every market stall from Borough to the dark, teeming byways of the East End. There was a happy wildness in Babble that the boys loved and concluded early on that they wanted for themselves. He uncovered every secret for them. One spring afternoon he had been with them when they saw their first adder dance, holding them back but urging them to enjoy the passionate ritual of the young snakes at the edge of the wood. He shared most of their memories.

Mungo listened to Abel speaking of his hopes for the visit, and gave him news of the house, the hill, the loch. His brother's voice was distant, coming and going in waves on a line that echoed, and Mungo was conscious as always of the limits to their intimacy in such calls. Before they parted, he returned to his first question. 'All well with you?'

Was there a hesitation? 'Never better,' Abel said. 'And I'll have some news for you when I come.'

There was no more, so Mungo went to find Babble. He was in the kitchen, organizing their supper, and their moods lifted. Only two weeks, and Abel would be back. So would Will, surely. Mungo said they should raise a glass. A Saturday to remember.

The phone rang again.

'Will! Now here's a coincidence,' Mungo said, back in the hall. He was flustered. 'Guess who else has just rung? I can hardly believe two brothers on one night.'

'What?'

Something was wrong.

'What did Abel have to say for himself?' His brother sounded tense.

Mungo spoke to him directly only once a month or so, and he was sensitive to his tone, the pace of conversation. Tonight there was no laughter in his voice. Mungo felt the return of the alarm that he'd encountered fleetingly a few moments before, and this time it settled.

'Only that he's going to be here soon. Briefly, I imagine. The dates have to be settled. Just himself – no Hannah, sad to say. But I was hoping it could be you, too, just as you've said. That's what I assumed when we were talking.'

'Why?'

'Well, you wrote. I thought you were planning...'

'But this has come out of nowhere,' Flemyng said.

'All the better for that, surely. Abel's thrilled at the thought of the three of us here.' He knew that his puzzlement must be obvious.

'I'm sorry, Mungo, I can't be sure that I'll be able to arrange it. Things here are busier than I thought they'd be. Complications, and so on.'

Mungo, who hadn't heard Will so uncertain for years, said that Abel had sounded like a schoolboy again. Full of excitement.

'And do you think that's why he rang?' Flemyng sounded agitated.

'I don't understand this, Will. What on earth's the matter?'

Flemyng spoke slowly, and to Mungo it sounded as if he was addressing someone whom he hardly knew, and not a brother. They were careful, hard words.

'Did he mention me directly? Ask what I'm doing? Mungo, I need to know.'

Babble had taken a drink from the kitchen and was placing it on the hall table. He stopped when he saw that Mungo was pale. The bonhomie of a few minutes before had evaporated. Without a word, he pulled a chair from the other side of the hall and slid it behind Mungo so that he could sit down. He remained at his station for the rest of the conversation, standing at Mungo's shoulder.

His brother's voice was cold. 'Tell me.'

'Will, I'm sorry about this but I don't know what's gone wrong,' Mungo replied. 'We don't speak often these days, and I'm thrown, to be honest. What's wrong? Abel wondered how you were – that's all.'

From Paris, his brother spoke sharply.

'Nothing. I can't talk now. But please let me know what Abel said, exactly. Perhaps we shouldn't speak like this. Write to me, would you?'

Then, after a pause, he said, 'Please.'

His voice had changed in a way that alarmed Mungo, because he picked up a tremor in his brother's voice that he'd seldom known. A touch of panic.

Of course he would write, Mungo said, though he was already worried about what he might say.

His brother's last words were, 'I'll explain in due time. I'm so sorry.' And he was gone.

Mungo, still wearing a shooter's long tweed jacket against the cold, stayed in his chair. Babble was standing by him, and asked if he wanted another drink. At Mungo's nod he disappeared towards the kitchen.

Mungo stood up, and shedding his coat he opened the front door and looked down the slope towards the loch. Darkness wasn't far away. The last of the sunset had thrown a fringe of pink on the rim of the far mountains and the landscape was dappled in the dusk, its black places already lost to view. Soon all the contours would disappear. He heard no sound outside. Taking in the silence for a few minutes, he turned back to the house when he heard the grandfather clock in the hall striking the hour, and it broke the train of thought that had taken him far away. Babble had another drink for him, and their supper was ready.

They sat together at the kitchen table. Mungo's round and jovial features were unnaturally glum and Babble's lugubrious face, surrounded by a dark red mane, added to the picture of anxiety, even sadness. Mungo's shirt was splayed out, and his thick hair, usually neatly swept back, had sprung up. He was uncomfortable as they ate Babble's pie. 'This should be a happy night with such good news,' he said. 'A great pity.'

'Why?' said his old friend.

'I can't really say. That's what disturbs me.'

Babble said that hearing only one side of the conversation with Will, he'd understood that there was a puzzle that Mungo couldn't unravel. He wanted to know what had been disturbing about the conversation. 'Both boys on one night. It should be a celebration,' he said. 'Will is coming back, isn't he?'

Mungo shook his head, and fidgeted with his fingers.

'We've been thinking that for weeks now, and Abel makes it perfect. But Will's troubled, more nervous than I've known him for a long time. Wary and unsure of himself. And that's not Will.'

Certainly not, Babble said. He was clearing the table, and he pushed a wine bottle towards Mungo. On Saturdays, Babble always brought one in from the old cold room that acted as an indoor cellar. Through the shooting season the wine racks had collected some stray feathers and a few streaks of blood from the carcasses hung above them, and Babble had plans to move his bottles to a proper home that he was preparing in the empty stables, but there was no rush. Their time was their own.

On this night, however, he had imbibed a measure of Mungo's alarm, and, because their closeness had bred such a dislike of disturbance in the weekly routine, his own worry seeped into the conversation and confirmed Mungo in his sudden gloom. The axis had tilted, and in a few minutes Altnabuie had been thrown out of balance.

Mungo spoke. 'Their lives have always troubled me – the obligations, the dangers I suppose, too. The way they disappear. You understand why, as well as I do.'

Babble nodded, and after a little time of silence, he said, 'What worries you most?'

'That's quite simple. I worry that he isn't safe.'

Mungo said he often wanted to talk to Will's people – or Abel's – but it wasn't easy, nor even proper. They were out of his reach. Babble knew enough of the history to understand. 'But that's not how it works, I'm afraid,' Mungo said.

Babble, as he began to clear the table, asked him, 'Is there no one?'

Mungo had been far away in his mind, but came back to attention at the question. He spoke softly and slowly. 'There is one man, though I haven't seen him for long enough. He cares about Will. I know that much. Now may be the moment. What do you think?'

Babble was leaning over the sink. 'Of course. Get on with it.'

And Mungo said, 'I'll ring. I have a telephone number upstairs for emergencies. I've only used it once, when Mother died.'

He was looking through the window by the door towards the woods. Darkness had settled but he could see that the trees were bending gently in a west wind that had picked up in the last hour. There was a rattle on the glass. 'Even when it blows, we're peaceful here,' Mungo said. 'We take the calm for granted, don't we? The certainty about tomorrow.'

Babble was at his side. 'What's thrown you?'

'His voice,' Mungo said. 'A feeling that, for once in my life, I'm not able to read him.'

Babble said that they had always known that Will and Abel were leading lives that couldn't be open.

Mungo spoke with sadness. 'I understand that. They love their secrets, and I have none. Perhaps that's why I'm feeling lonely tonight.'

He turned back from the window. 'I'm a brother, and I know when something goes wrong with them. I can't stand back from that.'

'It needn't be bad,' said Babble.

'But I'm sure it is.' Mungo turned to him, and there was no smile. 'I know Will too well.'

'What kind of badness?'

Mungo said, 'I can't tell. For his sake, I hope he can.'

*

Flemyng slept fitfully, rising with the light and finding a café that opened early, where they were still rolling the tables into place on the pavement and wiping them down. He walked to the stand on the corner of the Boul' Mich to buy his newspapers and spent a minute or two scanning the headlines and covers. *Paris-Match* had a fashion portrait, and he turned to the news magazines. A byline caught his eye, and he added the magazine to his pile.

Walking back to the café, he turned to the centre pages, and there was Grace Quincy. It was a valedictory to America at a time of agony before she resumed her European travels, a poem to her own feelings. Assassination and riots, the melodrama of humiliation and wild hope in politics, a wanderer's picture of home that expressed a child's feeling of loss and wonder. Flemyng stopped on the corner, leaning on a lime tree, to read to the end. There was a picture of Quincy in Chicago, on a burnt-out street in the dusk with police shields behind her, and he remembered the strength that he had seen in her at Hoffman's party. He had a habit of talking aloud to himself when it was safe, and as he stepped towards his table at the café, he said, 'I like you, Miss Quincy.'

The call from Sandy Bolder came to his apartment in the late morning when he was hoping for more solitude. He had excused himself from church and the ambassador's drinks, deciding to throw himself into serious work on his French, which he still thought underpowered. He'd been reminded in recent weeks of Bridger's ease and eloquence in, so it seemed, any language he chose. It persuaded him to improve.

He had bought an edition of *Madame Bovary* from a *bouquiniste* on the Left Bank that pleased him because it seemed to have passed through many hands, although he was finding his progress unsatisfying, and he was working his way into

Emma's first affair with distracting detours to the dictionary he'd placed on the sofa beside him. The sun was filling his drawing room as he tried to find a rhythm in his reading, and he was looking forward to a serene afternoon, alone. When Bolder interrupted he was irritated.

'Will? Sandy here. I think we need to get together this evening. No names, no pack drill' – Bolder's patter always made Flemyng wince – 'but there are things to say. Brasserie Lipp? Nice bustle on a Sunday. A quick something at about eight?'

And now he was side by side with Bolder in the back room, attended by a cadaverous waiter with a droopy grey moustache who hadn't smiled since they'd taken their places and who'd slid their table back into place so that they were pinned like a pair of flying ducks against the wall. At least they could see the rest of the mirrored room, Flemyng thought, and their position gave them a little privacy. Bolder had started with office gossip while he poured from a carafe of red wine and broke bread for them both.

'Poor Freddy. It seems to be such a struggle. How long, dear Lord, how long?'

Flemyng refused the invitation. His mind was flitting from the conversation to Mungo, and he felt flashes of guilt at his dyspeptic phone call the night before. Guilt, and anger at himself. Too much of his anxiety had been on display.

With Bolder, he had to hide it. They had moved from Freddy to the pernickety habits of Wemyss, the ambassador's private secretary – 'Wemyss, sounds like seems' was the label that Bolder never failed to pin on him – and then he had made Flemyng's flesh creep with a description of the new librarian, who was less of a bluestocking than her predecessor and therefore, as Bolder put it, held the promise of opportunity.

Flemyng avoided his leer by drinking, and thinking of Mungo. He also wondered why Bolder had summoned him.

'I don't want to talk about your friend on the metro, Will. Not the place for that,' he said in a schoolboy stage whisper. Flemyng stiffened with annoyance. 'But we're hearing a good deal about the other side at the moment. You'll remember I said in Freddy's room that Pierce has spotted *activity*.'

'Even Pierce,' Flemyng said.

For ten minutes or so Bolder rehearsed the office view of the NATO negotiations, spoke admiringly of the quality of material finding its way to the station from Prague and Warsaw, and gave a clumsy precis of cables from London about Berlin which Flemyng had digested for himself the previous week. Bolder also made a case for his own contacts in France in circles where sympathy lay with Moscow. Flemyng believed that Bolder could never sustain a conversation with such people without appearing ridiculous, whether in a philosophers' café or on a trade union march, and concluded that at best he had acquired a useful contact in one of the French agencies who watched Moscow's friends as best they could.

There was alarm about Russian intentions in Prague, Bolder said, and as a consequence a fear that France and Italy might face trouble from those whom he described simply as the undesirables. 'Trouble of a kind we haven't known,' he said with satisfaction and his sideways smile. 'I'm on alert. Standing by my bed.'

'So what's new?' Flemyng asked. 'We know all this, Sandy.'

Bolder tapped the side of his nose, and Flemyng was unable to prevent himself from laughing.

'Don't mock, dear boy, please. I do have one titbit. I think it may turn out to be one of the juiciest we've had in our time here.'

They watched the waiter clear their plates without a word, and Bolder waved him away.

'Plans of ours. Important plans. I think they have them,' he said in a whisper.

'Who?' said Flemyng, irritated by 'I'.

'Who do you think? Don't tease me.' Bolder's discomfort verged on anger. 'The reason I'm choosing you,' he said, 'is that you had that brush in the street. We know something, don't we? That your man and his compatriots, Berliners of the wrong sort, are just Moscow's cherished message boys. That's my point. There's a game afoot.'

'So you're telling me there's a leak.' Flemyng's incredulity was obvious. 'Where?'

Bolder placed both hands on the table, spread apart as if he were poised at a keyboard. 'There are so many places to choose from, I'm afraid. We may be talking military planning here – movements, how many people in the field...' and he dropped his voice. 'The things we're able to do in a time of trouble, along with our allies. Does the other side know much more than we've always thought, and at the worst moment imaginable, when Moscow and Washington are both in a spin? That's my question.'

'When, Sandy?' Flemyng said. 'When did you learn this?'

'Over the course of a week or two, and I think I've confirmed it this very weekend. I can tell you this much, Will. The French have found traces of a network. I'm told they have a list. A roster of spies, sent to get inside our secret places.'

Flemyng said nothing, because Bolder was heading towards his climax.

'They're not sharing names or places with us – yet. But they will, and I think I can say that it will be through my good offices.'

'The Americans?' Flemyng said.

'Exactly what I thought you'd ask.' Bolder was smiling, enjoying his moment. 'More your territory than mine, of course. Our French friends rather enjoy holding things back from Washington, as you know, but I'm told that the word may be out. I shall be learning more, in time. That's all I can say. But at this end, of course. I wanted you to be the first to know.' He ran the back of a hand across his lips. 'I'm going to London in a day or two. No cable. This is being done in person – solo, you might say.'

His triumph laid out, Bolder waved to the waiter sitting at his station by the bar and he rose to come to them, a long napkin trailing from his arm. 'Your ears only, of course.'

'Freddy?' said Flemyng, watching him.

'Not yet,' Bolder said and raised a glass, as if no other answer were possible. 'Only when I see the names.'

Flemyng concealed most of his shock, but the conversation left him staring at his companion in a state of wonder. Either Bolder was bluffing, in which case he had lost his bearings and was veering towards a cliff edge, or he was handling a precious prize with a fecklessness that Flemyng could barely comprehend. To arrange a rendezvous for such a revelation at Lipp, which Flemyng considered a gathering place for all the disgruntled waiters in Paris and their target customers, was an act of delinquency. To boast of having kept Freddy Craven in the dark was disloyal and shocking, and – Flemyng was cool and honest about himself – to trust him with such a secret before telling London was to court danger with the recklessness of a street drunk. Yet Bolder, summoning cognacs for them both, was oblivious.

Flemyng knew, too, that later, when he would lie awake as he had done each night for a week, he'd consider another possibility. That Bolder was playing his own game.

The curse and joy of all their lives.

He took the only sensible course, and changed the subject. Bolder reacted as if he had expected it.

'The students out at Nanterre?'

'A comic business,' Bolder said.

Flemyng smiled. 'Some of them call themselves *situationists*, whatever that means.' He shook his head.

'There you are.' Bolder was laughing now. 'Piffle. Some of them are twenty years old. We mustn't be distracted by them. The old Moscow hands are the real danger. They've been at the game a long time. The deeper undercurrents run strong.'

Flemyng was aware, he went on, as if he were talking to an outsider, that NATO was being tested. Russian intentions were hard to read, and therefore alarming. 'That is why I believe I have a duty to take myself to London, entertaining though these students may be,' leaving no doubt about where he stood on the subject of some of Flemyng's reports.

As if they were deliberately putting Bolder's revelation out of their minds as well as their conversation, they paid the bill quickly, Bolder counting out the francs in two piles to get the sums right, and made a hurried exit. Their apartments were only a few streets apart so they walked together on the first part of the journey home, heading west on the boulevard before they turned into a short street that would bring Bolder to his door. After a few minutes in which they'd said nothing, Flemyng stopped and spoke sharply. Bolder was taken aback by his tone.

'Let me be clear, Sandy. Who do you think is on this list that you are told exists but haven't seen, and why should we believe in it?'

'Please don't jump on me. I'm like one of your bloody stalkers in Scotland. Advancing slowly on my target, but not there yet.' He had reddened and anger was showing for the first time. 'If I knew names, I would be convening meetings with Freddy, unleashing the dogs, wouldn't I? All I know is that there is evidence of a network of agents who are starting, ever so slowly, to dig deep. The kind of thing we dream about. Except this time it's the other side doing it to us, and our allies. All of them, because we're in this together.'

'And you've swallowed it in one gulp,' Flemyng said quickly.

The barb hit home and Bolder's excitement showed its brittle edge. 'This may be my moment, Will. Trust me to judge if this is the genuine article.'

'I'm simply reflecting,' Flemyng said, 'on some of the dud leaks that have been sent our way in recent years. We know what happens when the service is forced to spend time chasing its own tail, and disappearing up its own backside. We're turned inside out.'

'You can trust me,' Bolder said, and, for the first time that Flemyng could remember, laid a hand on his shoulder. He was not a toucher, and it was a sign of his need for praise. His anger had passed, and he was the supplicant again.

'I hope you're right, Sandy. Believe me.'

They walked for a few minutes in silence, and reached Bolder's apartment building.

Flemyng knew what was expected. 'I'm grateful for your confidence, Sandy, but it's all rather troubling and puzzling. Let's talk when you're back from London. Do be careful there.'

Bolder looked crestfallen as they parted with a brief handshake. Flemyng watched him fumble for a key before he turned away for the five-minute walk home. Bolder called after him from the doorway as Flemyng pulled his trilby down and reached the corner.

'I'm so grateful, Will. Your trust is important to me.'

Afterwards, Flemyng reflected that if they had taken another route, a detour round the great bulk of Saint-Sulpice whose bells he could hear from his bedroom, and had walked first to his own apartment instead of to Bolder's, there would have been a moment of crisis to add to the strangeness of their encounter at the table.

But he had no warning of that thought as he pulled his jacket tight and wrapped a scarf around his neck, his thoughts elsewhere. First, he pictured Altnabuie where he could see Mungo preparing for bed and saying his prayers – the only one of the boys who had kept the habit – and then, as he found himself veering into a favourite narrow street, he brought to mind his lost love. He thought he would never see Isabel again, but she seemed to walk beside him. Once he had wanted her gone, but would it have been better if she were there? It was a question he believed he would never be able to answer.

He was passing the piano repair shop that she had loved, where only a few tell-tale fragments on the red cloth in the window hinted at what went on inside. They were never cleared away at the end of the day, and now a street lamp illuminated a tableau that stirred him. A row of felt-covered hammers on a wooden batten taken from a piano's innards, a thick metal string wound into a coil, two ivory keys side by side and, lying on its own, a shiny brass pedal that looked like an abandoned shoemaker's last. They were remnants of their affair, a few glistening shards of memory. He didn't pause, but found as he stepped towards the corner that the sight had unsettled him.

He reached his own street, and as he stepped off the pavement he caught a movement in the darkness of the passage that ran alongside his apartment building to the street behind.

He stopped, and didn't move. Watching for a moment, he saw nothing more in the stillness.

His first instinct was a stab of relief. Bolder had gone. Then he pushed his shoulders back and walked across the roadway, directly into the shadows.

Kristof said, 'Thank you, Mr Flemyng.'

EIGHT

On the stroke of ten the next morning, Bolder was at Freddy Craven's door to report the outcome of the inquiries that had occupied his weekend. He was spruced, polished and eager.

An earlier appearance would have been unwelcome, because Craven took his time in settling into his daily routine, shovelling the books and papers alone in his office and unwilling to be disturbed before he had gone through his mysterious and reassuring paces, but Bolder was determined to be his first Monday business. He gave a sharp double knock, and waited for the call to enter. In his declining days, Craven had rediscovered the advantages of order.

Bolder's habit was to open a conversation with an apology. 'Sorry,' he said. 'But I've had a busy weekend. I had to.'

Craven was seated at his desk, leaning over his papers. 'You'll have to explain, Sandy.' He didn't look up.

'Our talk on Friday was so odd,' Bolder said, 'and I could tell that you shared my view. No hint of why Will should be picked up? Not a clue from our East German friend? Freddy, I can't quite believe it. I care about him as you do, and we must protect him.'

So he reported that he had set some hares running, although with some regret.

Sitting down, he said that Freddy would imagine how he'd gone about it, because the old man knew Bolder's style. But he would describe his preparations nonetheless. He had exchanged messages with their mutual friend Sam Malachy, now a trader in the spies' bazaar in Vienna, using the NATO imbroglio with the French as the starting point. 'We had a little talk on the telephone. Carefully, of course. Then some cables. Funnily enough, he's in London as we speak. More language training, so he says, poor chap. Needs it, mark you.'

Craven smiled. Malachy was a favourite of his.

'I did, however, find him very useful,' Bolder said.

Then he had spent the rest of Saturday on calls to London on a variety of pretexts, making sure that Flemyng's name came up in every conversation. He assured Craven that he had been exceptionally careful in concealing his purpose. He and his wife had also given Sunday lunch to two younger embassy men who lived alone and needed weekend hospitality, and afterwards Bolder had led them on a brisk walk round the Île de la Cité which had got them talking.

'I've one question to begin with, Sandy,' Craven said. 'Why Malachy?'

There was only a slight hesitation. 'Ah. He's deep in the NATO business, and an old mucker of Will's, as you know better than anyone, Freddy. He watches Moscow's men, shall we say, with an eagle eye.' He fluttered a hand to suggest it was obvious enough to need no further explanation.

'Carry on,' Craven said without comment.

As for the embassy colleagues, Bolder said that he been careful to make sure that Flemyng was never the subject of a direct question, nor a dominating figure in their exchanges. 'No one would have guessed my interest, Freddy, I promise you. No one.'

'Bridger?' Craven said.

'Hardly saw him,' Bolder replied, and moved on quickly. Flemyng had been a presence in all his conversations, his moods and his comings and goings woven easily into the weekend social round. Bolder had later found reason to ring two French friends at home before they had dressed for dinner on Saturday, he said, so Freddy could tell that he was leaving nothing to chance. He had then spent an hour with a recently acquired friend in a café two streets from his own. Some last calls to London late on Sunday, and he had assembled his thoughts. 'I have a picture,' he said.

Having heard enough, the old man raised a hand to stop him.

'So you think Will is lying.'

Bolder shook his head, and spread out his short arms. 'Lying? No. A terrible word. I wouldn't use it of Will.' He ruffled his hair as if he was trying to get rid of an infestation.

'But?' said Craven.

'But I worry about him. There are signs.'

'Signs.' Craven sighed, and said that he'd better hear what they were.

'Malachy says he's been exchanging cables with him on the NATO business and that Flemyng's been terse. Monosyllabic. Wemyss tells me that in the last week he's been working in the library away from his desk and keeping himself apart. I hear from London that he's gone quiet. Bridger said the same thing after church. Not that Pierce has the advantage of knowing all that we know. Naturally.'

'Naturally,' said Craven.

Bolder delivered his conclusion. 'Not Will's style at all. And I've asked myself why.'

Craven said that he supposed the reason that Sandy had

come to see him first thing on a Monday morning was that he had come up with an answer to that question. Shouldn't he reveal what it was?

But Bolder was not ready to advance. He took a step backwards, like a fencer in retreat. Wiping his mouth again, he said, 'No such luck, Freddy. I merely say that it's curious, and curious to a degree.'

Craven, who had known Bolder for more than twenty years since he was a boy in the office after the war and went to Berlin for the first time, said nothing. He lit a cigarette and looked towards the window, inhaling with a wheeze. Bolder was standing in front of the desk, his hands clasped in front of him as if he were about to ask a favour. Craven took a few deep, rasping breaths.

After waiting for the old man to turn his head back towards him, a signal that they could resume, he said through the cloud of Craven's smoke that there was one piece of news he'd picked up over the weekend that had greatly added to his feeling of discomfort. 'A coincidence,' he said.

Again Craven said, 'But?'

'But one that's hard to ignore.'

Craven had stubbed out his cigarette in his Johnny Walker ashtray and was pulling another from the packet. He made no effort to direct Bolder, nor to hurry him along, but instead sank back into his own haze, his shoulders dropping and his chin almost touching his chest. To an outsider he would look like a man shrinking into himself; to all those who knew him, he was in the posture when he was most alert, missing no change in the atmosphere, no unexpected word. Far from abandoning the world, he was preparing to take it on again.

'My coincidence' – Bolder was always proprietorial – 'involves a fellow at the Quai d'Orsay, whom I see from time to time. We do business, not much to be honest, but I've found him useful at some of our difficult moments. I don't think you know him.' Then, in case Craven might be piqued, he added, 'Quite junior, Freddy.'

He raised a finger straight up to make his point. 'But he'll always guide me away from a misunderstanding. He's my man on the mood. My barometer.'

Craven said nothing.

'So I tapped the glass, you might say. I was in touch over the weekend. Managed to catch him on Sunday afternoon, and said I wanted to arrange one of our lunches. We spoke over a coffee. Not on the telephone.'

If he was impatient at Bolder's pace, Craven didn't show it. His spaniel eyes were watery and still, and he seemed to have all the time in the world.

'He's well connected elsewhere.' Even with Craven, Bolder observed proprieties that weren't required in his presence, and often used the euphemisms he and his kind had to deploy outside the office. 'Knows some of the strangers in town.' Then he added, unnecessarily, 'Of the sort that we're led to believe have approached Flemyng.'

Bolder said that he had spoken to his man about NATO troubles and suggested that they meet later in the week at their usual brasserie on Place des Ternes. 'Naturally I didn't mention anything from our end, our private business so to speak.' Realizing that he might be revealing more about the scope of his weekend efforts than he meant to, he speeded up to cover any embarrassment. 'And that's when I had my lucky moment.'

'Tell me,' Craven said.

'It came out of the blue.' Bolder sounded as if he might be about to wander again. But he had reached a climax, and couldn't stop himself.

'He asked me whether I'd heard of stories circulating, that might reach the press.'

'And you couldn't help?' said Craven.

'Not exactly. I was intrigued, that's all.'

'You'll have to do better than that, Sandy.'

'It chimed with something I'd heard from an American friend, that's all. One of the better correspondents.'

He took a few steps backwards as Craven got up. Behind his desk, beside the mechanical doll, was a hat stand on which he'd hung his black bowler hat, never worn in Paris but usually taken on visits to London, and he reached for a mahogany walking stick that dangled from one of the other pegs. He was preparing for a walk. But first he went to the window, and stood with his back to the room, leaning on the stick like a countryman in the field. His breathing was rough, and he coughed before he began to speak.

'Very thin gruel, Sandy. Here's the question I ask myself. Are we at the start of a new game? Or are we getting a glimpse of something that's been taking shape without us knowing? Maybe a game directed against us. Have you considered that?'

He turned slightly to catch Bolder's eye. 'That means trusting each other.'

And suddenly on those words, with a sharp movement that caused Bolder to jerk himself to attention again, Craven delivered a hammer blow to the floor with the ferrule on the end of his walking stick. The sharp crack might have been an alarm bell. Craven's apparent torpor was broken, and when he turned his eyes were full of life. He raised the stick and jabbed it at Bolder.

'You can say nothing – *nothing* – that suggests there is any worry about Will.'

And Bolder, shaking his head, responded with words that

surprised even him. 'I'm sorry, Freddy, but I have no such worry. And I make it my business to ensure that no one else does. But I need to know what to think. You're master in this house.'

'Have you seen Will since Friday?' Craven was quite still.

Bolder smiled because he was prepared for it. 'Briefly, last night. I thought it was right to be reassuring. We dined at Lipp, and we said nothing about Friday's conversation. Nothing.' He turned away from the steady gaze of his boss.

Craven's voice was quieter when he spoke, and he changed tack. 'Sandy, you must realize how much I'm hearing from home. They can't make head nor tail of Prague yet, but they know the cracks are widening. The student business in Warsaw is another puzzle, and there's a Pact gathering there this week, with all the old warhorses on hand. Moscow making a show. America's in flames, and troubled in the gut. And here, in this city – what can we expect? The old order shaking? Maybe. And the Americans worry about us, too, as well as themselves. The London demonstration was a whopper. We all know their war's going wrong. We, you and I, like predictability. But it's slipping away.'

Craven's face was a mask of weariness, his jowls drooping and his grey hair clinging to his scalp with sweat beginning to moisten his cheeks. It was mid-morning, and he looked as if he had already suffered a long, hard day.

He still spoke gently. 'We think our trust is so strong. It holds us together and sees us through. But it's fragile, Sandy. We're more vulnerable than we like to think.'

He stepped towards Bolder, who didn't move.

'That's what I've learned, and why I worry.' He snapped his fingers, a hypnotist jerking Bolder out of his silence.

And knowing there was more to come, Bolder responded, 'Tell me, Freddy.'

'Coincidences,' said the old man. 'Like troubles, they never come alone, do they?' And because the conversation had tired him, he went back to his chair and sat down with a bump.

'You had a busy weekend and so did I. I've been asking around, here and at home. Listening.'

'And what did you hear?' said Bolder, leaning across the desk for the first time.

Craven hesitated. He kept silence, then cocked his head to indicate that he had made a decision. It seemed to come reluctantly. 'A whisper that intrigued me.'

Bolder brought his head closer to Craven's to hear the secret. It came softly.

'Will's brother has been posted to London, and in a hurry. I smell trouble.'

NINE

While they were talking, Maria Cooney was lying in her bath and thinking of Abel Grauber. Another part of the city, a different trigger for the thought, but the same man. Flemyng's unexpected appearance at Hoffman's party had brought him to mind, because they had already shared so much, and he had been her companion throughout the weekend, a spirit on her shoulder.

She knew him to be Flemyng's brother, and had learned from him how he had come to use his mother's maiden name in New York. In the years of their companionship in the same cause, a robustly American one, the story had taken shape. She knew there would be other layers to be revealed, so the family had become a fascination for her. And Maria was certain that Will Flemyng was unaware of how much she knew. It pleased her.

Abel was dark, like his brother, but his features lacked the sharp lines that could give Flemyng a stern profile in the flick of an eye, because the furrows on the older brother's cheeks could deepen quickly, and his mouth turn down. For all his cheerfulness – and the eyebrows that were usually raised, the easy hands with those long fingers that he ran through his black hair – there was mournfulness near the surface. She knew it for what it was. Abel had softer lines, and had told her that he resembled his brother Mungo more closely, although he had always been a skinny boy and would never have the confident roundness of the oldest of the three. Maria had never met Mungo but in her mind he was the picture of a beaming Edwardian, comfortable and benign – unhurried by the world, and always the stabilizer. Abel had a straight back and a near-military crew cut, by contrast with her picture of Mungo, and Maria enjoyed imagining him allowed to relax into a style that might fit their age and his time. But they both knew that the moment hadn't come. His orders wouldn't let him.

She pulled the chain that released another torrent of water into the tub, and heard the clanking from the pipework above. Her apartment had high ceilings and crumbling cornices, and plumbing that had been left on its own since the twenties, but she played to the strengths of the old place with furniture that she'd picked up in forays to a run-down emporium in Montparnasse where she found sofas and two chaises longues that were scuffed and wobbly but could be brought to life with piles of richly coloured cushions and covers, and she softened the creaky floors with thick rugs. A warm nest. And in contrast to the contemporary posters that were on the walls, she liked the antique locks that took an extra turn to open, the rusty iron bar that crashed into place behind the front door to the building, and the brass lamps that were in every room. Unlike her space in rue de Nevers, the apartment was full of colour and light. She liked to think it had no dark corners.

Abel had seen it only once, on a swing through Paris earlier in the year when he had been bound for a difficult encounter in Rome. He'd been sent to plug a leak that might have become a scandal. Maria knew how much it had cost the office, and, in the course of silencing a political operator who had turned from friend to foe, Abel had sacrificed the friendship of a colleague who, they both knew, had begun to believe in his own invincibility and drank too deep from the fountain. His tongue had loosened, and as a result he would never work for the boss again. Abel had stopped off on the way to gather his strength for the confrontation in Rome, and he and Maria had visited some of his old Paris haunts. They walked in the woods, and spent a long evening together in a restaurant where she knew there was no chance of seeing anyone from the embassy. Afterwards, with Abel stretched out on cushions on her floor, they spoke of the war and their private despair.

The next morning, Abel had visited the embassy to make his courtesy calls and reported afterwards that nothing seemed to have changed since his departure, except the ambassador. 'Did anyone ask for me?' she asked.

He reassured her. 'Course not. They know you not, except as a reporter.'

Now Abel's name had surfaced again. She went through her brief conversation with Flemyng before he left the party, when he had appeared anxious. His questions had surprised her. Had anyone asked about Abel? Were people making inquiries?

Maria was confident that Flemyng's knowledge of the details of her precise connections and the routine of her days was incomplete. But he knew her as a friend of Abel's, and his partner in some of the battles in which they were all joined. They had an agreement that had never been negotiated, because that would have unsettled them both, but allowed them to know that they were secret allies, without the freedom to be open about their lives. One day, Maria believed, they would find themselves operating together arm in arm from the same bunker, though she couldn't say when.

When Flemyng had spoken to her at the party, his first question had been straightforward and delivered with a typical touch. She was a newspaperwoman, he'd said with a smile. Was Abel in the news?

There hadn't been much more. Flemyng had spoken of other things – presidential primaries, fire in the ghettoes, students in Paris, the east – but left one restless question in her mind.

Why was he worried about his brother?

She had no doubt that his conversation sprang from anxiety: mention of Abel at a party had been dangerous. Even a show of their obvious familiarity in that company carried a risk. Flemyng had turned his charm on Quincy – she had watched him carefully and thought she had missed nothing – but with Maria herself he had been unable to conceal a touch of concern. His habit of rubbing his shoulder, as if groping for his troublesome scar, was always a sign that he was tense, and she used to joke that he would never make a poker player, because a shadow of seriousness always came across on his face when he felt personal pressure. His words never gave anything away. His face did, a little more often than it should.

As she climbed from her bath and towelled herself dry, Maria tried to remember when she had last heard Abel's name in Paris. Nothing in her office, where there was no one who knew him. She didn't know details of any operation in which he was now engaged, in Europe or at home. Yet Flemyng was alarmed – she had seen it. Abel hadn't been in Paris recently, because even if he had passed through quickly without a chance to see her he would have sent a message. And in her careful contacts with the few French officials who were her special friends, his name hadn't been mentioned. As for his circle in the city from the embassy days, no one had been in touch with her. And if they had, she reflected, she'd have hoisted a storm cone because her cover had always been assumed by Abel and herself to be deep enough to give her all the protection she needed.

There were two possibilities. That Flemyng had been unsettled by an inquiry about his brother, leading to his question about whether Abel was in the news. Or that he was sending a warning. But if so, why use her? In his time in Paris, Flemyng had only once revealed any knowledge of her position and had done so in an elliptically elegant way that left no doubt, but no trace either.

One conclusion.

Flemyng was in danger, and knew it.

TEN

Freddy Craven had a pattern for his journeys to London which he took trouble not to break. It began before noon, when he would take a corner table in a restaurant a few streets from Gare du Nord which acted as a refuge for a rolling roster of men of his own age who liked to have lunch alone, or were obliged to. There were always half a dozen of them at their single tables in two rows in the small ground-floor salon, all in shirt and tie, facing each other like a guard of honour for the families who were steered to the noisy dining room upstairs. They kept a code of silence, eating seriously but without hurry, and seemed content in their solitude. Their eyes would meet, and familiar faces got a nod of recognition but little more. Craven fitted in and enjoyed the routine. By two o'clock he would be walking to the station. The ferry and the Dover train would get him to London in time for a late supper at his club.

They were days that reassured him, and their unchanging character was as much a part of his life as the eccentricity he protected in himself, flourishing only because of his devotion to the continuity underneath. One of the attractions of a last tour in Paris was his feeling for a past that had never slipped away, one he'd come to know in the heady years after the liberation, when he was first invited by his masters to explore the secret byways of the city.

He had enjoyed the spectacle of an old lady coming back to life and walking out again.

In the years that followed, Paris had been an anchor through his wanderings. In times of trouble, he'd reach for it, and feel the pull through the storm. He loved its smells and moods, and, because he was a reserved man by nature, he envied its arrogance. Flemyng had asked in the last few days if that was why he seemed out of sorts – that he couldn't bear the sight of Paris trembling.

Craven's decision to go to London on this Monday seemed impulsive, and Janet, his secretary, marked it down as another sign of his disturbance, which she ascribed to his creeping illness. But she couldn't be sure. Booking his passage, she took his instructions for absolute discretion without a murmur – her life was played out in closed compartments – although she noted his distracted manner and downbeat spirit.

There had been talk in the embassy about his unease at the thought of upheavals in the streets, and some amusement – Bolder said that for the first time in his life Freddy was getting frightened of the unknown – but Janet had sensed something underneath, and thought that she should watch the others with care. For what, she didn't know.

As Craven left the restaurant, two waiters holding open the brass-bound doors for him and giving him formal bows of farewell before they closed the other diners in, she would have seen another sign. He was unsure whether or not to cross the street.

He hesitated on the pavement, as if worried that he might not make it to the other side in time. Then he stepped back, his overnight bag seeming to pull at him, and moved along the line of shops that led towards the end of the boulevard. He walked slowly, carrying the burden of his weariness.

But he was fortunate.

Before he reached the junction, a figure appeared at the traffic lights ahead, turning away from him unawares, and looked towards the station, standing to attention with his head held high. He wore a wide-brimmed felt hat, a light grey suit and carried a small brown suitcase that was polished and gleamed in the sun.

Sandy Bolder.

And Craven knew, on the instant, that he was bound for London.

Bolder had said nothing when they spoke, only two hours before. Why?

Craven stopped at the window of a cigar shop, and gazed at the implements and painted boxes racked up on their silver stands, his reflection clear on the glass against the gloom inside. He was still. Without changing position he could see Bolder almost skipping across the street and setting a course for the station through the swarm of taxis honking down rue de Dunkerque. He watched until his colleague had disappeared through the stone arches and a crowd closed behind him.

When Craven began to walk again, he had slowed down, his natural response to shock. He stepped only a few yards to a dingy café on the corner and went to the bar where he had a coffee and cognac. Exchanging words with men in their fifties who smoked on either side of him and drank pastis, he appeared calm. There were two students in the corner, long-haired and laughing. Craven's companions snorted; one spat on the floor. After a few minutes, he checked his watch. The Calais train would be on its way.

Dropping a few coins on the zinc bar and picking up his bag, he hailed a taxi. He sank into the corner as it rattled over the cobbles, taking no interest in the streets nor the traffic pressing in on them.

'Mr Craven, sir.' The guard inside the embassy gate was

proud that they were both naval men, which made him enthusiastic for the formalities.

'George,' said Craven, touching his hat and upping his pace as he crossed the courtyard.

He sat at his desk for two cigarettes, and recast his plan.

He was interrupted after a few minutes by one of the Gurkhas who manned the communications room. 'Message from London, sir. We thought you'd left the embassy, and we were going to hold it. But George saw you coming back, so here it is, sir. Your eyes only.' He handed across a yellow envelope and Craven opened it as he left the room.

It was worth lighting his pipe. Craven smiled and, unusually, spoke aloud to himself. 'Well, who'd credit it? Freddy's luck strikes again.'

He asked the switchboard to place a call, and within a quarter of an hour he was put through.

Ten minutes later his secretary was surprised to see him coming through her door. 'What went wrong?'

'Janet, we need to have a quiet conversation,' he said as he shut the door and slid a chair towards her desk. 'Nothing's wrong. Quite the contrary.'

He sat down and lit up. She said nothing.

'I know you will have said nothing about my travel arrangements. But did Sandy Bolder have a ticket for London, too? For today.'

She had booked nothing for him. 'He would come to me in the normal way of things. But I have no reason to think that he's gone over. Have you?'

Craven shrugged. 'Never mind. I heard something, that's all. We haven't spoken. All right?'

'Of course we haven't.' She smiled. 'I wouldn't have let you interrupt my afternoon anyway.'

He said he wanted to make a request, on their usual terms. There was a London flight from Orly at four. 'Tight, but I can make it.' Looking across the desk, he seemed to Janet to be nervous, because he kept his hands off her desk. But his eyes twinkled.

'I've then got an arrangement that I want you to make, a rather unusual one.' He knew that Janet, like him, was a devotee of Thomas Cook's European railway timetable, which Craven treasured and sometimes picked up in order to get himself to sleep, so his instructions were simple and quick. She made a note on her pad, in pencil, which she would destroy at the end of the day.

'I'm sure the timing will work,' he said.

'I'm certain of it,' she said. 'And to make sure that you have a good journey the other way, shall I get you on the night train from Victoria on Thursday?'

'You read my mind,' he said. 'The *Golden Arrow* it is.'

She wished him good luck, and he rose.

Craven then made his way along the corridor towards his room, stopping at Will Flemyng's poky office on the way. The door was closed. 'Anyone in?' He gave it a slap with his hand.

Flemyng appeared, shirtsleeves rolled up. 'Come along now if you can,' said Craven. And then, over his shoulder, 'Bring that bottle with you. I see it's open.'

They sat on either side of the desk, and Flemyng poured two full glasses of Chablis.

'Cheers.'

Craven raised his glass without speaking, then savoured his wine for a few moments. 'We need to have a frank talk, you and I, don't you think?'

'As always, Freddy.' He sipped his drink.

'I'm going to tell you something odd. Bolder is on his way

to London, I'm fairly sure. Either that or he's got an assignation with a dame in Calais, but that's not very likely, is it? And he didn't ask Janet to book his passage. Nor did he tell me. What do you make of that?'

Flemyng asked how he had found out. 'I saw him at Nord,' said Craven.

'So you were on your way, too,' Flemyng said. 'Why?'

Craven laughed. 'That's my Will. But I'm asking the questions. Have you any idea?'

Flemyng sipped his wine.

'Have you?' Craven repeated himself. He had leaned back to pat the head of the wooden doll behind his desk.

'No, except that he's been behaving strangely. More excited than usual. And it isn't the students. He doesn't think much of them.'

Craven was watching him. Flemyng's longish face was serious, symmetrical dark creases highlighting a mouth that had turned downwards. He was well tanned, and on this afternoon looked swarthy although he had shaved carefully as usual and his black hair was smooth. After a few moments Craven turned away to the window, and drank. He spoke without looking back at Flemyng, drawing on his pipe.

'Sometimes I think I'm losing my grip here.' He waited until a cloud of smoke was settling round his head.

'I'm not going to push you, Will, because I hope it isn't necessary and I want to give you a little time; let you ponder things for a bit. But remember, my boy, that I can read you. You've noticed something with Sandy' – Flemyng was surprised by the switch to the familiar mode – 'and it may be troubling you. Well, I'm bothered, too, and I want you to come to me when the moment is right. Sooner rather than later. You understand.'

Flemyng's voice was quiet.

'I do, Freddy', and suddenly he had to look directly into the eyes of the old man who'd swung back to face him. 'But I don't want to make up stories,' Flemyng said. 'Castles in the air.'

'Certainly,' said Craven. 'Nor do I want secrets in the air.'

He stood up and stretched, his energy a signal that the conversation had refreshed him. Flemyng didn't respond.

'We have to live with the damned things,' Craven said, 'and we can do without manufacturing more of our own, just for the sake of it.'

Flemyng could see a red spider's web of blood vessels in one eye, and Craven's forehead had a tint of purple.

'I'll be gone for a few days. Back on Friday I should think. Then we'll talk.'

Flemyng wished him well, asked no questions and tried a smile.

Craven said, 'We do lead rather ramshackle lives, don't we? It occurs to me that if Sandy is away, too, you're in charge. Marvellous. Enjoy it, my boy.' But his expression was serious. 'Take these.' He handed him a brass ring with two keys. 'These will get you into the left-hand drawer of my desk. If anything happens to me when I'm away… or if there's a crisis of some kind, please don't hesitate. But take good care of these, please. Old men have to make their dispositions. You never know.' He smiled at him. 'Keep them. Even I can't go on for ever.'

Flemyng laughed as he put the keys in an inside pocket, but knew that he looked awkward in collecting the glasses and changing the subject – the spring weather, the latest from Nanterre, the preparations for May Day and talk of riot squads gathering at police stations across the city – and that Craven was watching him. The old man allowed him to speak, and said nothing more. Flemyng was dismissed from the room with a nod.

On his secure phone, Craven made some brief calls. Jonny Hinckley in Brussels, always on the inside track. Then an old friend in London who answered his question easily: a check with the office language school could be arranged at short notice. He was cheerful throughout, talking briefly but enthusiastically, as if he were happy to be making an unexpected visit home. When another message was delivered from the code room, he was even happier. Janet confirmed his taxi and his flight. His third phone call was to one of his boys who'd done well.

'And how is spring in Berlin?' he began.

*

Flemyng sat for some time in his own office. He finished the bottle of wine, which was unusual for him, and knowing that Craven would be wondering how he would react to their conversation he decided to veer away from Bolder and his trip to London. Instead, he called the embassy switchboard and asked them to book a call to Scotland, and his brother. The rest of the office had been enjoying direct calls to London for a year, but the luxury hadn't yet arrived at the Lochgarry exchange. He knew there would be a record of his call available to anyone who inquired, which was one reason for making it. Flemyng knew, too, that there was a good chance he would be overheard.

Ten minutes later his phone rang and Mungo was at the other end. 'I hope you're in better form than you were the other night, *mon frère*.' He couldn't hide his concern about Flemyng. 'This is not like you, ringing during the day. What's wrong?' They were back where they had left off on Saturday night.

'Nothing at all. I wanted to apologize for being off colour last time. This is a jumpy place. We're like animals in the field that know the storm's coming, but not when. So this is me asking you not to worry.'

'And Abel,' said Mungo. 'You'll want to know if I hear any more. He'll be here in two weeks. A flying visit as usual, I expect. But, Will, if you could come it would be special for me.'

'He hasn't been in touch since we spoke?'

'No.'

'I'll try to get back,' Flemyng said, and with good wishes to Mungo and Babble he said goodbye.

A minute later, along the corridor, Craven's phone rang.

'Scotland. He rang home.'

Craven's taxi for Orly was due in ten minutes, so he searched in his desk for the half-bottle of whisky he kept for airport emergencies and decanted it into a pewter hip flask. Then he was on his way to the embassy side door, bag in hand.

At that moment, Bolder was on the dockside at Calais, full of zest. There was a strong westerly breeze and he enjoyed the air and the spray as he watched a ferry leaning into the swell and turning at the harbour wall. It would be a lively crossing, so he would stay on the upper deck. He had checked the other passengers gathering beyond the customs shed and there was no one who seemed familiar, from the embassy or anywhere else. Had any acquaintance turned up unexpectedly, Bolder would have been the first to strike up a conversation because he was always ready, but it wasn't necessary.

It was one of his unusual traits that he liked to stand out in a crowd, going against the traditions of his trade. Where Flemyng would adopt a quiet and diffident pose in most kinds of company, giving out signals of ease, and Craven would mimic the demeanour of any crowd to become part of it,

Bolder had never tried to lose his natural swagger. He was showing off his new dove-grey suit for the summer and a tie brighter than any of his friends in London would choose. Most notably of all, he carried himself with a deliberate erectness, sometimes exaggerated by a habit of tilting his head back with his sharp chin jutting out, a pose that Flemyng once told him made him look as if he was being measured up for the prow of a ship.

At the moment the gangway was clattering on to the quay, and Bolder was shuffling into line, Craven was approaching Orly in the taxi, his hand on the flask in his bag. Flemyng was lingering in Janet's office.

He'd brought two memos that he wanted to send home in that evening's bag, to be taken by a Queen's messenger on the night train. One was a leisurely account of the Nanterre upheavals, in which he erred on the side of drama. Why not? Then he exchanged gossip with Janet about her Easter holiday in Normandy and his hopes to go to Scotland in May, events permitting. As he left he asked casually about Craven.

'Freddy's in London tonight, I gather.'

'You probably know more than me,' she said, which Flemyng chose to take as a confirmation. If Craven had other plans in Paris, she would probably have told him.

Saying that he was heading home early, he went to his room and tidied his desk, locking his briefcase away for the night. He carried nothing with him as he went downstairs, only a thin novel in his pocket.

George called out to him in the courtyard. 'Message, sir, come by hand. I'm glad I caught you.'

He took the envelope, gave thanks, and passed through the gate. There was a café on the next corner where he often stopped on the way home, and he went inside before he opened it.

The waiter who stood by him until he had read the short letter said it must be good news.

Flemyng looked up, smiling. 'Yes, it is.'

Grace Quincy was asking if they could meet, and soon.

*

Taking a sheet of notepaper from the tail-coated concierge at the Meurice, Flemyng wrote a short note to Quincy. His hand was easy and elegant and he took care to express his frustration at having missed her at the hotel where he'd hoped to make contact on the way. But he would be delighted to meet, whenever she pleased: sadly, it couldn't be that evening. But could she ring him in the morning? He wrote out the phone number at his apartment. Then he said he had read her piece in the *New Yorker* and it had moved him greatly. He signed the note 'Will' and, conscious that it was early days, 'Flemyng' in brackets.

Addressing the envelope with her room number, which the concierge had been happy to give him, he left the note and took one of the taxis at the front door to Bastille. From there he walked for nearly a mile, taking care to stop twice, at a *tabac* and a café. No one was following him. He sat at a table and took a second piece of notepaper from his pocket that he had picked up at the Meurice and wrote a few words, using block capitals.

'Eight o'clock OK?'

He signed it 'W'.

Continuing his walk for five minutes more, turning eventually into a street of high apartment blocks that ran towards the river, he found the building he was looking for, pushed back the high entrance gate and slid the envelope under the first door to his left. He walked to the other end of the street and took a new route towards Bastille, where he arrived about half an hour later and walked through to Place des Vosges.

He had time to eat. For more than an hour he lingered in a brasserie under the stone colonnade, producing a Simenon paperback from his inside pocket which he began as he waited for his cassoulet. Afterwards he took a table near the bar and read, taking his time with one drink. At a quarter to eight he paid his bill and was gone.

His destination amused him, because it took him close to the apartment where Jeffrey Hoffman had produced his birthday coup and he could see that the long curtains in his salon were pulled back. A shadow moved across a white wall on the first floor. Hoffman was alone again.

Five minutes later he was in a shady street away from the traffic, in a bar where it was difficult from the door to establish how many customers were drinking in its darkness. There were two women on stools at the bar, but they showed no interest in him. He moved through the gloom and there, sitting against a striped curtain nailed to the back wall, was Kristof.

'You call this dinner?' Flemyng said, looking around.

'My little joke. When were you last in East Berlin?'

'Don't worry, I've eaten. I knew what to expect. But I'm glad we're here. We have to talk.'

'Tell me,' Kristof said. 'Why the hurry? I had expected to wait a week, perhaps longer, since we met outside your apartment. And suddenly you turn up with a note. Our signal, as we arranged. Am I allowed to know why? This is not a complaint. I am glad to see you.'

The barman shouted towards them in the dark, waving like a conductor. Flemyng called back to him, ordering drinks.

'You see what I mean,' Kristof went on. 'This is new. You are making the running.'

Flemyng shook his head. 'I want you to explain yourself, that's all. I've nothing to give. I need to know what you have for me. Us, I should say.'

He noticed a change in Kristof. Flemyng had looked again that afternoon at the sketch he had made after their first conversation, and now he saw that the craggy outline of his companion – the edges that gave him an older look – was giving way to a face that he could see had taken on a youthful mobility, dimpled and soft. Even in the gloom of the bar he could see that Kristof's eyes weren't on the move, but steady. It was remarkable that there was no symptom of alarm.

'Why?' he asked.

'As I said, I have learned about your brother.'

'And I told you that there's nothing for you there. If you think he would play games with your people, you are a fool.'

'How do you know?' said Kristof. 'If I told you that there is evidence that suggests the opposite, what would you say?'

'Rubbish.'

Kristof laughed. 'Mr Flemyng...'

'Will, please.' Their drinks arrived, and there was a moment of quiet, Flemyng's acquiescence sealed. But in the first burst of intimacy he showed his anger for the first time. 'What the hell do you want?'

'I want to help you. In return I may ask for something, but I can tell you this. The favour would be personal. It would involve no danger for you, no betrayal. That is my promise.'

'Why should I believe you?' Flemyng knew a threat when he heard one and his face was hard.

'Because you have no choice. Just in case. We are going round in circles, are we not?'

Flemyng said that he could walk out of the bar, leave Kristof alone, and the curtain would fall. It would be over.

'How do you know? I have a note written by you – at the Hotel Meurice, I see. Careless. Perhaps I had someone watching you from a window when you delivered it. A Russian friend, who can say? Or on the metro when you followed me the first time. I repeat, how do you know? We are together now, Will.'

Flemyng's stiffness remained, but his voice was softer. 'My colleagues are now aware of you. I have done nothing to break their trust.'

'Then you are remarkable in our business, wouldn't you say? Can I assume that you have told them everything, or not?' He smiled.

Before Flemyng could reply, he went on, 'I understand you, because I've broken my own trust. I will not tell you now what I can give you, but allow me to tell you this. I don't want to jump, to take a train and a fishing boat to England and hide from my people. There are things I can tell you, but it will take time.'

Flemyng's answer accepted the change of key in their conversation. His voice was still soft, but his anger seemed to have passed. 'OK. You don't want to come over. So what do you want? Money, to help us?'

'You are not as good as you should be, you know,' Kristof said. 'When I was trained, that question would have caused laughter. Maybe more. Take what you can get…Will. Don't try to pull in the fish too soon. He might get away.'

Flemyng wore the same expression as Freddy Craven had seen in the afternoon. He was quite still, with his features fixed, and Kristof took it as acceptance. He resumed. 'I will arrange for us to meet again and we can talk about what I might have. And perhaps what you might give in return.'

Flemyng jumped up from his seat, without a word, but before he could move towards the door, Kristof stood and pulled him back, quite roughly, so that their heads came together. He whispered a sentence or two before he let go.

Flemyng remained rigid.

A few seconds passed, then he pulled back and walked quickly away from the table, almost stumbling towards the door.

Kristof signalled to the barman, who'd watched him leave. No need to worry; he would pay.

Outside, it was dark in the curved street that led away from the bar. The wet cobbles shone. Flemyng walked as if he had drunk too much and was taking no care, but his mind was clear. His thoughts were speeding – to Freddy Craven's office, to home where Mungo would be in his study catching the last of the light on the loch below, to Bridger commanding a lunch table, Bolder in Whitehall, then to Washington and Abel. The closeness of family and the companionship of his secret friends overwhelmed him for a moment, and he felt adrift.

Climbing into the taxi home, Kristof's last whispered word was a dismal echo in his head.

Quincy.

ELEVEN

'Guilty?'

Maria asked the question without turning round. She sat on the edge of the bed, and ran both hands high through her hair before rising to step, naked, towards the bathroom.

Quincy was propped up on one arm and laughed after her. 'Hardly. We're in Paris.'

Maria was standing under a shower that produced only a feeble flow and she worked hard to build up a lather. She sang a little. Drying herself a few minutes later on a thick yellow towel she called through the open door, 'You surprised me. Do you mind me saying that?'

Quincy had dressed quickly. 'You didn't,' she said. 'Not at all.' She was strapping on her watch, which showed nearly eleven o'clock. It was dark outside. 'I'm glad. I get little enough affection on the road, and I need it.' She was smiling into the mirror, buttoning up her powder-blue denim shirt. Her blonde hair was back in place, and she smoothed herself down. Maria came up behind her, wrapped in a long robe, and placed one hand on her back.

'Thank you,' said Quincy. Her shoulders relaxed and she reached behind her to touch Maria.

Always aware of the need for explanation, Maria said, 'These are bad days. Maybe that's it. Wildness everywhere.'

Quincy said she was proud not to have become a full romantic, though her life had given her the chance, and she was sometimes moved by the idea of such connections. 'The cards fall and that's it. Tomorrow they'll tell a different story.'

Maria recognized the defences of the woman whose passions she had so easily roused, and made no challenge. Instead, she allowed Quincy to take command. 'I guess we'll see each other around town this week. Who should I meet at Nanterre?'

Maria gave her some names – 'you'll like Danny' – and suggested they make a trip together. Wednesdays were good; there was usually a strategy meeting, a rambling and disorganized affair in the canteen, where anyone could turn up. A week from May Day there would be a crowd. 'It's chaos. Two strangers won't make any difference, even Yanks.'

'OK, we have a date,' Quincy said.

She turned away to the corner where she had stowed her bag. Alongside, in a brown leather case, was the portable Smith-Corona that travelled with her. Her story machine, which she played like a piano. She placed it on Maria's dresser. 'I'm going somewhere tonight where I don't want to take this. Can you hold it here till tomorrow? I'll call when I can.'

'Sure. You'll feel naked without it.' They both laughed.

'You're right, but there are places where I don't want to take it. Too precious. Watch it for me.'

Maria picked up the typewriter and they both stepped into her living room, where she placed it in the bottom drawer of her desk, under lock and key. 'Your friend is safe with me.'

Quincy said, 'A companion I trust.'

Three days before, Maria had never met her, not seen her. She was a name beyond reach, a distant star in a trade that still cherished glamour and a feeling for the untouchable. But in the whirl of one long weekend they had been thrown together and – so Maria saw it – had drawn energy from each other. She knew, as well, that the speed of it all couldn't last. The pulse was too fast. Her experience told her that there would never be another afternoon like this one. They might try, and perhaps re-create some of that mood. But not for long. She knew herself too well. Like Quincy, she was a gypsy travelling on.

She attached no sadness to the thought. The pattern had long since shaped her life, and she had absorbed the lesson years before. Moments of surprise, even hints of ecstasy, then the days would resume their familiar flow, with no promise of a next time. It was why, Maria well knew, she had been first attracted to a secret life. Her most precious possession was the thrill of concealment, and the excitement of the dark.

She said to Quincy, 'Grace. Why are you here?'

A sudden question. Quincy stiffened before she laughed, and put on a quizzical face. 'I love Europe. Barricades going up east and west. Where else would I be right now?'

'At home,' Maria said, watching her from the sofa.

'You sound suspicious,' said Quincy, putting out her arms. 'Why?'

She was standing in the middle of the room, holding her ground. 'For wanderers like you and me there's always the road. It pulls at you, takes you away. Right?'

'I know it,' said Maria, 'but I sense that it's different for you. This time, I mean.'

Quincy had a serious expression, and she had picked up Maria's change of tone. For a moment, she was hard.

'Today wasn't about you getting under my skin, for God's sake, was it? Getting questions answered. Tell me it wasn't.' Her smile had gone.

Maria saw how easily her fragility had revealed itself.

'Of course it wasn't. It's been one of my best days. Truly.'

Before Quincy could reply, she went on, 'And I've got a feeling that you're working on something out of the ordinary. I may be able to help, who knows? Even in our trade, that's possible.' She laughed, and Quincy responded.

'I'm sorry. I'm tense… maybe the reason for this was…'

'Don't explain. That's better,' Maria said.

Quincy shook her head. 'No, I do want to tell you something. I need your promise, though…'

'Of course.' Maria put both hands on the low table in front of her as if she was preparing to turn over all her cards.

'Maria.' It was the first time she had used her name that day, and signalled a change of voice. Maria stood up. They spoke as if they were facing each other across a desk, perhaps one of them picking at a typewriter and the other lighting a cigarette, with a chattering office around them. Their eyes were dancing.

'You're right,' Quincy said. 'You've seen it, because I guess you know the signs. I do have something in the wind. Taking shape in the storm, I'd say.'

'Big.' Maria wasn't asking a question, but making a statement.

'I'd say so,' said Quincy. 'Certainly.'

Maria waited.

'I'm tempted to say I can break a story that will change our lives. But that's fantasy, as we know.'

'How often do we say that?' Maria said. 'The thought that keeps us going.'

'I know. This is different.'

'How?'

'By telling us how little we know. How very little.'

Maria stood up and walked across the room to the window.

She turned to face Quincy. 'We can talk some more, if you want.' Quincy shook her head to signal that it was too soon. 'But something strikes me right now,' Maria said. 'Is this dangerous?'

'Oh yes,' said Quincy, and smiled at Maria. 'But not for me.'

TWELVE

No car awaited him at Heathrow, because Craven had told no one in London of his coming. He took the airport bus to Cromwell Road, and it was empty enough for him to settle himself on the back seat in the shadows and finish his whisky discreetly, without appearing to be a man with a habit. Checking his watch as the other passengers got up, he confirmed that there was time for a quick supper at his club before he had to make his connection. He took a taxi to Pall Mall, enjoying the rattle down Constitution Hill and the faint glow from the ring of lamps that marked out the edge of the park in the dusk. He had his black leather Gladstone bag held between his feet on the floor, and out of a habit formed in Paris he clung firmly to the strap hanging by his head. As the cab slowed down at the steps of the club, he reminded himself that he should replenish his flask for the night ahead.

The porter took the flask from him and said it would be ready when he got a taxi an hour and a half later. Craven hung his coat, scrubbed up at the schoolboy sinks downstairs, tightened his tie and headed to the bar.

He concluded quickly that he had probably avoided the danger of an office encounter. A Monday night – slower than ever, said Dilys across the counter – gave him a good chance of anonymity. He had an easy story ready if required, but a scan of the five others in the cramped basement room reassured him that it wouldn't be needed. A Treasury panjandrum of long ago was entertaining two friends of his own generation, and the two others who were passing the time together had none of the signs of office men. They didn't recognize him. Smiling, he gossiped with Dilys for a few minutes over a schooner of sherry. 'Still travelling, sir?' she said, which was as far as she would go.

'As ever,' said Craven.

He didn't ask whether Sandy Bolder had been in. Part of him wished, for the sake of wickedness, that Sandy had taken the risk. He realized that the thought was a measure of his unexpected exhilaration, as if one secret journey was a release from all his woes, and wondered if he was rediscovering his taste for excitement.

During supper, which he took in a corner table in a sparse room with the diners spread out to avoid intimacy, he assembled his thoughts. He made no notes, but reviewed events of the last forty-eight hours and made his plans.

The waiter, who greeted him warily and whom Craven was surprised to see – he had evidently survived the spicy clubland scandal that had entertained the members for months – knew better than to open a conversation. He brought trout and a steamed pudding and poured wine for Craven, paying no heed to the dusty glasses.

In his mind, Craven began with Flemyng. Will had been troubled rather than excited by his first conversation with Kristof. Why?

Knowing Flemyng from his green days in Vienna, he had recognized much of his old self – the nose for the chase, a love of the game. So why was his boy cast down by the possibilities? His love life with Isabel had been rocky, but Paris promised them thrills to come. And for Flemyng, the politics of the street had always been a tonic. Why the nervous gloom? And Bolder, although frothing with excitement, was behaving oddly. An unannounced trip to London, and a Sunday-night dinner with Flemyng where they'd apparently discussed nothing of substance, with Bridger stirring the pot in the background. Craven twitched with curiosity, giving him more satisfaction than distress. He was being lured back into the field. Time for a brandy in the smoking room.

Collecting his flask from the porter, he stepped into the hall feeling the return of the energy that had drained away in recent weeks. The question that he knew would linger with him through the night was the most familiar of all: what didn't he know?

'Farewell,' he said to the porter as the door was pulled open for him. 'A lovely trip ahead.'

'The driver knows it's King's Cross, sir', and Craven ducked into the cab.

On the side of the train he found his name on the passenger lists gummed to the window of each sleeper carriage and checked the number of his berth. There were no other names that he recognized. Settling into his tiny compartment, he took in the familiar accoutrements as if they came from a corner of the family home – hairy blankets, the china chamber pot that slid out of sight beneath the sink, the blue nightlight that would stay on, and the temperature control that he expected not to work. He sniffed the metallic warmth of the steam from the heating system, and let memories flood back. Placing his flask on the little shelf that folded down from the wall, he hung his watch on the hook at the side of his bunk, and allowed the blind on the window to ride up to see the moment of departure. Just as the whistle blew and the whole train creaked into life, the attendant knocked at his door to check off his name on the list and take away his ticket.

'Breakfast, sir? I'm assuming an early cup of tea.'

Craven thanked him.

'Good night, sir. Edinburgh by half past seven. Windy, but a fine day all the same, so I'm told.'

*

He was awake before they crossed the border, and let the low eastern sun stream in. Mist on the fields and a landscape that seemed free of any movement.

He reached for the jumbled, garish dream just gone. He had imagined himself in Vienna, in wild and easy days. Flemyng had flitted across the scene like a dancing wraith, and there was no sense to the pictures that had flashed in his mind. He and Flemyng were their other selves: it was Craven who'd been stabbed in a bar, Flemyng who'd waited for him to come home and bathed his wound. Bolder, who'd never served in Vienna, was an itinerant street singer who seemed to have a lute, and Sam Malachy appeared as a pantomime ambassador, wearing a blue sash with a sword at his side. Bridger was pouring drinks, wearing a waiter's jacket, his arms up in the air in a gesture of welcome to the crowd. Mad. Straight from a school play, thought Craven. A torrent of nonsense and topsy-turvy memories. But the picture of Flemyng's serious face was sharp, watching him in his distress through the dream. As he cleared away some of the mist on the inside of the carriage window with a handkerchief and looked to hills splashed with sun, Craven imagined that face reflected on the glass, questioning and anxious. The more seriously he pictured Flemyng, the more mysterious his face appeared.

But the spirit awakened in him the previous night was running strong. Years had fallen away. When he'd dressed in the casual trousers and blazer folded carefully at the bottom of his Gladstone bag, and stowed away his pinstripes, he was eager to step out. He did retain his naval tie, because he found it difficult to abandon it without strong reason, and when he brushed his hair he neatened it with the cream he always used for the office. There was a flattened fedora in his bag, and he got it into shape, ready for the day.

There were warm rolls for breakfast and a miserable piece of fish, but Craven was happy. On the road, the alarms that had taken him from Paris were overtaken by expectation. At Edinburgh, he was packed and ready before the train clanked to a halt, and he was on the platform in a moment, his fedora squarely on his head with the front rim folded nicely down, almost to a point.

He slammed the door behind him and stood still on the platform. A few passengers ambled past, one with pyjama bottoms showing below his long coat. There was no rush. A porter wheeled a heavy cart carrying suitcases and two wicker cages of racing pigeons. After a minute or two he was alone. From a wooden bench near the taxi rank, he saw a figure rise and approach him steadily, an arm raised in greeting.

'Freddy Craven.'

'Hello, Mungo. This is such a pleasure.'

'All mine, I assure you.'

They shook hands and seemed an ordinary pair of old friends, Mungo Flemyng beaming as he picked up the Gladstone bag and waved towards his car, parked only a few yards from the platform in the waiting area, next to a long barrow piled high with milk churns. The station was quiet, and they looked like men in no hurry.

Mungo placed Craven's bag in the boot, and a young dog on the back seat jumped up to press his nose against the window. 'Rousseau – because he thinks for himself. Don't mind him. He'll settle.'

Soon they'd driven slowly up the ramp and out of the station, Craven leaning forward to catch his first glimpse of the cragged city skyline above them.

'We're going home,' Mungo said. 'You're sure that's what you wanted?'

'Very much so,' Craven said.

And quietly, with no air of alarm, he began to explain why he'd come. The message relayed from London, letting him know that Mungo needed to get in touch, had arrived at a happy moment. He guessed that it must be a request for help, and he was in the same predicament. 'So you see, it all made sense. We needed to talk. And Will, of course, doesn't know I'm here. So we have a chance.'

Mungo nodded. 'This means a great deal to me. Thank you.'

He said he had hesitated before using the number that he had been given for emergencies. 'It's all the stranger because there's nothing wrong that I can put my finger on. No crisis, just a sense that things aren't right. Was I overanxious? I confess I was a little alarmed at your reaction – that you wanted to come straight here – because it rather confirmed my worries. I'm afraid I hardly slept last night. The relief that it's you in person is – well, very great indeed. I had hoped for it.'

Craven laughed. He recalled the first weekend they'd spent together, at a history conference in London eight years before. Mungo had given a paper on Roman Scotland, and found Craven an enthusiastic member of his seminar, revealing that he knew every fort on Hadrian's Wall and relished the mystery of the whereabouts of Mons Graupius, the battle where

Agricola's legions had crushed the Caledonians before taking their leave. 'Perhaps I'll show you the marching camp near home,' Mungo now said as they drove. 'For them, a temporary stop along the way, but full of interest. Tacitus mentions it in passing. When the light fades, you can see the layout quite clearly against the hill.'

Craven's presence at the conference where they met had come about as a consequence of another mystery, involving a Polish historian who had signalled that he might be a willing informer, and Mungo would have been surprised to learn that Craven spent each of the three nights in a cramped room on the attic floor of the Regent Palace Hotel off Piccadilly in conversation with his potential recruit, well supplied with cigarettes and vodka, to decide whether or not he was a genuine catch. Two of Craven's juniors, one of them the young Sam Malachy, were listening on headphones in the next room, perched side by side on a creaky bed and drinking instant coffee through the night. The Pole turned out to be a star who was still shining, and so the weekend had a happy place in Craven's memory, alongside the pleasure of his first acquaintance with Mungo, to whom, as a result of high spirits at his success with Warsaw, he confided before the weekend was over that he had a professional connection with his brother. No more than that, but enough.

They'd met again three years later, when Mungo had come to a lecture in Vienna. Will Flemyng had returned for a month to Berlin, so Craven made sure that he was in the audience to welcome Mungo, and that a good dinner followed.

But they had never met in Scotland.

'I'll take you the back way,' Mungo said as they dropped down on the other side of the castle rock and the Old Town and headed west with the morning sun at their backs. 'We'll have a small detour. I do enjoy a city with hills, don't you? That's the hospital, on the slope there, where Sassoon and Wilfred Owen were confined together in the first war. Such strange luck.' Then Craven learned why they had taken that route. 'We're not too far from Will's school here,' said Mungo. 'You can see the rugby posts through the trees. He was happy there.'

And Craven asked, 'Abel's too?' although he knew the answer.

'Abel's too,' said Mungo, and so they began to talk, as decisively as if Craven had said *open sesame*.

He asked Mungo what was wrong.

'We talk sometimes on the phone, though not very often and rarely on a Saturday, just because that's not been our habit. I was thrown a little because Will was very agitated. Extraordinarily so.'

'About anything in particular?' Craven asked.

'Yes, that's the point. Abel.'

Mungo asked Craven if he could offer any comfort, cast any light. 'You can see why I'm worried. Will is usually calm and clear. Not at all the mysterious man, if I can put it like that.'

'You certainly can,' Craven said, and laughed by way of encouragement.

'Brothers have a sixth sense with each other, I suppose,' Mungo went on. 'Maybe historians, too. We spend our lives looking out for turning points, don't we?'

Then Craven surprised him. 'Are you expecting to see Abel soon?'

'How did you know? He's coming home in a couple of weeks, and I was hoping Will would be with us, too. But he's not sure. Paris edgy he says, and I do see the newspapers. But, Freddy, what do you know about Abel?'

'That he's heading our way, that's all. And for rather longer than a weekend, I'm told.'

'Oh.' And the intimacy was interrupted, Mungo aware of the doors that couldn't be opened and Craven that he had broken a piece of news. There were some minutes of silence, then they spoke instead about spring, and the fields around them, the shadowy hills ahead of them to the north. They settled back, and Mungo drove happily for more than two hours. They spent equal time in conversation and silence.

Having made a loop of a few miles to get a view of the marching camp where a small excavation team was setting to their day's work digging and scraping, Craven got his first sight of Altnabuie.

'I've heard a good deal from Will,' he said. 'How satisfying this is.'

Mungo was moved by the intimacy, and let Craven continue. 'When you know your time is limited, you treasure the things that are fresh to the eye. They lighten the days.'

Mungo's old car had carried them on the twisting road that came to the house from the east, and as they took the last bend through the trees Craven saw the rooftop with its crooked chimney on the western gable and beyond it a flash of water. The wind was picking up from the west and the loch was streaked by ripples that shimmered and seemed to race towards them. On its fringes were the thick woods that brought an emerald softness to the glen – birch and alder, holly and fir – and on the rocky heights above the lochside a forest of broom had burst into colour, as bright as splashes of ochre laid on the landscape by an artist's hand. The scene was alive, yet still.

'You see how peaceful we are,' Mungo said.

He turned the car to park by the back door, and Babble raised a hand in greeting. Taking Craven's bag, they laughed together at the picture Flemyng had painted of him when he first spoke of home in Vienna. 'He still tells the old stories, I suppose,' Babble said. 'Well, we wouldn't want it any other way.'

The sun was high and Mungo said it might be worth walking for a little while before lunch, to get the best of the day. Rousseau leapt ahead of them and disappeared in a thicket. Another dog came from the house and chased him.

There was a rickety bench by the high wall on the garden's northern side and they stopped there.

'You were right that I have concerns,' Craven began. 'Your message that was passed to me was a godsend really, timing that made it seem *meant*, if you follow me. I want you to help me, and then I'll do everything I can to help you.' It was a gentle instruction, sympathetic but firm. 'Tell me the whole story.'

So Mungo spoke of the twin phone calls on Saturday night, expressing embarrassment that such a family episode, apparently small and insignificant, should have brought them together to share their alarm. But being a meticulous man, he reconstructed the two conversations with accuracy, getting the timing right. Abel's excitement at coming home and Will's discomfiture at the fact. He remembered Will's very words – 'Did he mention me directly? Ask what I'm doing? I need to know.' As Craven would understand, Mungo said, the questions had lodged stubbornly in his mind.

'Of course I told him that Abel had said nothing of the kind. Nothing but the news of his homecoming. Babble and I were celebrating the fact when Will came through a few minutes later, and d'you know, I still can't understand why he rang me. He didn't say. But he was in a state of alarm.'

Craven asked if he sometimes felt that, as the third brother, he was used as a conduit between the others, or asked to keep a secret, and whether he minded.

'I know that I am and, Freddy, I can say to you that I find it difficult. It helps them, no doubt, but I know nothing of their lives and that sometimes disturbs me. I'm a man who likes order. History offers no certainty, as you know, and that excites me. Away from my books, I am quite different. I want to know exactly who I am.'

Craven said, 'I understand. But you are doing them a great service. Because of what they do, they need you.'

'Abel once explained it to me, in a letter,' said Mungo. 'Obliquely, but it was clear enough. He said that hidden knowledge was always the most precious kind. As a historian, he thought I would understand that. The belief in a secret had great power, he said, even if the secret didn't exist. We need to have them.'

Craven said that he wished he had met Abel.

They stood for a while, taking in the sunshine. 'You can see the colours changing,' Mungo said. 'That hillside will be a riot of yellow in the first week of May. It's when everything starts to turn.'

For a few minutes they didn't speak, and listened to the birds and the rushing water close by.

Craven had lit a cigarette, and drew deeply. 'I think I can tell you that Will has been troubled,' his voice rough. 'Of course there was the Isabel business, upsetting to a man who cares about his feelings, but there are other matters that you'll realize I can't delve into, even for you. But you know enough for me to be able to say that he is involved in a sensitive piece of work that is bound to take its toll. All of us learn that along the way.'

They spoke for a few minutes about Flemyng's love of his trade, the excitement that had lifted him up from the start and which he was able to transmit to Mungo. 'I have never known any detail,' his brother said, 'and I understood that from the start. I've asked him nothing. But I've let him confide his feelings when he has needed to, so I've learned a little of the pattern of his days. The accidents, the satisfactions.'

The two men walked to the lochside, Mungo saying that they had half an hour before lunch, and they fell quiet as they dropped down the long slope. The wind had settled into a gentle breeze that lifted the trees at the garden's edge, and in their shelter they absorbed the spring warmth. Craven could smell the woods, and a freshness that he hadn't known for months lifted his spirits as they reached the carpet of late daffodils that lay between them and the water. There was a rowing boat out in the loch and in it they could see the motionless figure of Tiny, the ghillie, with his rod. 'We have a heronry in the trees yonder.' Mungo pointed. 'No sign of them this morning.'

Content, their anxieties shared, they spent a little time walking on the bank. There were birds wheeling above them, and from the hill to the south came the sound of a tractor starting up. As if it had been a signal, Mungo said that Babble would be ready with lunch. They turned for home.

A few steps up the slope, as they approached the gate in the garden wall and Mungo leaned forward to open the way, Craven said, 'I'll explain why I'm concerned, Mungo, as best I can, and I know you will understand. Then I must rest, if you don't mind.'

They stood together facing the house, and Craven, a little tired from the walk, put his weight against the wall.

Mungo said, 'Look, you've had a long day. Have the afternoon to yourself and we'll have an early night. We can talk properly tomorrow – you'll stay?'

'We must talk, and I shall stay, with pleasure,' Craven said. 'You know that I care about Will deeply, and that's what pains me. For the first time, I know he's not telling me the truth.'

Thirteen

Quincy caught Flemyng a few minutes before he left his apartment to walk to the metro. He was in his small kitchen, a cup of coffee teetering on the edge of the table and two newspapers open in front of him. The ringing of the phone from the high iron stand in the lobby surprised him. With both Craven and Bolder away he wouldn't expect to be troubled before work. Memory kicked in with a shock: as a consequence of their absence he was in charge of all station business. Why hadn't he prepared more carefully for the possibility of trouble? A message from London that demanded action and a request from Janet to pick up one of Freddy's tasks of which he had previously known nothing. So he was quick to the phone, schoolboyish with guilt as he picked up the receiver.

Relief. The voice said, 'Will, it's Grace.'

'Well, hello.' His excitement showed. She spoke as if their conversation at Hoffman's party had only been interrupted for a minute or two, enthusing about the company they'd shared, wondering how his weekend had been. 'Partying again?' His account of a solitary and disjointed couple of days produced laughter at the other end, and he found himself in a conversation that had turned flirtatious from the start.

'You mentioned lunch,' she said, grasping the moment. 'Can we do it as soon as we can? Like today.'

The tasks he had set himself for the office shrivelled away in his mind. They could wait. He had the ambassador's round-table meeting – to everyone in the embassy, morning prayers – where he'd have to listen to Bridger's account of a trip to NATO in Brussels the previous day, but there was nothing else that couldn't be shunted into a long afternoon. He had his eye on one Sorbonne student who looked eager to talk, but he could wait until the evening. 'I'd love that. You understand that something may come up, but there's no reason to expect it. I've a place here on the Left Bank that I like, and you would. One o'clock?' He gave her the address on the rue de Seine and promised a good glass of wine.

Ringing the restaurant, he asked for a quiet table – he was happy to say that it was because he would have a woman friend coming for the first time, and all was understood – and in double-quick time he prepared for the office. Leaving the apartment block with a cheery word to the concierge at her post, he set off for rue du Bac and the metro with a new light-ness of foot.

Janet had some telegrams ready on his desk, Freddy Craven's morning bundle as well as his own, and he closed himself in with a pot of coffee and, unusually, an open packet of cigarettes. There was a copy of a telegram from Prague that was the most interesting overnight news, because the resis-tance to Moscow was said to be hardening. Warsaw was quiet and with heavy political traffic from Washington he sensed that the office in London had turned westwards for the moment. But there was an account from Jonny Hinckley in Brussels of NATO discussions on deployments in Berlin that he read with special care, knowing that he would hear Bridger on the subject in a few minutes. He thought of Jonny, near his age, skinny and dark with thick round glasses that made him look like a librarian. But when it came to missiles, he knew everything.

The ambassador summoned his troops three times a week to a long dining table in his outer office that was swathed in green cloth and used as a gathering place. The glass cases along one wall were filled with richly patterned china plates and tureens, so that Flemyng often felt he was on a visit to the V&A. Ten of them sat down on this Tuesday, a mixture of the powerful – Bridger was at the ambassador's right hand – and minor *fonctionnaires*. Flemyng, because he was acting up, found himself placed on the boss's other side and remembered that he would have to give a report, Craven-style. Having watched the old man at work as bag carrier he knew that brevity was cherished at the top of the table and a pithy sign-off could leave the impression of a job well done, even if nothing of substance had been said. As he sat down, he rehearsed in his head.

Across the table was Wemyss, notetaker. As always, he was meticulously turned out, pale and serious with three spare pencils lined up beside his notebook. He wouldn't miss a word.

The parish notices were brief (a Treasury deputy secretary was staying at the residence overnight – no sign of extravagance would be shown, even at the ambassador's table) and Bridger took the floor.

'Sir.'

Flemyng wondered how long the old conventions would last, like the coal fires that were still banked up on demand for the likes of Bridger in their rooms in London looking out on the park. But he knew he should concentrate.

'You will understand,' said Bridger, his great bulk hunched over his papers on the table, 'that NATO deployments are exceptionally sensitive as things stand. There is a

Pact gathering in Warsaw coming up in the week – so we're led to believe – and all the signs are that the panic in Prague has spread. Moscow knows that it's a sticky wicket.' He quoted from some of the reports Flemyng had already read, none attributed.

'So what are their tactics?' Bridger went on. 'I can tell you truthfully, as a consequence of some long and serious discussions yesterday, that we just don't know.'

Flemyng found it hard not to laugh. He imagined what Craven would have done in his seat, and realized that he couldn't risk any display of incredulity – although it was the old man's speciality – when Bridger was in mid-performance. A junior, he kept a serious face.

'Here is our difficulty.' Bridger's account, he knew, would be banal by comparison with the telegram he had a read a few minutes earlier from Hinckley in Brussels, who had painted a lurid picture of turmoil: the French offside and grumpy, the Americans lost in their own trauma, London uncertain as a result and floundering. Above all, the West Germans in Bonn in a state of electric anxiety. Bridger was determined to be formal. 'We must display calm fortitude – that was the foreign secretary's phrase last Thursday, you will all remember – in the face of great uncertainty on the other side, and therefore potential danger for us. They are alarmed for their own security because of the Czechs. Understandable you may think, whatever our differences.'

Differences! Flemyng was enjoying himself.

'I notice it is beginning to be called the Prague Spring in some quarters,' Bridger said. At that he paused for effect, looking both ways along the table, and in the silence that followed Flemyng realized how much had been lost in the course of his rise. He couldn't excite his men any more.

'The consequence is that they are more watchful and nervous, and rather obsessed with us, in Berlin and other places of significance. A wrong move on our side would be problematic, because it would be misinterpreted. So' – and he brought his hands together to indicate that he was making his bull point – 'we must do as we were taught as boys – be prepared.'

And do nothing, Flemyng said to himself. His judgement was that the ambassador thought it as much of a vacuous performance as he did, because he addressed no question to Bridger and threw it open for discussion, by order of seniority. Flemyng came third.

'Pierce is correct in speaking of misinterpretation on the other side,' he said, nodding towards him. 'It is the great unknown. They probably think that at a time of crisis we're prepared to do something mad, when we aren't.' The ambassador shifted back and forth in his seat, to indicate that he didn't approve of the word.

Flemyng went on, 'My question is this. How much do they know – *really* know – about our options and our plans?'

He couldn't resist annoying Bridger with a flourish, and gave an addendum for the ambassador's benefit. 'That is the *fons et origo* of the whole business.'

The ploy was deliberately aimed. Bolder was in London, and even as they spoke in Paris would be spreading his news – that he thought there was a leak, and that much more was known in the east than Bridger and his muckers suspected.

He watched the table. The ambassador was impassive next to him, keeping still, although he had murmured approval at the Latin tag. Bridger gave no sign that he recognized Flemyng's comment as a reference to Bolder's story. Therefore, he knew nothing. His chancery outriders were blank, and no one else contributed on the question, except the head of press who wanted to check that it would be fine to spread the word that the embassy was taking the lead in the NATO discussions. 'Absolutely,' Bridger said. 'Vital. Thank you, Hargreaves, for the prompt. Because of the sensitivity of the French position – awkwardness, the pig-headedness at the Élysée one might say, sir, if you will forgive me – we are in the lead here. I shall circulate our embassies this afternoon to make the point.'

Wemyss was writing.

Prayers were almost over. The ambassador's benediction singled out Flemyng heavy-handedly – 'Freddy does look rather younger today, doesn't he?' – and they were free.

Bridger took the stairs beside him. 'I wanted to be measured at prayers, Will. One is, you understand that. But the other side's problems in Prague and so forth are for them to solve. We have no interest in making them worse. Our rule for life – never poke a stick at a bear when he has a sore head. That's the alliance view, hot off the press.' He swung round and was gone.

Fleming thought of Sandy Bolder as he went through the security door to the station's rooms, and wondered if Craven had tracked him down yet. His mind turned to Quincy. He would clear Freddy's papers within the hour and walk to the restaurant.

He was pleased with his choice, a small place where he was recognized and where the *patron*, who had a wicked smile and the belly of a Buddha, was pleased that he was bringing a new woman to lunch. And an American! He would do his best in the kitchen, and protect their quiet corner. He brought Flemyng an invigorating aperitif without being asked.

There was a pile of magazines in a rack beside his table – most of them out of date – and Flemyng picked up *Paris-Match* from the previous week. The cover showed a flaming jet on the runway at Heathrow, from which the passengers had scrambled from disaster, and inside there was another American gallery of pictures. All the world had now seen the grainy black and white images of the cortège in Atlanta, with the coffin on its wooden cart – *une charrette du pauvre* – surrounded by the faces of the famous, set in agony. The portraits of burnt-out streets in Washington and Baltimore, with helmeted soldiers and the National Guard gazing at the ruins with useless guns in their hands. He remembered Quincy's essay, with its effort to find a spirit of innocence and belief.

Then she was there. In white shirt and jeans, she was greeted by the *patron* as a vision that lit up his little corner of the city. Shepherded to her place with simple ceremony, she slid round the table to kiss Flemyng on both cheeks. 'When in Paris,' she said, and put two hands on his.

Flemyng's humour was high. They ate, laughed and spoke of Paris. At first Quincy avoided direct questions about his life – he had expected that kindness after their joust at Hoffman's party – but they both knew that the moment would come. For Flemyng, the conversation sped by and made him happy. She was funny and quick, full of stories from Vietnam and the American street, absorbed in the story of Prague, where she'd marched with dissenters and watched the citadel shake. Not for the first time Flemyng wondered whether he should have been a reporter. All his antennae were alert; he was lifted by the talk of a natural observer, and ready for anything.

It came. 'Let's be honest with each other, Will. You don't have to tell me what you do. I've been round this racetrack often enough.'

To his surprise, she added, 'And you couldn't have been where I've been through the years and not heard of Freddy Craven, a master. I wish I knew more. Meet him?'

He shook his head. Over the years he had deployed different

stratagems to deal with the question, knowing that the blank denial was never enough for Quincy's kind. With her it was clear that while she would not expect him to break his code, because she respected it, they both had an instant and relaxed understanding that the truth lay between them, and would lie there undisturbed.

As a result, they would have fun. He told stories of Vienna in the cold, and of games on the front line in Berlin, well edited to reveal almost nothing but bristling with atmosphere. She described her last adventure with the Czechs, and the difficulty she had in fending off the lunges of a politburo apprentice whose friendship she wanted to cultivate but whose bedroom habits she didn't want to explore. They spoke as if they had known each other for months, and tried to find experiences they had in common, in the old habit of potential lovers searching for crossing points that led them to common ground.

'Here's one for you', she said. 'Last time I was here – January – I caught Jimi Hendrix at l'Olympia. Beat that. Are you young enough?'

Flemyng's eyes sparkled. 'I am, and I was there. Don't be surprised. It's safe to say I was the only member of the British embassy on parade. I even remember the date – 29 January, a Monday. It was my girlfriend's birthday.'

Then he added, almost too quickly, 'She's away now, in New York.'

'For good?'

'For good.'

'I'm sorry. But you're not going to find it difficult to have fun in Paris,' she said, 'maybe in a purple haze', and they both laughed.

He responded with a suggestion that they should have dinner on Thursday. Could they meet at his apartment? Quick, exhilarating and definite. She said yes, and satisfaction surged through him. They raised glasses and touched them across the table.

Then, as if the conversation had been a necessary prologue, Quincy turned serious. It was done gracefully, with confidence that enough of a relationship had been established for it to be safe. They were at the beginning, and would be travelling together. Fleming was ready, expectant.

'Help me, Will.'

'With what?'

'I'm going to be frank. I know that you of all people won't tell.'

He laughed. 'You're dead right.'

'I'm watching some interesting people, and I think folks like you underestimate them.'

'How do you know?' he said.

'I'm hearing an astonishing story, learning it. From French friends.' She drank. 'And others, from everywhere. You'd love it.'

'You intrigue me,' Flemyng said.

Quincy said that they could make discoveries together.

'About whom?' he said.

'The East Germans, that's who.'

Flemyng gripped his wine glass so hard that it nearly· cracked in his hand.

FOURTEEN

The three men of the Paris station were unsettled, thinking about each other.

Freddy Craven had accepted Mungo's offer of sanctuary in his study on the first floor at Altnabuie and he had spent much of Tuesday afternoon on the phone. On Wednesday morning he was preparing to track Sandy Bolder's movements with the help of friends whom he'd alerted. Despite the warmth of the morning scene from the window, the bright flicker on the loch and the patchwork hills beyond, the prospect was irritating. Bolder himself had succeeded in assembling a meeting of East European foot soldiers in the office conference room, but was troubled by the sharp question that had been relayed by a friend, straight from the chief: was Craven in the picture? And at the embassy, Flemyng, whose anxieties had led him to open the locked drawer in Craven's desk, was wondering how to deal with what he had found inside.

He tried to suppress his guilt, using the dubious justification that he was in charge of the station for a day or two, and at a moment of alarm. But he felt a flood of shame.

In front of him was Freddy Craven's secret diary.

There were several volumes, in a deep box which he had opened with the second, smaller key on the ring Craven had given him. He could see that they were a spy's travelogue

– two books marked 'Vienna', three more for Berlin, the London interludes placed between them in date order. Earlier, thinner books traced his first exploits in Helsinki and Prague. With the dark thrill of a voyeur, he picked up the book on the top of the pile, 'Paris' written in block capitals on the black cover.

The entries were a mixture of sketches and reflections, people and places, in Craven's clear copperplate, with long loops. But most passages were rendered in skeletal form, with only a few names spelt out, and those pages looked at first like random jottings with no linking narrative. But a few minutes spent with the entries from March, applying his own memory of events, allowed Flemyng to crack the shorthand, and translate. He realized quickly that Craven intended the record to be confusing to outsiders but daylight-clear to him.

They each had a number of work names to be used outside the office when some cover was required, just as operations were routinely coded, and from their abbreviated forms in Craven's notes he could piece together a story, week by week. Having also worked out the identifiers for his restaurants, his friends and embassy staff, his contacts in London and a few other embassies, Flemyng saw the picture swimming into focus. Times and places, the round of useful friends, and a map of Craven's days. He noticed that his meeting with Kristof made a heavily disguised appearance on the previous Friday, the 19th, with no names.

But through the excitement that he still carried from the previous day's encounter with Quincy, and the prospect of their dinner to come, Flemyng felt the pain of regret. This was the book he was meant to read after Freddy Craven's death.

His guilt was compounded by the memory prompted by the diary, Kristof's promise to prove – in his words – his suspicions of Abel. Whatever the accusation turned out to be,

Flemyng knew that he would have to tell Craven in the end, who would know how much he had been concealing. The old man might be merciful, but would feel the hurt.

His phone rang. The clock showed eleven as he sat back in Craven's chair and answered, with the notebook on the desk.

'Mr Flemyng, Pamela here.' Bridger's office. 'Might you be able to pop along a little later? Are you lunching?'

'No.'

'Shall we say at two?'

'Say to Pierce that I look forward to seeing him. Thank you, Pamela.'

He pulled open the bottom drawer, but before he put the book away he read, for the first time, the pages for the previous few days.

'April 21 – AG to G soon,' he read. Then a version of one of Flemyng's own work names, with two question marks and 'x', all underlined twice.

From his reading of earlier pages he knew that Craven used 'G' to represent the American embassy in London. The references in the diary to the anti-war demonstration that had choked Grosvenor Square on 17 March made that clear. Elsewhere, Flemyng had worked out from his own knowledge of office business that Craven placed 'x' after a name when a piece of information had been concealed from an individual or held back, or sometimes in relation to a fact that was unknown or couldn't be verified.

Everything was open to him, and he felt a tremor in his hands from the shock. The connection between 'G' and Flemyng was something unknown to him, contained in the letters 'AG'.

Abel Grauber.

He was coming to London. Craven knew it, and Flemyng didn't.

He locked the book away, put on his jacket and went to sit in the garden.

*

Maria spent the morning preparing for May Day, a week away. She had spoken to three trade unions in the previous few days, and with one more call she was ready to write a despatch predicting that the annual marches in all the big cities would be powerful anti-government protests. She got the necessary words from the president's office and the interior ministry and wrote a brief, cool account of what was planned, laying out the prospect that with some students playing their wild cards for the first time, the May parades would be a physical challenge to the authorities. The campus revolutionaries and the factory workers might have little in common in style and discipline, she wrote, but even that unlikely alliance could be powerful.

She had filed by twelve. New York would be happy to have a piece in hand before breakfast.

In the afternoon, she would go to the strategy love-in at Nanterre, and hoped that Quincy would remember her invitation to come along. She did know that she'd meet her English friend, Edward Abbott. She had managed a brief word at Hoffman's party about his two-day train journey from Prague and caught his excitement. Working for a Sunday newspaper, he was able to play a longer game than most of their colleagues: there were no daily deadlines and scrambles in the evening, although in the weeks when London came late to a story on a Friday his life turned turtle. He was feeling lucky. His paper thought Paris was pregnant with possibility for the weekend, and he could expect a page to himself.

Maria enjoyed him because his conversation, like his prose, was measured and his romantic streak glowed when he found himself in political tumult. He wrote beautifully because he was connected to events. When the tide raced, he surrendered to its force and never swam away.

Ringing him earlier at his hotel in Oberkampf, they'd agreed to meet at the café on Maria's corner and drive out to the Nanterre campus.

She left the office and took the metro across the river, reaching rue de Nevers quickly. Within a few minutes she had a line to Washington and it was arranged that Abel would ring her back. She was curled on the sofa with her feet tucked under her, reading Mailer in *Esquire*, when his call came through.

He was down. The office was infected by the cloud of despair that had darkened the skies and wouldn't clear away. She knew of Abel's private feelings about the war – Hannah's brother had been drafted at Christmas and had been thrown into the chaos that came with the Tet offensive as soon as he got to the front line. Abel spoke of a month of despair and uncertainty at home. But there was something he could pass on that would cheer them both up. 'I'm coming to Europe. A posting.'

Maria was smiling, and squeezing a fist with delight. 'I was hoping. It fits. Back here?'

'London for me. That makes sense. What did you want?'

'You can probably guess. I've been seeing someone who's close to you.'

Abel's mood was changing for the better, and he teased her. 'Seeing him? Don't tell me you're…'

'Come on, you know better. Not in the English sense. Just around town. And he's in good shape, so far as I can tell.'

'Look, Maria, I'll be seeing him in the north, if you follow me, before too long. I'm sure he doesn't know yet what I've just told you, so let me deal with that.'

Maria said he could trust her to play dumb if she saw Flemyng, and asked him to let her know his dates when he had them. They gossiped with care about Washington and Maria ran through her thoughts about what might happen in Paris in the following week. 'I'm heading out to Nanterre in an hour or so. With Edward Abbott. Know him?'

'Only to read. Beautiful pen.'

'Maybe Grace Quincy, too. I told you she's around and she wants to come.'

'I bet. So the gang's all there,' Abel said. 'I wish I was with you. It's wearying here; so damned wearying.'

They rang off, and Maria walked to the café round the corner where Edward was waiting. He was thin and bony, wearing perfectly round spectacles, and although he seldom dressed to impress – when he wore the jacket of a suit it was often with the wrong trousers – he did wear a tie on most days, because he was a rich mixture of flair and convention. In his writing he took flight; in manner he was gentle, even deferential. She loved his mind, because it reminded her of her brother, who taught history in Dublin, and they always began to catch up – in Warsaw or Paris or Washington – by talking about new books they were reading or favourites they had dusted down. As she kissed him and sat down, he held up a paperback that was falling apart – the autobiography of Alexander Herzen. Russia on the cusp of alarm and decline. 'It seems appropriate,' he said, 'to read about the Tsars tumbling into disaster.'

They fell happily into each other's company and caught up on their friends. Who was in Prague, where the trail led next, who'd been assigned to the primary campaigns. 'I'm here for a bit,' he said. 'Friends say we're going to have quite an event on our hands. Let's go to see them.' Her green Citroën 2CV was parked lopsidedly in the next street with two wheels on the pavement, and it was unlocked. Pulling her flimsy door shut, she jerked it on to the street and they headed west.

Ten minutes later, creeping through a lunchtime jam, they passed the British embassy. Abbott played the schoolboy and waved at the flag. Inside the building, the scene was serious. Flemyng had arrived at Bridger's office on the stroke of two and found him on wooden library steps replacing a book on the top shelf. 'Make yourself at home. We have a tiny problem, I fear.'

Stepping down, he stood beside his globe and dusted off his jacket.

'It's unfair on you, Will, because you're only acting up for a day or so.' He sighed. 'But we've got to know what Sandy Bolder's up to. You won't believe this. He took himself to the European desk in London this morning, first thing – having scuttled over the river from your place, I assume – and made a perfect nuisance of himself. More or less squatted in our corridor. Pompous and mysterious, Patrick Ingleby tells me, whatever that means. He's now running Europe, incidentally, and it's going to his head. Anyhow, Bolder has been saying that he's on the brink of a discovery that will startle us all. Extraordinary. Out of the blue. No procedure, no arrangement made from this end. I know you'd have told me.' He checked with a glance and Flemyng shook his head.

'If he's in London to see his own people – yours, I should say – that has nothing to do with me, in theory at least. But we can't have him wandering the halls willy-nilly, flaunting that ridiculous hair of his, stirring things up. Shocking. He just doesn't have the seniority on our side of the shop, and these things do matter, Will. We have rules for a reason.' He folded his arms.

Flemyng said, 'It's awkward for me, Pierce, because I didn't even know he was going until after he'd gone. The same goes for Freddy.'

Bridger shook his head and dived in. 'And that's another thing. Where *is* Freddy? Off the face of the earth as far as anyone here can tell. The ambassador is perturbed, I must say to you. Doesn't know what to make of it. Says your ship seems to have run aground this week.'

Turning away to the window to show that it was a painful scene, he said, 'It's a pity for you that you're at the helm, so to speak.'

'I can only apologize, Pierce,' Flemyng said. 'Normal service will be resumed, I promise.'

'Soon, please,' Bridger said. 'I speak as our master's deputy on this matter. And as I said at prayers yesterday it's a moment for calm, everyone in his place and keeping his nose clean. Nothing untoward.'

Flemyng said, 'And what exactly was Bolder supposed to be bringing to your colleagues, the chaps on your corridor? Was he peddling names, by any chance?'

'No. That's the thing. Nothing anyone can put a finger on. Just making himself sound important.'

'Sometimes it comes with the territory,' Flemyng said, looking away.

Bridger was oblivious. 'I have a visitor soon. Sorry. I must send you on your way.' He spun the globe with one finger.

*

At Nanterre, the canteen in the student building was filled with a rolling crowd and had the air of a cavernous bar in the early hours, a dance hall with the lights down. There was a group in one corner listening to a guitar, some of them flat out on the floor, and across the room an argument was threatening to turn into a struggle. Somebody ran shouting from the room. At least five people were handing out newspapers and campaign sheets at the door, one of them wearing a Mao cap, the others in black. Maria and Edward could smell some joints smouldering behind the counter, from where the staff were long gone, and there were pungent clouds of rough tobacco everywhere. Someone was cooking in oil. A few on the floor looked as if they'd slept there for days and the place reeked like a school gymnasium on a wet afternoon. They'd rigged up an urn to boil water for coffee, and people were pulling stale bread rolls from a cardboard box. Someone had brought in a cat, which sat on top of the juke box with its tail rigid in the air and its eyes wide. Edward, who'd rolled his tie up in his pocket, was smiling. He sat at a trestle table under the skylight and wrote in a neat and tiny hand. As he did, there was a commotion near the door and somebody began to speak.

He was burly and black-jacketed in leather, with a thatch of fair hair. Maria thought his accent placed him somewhere south of Lyons but he had the air of an urban soldier. The riot squads were getting ready for them in the streets, he said, and they'd fight for their government of old men, but the eyes of the world would be on the coming resistance. Around him a gang of listeners turned into a solid crowd, bound together and quiet. They were a disciplined platoon, about three dozen strong, energized by the smell of battle.

Their university had already been sealed off once by the police after the March events, and they could expect it to happen again. But next time they would have to contend with students across Paris and beyond. He fired them up, and ended with the slogan that someone had painted across the roof above them and which was scrubbed out by the authorities, then painted on again. 'Be realistic! Demand the impossible!'

They cheered.

As well as the crowd that hemmed him in there were others who lay bored along the walls, or laughed to themselves. Now and again there were shouts, with everyone joining in, and someone sang for a few moments. There was a pile of clothes and shoes in the corner, and people picked up T-shirts and jeans as if they were going on a country ramble and needed gear. There were men in their thirties and kids who looked sixteen. All of them moved in the same throng. Someone else tried the Internationale, not getting far. The crowd began to thin out quickly, a few waving red flags as they walked into the sunshine. There was a fire burning in a waste-paper bin in the courtyard.

Maria and Edward hung around, and soon they were with about fifteen people, half a dozen of them women. They were intense, though Maria got a handshake from several of them who smiled and gave her a hug. Edward began to talk to them, and listened. They spoke of the messages they were getting from London, Washington, Berlin, of the newspaper they were putting together – soon it would be a daily, they said – and their plans for May. A couple of them were German, there was an American from Chicago and a good deal of the conversation was in English as a result.

'How do we know this will happen?' Edward asked.

'No one believes in revolution until it comes,' someone said.

'It's coming,' a blond boy said. 'Believe me. It can't be stopped. This place is ours – we're in control – and it's going to happen next week. The movement is taking shape. Come to the café tomorrow. She knows where it is' – smiling at Maria.

Abbott saw that Maria was distracted. 'OK?' he asked.

Maria apologised. 'I thought Grace Quincy might come, that's all.'

*

When he had checked that the black iron gates were bolted, and rattled them by habit to make sure, Georges Lebosquet began his evening ritual. He set off along the cemetery's principal boulevard, picking up a few pieces of rubbish as he walked, and looked to each side as he progressed. As a deputy keeper at Père Lachaise his duties were straightforward and unchanging, and he got his satisfaction from ensuring the calm of the place when the living went away and let the dead look after themselves.

At the end of each day, when the last visitor had disappeared – sometimes a little later, when the gravediggers had finished their business following an afternoon burial – he walked for half an hour or more to look over some of his territory. His route varied, so that over the course of a month or so he visited every corner of the burial ground. He noted down evidence of any mausoleum that needed attention, or a railing or gate that had rusted away, and his observations were entered next morning in the logbook in the keeper's stone lodge near the main gate. The families responsible for the upkeep of their own tombs would be contacted and asked to attend to them, or, in the case of a prominent resident – Chopin, Proust, Piaf – the staff would take charge.

Sometimes M. Lebosquet worried that he was trying to make water run uphill, because in his twenty-seven years at Père Lachaise he had watched material decay take hold and advance. There were many memorials whose angels and cherubs had lost arms and wings, and tombs with gates that swung free when they should have been locked fast. Heaps had built up of jagged stone fragments long separated from their monuments, waiting for someone to cart them away. So many repairs were needed that the list in the logbook was never cleared. The gravel and cobbled paths were well swept, because funeral processions still came through on most days and pride still had a place, but much else embarrassed him, particularly the state of the columbarium. How many urns did it contain? No one knew, but he and his fellow keepers thought that the cemetery held the remains, in one form or another, of more than a million souls.

As he turned up a slope, near the bust of Balzac, he saw the owls waiting for the evening in a favourite chestnut tree that was heavy with blossom, and there was a convocation of young starlings on the high tomb ahead of him. Despite the army of cats that patrolled the graves, the sparrows of Paris were everywhere, enjoying the freedom of a hundred acres and all the high perches in the monuments and the trees. The April light was bright. He savoured the fragrance of spring, but he liked his walks most of all in the early autumn, when the evenings began to draw in, because then he could enjoy the cemetery as the light disappeared. The animals crept out, and the birds sang a chorus for the end of the day.

M. Lebosquet had just turned sixty, and, although he was in decent health, he carried too much extra weight and often felt a little tired by the end of his walk, having been in the cemetery since eight o'clock when he and the two other deputies breakfasted together before they began the day's rounds. On the southern perimeter he started on the path home. Within an hour he would be at the table with his wife.

He turned left at a group of graves that he knew well, because he passed them every day. A fox was barking in the trees behind him and he noticed that someone had left a rucksack propped up neatly against an obelisk. As he bent down to pick it up – he'd lock it away before he left, having made a note of its contents – he was aware, all at once when he straightened up, that something was wrong.

He was puzzled. There was a change in the scene that he couldn't immediately identify, but he knew it was there. He looked around. The grave in front of him was undamaged, and he noticed that it had been tidied up in recent days. The memorials on either side looked as they always did.

Then, from the corner of his eye, M. Lebosquet caught sight of what had caused him to stop.

He swung leftwards and stood motionless for a moment, like the statues behind him.

He dropped the rucksack at his feet and ran, as if for his life.

FIFTEEN

The driver of the ambulance said to his companion that it was unusual for a body to be driven through the gates of Père Lachaise into the outside world, instead of the other way round. They laughed together as they switched on their red lights and took the roundabout at speed.

The ambulance was on its way to the Hospital Pitié-Salpêtrière and not the city morgue as they had expected when they arrived at the cemetery. From the start, there had been no question of resuscitation, but they were aware from the moment that they were led in procession from the keepers' lodge to the grave that the circumstances were unusual. Two senior police officers were already on the scene when they got there, after a struggle with traffic that held them up for twenty minutes, and they had spent more than an hour and a half on the scene. They were now heading south-westwards to the Pont de Bercy and they assumed that there would be a welcoming party at the hospital on the other side of the river. They had made sure that the back of the ambulance was neat and tidy, with the white-covered stretcher properly bolted down and its passenger strapped firmly in place.

Soon afterwards, while the first examination was beginning at the hospital, the guard at the British embassy gate rang the office of head of chancery. He knew that Bridger was working late.

'Sorry to disturb, sir. George at the front door. A call has come through the switchboard and I think it needs your attention. Police, sir.'

Bridger was working on a speech for an awards ceremony the next day where he was deputizing for the ambassador, and had been timing his remarks in a private rehearsal, but George's tone was such that he expressed no irritation. Within a few minutes, having spoken on the line to one of the inspectors at Père Lachaise, who was as surprised as he was that they were having the conversation, he summoned Wemyss,

'A flap, I'm afraid. I need Flemyng, and, failing that, Freddy Craven, wherever he is.'

There was no reply from Flemyng's apartment, and Wemyss reported that he couldn't raise Craven, who had evidently not returned to Paris. 'Bolder?' he suggested.

Bridger showed his fiery side. 'Forget him. He's in London on a jaunt of his own. We'll have words when he's back. I knew it! The station is in a mess this week, Wemyss. We have a long night ahead.'

'Janet, sir?' said Wemyss.

'Precisely. She will know how to proceed.'

Wemyss was despatched to the apartment a few streets away where Janet Phillimore had lived for five years, since she arrived at the same time as Craven's predecessor. Unlike the men in her office, she was ready for action. Asking Wemyss to make himself comfortable, she prepared quickly and efficiently to return to the embassy, wearing the pearls that were her badge and without which the station would seem to be losing face. Wemyss knew her reputation for loyalty and iron discipline over many years and, as a junior on only his second posting, he was content to let her give orders. In less than ten minutes they were ready to leave, and she led the way. At the embassy gate she told him that she would visit Craven's office, then meet him in Bridger's room. 'I'd say that I shall be with you in five minutes and no more,' she told him.

She was, and having been briefed in a few sentences by Wemyss about the nature of their problem, although he hadn't mentioned a dead body, she brought them a solution.

Bridger, whose attachment to hierarchy involved a degree of old-fashioned gallantry, expressed his gratitude for her attendance. 'I'm afraid, Janet, that in the absence of all the men you are required to steady the ship once again and steer us through the storm.'

'I'm delighted to be able to help,' she said. 'Mr Flemyng is in the city, as far as I am aware, but I know that he intended to meet a friend this evening. So I expect he is dining – with whom, I don't know. We can hardly expect to visit all his favourite places in search of him' – Bridger smiled as if it was a dig at Flemyng – 'and he will not be available at his apartment, I should think, until after ten. Mr Bolder is in London, but I am afraid that he did not ask me to make the arrangements, so I am not aware of where he is staying. We could try his club. I have the number here.'

Bridger shook his head, saying nothing.

'As for Mr Craven, fortunately I can tell you where he is. There is some awkwardness here, because he did ask me to keep a confidence. Under the circumstances, however, I feel justified in breaking it. He is visiting Mr Flemyng's family home.'

Bridger sat up straight. 'Why on earth has he gone there?'

'That I can't say,' said Janet firmly. 'I don't know, and I should tell you that the same goes for Mr Flemyng. Mr Craven arranged the visit with discretion. However, I have brought with me the telephone number of the house in Scotland. That is where we shall find him.'

Bridger asked Wemyss to find a bottle of sherry, and thanked Janet for her help. 'We may need you during the evening. Are you able to be with us?'

'Of course.'

'Very well,' Bridger said, 'I shall tell you what has happened. It is distressing, and a little mysterious, but there we are.'

Wemyss poured three glasses before making the call. Aware that the direct dialling to London which they had enjoyed for a year or so was not available to Scotland, he went to his own room to speak to the international operator, and asked for Lochgarry 220.

'Let me tell you quickly where we find ourselves,' Bridger said. 'There is a suspicious death, here in Paris.'

Janet showed no surprise or embarrassment.

'Rather senior police officers are at the scene because of the circumstances and, unfortunately and surprisingly to us, they wish to talk to Flemyng and Craven as a consequence. I know not why. But nonetheless we must be in touch. I should say, incidentally, that there is no indication that these policemen are yet aware of the positions Craven and Flemyng occupy here. That at least is a relief. I can talk to Freddy, and perhaps he will want to speak to Flemyng later tonight, assuming that he returns to his apartment from wherever he might be.'

'Would you like me to speak to Mr Craven first?' Janet asked.

'I think it's one for me, thank you. But I may need you here. We are most grateful, Janet. It is typical, if I may say so.'

Wemyss was back in the room.

'The call should come through to your desk in a minute or two, sir.'

They sat in silence. No one spoke until the phone rang.

'Bridger. Thank you, operator.'

Then, after a pause. 'Mr Flemyng. How very nice to hear your voice once again. This is Pierce Bridger at the embassy in Paris. You may remember that we met many years ago when Will and I spent a weekend in Perthshire. We were doing strange things in Fife at the time. Young blades and so forth. Do you recall?'

It was clear that Mungo was alarmed, because Bridger had to leap in quickly.

'He is fine and dandy, and there is no need for you to be concerned. This is not an emergency. The reason for the call is simple. It is our Mr Craven to whom I must speak. Mungo, if I may, I'm sorry to trouble you, but the embassy here is aware that he intended to visit you and I wondered if indeed he had succeeded in making his trek to the hills.'

He listened, staring at Wemyss.

'May I speak to him? I am most grateful.'

He smiled at Janet, and signalled to Wemyss to replenish her glass.

'Freddy? Pierce here. Thank God I've found you.' He listened. 'Never mind that. There is a teeny-weeny flap here and I need your help.'

He explained that Flemyng couldn't be found, that Bolder had taken himself off and, excusing himself for saying more on an open line that would usually be wise, he said that he wanted to outline the story. Watching him, Wemyss and Janet could see from his reaction that Craven was taking command from the other end.

'I agree, Freddy. I would be very happy for you to be the one to tell Flemyng. I shall keep Wemyss with me here.' He looked at his watch. 'We would expect him at his apartment in perhaps an hour and a bit, don't you think. And then here at the embassy.'

Agreed.

And Bridger, quickly and concisely, told Craven what he needed to know.

'We have a death here in this city. Violent, the perpetrator unknown, and the deceased a person of some significance. The police have made a connection, of what kind I do not know, with Flemyng and with you. Others, too, I'm told. Without knowing the nature of their interest, I am aware that this is likely to come as a shock to you both.'

Craven said something at the other end.

And Bridger replied, 'Grace Quincy.'

Sixteen

Maria watched for Flemyng from a café across the street, with a view of his apartment door. Darkness had come. One person had already rung his bell, the concierge having disappeared for the night, and was driven away when he got no reply. The embassy, Maria assumed. She waited.

At about half past ten she saw him appear at the corner and turn into the street, approaching his door with a brisk step, but by the time he stopped to find his key she was coming up behind him. He was startled, then smiled as he turned round. 'What brings you to my door?'

Maria's dark expression was enough. He reached out a hand towards her and stopped when she spoke. 'I have to come in, please. I'll explain everything. It's bad, Will.'

Unbuttoning his coat, he took off his hat and they climbed the stairs without a word.

Sitting on two sofas on either side of a low table piled with books and topped with newspapers, they faced each other and Flemyng made no move to get a drink or make coffee. His black eyes were bright and fixed on Maria, whose face was marble-white. Her words were stark.

'Grace is dead. She's on a slab at the hospital. The world's going mad.'

Even in her grief, Maria was watching for any sign that

Flemyng knew what was coming. There was none. The shock passed across his face as if he'd taken a punch from nowhere. His jaw sagged and his eyes narrowed. Putting a hand to his head he ruffled his hair violently as she'd often seen him do before, a gesture that made it seem as if he was waking from a dream.

'God Almighty, where? How?' His eyes were bright.

'It's a bad story, though I know little enough about it. I had a call at the office from the police because they found my name and number in a notebook where she kept her Paris contacts. Friends, people she might call. It was always in her bag. I've talked to them, and they may have gone to the embassy, too, because there's something with your name on it. Get us a drink and I'll tell you what I know.'

He went to the sideboard, and, pouring two glasses from a bottle of red wine without asking Maria what she wanted, he told her that he was only getting to know Quincy. He turned, and made his first admission. 'We had lunch – only yesterday, for God's sake – and we were going to see each other tomorrow. Maria, I had hopes. This is beyond me.' When he sat down he put a hand over his eyes.

As Maria took the drink, she said, 'I know how you feel. She was warm, and a woman who was... magnificent in a way. I've been weeping for her.'

Together, they concentrated.

Flemyng said, 'Everything you know.'

Maria's story was concise and organized. She might have been dictating to her editors, placing events in order of importance and leaving nothing out that might reveal the reasons for what had happened, or help draw back the veil that had been drawn down on a life which had touched both of them quickly and left its mark.

'She was found in the cemetery – Père Lachaise, where they're all buried – laid out on a gravestone, as dead as dead can be. A keeper came across her after the gates were shut for the day. He knew instantly she had gone, but there was no sign of violence. No blood, in other words. She was fully dressed. Looked normal, except – and this is hard, Will – her face was awfully contorted. The keeper was terrified. He's surrounded by death every day, but none of it unexpected. He rang the alarm bells and the police were on the scene pretty fast. They found her rucksack with all her things – passport, reporter's card, everything.

'I got all this from the inspector who rang me, then came round to my office. Told him I'd have to write the story, which I've done. You can imagine the mayhem in New York. I learned a good deal from this cop. He asked me not to write this, but they believe that she was poisoned in some way. It would explain her face. They're convinced that it's not a heart attack, which was their first thought, but apparently the police doctor who examined her in the place where she lay, said no. It was something else. Will, I can't bear to think of it.

'She's at the big hospital, and he told me they would do toxicology tests. Our embassy is with her – I've spoken to a friend of mine there, Butterfield he's called – and they're in a panic. First of all, she's famous and, second of all, what the hell was she doing in a cemetery, getting knocked off in a way that has assassination written all over it? She's been targeted. The cops know it isn't a street murder, nor an accident, and they're trying to find something in her notebook or her papers that would give them somewhere to start.

'My name was there, and they found a letter you had written her suggesting lunch, with your phone number on it. They asked me who you were. I told them where you worked – there wasn't any point in pretending – and I guess your people have been trying to get you. A lot of folks will be having visits tonight. She knew everybody, and she's been in and out of this city for months.'

Flemyng's hands were behind his head and he was leaning back on the sofa, his eyes focused on something above him. He'd said nothing during Maria's account, and when she finished he let out a deep sigh as if he had been holding his breath. Standing up, he sipped his drink and brought the bottle across. 'Let's at least drink to her before we get carried away in everything that's going to come our way.

'Quincy.'

Maria began to tell some stories that had followed Quincy round the world – how tough she was, the way she always seemed to get to places before the trouble started, her style, the fear that she put into the men that were on the road with her. Her natural body armour. Flemyng smiled.

The phone rang. His eye was fixed on Maria as he picked up the receiver.

'Freddy. My old friend.'

Then, 'You're *where*? But why?'

His face was as mournful as it had been when Maria first gave him her news, and one hand was clenched in anxiety. She had never seen him so possessed.

'Before you go any further, I know about this. I've just been told by a friend. It's dreadful, Freddy, and I really don't know where to start.'

He listened for a short time.

'I'll go there now. Mind you, American journalists, celebrated or otherwise, aren't our responsibility, and this is France. But I can imagine Bridger's panic if the police have found my name. And yours? What's going on here?' He frowned in

163

Maria's direction. 'I'll go now. And I'll try to ring you later. Stay up, and tell Mungo, as best you can, not to worry.'

His mood had changed. Instead of the dark silence that had come over him when Maria arrived, he'd found a vigour that quickened his movements but gave his face a serious set, the lines on each cheek standing out. He was on the move.

'I'm going to the embassy, and I've got a suggestion. Please stay here – all night if you want. I'd like it. The spare room is always ready. Use the phone, and have something to eat. There's cheese. I'll be late. But I don't want you to be alone, and I want to talk when I get back.'

'Me, too,' said Maria. 'Thank you.'

Without looking for his bag, throwing Maria a set of apartment keys, he was gone. She walked to the window and pulled back a curtain, looking down to the street. He was walking fast to the corner where he could pick up a taxi in a minute or two, and she saw him button up his jacket against the chill of the night. There was no one else in the street, and he passed through pools of darkness as he crossed to the other side, his own shadow stretching out behind him and then disappearing as he reached a lamp post with a bright light from above him. He stopped for a moment, as if to catch breath, and marched into the blackness at the corner where he was lost to her.

Letting the curtain fall, she took her drink and lay on the sofa, thinking of Quincy and the graveyard where murder had been done.

*

Flemyng saw the twinkling green light of a taxi soon after he turned the corner and ten minutes later he was at the embassy gate. George saw him in, and looking up from the courtyard he could see the only lights in the building coming from Bridger's office. A profile that might be Wemyss's was on the blind at the window, and he imagined him getting his orders. As he stood quietly, preparing his thoughts before he went upstairs, a side door opened and a figure emerged.

He spoke softly – 'Janet, it's Will' – and came out of the corner where he had been standing.

'Oh dear,' she said. 'I am so sorry. This was obviously someone you knew. How terrible. Did Mr Craven get through to you?' Outside the office it was always 'Mr Craven', even with one of her own.

'We've spoken, yes. I assumed you were on board. Well done.'

'It hasn't been much, but I know that this is not over. Quite awful, and no doubt quite complicated, too. Mr Bridger has kindly released me for the night. I shall see you in the morning. Mr Bolder is still in London, so you'll be in command. Good night. Please ring if I'm required.'

And in a moment she had stepped into the street.

Flemyng took the stairs quickly, and Wemyss opened the door for him, gesturing towards Bridger behind his desk.

'Will, thank goodness. The station has been rather under-represented this evening.'

Suppressing a spout of rage, Flemyng apologized for having been out of contact. 'What more do you know, Pierce?'

'That they have no idea what happened to her, but it is certainly a suspicious death. The Americans are having fits, of course. She was so well known that it's an embarrassing story all round. Every American journalist in Europe will be heading our way, damn them. They're her friends. From our point of view, it is simply a matter of working out why two rather important figures in this embassy are caught up in it, and how we get you out of it. Then we can let those whose responsibility it is get on with the investigation, and turn to our own business. That's what we hope.' It was obvious that he didn't believe himself.

He went on, 'I should say that I have been trying to maintain an even temper this evening. It hasn't been easy.'

Ignoring the invitation to apologize, Flemyng shook his head. 'It won't be so simple. Let's take it step by step.'

He was struggling with himself. 'I may be able to help a little, although I didn't know her at all well. We met at a party last Saturday, and I should tell you that I had lunch with her yesterday.'

'Lunch!' Bridger said, as if Flemyng had confessed to adultery. 'Dear God. Why?'

'Because she wanted to,' Flemyng said.

Bridger was in a more formal pose at his desk, the conversation having taken a turn that he hadn't expected. 'Let's be quite frank here. Did she know of your role in this embassy?'

Flemyng was quick, looking straight at Bridger. 'Not from anything I said.'

'I ask this' Bridger said, 'because I have had a call from the Americans. One of my opposite numbers. It's the reason for my sadness that Freddy Craven isn't with us, because he might have been able to help. Will, there is talk of a security problem here.' He took a long breath as if he were preparing to sing. 'I was given no more detail, but my impression is that you and your people may be required to co-operate with our friends. Rigorously.'

'We always do, as you know,' Flemyng said.

'Quite,' Bridger said, 'but it's important that with Craven away – I know where he is, by the way, and I'd be grateful for your explanation – and Sandy Bolder prancing round London for reasons that are beyond me, that you are aware that the burden will fall on you in the first instance. Speaking on the ambassador's behalf – we have talked frequently this evening, as you can imagine – we require maximum co-operation. Files and so forth.'

He added, 'Up to a point.'

Flemyng, who was anxious to leave, said that he could rest easy. Requests would be satisfied. 'I shall be here early and, Bolder or no Bolder, I'll do what is necessary.'

Bridger stood up, and got a bottle and glass to pour him a drink. 'I am sorry that you have lost a friend, however brief your acquaintance. My condolences. But you can understand my feelings about this embassy. Tell me, Will, since this is alarming the Americans so much – do you have any idea why it happened?'

'None at all,' said Flemyng. After a quick glass, he excused himself. 'I shall see you at morning prayers.' He nodded to Wemyss, who held the door open and walked silently behind him as far as the courtyard, where they said goodnight. In a gesture of sympathy, Wemyss shook his hand firmly.

Flemyng walked home. It took him about twenty minutes. From Concorde he walked east along the railings at the Tuileries Gardens and crossed the Pont Royal. On the Left Bank, with the noise of the riverside traffic subsiding behind him, he slid into the narrow streets around the university, passing close to the Brasserie Balzar where he'd spent the evening with two students from Sciences Po, and where he had learned how convinced they were that these streets would come alive the following week, with the arrival of May. He had people to talk to, but first there was the death of Quincy. Through the sense of shock that clung to him through his walk and made him cold, he thought of Bolder playing his games in London, and Freddy marooned in Perthshire, perhaps having a last pipe with Mungo in the drawing room at Altnabuie. It was his story to unravel.

Recollecting his excitement the day before when he set out for his lunch with Quincy, he felt a surprising clarity of mind in recalling an encounter that had moved him with unexpected force and had become, because of her last words to him, a challenge fired with uncertainty and promise.

What had she known that caused her to die?

He turned into rue de l'Université and, realizing that he was almost home, Maria came to his mind. They would talk, probably long into the night.

He climbed the curved stair to the first floor, and pushed the switch to extinguish the last light in the lobby. As he felt for the lock he heard voices, and stopped.

The door opened, and Maria smiled at him, kissed him on the cheek.

'A friend of yours has come.'

She moved aside, and Kristof smiled from the sofa.

SEVENTEEN

The morning light had come up before Kristof left the apartment. Flemyng opened a window to clear the air and the chatter of congregating birds filled the room. They could smell bread from the bakery across the way and hear the distant clatter of the street sweepers. Maria lay on the sofa where she had been for most of the night and Kristof coiled up in the most comfortable chair, shoes off and shirt open, and looking to Flemyng like a young man for the first time. 'I will leave you now. I have a long walk ahead.'

He touched Maria's hand when he had dressed, and she smiled. She didn't rise, bringing familiarity to the scene, as if they were a family. 'Thank you. Until we meet again.' She allowed Flemyng to take him out. They would want to talk together, without her.

As the two men reached the front door, Flemyng took Kristof by both shoulders, almost pushing him against the wall. Insistent, but gentle. 'I want to express my gratitude. I'm in your debt.'

Kristof, whose smile had lightened their night and their darkness, said he understood. 'I would never mention your brother in the presence of anyone else. I am glad you appreciate that. Perhaps it is evidence that you can trust me.'

Flemyng didn't reply.

Kristof said, 'I have told you that I may need help from you. The time may be coming.'

'I can't, and you know it.'

'But we're friends now. I know your apartment. We're involved in the death of someone we both know, and that makes us close. Whether you like it or not.'

Flemyng absorbed his words. He let Kristof open the door and leave the building on his own. The concierge hadn't yet arrived, and he made sure that he wasn't seen. Standing back in the shadows of the lobby, he saw Kristof close the door behind him, without a last goodbye. Back in the living room, Maria said, 'I watched the street. No one.'

A few minutes passed before they were ready to talk it through. Flemyng made a fresh pot of coffee, and cleared away the glasses and two empty wine bottles. Kristof had filled the bowl that was his ashtray and as Flemyng swilled it out under the tap he called to Maria through the door from the kitchen, 'You start.'

She was ready. All pretences between them had fallen away, and they were sworn as comrades without need of ceremony. In the depths of the night, feeling the cold, she had found an old shirt of Flemyng's hanging in the hall and she still had it round her shoulders on the sofa, her feet tucked up and two fat cushions gathered around her. She was a picture of comfort, although her face was serious. 'Let's go over what he said, from the beginning.'

Kristof's story had begun with an explanation of how he learned that Grace Quincy was dead. They reconstructed what he had told them, hearing his voice in their heads again.

He had described a knock in the night. 'I have a friend – let's call him that – who found the police at the door of his apartment this evening. It is far from here, in a different part of the city. But they came. I cannot say why – an address, a telephone number? Something in Miss Quincy's possessions, certainly, because they told him what had happened, and that his name had been found. I know this because afterwards he called me. He was a worried man.'

At this point, Flemyng had considered whether he should make a show of asking Maria to leave the room. But the assumption that they shared secrets was there from the start. Why pretend? He wouldn't break the spell.

Kristof gave no more details about his friend, but he spoke of the speed with which the news had spread. 'We knew of her, of course. She has been writing from Berlin, Prague, everywhere. I think she understands – understood – everything. I should say that I have met her.'

'Been in her company or spoken with her?' Maria sounded sharp.

'Oh, we have spoken together, more than once.' Flemyng looked as if he had received more bad news.

Maria let it pass, and for a while Kristof talked of the fear that his friends carried with them, all the time. The uncertainties that surrounded them. 'You Americans' – this to Maria – 'are living with your own chaos. Ours is a different kind – we can't give it a name – but it infects us. We have the same fever.'

They spoke for two hours before each of them, in turn, dozed off. Maria and Flemyng let him describe his feelings for Paris and the West. He asked no question that was awkward for them. They never had to raise a hand and say – stop there. He talked about his country and the system, a visit to Moscow, life in East Berlin, the alarms from Prague, Vietnam. But about his family and himself there was nothing.

For Flemyng it was a performance of skill and grace, and he wondered where he had learned his trade.

About four o'clock, with the first light brightening the window ledge, Kristof said that he wanted to give them something that might be helpful. 'I hope so,' he said. Maria pulled Flemyng's shirt around her on the sofa, and he sat still at Kristof's side, watching his hands and his eyes.

He took them to the cemetery. 'Père Lachaise is one of the strangest places in Paris. You may know this fact, or perhaps not. In the grounds are some hiding places where messages can be left. It happens. Sometimes I wonder if everyone uses it, from many places around the world, and the visitors to the graves are mostly spies, going about their business. It is an amusing picture. All of us, waiting to be alone with the dead so that we can collect our mail.

'I know where Miss Quincy was found, and I am aware that one of these places is close to that spot. It is a favourite of some friends of mine. I have used it myself from time to time. I don't think it would be a good idea for either of you to accompany me there, but I can describe it. As you will know, the instructions for such places are easy to remember. That is the point.'

And he gave them directions, repeating them quickly to leave no doubt.

'You will ask me whether Miss Quincy knew of its existence. Perhaps. All I will say is that my friend who found himself talking to the police is a man whom I have not known to be afraid before. Tonight he was terrified.'

Recalling the conversation with daylight brightening the room and Kristof gone, Maria said that he had taken a great risk in coming to Flemyng's apartment. 'You tell me that he's been to this door before, to meet you, but never came inside. I just invited him to wait for you. He didn't hesitate. Thinking how I would do this, if it was some kind of set-up – they hear Quincy's dead and try to draw you into some kind of trap –

I just can't see why they would do it like this. When I spoke with him here before you got back from the embassy – for a half-hour maybe? – I was sure he was genuine. He didn't interrogate me, just talked.'

Flemyng said that he wanted to hear about their first words. 'How did you explain yourself?'

'I didn't. Said I was a friend of yours, and he was welcome to wait here. It seemed natural, and that was the odd thing. He assumed that we were together, and that I knew your business. So he didn't hold back, but never asked me to give him my story. Told me who Quincy was, and that you knew her, and that she was dead. I said I knew her, too, because I was a reporter and we were off. I played along. I think he wanted to believe he was safe, and was scared to test me.'

Flemyng nodded. 'You're right. He wants reassurance. So anxious that it doesn't go wrong that he's thrown the rule book away. For us, it could be a prize.'

'Pure gold,' she said. 'Later we need to try to write it all down, both of us. Then we'll compare notes. Get the best version. A deal. OK?'

'OK.'

Such gifts seldom came without a little mystery attached, Flemyng said. 'He knew I was acquainted with Quincy, and that's why he came. Did he say how he knew?'

'No.'

Flemyng said, 'He's given us some help. I wonder what his price is going to be.'

Through the horror of Quincy's death, they'd shared the strange excitement of Kristof's appearance, and his willingness – Flemyng thought it was closer to desperation – to talk. When he had said everything he knew about Quincy, and his suspicion that her death was connected to the people he called

173

friends, he had taken them into his own world. Their minds went back a few hours and they heard his voice again, recalled their own reactions and their questions: 'I am protected by Russians, but in another way I am alone. Almost stateless. Although I am loyal, I hope to escape. I trust my friends, and I fear them.'

Most of all, he said, he had sympathy with his fellow foot soldiers who did their duty because their instinct was to believe in friendship and not to betray. But they knew that a crisis was coming. Prague? The Czechs wouldn't turn back. Students in Warsaw were having to be driven from the streets. Who would trust the Hungarians? And in East Berlin everyone was watching TV programmes from the other side of the Wall. Could Flemyng and Maria imagine what it was like to feel the thump of artillery on the castle ramparts?

'Think of it. The fear.'

Maria said he should remember that she was an American, living with her own nightmares. That produced his observation of despair that seeped across the divide. He asked her about home. Flemyng admired the delicacy of her answers, which hid so much of the truth.

Gesturing to the window and the river, he said, 'The government, over there. What are the old men thinking? Remember – this is a city of revolution. It knows its history.'

Another shower of rain had come, and the dampness on the roof across the street gleamed in the early sun.

Kristof turned to the places he knew at home, and Flemyng shared memories of Berlin. 'Did you grow up there?'

'I am a country boy, from a place you wouldn't know,' Kristof said. He returned to his commitments. 'I accept that there is a price to pay. My choice.'

'Choice?' Flemyng said. 'The word surprises me.'

'It's the one I use, that's all.'

Flemyng asked, 'Your English is remarkable. Have you lived with someone from London?'

'Perhaps,' said Kristof, and dismissed the question with a smile.

'How old are you?' Maria asked.

'I am thirty-four.'

'So you remember the Russians coming, in the war,' she said.

Kristof said they were times he would rather not remember. They took his lead, and turned to other things.

For a while they spoke about music, and films Kristof had seen in Paris. Maria told him of the coincidence that she and Flemyng had both heard Jimi Hendrix not far away at l'Olympia, though neither had been aware of the other's presence – 'Quincy too. She told him' – and Kristof's eyes brightened. 'So you don't live or work together?'

'We're friends, that's all,' Flemyng said. 'You understand the way.'

When the light came and it was time for him to go, the three found themselves grasping at the illusion of normality that they had created in the night. Just as they couldn't allow themselves to be flattened by Quincy's death, so the strangeness of Kristof's arrival, and the mysteries he trailed behind him, had to be managed without panic or drama. They felt the presence of danger, but it was more important that he became part of their lives like any new friend, with no alarms. They would take their time, and deal with him together.

With Kristof gone, and when it became obvious that she would have to leave, Maria asked Flemyng to sit at the table. 'Go back to Quincy, and what she said to us. There's something serious I want to say. I am not sure yet what it means, but she told me she was working on a story that was big, might change our lives. Must have been something more than student leftists.'

Turning his own cards over, Flemyng said that she had given him the same indication at lunch. 'She wanted my help with something, and I think it took her on to Kristof's territory.'

'That's where we are,' Maria said.

'We are, and it means we have to make a journey together,' he said.

Maria smiled. 'To the cemetery.'

'Of course,' said Flemyng. 'But not yet. The place will be crawling with police, and half the reporters in Paris, for a few days.'

He helped her on with her coat. 'We wouldn't want to be caught in the act, would we?'

Eighteen

Bridger's call with news of Quincy's death came to Craven at the end of the second day of his stay at Altnabuie, where he had found rest.

He had offered no resistance to Mungo's invitation to take a bed for a night or two, and without fuss he abandoned his plan for a visit of only a few hours. There was a sleeper to London every night – why rush? He had begun the journey with a tingle of urgency, then relief took over.

On Tuesday evening he and Mungo had shared a hotpot and talked history for a while, each of them aware that most of the personal business to be done might make more sense in the morning, and would be easier after a pause for breath. Craven laid the ground with hints about Flemyng's dark moods, and left the thought to mature with Mungo overnight.

He got strength from surroundings with such a capacity for peace. The advancing weakness that everyone was watching in the embassy had been less obvious, as if it had decided to allow him a little more time. When they tramped towards the hill after breakfast the next morning, his grey hair flying free and his blood up, he was aware that he had cut his moorings and might sail away. He was matching Mungo's tread, step for step.

They had talked about his brother, and Craven told Mungo more than he had ever known about the life he had chosen.

In the afternoon, Mungo gave him time and let Craven read in the library. He found Flemyng's complete set of R. L. Stevenson, the Tusitala edition, which he had collected and valued enough to keep safely at home, though the thin dark-blue volumes were made for a traveller. Craven lost himself in *Treasure Island*. Rest came easily, and afterwards he made two telephone calls from the hall, with Mungo taking a diplomatic walk through the garden while he spoke. Later, over Babble's simple supper, Mungo spoke about their family, happy to have a listener who encouraged him to delve deep. Craven confessed that he had expected to be on the way to Paris already. 'But I've discovered I needed this. Thank you. No doubt I'll pay for it eventually.'

The two were enjoying a late-night dram together when Bridger's call came.

Mungo closed the door to the hall while Craven spoke to Paris. It was some time before he returned to the sitting room. He picked up his pipe and his glass, and his eyes were bright. The tiredness he'd brought north with him had gone. 'I'll be leaving for Paris tomorrow, on the night train from London. You've met Pierce Bridger, he tells me. That was a summons of a sort. I'm afraid the embassy is in a tizzy. But I would like a last turn round the loch if we can in the morning. Do you mind a very early start?'

He added, 'I should tell you, Mungo, that I've just had a word with Will, too. There was something he needed to know – although he'd got there before me. Don't fret. He's fine.'

Mungo went upstairs a worried man.

But Craven spent a dreamless night in Flemyng's bedroom, with his friend's books at the bedside and one of his mother's landscapes on the wall, waking with the exhilarating feeling that he had snapped out of a trance, refreshed and restored.

He prepared himself quickly, putting on a pair of Flemyng's boots. Mungo lent him some rough tweed trousers because of the thorns, and the two men set off in the early light, their senses sharpened by the chill of the morning.

Mungo led him to a favourite trail that took them the short way through the woods, then to a path running between the fields that rose steeply from the southern side of the water. Craven had a long day of travel ahead but he was enthusiastic when they set off, the grass heavy with dew and swirls of mist coiling low over the water. Under the canopy of the trees, where the freshness in the air took on the sharp odour of pine and fir, they felt the musty damp of moss and fern in the shadows where sunlight never fell, and Craven was alert to every sound and smell as they moved from light to darkness and back again. Having left the trees and tramped to the top of a rise where they could look through a pass between the hills to the mountains beyond, they turned to follow a dry stone dyke down to the waterside, on a narrow path lined by wild flowers, through high clumps of willow and hazel, with a spiky hedge stretching ahead of them and marking out their route. Everything glistened with the moisture of the morning. By the time they reached the loch, and paused at an old upturned boat beside the wooden jetty, Craven said he felt as if he had sipped an elixir that cleared his mind and lifted his spirits. 'Bring him home when you can,' he said to Mungo. 'I'll help. He needs this.'

The breeze was lifting the mist away as they watched, and Mungo found himself released from his last inhibitions. Craven sensed the change and returned to the subject he'd raised gently the night before.

They spoke about Flemyng without embarrassment or reserve. At the kitchen table the night before, Mungo had expressed his worries, and the anxiety he felt at being unable to discuss his brother's business. 'I understand,' Craven had told him. 'I've known it all my life, from the other side. We have to live with it, and it's our choice, so I know not to let it gnaw at me.' He had added, 'Why should I complain? This is what I've always wanted.'

Mungo spoke about Abel – the decision as a young man to root himself in New York, where he felt his mother's flame still burning, and his own awareness of the circle of secrets that surrounded a second brother. The move to Washington. Abel's passionate nature, and his commitment. 'I'm sure he's never let a friend down in his life,' Mungo said.

'You're the one who didn't choose a secret life. Does that make you feel alone?' Craven's question was gentle, with no obvious edge.

Mungo spoke as if he had prepared for the question. 'Yes. I just remind myself that I'm the lucky one, being here.'

'It's terribly important, Mungo, that you tell me anything that might help to explain Will's anxiety about Abel. Anything at all.'

With Craven's departure approaching, Mungo was determined to approach a last question in his own way – through the melancholy that sometimes infected the middle brother. 'I spoke about Will last night, and he is worrying me. The darkness. There's part of the true Highlander in him, you have to realize, from our father's side. He had blood from the islands in him, too. Even worse!' He laughed.

'But Will learned to love that. They walked the hills for long days, far away in the northwest: camped in the back of beyond, and took to sea in a leaky black boat that we kept there. He treasured the connection with our past. You hear it in the old songs, you know. A longing that's so powerful, for something gone. Everything's about loss. He's had that all his days, although we grew up in these gentler parts – still in the Highlands, though only just – and it's what makes him attractive as a man. You can't predict. He often leaves you wondering, like a musical chord that doesn't resolve.

'A generous nature but touched by something else, which I've known to be destructive in many people. So I worry.'

'He's one of us, you mean,' said Craven, and laughed. 'I recognize the type, don't forget.'

'Only you can say that.' Mungo smiled back at him. 'With Abel it's different, although he chose the same game. You know I'm aware. He has his moods, and sometimes in appearance he's an open book, just like Will – you can see everything in their faces – but I think Abel has always been more single-minded. It's hard to explain, Freddy, but I think he worries less. Married, of course, and perhaps that helps.'

'By single-minded, do you mean ruthless?'

'I'm not sure. I think of him as a baby brother.'

Craven was leaning against the old wooden rowing boat, its fishing days over. Cracked ribs had sprung up from the keel and it was going to rot away where it lay, bottom-up, and turn into a little wreck of memories before the year was out. 'We'll burn her on the fire when the time comes,' Mungo said, slapping the dry boards.

Craven had work to do, and the calmness of the scene made it easy. 'You're sure there's nothing that explains why Will was so anxious on the phone? Any change you noticed at the time, or before?'

'I'm sure not. There's been no sign of trouble between us. It's an old-fashioned thought really, but you do know that we love each other? I'm sure of that.'

Craven asked if Flemyng, in darker moments when he was

at home, had expressed any worries about the life he had chosen, his trade. Was he regretting everything? 'Have you sensed any doubts of late?'

Mungo, the historian who spent his days sifting evidence piece by piece, was emphatic. 'I've thought about that, and watched, and the answer is no. He cares, and especially about you, if I may be personal.'

'I know that.' Craven pressed on. 'Was there any talk about Abel before that phone call? Anything?'

'No.'

'But you know something's happened, don't you?'

'Yes.'

'Did you expect it? After a visit, a phone call, anything?'

'There was nothing.'

Although long weeks often stretched between their conversations, which were short except for Flemyng's times at home in the summer or at Christmas, Mungo said the brothers had preserved their intimacy. 'What alarmed me was that the pattern was interrupted, all of a sudden, with no warning. Such a little thing, but so obvious to a brother. Almost violent.'

Craven asked him to try to explain it.

'I believe it must have happened in Paris, and recently. This hadn't been smouldering. I felt that his anxiety was new – fresh in his mind.'

Craven said, 'You should have been in this business, too, Mungo. I'm sure you're right, and I think I know where it came from.'

Mungo looked at him directly, but when it was clear that Craven was saying no more he stepped out to signal the start of the walk home. They turned back to the house in silence.

Babble's voice interrupted them as they walked through the garden.

'The phone. It's Will.'

Mungo's nervousness returned. 'It's only ten o'clock.' After a few words, he passed the phone to Craven. Flemyng's voice was heavy with emotion that couldn't be disguised. 'Please, Freddy, come back. There are things I need to tell you.'

Craven said, 'I'm on the train from Victoria tonight, and we can talk through the weekend. That would be useful, away from the office, don't you think?'

Mungo had taken himself out of range, but he was ready when Craven came away from the phone and found his way to the back of the house. 'News from the front,' he said to Mungo. 'I should tell you what's happening. There's been a strange event in Paris. Bridger told me about it when he rang last night. You'll be reading about it. An American journalist – Grace Quincy – murdered, it seems. All hell's broken loose.'

'And are you going to be involved somehow?'

'Perhaps. She knew everyone, you see. That's the problem.'

'You don't mean Will?' Mungo said.

Craven smiled at him. 'Oh yes, I do.'

The sun was splashing light on the hill, and as they passed through the garden the warmth of the day comforted them for the first time. Craven changed and got his bag to the back door and, while Mungo went to prepare for the drive to Edinburgh, took a few steps to the dining room and found the orrery, which Flemyng had often described to him and which Mungo had taken him to see soon after he arrived on the day before. The planets on their spindles were still, but the light coming through the eastern window was bringing the machine to life and its brass and copper glittered, the clockwork mechanism ready to turn at the touch of a lever. Craven stood motionless beside it, with a hand resting on the glass case, and thought of Flemyng. The man he knew, grown from the boy he had nurtured, had taken on a new colouring in these surroundings. Darker than before and, far from being revealed, more mysterious.

Rousseau leapt into the room. Time to go. On the road to Edinburgh, Mungo spoke again about the Flemyngs – their mother most of all, whose family name Abel had adopted in America and whose temperament was obvious in them all, in different quantities. 'We're all hers, but so different. An American, a painter. Mixed with that dark blood from my father. You have to understand the kaleidoscope of our nature – all the different pieces coming together in different shapes, and always on the move. I know I should find that reassuring because it's natural. But I'm uneasy now, to my bones.'

By the time they drove down the ramp into Waverley for his train to London, Craven had a picture of the Flemyngs that was richer than he had expected. As Mungo clasped his hands on the platform, moved by the long journey he had undertaken in his frailty, Craven's mind returned to Flemyng's phone call to Altnabuie from Paris, and the pain his older brother had heard in his voice.

'I'm taking the chance for a brief rendezvous in London with a friend. On the hoof, you might say. Then Paris. Thank you so very much. Your account of Will's anxiety has helped me, and him I'm sure.'

Mungo wished him well, asked him to care for his brother, and said he could only hope that their alarms would subside soon.

'I agree, for all our sakes,' Craven said. 'Try not to worry.'

But Quincy was gone, and had changed their lives. So, he knew, had Kristof.

*

184

In Paris, Will Flemyng arrived at Craven's apartment just before noon on Saturday. There was evidence of upheaval. 'I'm having the place cleaned up for a party. I'll tell everyone on Monday morning. Sit where you can.'

'How did you find it? Home.' Flemyng asked, moving a pile of books from an armchair before he sat down. 'I hope the sun shone.'

'That hardly mattered,' Craven said. 'You're lucky boys. I won't forget that crystal air, the hills, and it was good to talk to Mungo.'

'About me, I suppose.'

'Indeed. Now what have you got to say? Kristof first, please, then Quincy.'

Flemyng made his statement. 'Freddy, I said I needed you here and it's true. I haven't been entirely straight with you, and I apologize. I hope you will understand. It's time.'

Craven didn't wave away the apology, nor did he reveal any anger or hurt. The sphinx didn't blink. He was sunk between the wings of his favourite chair, and didn't move. There was tiredness obvious in his limbs, and he looked thinner, more hollow around the eyes, but they were bright and alert. Flemyng had to continue.

'Our friend Kristof. There was a hook, from the start.'

'Of course there was,' Craven said. 'What did he say about Abel?'

Flemyng got up from his place, his face drawn. He turned away in frustration. 'How did you know?'

'Mungo was alarmed by your phone call last weekend. He got a message to me. It turned out that we wanted to speak to each other for the same reason, without knowing it. Why else would I have gone to Altnabuie? And it's obvious Abel is in the middle of it. A schoolboy spy could have worked that out.

A famous American is dead and your brother is coming to Europe. Mungo got it right. Something alarmed you quite recently, and we both know what it was.' For the first time since he had sat down, he smiled.

'Before I tell you,' Flemyng said, 'I have another admission that involves my brother.'

'Ah,' Craven said, smiling for the first time. 'You're going to tell me that you've been reading my notebook. There's an entry about him from the other day, in my childish code.'

'Oh God,' Flemyng said, as if it was the confession he had never intended to make. 'I have, and I'm sorry.'

'I know you are. But I would have done the same – have done, indeed, in even more awkward circumstances. I want you to sit down, Will, have a drink and talk it through. Abel, Grace Quincy, everything.'

He reached behind his chair and produced an open bottle. 'Have a drop of red.'

Flemyng talked and out it came. The story of their second encounter in the metro minute by minute, the first mention of Abel in the café, and then the glistening, frightening lure cast by Kristof to pull him in. 'He said his people knew Abel well. Implied he was working with them. As brutal as that.'

Craven watched from his chair, and Flemyng noticed the old quickness in his eyes. He also thought there was fear.

'Repeat that please.' Craven's tone had changed, and words came quickly.

Flemyng said that Kristof had described a relationship between Abel and the other side, and left no doubt about it. 'He accused my brother of betrayal. I couldn't read it any other way.'

'Stop there,' Craven said. 'I want the exact words. And did you ask how he could prove this?'

Flemyng repeated the phrases that were etched on his mind, and said, 'The first thing I said was that it was obviously rubbish. The stupidest thing I'd ever heard, and hurtful. He then said he could produce evidence.'

'Did he offer any clues about what that proof might be? Anything at all? A name?'

Craven's mood had changed utterly. He got up and turned away. To Flemyng's surprise, he thought he heard him speak under his breath.

Turning round, he said, 'Anything else?'

'Only a hint from him. A threat, maybe. He says he might ask me for help. Something personal.'

'Nothing is personal with them,' Craven said. 'We know that.'

Flemyng said they all understood that. He would never co-operate. 'But it's hard to step back. You can see why.'

Craven said he was sorry, and picked up his wine glass. Flemyng could see shadows on his face, and a trembling in both hands. 'You seem shocked, Freddy,' he said. 'I was angry. But the idea that I'd take it seriously is absurd. Abel? Ridiculous.'

'I know,' Craven said. 'I'm shocked, of course. How could anyone expect this? Will, I'm so sorry.'

'For what?' said Flemyng. 'It's hardly your fault. Our world, that's all.'

He spoke of a crisis whose dimensions he couldn't gauge, and turned to Quincy. 'One of the reasons that this is so difficult for me, apart from the anger, is her. Freddy, she confided in me.'

There were newspapers on the floor of Craven's apartment. He waved at the heap. The murder still commanded space on the front pages – had her life been taken by a lover, a rival, a gangster? – but there was no conclusion from the police that was yet public. Everyone now knew the victim, but it was still assumed that her attacker had a grudge that was unknown.

Flemyng picked up a paper, and threw it down. 'She told me she was excited about a story that would somehow touch… people like us, I suppose.'

Craven was watching closely. 'You have to tell me everything. A story. About whom?'

'Kristof and his like,' Flemyng said, 'though she never used his name.'

'Her words precisely please, Will.'

'The East Germans.'

'That was all? No detail? People?' Craven was holding both arms of his chair.

Flemyng said, 'What she had found out, I have no idea. I had hoped to see her again.'

Craven took the cue to alter course, as if they needed a break. 'For personal reasons as much as this stuff, I take it.'

'You can be a hard man, Freddy.'

'Observant, no more than that. Mungo said to me the day before yesterday, before I left him: your face is easy to read, for those of us who live with you.'

Flemyng said that he was willing to confess his attraction to Quincy. 'But I was intrigued and alarmed, as you will imagine.'

Craven looked straight at him. 'You're in the firing line. Family, friends, the lot. And now your friend – your acquaintance, anyway – is dead. And you wonder if her murder could be part of this whole business. That's natural. And it means we have to consider, don't we' – in a theatrical pause, he filled his glass – 'that this may be a state crime, and nothing less. Even without a shred of evidence.'

Flemyng nodded. 'I suppose we have to. But by whom and why?'

'Anything else?' Craven was still more interested in his knowledge and his reticence. But Flemyng was done. About Bolder, his extravagant story at Brasserie Lipp and his trip to London – nothing. And Kristof's visit to his apartment after Quincy's death could wait. Another betrayal to add to the pile, but he convinced himself that Craven had heard enough for one morning.

'Surely that's a good start?' he said.

'Very well,' Craven said. 'We'll return to the politics of this murder in the office,' as if his flat was no place to discuss assassination. 'The police will have to say more, and colleagues will hear things, no doubt. She spoke to you about our East German friends, so the investigation is important to us. It's not only an American affair, although for public purposes that is how it has to be, and they don't want to give too much away. But we know something that they may not: what she told you at lunch about her story. And we both know that Bridger need not be told about this conversation, at this stage anyway, and with any luck – never. Let me worry about that, but meanwhile keep out of his way.'

They returned, finally, to Abel.

Craven said, 'He's coming to London, I gather, this month. A proper posting, not a fly-by, so a friend tells me. The question for us is obvious. Should we tell his people what has been alleged? Obviously not. It's an accusation against your brother that you consider to be vile. I cannot disagree with that. But do we keep what Quincy told you under our hats? We want their help to crack it, and we do have a lever. A knot, and a nice little problem.'

Flemyng said that nice was not the word that came to mind.

*

Like most political manoeuvres dressed up as entertainment, Freddy Craven's May Day party was expected to be a disaster.

His announcement came at Monday morning prayers, deliberately giving only two days warning, so that it was awkward for anyone to refuse the invitation. The ambassador had already departed for an official visit to the Midi that he said couldn't be postponed, Flemyng's only cause for relief. He was back in his place at the end of the table and could watch every face when Craven said he had decided they might as well celebrate, since Paris appeared to be preparing for a drama of its own. 'My terrace is rather small, as most of you know, but we can take turns looking over the city, and enjoy the day.'

Bridger, looming out of his wide chair, said they might smell some cordite. 'Bracing.' He would look forward to it and he hoped that he might bring Grizelda. 'Of course,' Craven said at his side. 'A welcome adornment at any party.' Bridger bowed his head in thanks, and, stiffening in his place, he tossed back a lock of blond hair that had tumbled down, and said he could tell them things about the preparations being made by the riot police that would make their own hair stand on end. Bending forward to peer along the table, he laughed in Bolder's direction. 'Even Sandy's.' Bolder beamed, touched and evidently deaf to the tone.

'I'm happy to say I have some sources of my own,' Bridger went on, his eyes still on Bolder to make the contrast. 'They tell me the coming days will challenge us all.'

'It could still be a slow boil, Pierce,' Flemyng said, raising a hand. Bridger frowned at the papers in front of him, and Flemyng added, 'Perhaps you know best.'

Craven, concealing his anger, picked up quickly and said he

would lay in a decent supply of drink and they were all welcome to lose themselves in the afternoon with his books and his jazz collection. 'No one will be thrown out, and you needn't leave until the last of the tear gas has dispersed.'

In truth, Craven had told Flemyng the night before, the point was to repair the damage in the station's relationship with the rest of the embassy. 'Especially between you and Bridger. It's bad for you both, and this place, and I want it to stop.'

Flemyng said that he had no interest in perpetuating a feud, but found it impossible not to respond to Bridger's barbs, which had become more wounding in recent days. 'Janet knows, from the talk on her twinset circuit, that he's been whispering in the ambassador's ear. Dropping poison. I'm sorry, but the Quincy business has tested me to the limit.'

'Him too,' Craven said. 'Remember that. He's shaking like a leaf.' They may have been boys together, he said, which made their later struggles worse, but the time for pain had passed. 'Surely?'

Flemyng didn't answer directly. 'You say I'm a man for a party, but I'm not looking forward to this one. You're kind to lay it on – don't misunderstand me.'

'All the more reason for my having it,' said Craven. 'We need to clear the air.'

'I can't see it working. I'm obviously driving him up the wall,' Flemyng said. 'He also seems to think that Sandy's off his head.'

Craven replied very quietly. 'And what do you think about that?'

Flemyng showed his embarrassment. 'We still haven't got to the bottom of his London trip. But steady on. He tends to get overexcited. That's his style.'

Flemyng threw himself into work for the rest of the day,

avoiding Bridger's office, and writing an assessment of what the government in Paris thought of the students and their plans, how the French communists would react to unpredictable interlopers on their turf and where the weight of the unions would fall. Having done that, he used NATO as another diversion and read the latest cables from Brussels. But on Tuesday, after a night disturbed by unexpected dreams of Quincy, he sent a message to the language school in Hertfordshire for the attention of Sam Malachy, attending an office course, on leave from Vienna.

Would Sam like to make a short trip to Paris? It would be good to see him, and, anyway, Freddy Craven was having a party.

He heard the bells sound the hour. It was May.

Nineteen

Abel's message was passed to Maria after she walked in the early light to rue de Nevers and rang Washington. He had left for London, and wanted her to come to him. The answer was no. There was trouble, and it was the worst moment for her to disappear. Could he come to her? She hoped for an answer before the day was out.

Taking a route to the office that cut through Place de la République she saw dozens of union banners on poles already propped up against the high statue like lances ready for a joust, and a body of marchers swelling up in the streets around the square. The men around whom the early crowd clustered were wearing dark suits and ties, or black leather jackets to show a little extra fight, and she noticed that the hundreds of students, most of them sitting on the ground, were keeping to themselves on the far side. They presented a more vivid picture. Their flags were a riot of red and black, painted anti-war placards were everywhere, and people were singing. She saw Edward Abbott listening at a table outside the café they'd colonized. He smoked as he wrote smoothly in his thin note-book, ignoring the noise, as if he were in a library instead of the street. There might have been no one else in the square.

She paused at another café near the metro to watch. There were faces that she knew from Nanterre, but she kept her distance. As she drank her coffee standing at the bar, where a few old men moved away from her, a loose procession began to form – orderly at the front, with an established hierarchy lining up behind the first banners and, farther back, a mass of followers that stretched out of the square and grew to fill every opening as she watched. It would take time, but they'd be marching within the hour, and she could join them further along the route.

When she reached her office, they were looking at wire service pictures from a memorial service for Quincy in New York which her colleagues had decided to arrange quickly. Two withered parents were on the church steps, the faces around them making up a tableau of writers and editors whom Maria recognized. But the family's glamour had gone, to be buried with their daughter when the French had finished their business with her. Quincy's mother shielded her eyes from a cruel sun, and the scene was bare and painful. On the wires, the stories repeated what everyone knew, that the Paris authorities hadn't yet found a trail that might lead to her killer. And how she had died, no one knew.

She went into the glass box where the teleprinter had spewed out the morning news, and picked up the phone to Flemyng.

'Are you marching?'

They both laughed. 'Believe it or not, I'm going to a party.'

'Well, I've just been in République and I see trouble. Our friends from Nanterre aren't at home with the old guard, especially the ones with dark glasses. They're going to be trampled. I'll let you know.'

Flemyng said he was going to get a bird's eye view from the apartment of Freddy Craven. 'You know who I mean, don't you?'

Maria said that it was painful to hear the name. 'Quincy asked me the same question, on the last day we spoke...'

'What did she say about him?' Flemyng's voice was quite calm.

'That he was a legend. I said I knew of him, like any reporter who's knocked around Europe, but that was all. She bought that. There wasn't much else.'

Flemyng said, 'I'm sorry to push you, but nothing?'

And Maria, feeling his anxiety, said she thought they should talk it through. 'In the evening? I can come to you.'

'I'd like that very much,' Flemyng said. 'Freddy's party's going to be quite a trial. Come at eight.'

He put down the phone. It was an embassy holiday, with Wemyss as duty officer sitting alone in Bridger's office, and Flemyng had been reading in his apartment. He put his book away and sat at a narrow desk at the window, going through a routine that he enjoyed. He took two sheets of writing paper and unscrewed his fountain pen, which he used when he was trying to think hard. He began to write a list of questions. Some of them were scratched out immediately, as if it would be dangerous to leave anything misleading on the page, and others were underlined. Alongside he had a list of names, and as he began to juggle the fragments in front of him like pieces of a jigsaw, looking for connections that might be hidden, he started on a second page. At the top he wrote the names of Freddy Craven and Grace Quincy, and underneath began a second list of questions. But they were a mess. He was sowing confusion where he should have been clearing it away.

Taking a clean sheet, he wrote another name. Abel.

No connections worked.

So he found himself picking up a pencil and drawing faces, adding an ornate gravestone to represent the cemetery, with Quincy's ambiguous smile dominating the page. But there was no shape that made sense. He was out of ideas.

Restlessly, he got ready for the party, slamming his bathroom door in irritation as he thought of the two Bridgers waiting for him. He had a grey linen jacket and he chose a red tie, knowing it would prick Bridger. He took a bottle of Côte du Rhône from his store in the lobby cupboard, found a brown paper bag and set off. Craven's apartment was less than a mile away and he walked, with the bottle under his arm.

Some streets were blocked off, and CRS troops were lounging on their own barricades, smoking in the sun. Flemyng could see trucks that looked like prison vans in the side streets, with helmeted heads moving at the windows, and packs of motorcycles ready to run. There was a flow of people heading eastwards towards République, where he imagined the traditional march was about to set off. Many of the women were carrying lily of the valley, the traditional May Day decoration. He checked his watch and walked a little faster. Freddy would be expecting him.

Craven's apartment was on the top floor of a block that gave a view of the river, one that was two steps up from Flemyng's in the embassy pecking order to reflect the old man's seniority. There was a concierge in a uniform, who called the lift, and when Flemyng arrived upstairs he saw that Craven had stationed a waiter at the door of the apartment holding a tray of cocktails, to give the party a touch of holiday glamour. From inside, he could hear Bridger's commentary.

'I'm told they always claim a million on May Day. Fantasy, I'd say. Nonetheless, my friends predict that this will be rather impressive. Worrying, of course, in its way. Freddy – are you listening? I imagine it reminds you of the Red Square parade.'

'Hardly, Pierce. There aren't missiles pointing our way.'

Craven saw Flemyng come in, and pulled him over.

'Now, Will, let's have a wee game you and I. How much trouble?'

They played along for minute or two, Flemyng regurgitating Maria's phone call and wondering aloud how the students would rub along with the old disciplinarians whom they had to follow. Bridger passed on a story from the interior ministry that there was a degree of panic about the unpredictability of the young leftists.

'We're accustomed to thinking that communists need *order*. There has to be a *structure*. That's what the whole business is about, after all. But this new crowd – none, apparently. Very odd.'

Craven said that perhaps Bolder could explain. He'd served more time in the east than any of them.

'Half of them are Maoists,' Bridger said. 'Heaven help us.'

Flemyng could see that Sandy was out on the balcony, with Grizelda.

Mrs Bridger was tall and fairly broad, a natural partner for her husband. But with her sturdy beauty came a natural elegance, flowing from the confidence with which she moved. More than any other woman of her height that Flemyng knew, she seemed comfortable. Her hair was a golden red, and long, organized in tresses. He often thought it was because she was German by birth that he imagined her on the opera stage in a heroic role. In her bearing and the timbre of her deep voice there was simmering drama. And from the unlikely combination of her size and her gracefulness there came a surprising lightness of touch in conversation. Their acquaintance was slight, but he enjoyed her.

When she and Bridger had met on his UN posting in New York, she had been a translator for the secretariat and at his young age there had been no social barrier to their liaison. Early on, he had secured his ambassador's blessing. Their walking-out was notably happy and quick, and they married in the episcopal church on Fifth Avenue with the British mission cheering them on, and Grizelda's German relatives from Cincinnati putting together an oompah band for the celebrations afterwards. If she turned out to be heavy going at the dinner table, as he thought she did, she was usually forgiven because her brain and her loyalty to Bridger were assets that he was rightly proud to have. An imperious hostess was always an advantage. Wherever they might be sent, Grizelda would cope.

Swivelling away from Bolder, who was leaning over the balustrade, she stretched out an arm as she stepped back from the balcony. 'Will Flemyng. We have seen too little of you since we arrived. Have you visited our house yet? I can't quite remember.'

'No,' said Flemyng, as she smothered him in her arms.

'We have some dinners arranged before the Parisians decamp for the summer, to their various boltholes here and there. Pierce has established himself quickly, I think I can safely say, in the right places. I shall ensure that you are on the list, and high up.'

'You're very kind, Grizelda.'

She turned towards Bolder, still on the balcony and standing on tiptoe because he was leaning over the iron railing towards the street. 'Sandy is a friendly soul, don't you think?'

'Always,' Flemyng said.

'Perhaps a little unsure of his place... his *status*, however.' She was watching Flemyng for a sign of agreement. There was none.

He said, 'I really shouldn't worry about Sandy if I were you, Grizelda. His is sometimes a lonely furrow, but he does plough it thoroughly.'

Craven came behind them, as if he had been given a cue, and gave Grizelda an old-fashioned gentleman's bow. 'My dears. The party is taking shape. And the march is getting close. Shall we watch?'

They crowded on to the balcony, much as they would line up for morning prayers. Bridger was in the centre, with Craven next to him and Grizelda at his shoulder. When the first rank of the march appeared, thirty-men-wide with a forest of red flags behind them, the watchers absorbed a little of the festival atmosphere. Grizelda had a lily of the valley pinned to her dress, and Bridger even raised a toast, tilting his head to the sun. 'Paris – how we love her.'

Flemyng laughed, and pointed to the phalanx of students who were appearing on the boulevard towards the back of the crowd. Different chants came through the hubbub, and they watched as someone set light to a Stars and Stripes. It was snatched by one of the stewards and the flames stamped out. There was some scuffling.

'Do you notice,' Flemyng said, 'how different the younger ones are from our own, let alone the Americans?'

Rows of pale young men in shirts and ties walked with arms locked, well-turned-out girls beside them. Pullovers and sober jerseys were more common than ragged T-shirts, and many wore black polo necks, like refugees from a jazz club.

'I was expecting a scene from Grosvenor Square,' Bridger said. 'It's surprisingly old France, is it not? Reassuring in a way. Where are all the jeans?'

Craven said that he didn't know whether to be thankful or not.

Grizelda leaned over them and said that the students seemed unlikely allies of the Viet Cong.

'Or the unions,' said Flemyng, pointing to a fight that had broken out not far from the front of the column. Four or five students were on the ground, and as the marchers moved forward they could see that they were bloodied. Fists and feet flew for a minute; then it was over. The injured were dragged on to the pavement and some students signalled to an ambulance parked at the end of a side street. The crew responded lazily, making clear as they crossed the road that they considered the fracas a fuss over nothing.

The march moved forward without a break at its established walking pace, as if nothing had happened. They would soon pass into Concorde and move towards the Champs-Élysées, where a vast tricolour was swinging to and fro under the arch in the distance.

Inside Craven's apartment, someone had put jazz records on his rickety turntable and Janet was watching two of the secretaries dancing together. Bolder had positioned himself in Craven's chair by the high bookshelf and was reading, with a dry martini in his hand. There was a conclave of junior chancery men in a corner. Bridger broke them up. 'I must speak to Wemyss. Will someone rouse him, please?'

He was handed the phone, and spoke as if he were addressing morning prayers. 'Wemyss, what news?' After a brief pause to listen, Bridger added, 'I do, however, have some for you. There has been an altercation here between students, I assume from Nanterre, and some of the old guard who organize this march each year and therefore think it to be theirs. Perhaps you should check the news wires, Reuters and so forth, and write a telegram simply noting the violent event, making clear that I have observed it personally, and telling London that I shall write a considered note in the morning. This may be the cloud no bigger than a man's hand that will one day fill the sky. Thank you, Wemyss, as ever.'

He turned away, satisfied.

And Craven appeared at his shoulder.

'You may be right, Pierce. I have some information from a friend.'

Bridger frowned at him. 'I've just informed Wemyss of what we saw. He is composing the embassy telegram.'

Craven said there might be more.

'Well,' said Bridger. 'Perhaps you'd favour me with whatever morsel you have in your knapsack. I won't ask whence it came.'

'They're closing down the university tomorrow,' said Craven.

*

Flemyng walked home after two hours in Freddy's apartment, crossing to the Left Bank with students who were carrying their marching flags and pushing into cafés that were already overflowing. Waiters in their long aprons were trying to control the crowd outside, black-suited cowboys circling a runaway herd. He cut away from his usual route, went towards rue de Tournon and found a space in a favourite café, where the atmosphere was high. There were clusters of police on the corner outside and a crowd of students under the awning, guarding the door, but he squeezed into a place at the bar and listened for a while to the talk shooting past him. Word of coming trouble had spread, and they spoke of where they would meet the next night. There would be a crowd coming in from Nanterre and they'd be together to face the police. Someone shouted one of the slogans, and a chant was taken up. In Café Tournon, the *patron* had given up on propriety. It was the way of things.

His woman – no one knew if they were married – had a lurid wig which everyone said she had worn since the end of the war, because her head had been shaved as the penalty for consorting with Nazi officers in the night. Afterwards nothing had grown back, making her punishment eternal. She was behind the bar, shouting at everyone.

Walking away, Flemyng found himself outside the barracks of the Garde Républicaine along the street and as he passed he heard the prisoners sending out their nightly message, playing with spoons on the iron bars at their windows. Their cells were turned into a grotesque xylophone, and the ringing followed him down the street.

In his apartment, with windows propped open to keep the warm air moving, he thought of Maria and put some wine in his little fridge to cool. He cleared the papers from his desk, and watched Quincy's face torn in two as he ripped them up. There was nothing to see, nothing to keep.

She arrived on time, and they touched cheeks. Quincy's death had granted them more intimacy.

Opening a bottle, laying out some pieces of ham and breaking bread, he spoke to her of the parade. Maria had seen more trouble between students and older marchers for whom May Day was as much a part of their year as Mardi Gras, and as unchanging.

Then they began.

'Quincy and Freddy,' Flemyng said, straight out.

'I was surprised when she mentioned him.' Maria had come prepared.

'I've no reason to think that she had any idea why I should know him. She thought I might make guesses about these people, that's all. She's been spook-watching for years, like all of us. I speak as a reporter.' She laughed.

'You said on the phone that there was no more to it than that,' Flemyng said. 'But there was something, wasn't there?'

Maria got up to get some water. 'Let's come back to that.

I promise I will. But let me ask you something. Did she talk about what she was working on?'

Flemyng said 'Yes' from the sofa where he lay.

Maria was managing the conversation, step by step. 'Thanks for that. You said when Kristof left both of us – the morning after – that she'd said something to you that took us on to his territory. What was her message?'

'This is difficult. You know that.'

Maria sighed. Like Flemyng's, her face was serious, all the fun gone. 'We're working together. That's the fact.'

'I know,' he said. 'But we have loyalties that we mustn't break.'

She got up and walked across the room. 'Will, we both want to know what happened, and that can't be a secret between us. Agreed?'

He said nothing.

'When you say "Kristof's territory" you mean East Germany?'

His reluctance hadn't disappeared. 'You know that I'm constrained.'

Maria ploughed on. 'She told me she was working on a story that might change our lives. She was a bit embarrassed by that phrase, but meant it. And if she mentioned the East Germans to you, we're both aware of where she was heading, and we have to do something about it. For God's sake, she's dead.'

After a few moments' pause, he said that it was time for them to visit the cemetery, and to find Kristof's dead letter box. The police would be gone by now.

'First thing tomorrow morning?' she said.

'And now you'll tell me what else Quincy said about Freddy,' he said.

'Sure. I was intrigued, but it didn't seem a big deal.'

'Tell me.'

Maria said, 'She asked me if I knew Craven's wife. That's all.'

Flemyng turned on the sofa and jerked his head sideways towards her across the low table. His hand was ruffling his hair. 'What?'

'You heard me.'

'Just say it again. Her exact words.'

'She said, "Have you met his wife? Could I find a way to meet her?" That was all, because I said I knew nothing of her.'

'I'm not surprised,' Flemyng said.

'Why not?'

'Because Freddy's never had a wife in his life,' he said.

TWENTY

When the gates at Père Lachaise opened at eight o'clock, Flemyng and Maria were watching. Each carried a small bouquet, bought from the flower seller who had pulled her wooden cart into position in time for the early visitors and was dousing her blooms from a giant watering can. They had spent a few minutes in a café across the street, almost alone, to confirm their plan. Even before the high gates were firmly chained back for the day, they were inside and walking towards the place where Quincy had died.

Every journalist in Paris knew the gravestone. Max Anderson had led a posse of Americans for a wreath-laying and a eulogy from him on the day after her body was found, and when Flemyng and Maria turned into the pathway leading to the stone they saw a collection of flowers that were still bright. Placing their bouquets at the side of the pile, they read some of the messages from her colleagues and the family. Many were anonymous, but there was a large wreath from the American embassy. They stood for a little while, in unfeigned sadness, until they saw a member of the cemetery staff moving along the adjoining row of graves.

They had agreed that Flemyng would speak first, since in such a place it might be thought to be a man's business.

Explaining that he and his friend had known the late Miss

Quincy, and they were greatly saddened by her death, he wondered if M. Lebosquet was at work and whether they might speak to him. They knew he had found her body, and it would be a comfort to see him. Flemyng's French passed muster without comment from the official – maybe because he was not *Américain* – and he felt a gratifying tremor when the cemetery man said, after he had expressed his condolences, that it would be easy to meet Georges.

'He will be here at nine, coming along that path. He begins each morning over there.' He pointed over their heads.

They thanked him, and each took his hand in turn. There would be no difficulty in recognizing Georges Lebosquet. His photograph had been on the front pages, and Flemyng had read every word written about him.

'First,' said Maria, 'a treasure hunt.'

Each of them remembered Kristof's precise directions for the dead letter box he had revealed to them in their early-morning talk. They found the junction of the two walkways he had described, and counted the plots as they walked south towards the edge of the cemetery. Sheltered behind the yew tree and a high memorial, they found the section of wall that was hidden from passers-by, a gap in the curtain of ivy and the loose stone at head height. It came away easily.

By way of preparation, they looked at each other with deliberation, and didn't speak. Maria put her hand into the cavity.

She took out a sealed envelope and turned it over. There was no inscription. Flemyng remained silent. Maria held it close to her face and, in the morning air, she said she imagined that she could pick up the odour of Quincy's perfume.

Flemyng's eyes welled up and, breathing in, Maria turned away.

As she did so, she heard footsteps on gravel, and leaning back to whisper to Flemyng, with one hand on the high memorial beside them, she pushed herself away and moved fast. The envelope disappeared into the bag over her shoulder and she walked briskly along the line of the wall. Without a word, Flemyng replaced the loose stone and set off in the opposite direction.

They emerged on to the path about sixty yards apart, looking away from each other. The young couple whose footsteps had alarmed Maria had already turned right to join another path and were walking away with their backs towards the wall, hand in hand and taking their time. Their clothes gave nothing away. They could have been visitors touring some famous graves, or students in search of solitude. Caught up in themselves, they didn't look back.

With the interlopers gone, Flemyng and Maria found each other and she patted her bag. They would open it later, after they had seen M. Lebosquet. It was nearly nine o'clock.

They walked together along the perimeter path, through a maze of obelisks, memorials and ruins, and ahead of them they saw the deputy keeper beginning his early rounds, which he would repeat at dusk. M. Lebosquet turned towards them and, keeping to the centre of the path, approached with a steady tread, obviously bent on an assignation. Flemyng said to Maria that he seemed so determined that he could be an ageing gunslinger on the dusty set of a western, ready for anything at high noon. But when they shook hands, he was practising propriety, not bravado, and gave an exhibition of politeness.

'I am told you are looking for me,' he said.

Despite the season, he was in a dark blue woollen suit. It was worn away in patches but a working uniform that was also respectable enough for any conversation with a widow or a priest. He had springy grey hair, with tufts high on each cheekbone, and a natural expression that was heavy jowled and serious, turning avuncular when he smiled. Flemyng and Maria introduced themselves, and he dipped his head. They explained their friendship with Quincy – by their description it might have stretched back for years – and he said he understood perfectly why they might want to talk to him. Sometimes, he said, comfort was his business.

They found a bench and sat side by side, M. Lebosquet between them. He gazed across his tombs.

When he began to speak of the shock he felt at the event, they commiserated with him and encouraged him to give his feelings full rein. His relief at their gentleness, and their apparent lack of interest in gruesome detail, meant that when they began their questioning slowly he dealt with them as if they were sympathizers, with no interest in interrogation. They were so much easier than the journalists who had queued up for him a few days before.

M. Lebosquet was proud of the cemetery, and its place in the history of his city. He respected the graves of the famous and cherished their memorials, but most of all he treasured the family plots and mausoleums that held the story of Paris through the generations. Each time they opened one up for an urn or a new coffin he heard the turning of a page. This was the first time in his experience, he told them, that death had besmirched Père Lachaise in such a way. Even the loss of a child, heart-draining though it was, was part of the natural rhythm in the cemetery. The cry of murder – heard around the world! – disturbed everything. Revealing the romance that was part of his nature, he said that he felt as if a mirror had been smashed, breaking his own image into pieces and promising him seven years' bad luck.

'That is why I refuse to believe that she was killed here. I cannot.'

For Flemyng, it was a moment to hold back. He didn't ask why, nor push M. Lebosquet for a reason. There was time.

After a few moments, he said that it was poignant for them to remember Quincy's rucksack, because they had often seen her carrying it. Did he think it had been thrown aside, or placed carefully where it was found?

Definitely not cast off, said M. Lebosquet, but laid deliberately against a neighbouring stone. He could show them where, if they wished. Clearly, she had put it there herself.

Flemyng said, 'The gravestone where she lay is quite high off the ground. We have been there. It would require effort to get up there. You know that the police – and the newspapers, of course – think she was lifted there. It's part of their murder story. Is that how it seemed when you saw her – that she had been taken there when she was dead, and laid out?'

They could see that it was still painful for him to remember the scene. He tossed his head as if trying to rid himself of a thought. 'They like to think that, but that is not how it was. I told you.'

Flemyng said that he knew it was difficult for him. They were thinking of Quincy, too. If he didn't mind, it was important for them to know how she had looked at the end.

'I don't believe she was carried there as a corpse. Do you understand? This is why I am so angry at the suggestion of murder in this place. I felt very strongly at the moment I saw her that she had died there, sitting on the stone. Unaware of what was happening. I have no explanation for that feeling, but I know I am right.'

'That comforts us,' Maria said. 'Thank you.'

And Georges Lebosquet made his confession. 'I have something I must tell you.'

Terrified by the unexpected arrival of death, he had run to

his office. In the nights afterwards he dreamed of what he had seen, unable to remove the image from his mind. 'I am sorry to say this, but it was like a photograph in my head. The surprise on her face. That's what it was – shock. As for pain at the end, I hope not.' But long after his interview with the police – it had been straightforward and wrapped up in an hour – he remembered a detail in the scene that troubled him because it had slipped from his mind in the turmoil afterwards and, after deliberating with himself, he had said nothing about it to the officers.

When he first saw her, a cigarette lighter was beside her body on the gravestone. It was silver. But when he returned with the police after the alarm call had been made, perhaps twenty minutes later, it had gone.

'You mean that when you found her, although the cemetery was closed for the night, there must have been someone else nearby?' Flemyng said gently.

'Yes.'

'Watching you, perhaps,' Maria said.

Flemyng said he assumed there were people who crept into Père Lachaise to sleep for the night. Tramps, street wanderers, maybe students with no home.

'Indeed. We know this,' M. Lebosquet said.

To be frank, he went on, he was fearful of going to the police to change his story and tell them about the lighter. 'It was stolen, that's all. Am I right? She is dead. I cannot bring her back.'

His refusal to believe in murder was absolute. He was sorry to remind them of how she had looked at the end, but he was certain that she had been taken by a seizure that came from nowhere. *Un grand coup de sang.* These things happened. He waved at the sky.

Flemyng said mildly that he was surely right. Newspapers liked to make up stories, because it was always easier to write about a mystery than the truth. And everyone knew about the police – they ignored the obvious because their lives were governed by suspicion.

He noticed that Maria was holding her breath.

'Thank you,' said Georges Lebosquet. 'I will say nothing. May she rest in peace.'

They spoke for a few minutes about Quincy. Maria told him that in her trade she was a person of unusual gifts. 'A woman in a man's world, an adventurer. She wrote like an angel.'

They walked with him to the keepers' lodge and enjoyed the sun. The cemetery was fresh, green and bursting with buds on the bushes and the horse chestnut trees. The May blossom was coming. They prepared to part, with thanks and in good humour.

As they shook hands, M. Lebosquet said he was glad he had been able to help them deal with the sad event that had taken their friend away. Then he added, 'There is something else I should say.'

'Yes?' Flemyng said.

'I think she loved this place.'

They waited, giving him time.

'I have thought about her very often. Long after the police went on their way. And my memory is clear. I saw her before, when I was walking the paths. She came here – at least twice, maybe three times – in the days before she died.' He put a hand across his chest, as if he was taking an oath. 'I know this. You may think it odd, but I am comforted by that.'

'So are we,' said Flemyng. 'Thank you.'

'It is the kind of information – so personal – that we must keep private,' Maria said.

'Certainly,' M. Lebosquet replied. 'I have told no one but you. Her friends.'

They thanked him, shaking hands formally, and turned towards the gates. As they passed through, Maria unzipped the bag on her shoulder and pressed her hand on the envelope inside.

TWENTY-ONE

When they arrived at Flemyng's apartment, they found a telegram from Sam Malachy that the concierge had slipped under the door.

> Sorry missing party. On night train.

'In the old days it would have come yesterday, even before Sam got to Victoria,' Flemyng said. 'Never mind, we can all have lunch. I'm not expected at the office. You'll like him.' He watched her place the envelope from the cemetery on his square kitchen table, sliding a bowl of fruit to one side.

Maria said they had a dilemma which at another time might amuse them. 'Mine or yours?'

'Washington's or London's?' Flemyng said. 'Sometimes the spoils of war have to be shared.'

Maria opened it carefully, sliding her thumb under the gummed flap to ease it up slowly. There was no writing on the envelope but they could see that it was creased, scuffed with dirt, and had been resealed at least once. Flemyng deliberately put his head down, so that he was close to the table and sensing the perfume that Maria had imagined clinging to the envelope. Her fingers went into the envelope, and she slowly pulled out the wafer-thin package that was inside.

A sheet of rough copy paper, the same kind as Maria used in her office, had been folded in four. Making the point that it was a joint enterprise, Flemyng took over. Unfolding it, he pressed it flat with his hand and they looked at it together.

Before them lay a list of names. All appeared to be German.

'Recognize any?' Maria said, after she had read them twice.

'Not one.'

'Me neither,' she said. He was watching her.

There were nine of them, typed, arranged alphabetically and showing no other pattern. Three women were listed, and six men, but they weren't grouped by sex and the names were written with surnames second, so that they didn't seem to have been taken from an official document.

'There's something else,' said Maria. 'This wasn't typed by a German, or at least not on a German typewriter. Some of these names need an umlaut. Other accents for all I know. There's nothing.'

Flemyng was looking down at the paper, both his hands on the table.

'And we still have to answer the big question.'

She put it in words. 'Whether Quincy was supposed to pick it up, or whether she put it there.'

'Quite.'

Maria added, 'And there's another decision we have to make.'

Flemyng smiled at her.

'Who gets it?'

The doorbell rang, and a voice came through the letterbox. 'Wakey, wakey, Will Flemyng. Still in bed?'

The night train had delivered Sam.

*

Freddy Craven was very angry, and Sandy Bolder was curled up in his chair like a furry animal in retreat.

'I wouldn't be so unhappy if Bridger didn't have a point.' Craven's voice was cracking.

His grey hair was greasy and dishevelled, spiked and unruly, and the bloodshot eye more obvious than the day before. He hadn't risen from his desk since Bolder had answered his summons, and his headmasterly dressing down was costing him energy he could hardly spare.

'Have you any idea how embarrassing it is to hear that you've been parading up and down King Charles Street, bawling like a costermonger and stirring up the crowd, without telling me you were even in London? I think much the same of Patrick Ingleby as you do, but unfortunately for us he's now in charge of Europe in the Foreign Office and his cables are read all over the place. In this case, by every ambassador on this whole bloody continent who's up to it. Thank God ours is away, and Wemyss can lose the damned thing in one of his files.'

Bolder, flirting with pathos, said he had no idea that anything he said could have been taken so seriously. 'I promise you, Freddy, I was careful to avoid detail. I tried not to leave traces.'

'You might as well have worn a sandwich board up Whitehall.' Craven was shaking. 'Spreading rumours like a fishwife, spraying hints and winks all over the place, in the bleeding cabinet office if you please, and then decamping to the Travellers to finish the job, making such a fool of yourself in the bar that you might as well have dumped a dog mess on the carpet.'

With effort, he pulled himself up to stand. Propping himself against the wall with one hand, he reached for his stick before he walked to the window. 'You are claiming –

do correct me if I'm wrong, won't you? – that there is some kind of leak. You don't know whence it sprang, which government or even which bloody capital, except that Moscow may know something that it shouldn't – *may know!* – about alliance plans. Which ones we don't know. What may have leaked, you have no idea. When the information was passed, if it was, you don't know. In other words, you know bugger all.

'But you claim that it's evidence of a network of agents, of which the French are aware and are keeping to themselves. I expect they'll be delighted to hear that you've been spreading the story across London.

'And as for our own dear service – I'm thinking of Duncan Gilfeather in Berlin, poor Jonny Hinckley at NATO – what the hell have you done? Left them in the bloody lurch. Didn't speak to them, and gave not so much as a by-your-leave before you tossed them on a dung heap. From which, incidentally, they will have great difficulty crawling out.'

Bolder said, 'I'm very sorry, Freddy. Really.'

Both men were exhausted. Bolder's hair had collapsed and the thatch lay matted across his forehead. His crisp white shirt was sweat-stained and in an unthinking nervous spasm he had undone his shoe laces. Craven was erect at the window. Without his stick he would have been on the floor.

Swinging round slowly, he said, 'Sandy, this hurts.'

Bolder said, 'I understand.'

'I want to salvage what we can, for the good of this station,' Craven said as he sat down at the desk. 'I've drafted a telegram which indicates exactly how I think this suggestion or rumour, or whatever we call it, should be treated. With exceptional caution. Exceptional. I have said that my own conversations indicate that at a moment of tension it's natural to have claims from the other side that the balance has shifted

– intelligence-wise, I mean – and we have to remember that it's in their interest to set some hares running. One of which may have crossed your path.'

'Are you putting me in the public stocks?' Bolder's head was down, and he was whispering.

'Oddly enough, no. Though God knows why. Your name isn't mentioned.'

'Thank you, Freddy. You're a good man.'

'I may regret it,' Craven said. 'But I want this place intact. Especially with what's coming our way. It's not the Russians we're going to be talking about here.

'The Nanterre faculty is being shut down today. The police are all over the Sorbonne. A right-wing bunch set fire to a lecture theatre early this morning, and you can expect the riot squads on the street. They'll be rough because that's their way. The army's round the corner. And half the lecturers are going on to the streets with their students. They're serious. Flemyng says there's a dam that could burst. Sandy, for God's sake, don't you care?'

'Of course.' Bolder sounded sad. 'But maybe I have Russia on the brain. You know, my life.'

Craven said that he wouldn't expect Bolder, even in these circumstances, to tell him the names of everyone he had met or listened to in recent days. Secret servants' rights were sacrosanct, almost always. But he added, 'I deserve a little more, don't you think?'

Bolder nodded. 'What I would say is this, Freddy. There was no moment at dead of night. Not a knock on the door. It was talk, that's all. I speak to the French, all sorts of people around this town. Even the Americans.' If it was meant as a joke, it failed.

'Talk!' Craven was shouting now. 'And you pranced off to

London as if you had the bloody Holy Grail in your suitcase. Grow up, Sandy. This isn't what you were taught to do.'

'I have no words,' Bolder said, miserably.

The old man looked him in the eye. 'If I'd built my reputation on talk of that kind, I wouldn't be here.'

They were both exhausted, Bolder folded up in his humiliation and Craven drained of all his fuel.

'And by the way,' he added, delivering a last uppercut, 'I knew you were slinking off to London. I saw you at Nord.'

'Why were you there?' There was a last sliver of defiance in Bolder's voice, but no more.

'That, my dear Sandy, I'm not going to tell you. Now get on your way. I'm going to finish the telegram. And, no, you're not going to see it.'

Thus dismissed, the weary Bolder left the room without another word.

Craven lifted his phone and, after a moment, asked for a cipher clerk.

*

Quincy's envelope was back in Maria's bag, the paper with the list tucked away while Flemyng welcomed his old friend at the door.

Sam Malachy had kept all the rough edges that Flemyng had lost. He was short and beefy and his dark brown hair never looked the same from one day to the next. His features were rounded, except for a pointed nose that gave the impression of turning upwards at the end. Flemyng always told him he had the look of an eighteenth-century squire who'd led a raddled life, and he did carry the air of a good-time boy, which he was. The broad Yorkshire voice had never softened in his time away from home, and it misled some colleagues, who were deceived into thinking that as a consequence he was no linguist. But Sam was one of the best in the business. At the language school he was polishing his Czech again.

They came into the room together, Flemyng's arm across Sam's shoulder.

'This is Maria. Rest assured we can talk as friends.'

Sam took her hand. 'That's saying something.'

Flemyng got a kettle on the boil, and asked Sam for news of Vienna.

'You know how it goes. Sleepy old town, set in its ways. Fur coats on the Staatsoper steps, picnics in the woods. *Sachertorte* for tea. Then – bang! – it's all excitement.'

He was watching Maria, as if wondering whether to continue, and when she caught his eye she nodded quite deliberately.

Sam smiled. 'We get news from Belgrade or up the river from Budapest. Bit of trouble in Warsaw maybe. Everyone gets worked up and we scamper around. Talk to each other and let the rumours breed. Then we all go quiet again. Except this time, Will, it's different.'

'Prague, you mean?'

'I do,' said Sam.

'Can they keep the lid on?' Maria asked.

'I doubt it. We can feel the heat in Vienna.'

Flemyng was pouring tea. 'We're going to have lunch, but let's talk first. Sam, I need to let you know that Maria is in on all this. Don't hold back. We're working together.'

'In whose interest?' Sam said, and laughed.

'You needn't worry about that,' Flemyng said. Sam picked up his serious expression and sat back, ready to listen.

'It's the old story, Sam. We've got a puzzle, it's in two parts and maybe more, and the pieces don't fit. The only thing that we can be sure of is that we've found ourselves walking into a minefield wearing hobnailed boots. I'm going to start with a name that you'll know. Grace Quincy.'

'Murdered in this very city,' Sam said. He got up and began to pace the room. 'And known to you?'

Maria said she had been. As at the cemetery, she gave no hint that their acquaintance had lasted no more than a few days. To make Flemyng's point, she said, 'Together, Sam, Will and I have discovered something important. That's why we can talk openly to you. When Grace died, she was working on a story about the other side. Vienna's the gossip capital, and she passed through recently. Hear anything?'

Sam said he'd like to ask another question first. Looking at Flemyng, he said, 'How's Freddy?'

Flemyng was alerted by the sharp tone of someone who thought he was getting to the point. Catching his eye, he detected in Sam a seriousness that hadn't been there a moment before.

'Have you talked?' Flemyng asked.

Sam had turned away and moved to the window. He said nothing, as if he had missed Flemyng's question.

Aware that the atmosphere had changed, Flemyng continued without asking again. 'Put it like this, Sam – Sandy Bolder's not Freddy's favourite boy at the moment.'

Repeating himself, he said that Sam shouldn't worry about Maria. 'Please. She knows this story from me and no one else.'

'OK,' Sam said. 'Sandy rang me. When you pulled me over from London, I couldn't think why. But I heard a whisper afterwards that Sandy was causing trouble back at base and I wondered. Did he tell you that he spoke to me?'

'He did, and Freddy knows, too.'

'It was odd,' said Sam. 'One of his conspiratorial calls. Said there was talk in Paris of leaks. Russians smirking all over the place. Knew more than we thought they did. Had I heard anything in my outpost, where all the wires seem to cross. No was my answer. I did tell him he had Moscow on the brain. They're panicking so much about Prague, believe me, that everything else is for the birds.'

Then, he said, Bolder had sent a telegram. Eyes only for Sam. He was convinced that the key to his puzzle lay in the east. But there was nothing Sam could offer in return.

'Put it like this, Sam.' Flemyng stretched back as if to give a summing up. 'Maria and I are caught up in the Quincy business, which makes it awkward for us both. We knew her, and everyone's trying to find out why she died. There's a coincidence here that's impossible to ignore. Bolder thinks there a game afoot in this city. Quincy's on to something. And suddenly she's dead.'

Sam said that he had the same attitude to coincidences as Flemyng. 'They're never what they seem.'

But he could be emphatic. He hadn't seen Quincy in Vienna recently, and no talk about her had come his way. 'They all pass through, back and forth from Prague and beyond. She's a regular on our patch. A sparkle of Hollywood in the gloom, people say. But this time, nothing.'

Maria said they must be thinking about lunch. 'I've got a suggestion. We head into the quarter first, and spend a little time. There's a place in rue de Seine where I'll find some people I know and you can go on from there.'

'Students by any chance?' said Sam, all smiles.

'Sure. Kids with armour on.'

Flemyng was clearing away and getting his jacket.

Sam said, 'And what do they say will happen next?'

'The revolution starts tomorrow,' said Maria.

TWENTY-TWO

While Flemyng and Sam were preparing for a night in the streets, Abel Grauber was inhaling the remembered smells of London, soothing the last of his transatlantic weariness. He did little on his stopover except to contact the brothers, Mungo by phone and Will by telegram. He stayed clear of the embassy. Whatever the coming days held, he was determined that his presence itself shouldn't become another secret. There would be enough of them.

Mungo was subdued when they spoke, but Abel felt the pulse of relief in his voice. 'I'm looking forward to having you here, whenever that might be. Your room is waiting. Come when you can.'

He left his telegram to Paris until the end of the day, to make sure that it wouldn't be delivered until the morning, and said that he expected to be able to call Flemyng from the city the following evening.

Steering away from embassy tracks, he dined at Bianchi's in Soho, where the clock outside the first-floor window was still stuck at half past one, as it had been for years. Elena, doyenne of eating places for a mile around, remembered him and pampered him at a table in the corner, like one of her actors whose bills never needed to be paid until they were back in work. Later, he decided to walk to his dingy hotel near

Victoria, with creaky beds and no night porter, to be ready for the first boat train of the day, paying in cash and confident that in all London Elena was probably the only person who knew he was passing through. She never told tales.

On the crossing, smooth with a spring breeze light enough to leave hardly any white traces on the water, he sat on deck and looked back to the cliffs until they disappeared, only turning towards France at the last. Where was home? Mungo's voice had cheered him and he felt the lure of the north, where there was solace. London? Friends and memories, but for Abel the embrace of the city had lost its warmth. In the months ahead, however long he was required to stay, he wouldn't be resuming a love affair, but trying to rekindle its flame.

He bought bread and cheese in Calais, and took a sheaf of morning papers to the train. Then he found time to sleep. He stirred only once on the journey, so when he took time for a coffee at Gare du Nord he felt rested.

Leaving the metro at Odéon, he dropped his bag at a hotel a few minutes' walk away, and in a café on the next corner rang Maria's office from the phone under a wooden hood on the wall. It was late afternoon, and in their brief exchange – anonymous and almost monosyllabic on both sides – she told him that she could be at their old place within the hour, not naming it. He rang off, knowing that he had time for a walk through some of his old streets before turning up at 36, rue de Nevers.

They hugged, and Maria poured the coffee she had ready for him on the gas ring.

'Sleep here if you like,' she said. 'You know it well enough.'

'Don't worry. I'm at a *pension* three streets away. But, have you...?'

Producing a key from her bag as he spoke, she dropped it on the table. 'I have a surprise for you,' she said.

'Me, too,' Abel said. 'Isn't that how we like it?'

'Whether you're going to like this or not, I can't say.' She laid one folded sheet of paper in front of him. 'Here's where we are. Read it.'

She gave no description, no explanation.

Abel flattened the sheet, and looked at the list taken from the hiding place in the cemetery, the copy typed out by Maria in her office. She sensed his excitement.

As he looked at the names, his face took on such intensity that Maria almost believed that for the half-minute or so that he scanned the paper he didn't blink. Concentration had kicked in, and he didn't speak. He breathed in slowly. Then, looking up, 'You know any of these names?'

'No,' she said.

'Nor me.' He shook his head. 'Who knows?'

Maria said she had checked at the embassy without leaving any fingerprints – 'our lovely Butterfield' – and had established that the names were in none of the obvious files. 'None on the usual lists, and no trace among people we've come across in the last few months. The old regulars, trade delegations and so on. Not one of them turns up in any cables. Zilch. But we've only started.'

'Berlin?' Abel said. 'Has Hershkoff seen them?'

'Not yet. I need to work out how to get it to him. We may need a courier of our own.'

Abel said, 'Begin at the beginning. Is this something Quincy left behind?'

'That's why I love you,' Maria said.

'Tell me.'

Abel was dark-haired and sun-browned, slim and easy with himself. His rounded face had a touch of Mungo's cherubic style, but he was narrower, taller, and his eyes were darker. Jet black. When he was serious, everything about him seemed to draw in so that he became thinner, and his face longer, but for now he had thrown his shoes aside, and showed through his excitement the readiness of an athlete on the blocks. His jeans were blue and a dark green shirt open to his chest. He wore a gold ring and his sleeves were rolled up to the elbows. Watching him, Maria said quietly, although he heard her, 'Every inch an American.'

'On with the story, Miss Cooney.'

Maria said, 'This list was in a dead letter box in the Père Lachaise cemetery close to where Grace Quincy was found on her stone. She died on the Wednesday, as you know, and these names – in an envelope – were left there in a hiding place. Was she meant to collect it? I don't know. But we believe the envelope was handled by her.'

'Why? I'm assuming you didn't find this by chance,' Abel said, showing no surprise at anything she had said.

'No.'

'So who told you where?' There was almost no pause between his questions. 'Quincy herself?'

Maria shook her head. 'OK. Here's the first complication. I wasn't alone when it was found.'

He said nothing, but stretched out an open hand. 'Give it to me.'

'Your brother was with me.'

They were sitting close, neither missing any change of expression in the other. Abel's face didn't alter, but his eyes turned away from hers, to a window and a brick wall in shadow outside. He stared. In Flemyng, Maria had seen something of the intensity that the brothers preserved for their dealings with each other. She said nothing.

The men lived far apart, but Flemyng had told her that at

each connection the power came flooding back, unbidden. A complication, but they lived with it. She had once wondered aloud with him whether he would describe it as love, because she knew from them both that with their energy came nervousness and even suspicion. Sometimes, a reluctance to trust.

'Of course it's love,' Flemyng had said to her. 'Not the word we use, mind you. We're one, whether we like it or not. Some day we'll find time to talk about it.'

Now she had placed him at her side in the Quincy story, and Abel would have to find out why. She saw that his face was drawn, which brought the shadows back.

'Did Will know her?' he asked.

'I introduced them four days before she died.' Maria told the story of Hoffman's party, Quincy's arrival and her introduction and Flemyng's fascination. His excitement. With the care that each expected of the other, she added, 'If he did know her and concealed it, he did it bloody well. I'm sure it was a genuine first meeting. She said so, too. I know it wasn't the last.'

'When was that?' Abel asked.

'The day before she died.'

'He told you?' Abel was stating a fact with his question and didn't wait for an answer. 'And now you can tell me how you came to visit her death place together.' For the first time, his voice lost a little of its confidence. 'You'll realize this is a big surprise.'

He rose and poured himself a glass of water, drinking it down slowly in one. 'I'll give you mine now. The reason I'm here is to talk about Quincy, as it happens, but I can't start till I know the whole story of you and Will. Tell me all.'

Taking the floor without asking another question, Maria drew a picture.

'When I told you I'd met him last year I said that he'd probably marked me down. He hasn't mentioned you: I'd have told you. We've walked together, had dinner. Gossiped. Things known, and never said. Then the last few weeks came along. And Quincy, too. She brought us together and pulled back the veil. One of the last things she did.'

Abel asked what Quincy knew about her.

'Guesswork. But she knew all right.'

'And Will?' he said.

'He was attracted to her. I saw it immediately. They were playing a game, and he was willing to let her.'

'So she knew,' he said.

'They'd hardly begun,' Maria said, 'but I'd say so. And Will would, too.'

Abel said he'd interrupted her flow. She took up the story.

'The night she died, we got information afterwards pointing us to the dead letter box. It came from a source of his, and I was there. This is where it gets difficult.'

'Why?' Abel said.

'The source is his.'

'So what? That's how we got the list,' said Abel.

'Yeah.'

'So he's ours, too,' he said. 'Who's the source?'

Abel was still standing, and she went to him. Holding both his shoulders, she said that she was depending on the trust between them. 'There's a history here that I don't understand yet, can't put together. Give me time. Let me come back to the source later, and put him aside for now. Please, for me.'

He said, 'Do it your way. Your town.'

With Kristof off the stage and safely stowed in the wings, waiting for his cue, Maria went back to the cemetery. She described their discovery of the hiding place, the encounter with M. Lebosquet and his revelations. 'Two facts. The missing cigarette lighter, taken from the scene, and his memory of Quincy's previous visits.'

'Helpful,' he said.

Days later, Maria would remember Abel's response with crystal clarity. Quincy was in the room with them – teasing, determined and, as she had learned with her death, in thrall to a secret life.

Maria felt pain, but understood.

Abel, younger than Maria, was in control. The knowledge that he brought from Washington changed everything. He began with his memories.

'I met her in Europe, a couple of times, and got the full treatment. I remember a party in Vienna where she came on strong. Almost ate me up.' He smiled. Maria spoke of the folk-lore that was attached to Quincy and her travels, the guile and gaiety, and her capacity to appear from nowhere and seem at home. Always one of the band, longing for the road. She said she found it hard to imagine such a lonely death.

'But she *was* lonely,' Abel said.

'How do you know?'

At the moment of revelation, he smiled again, as if it might be a relief to Maria. 'Because she was playing the game on both sides, where there's no hiding place. No trust.'

He got up. 'I'll go back about eighteen months, after you left for Europe. There's a young guy who climbed on board with us around that time. Name of Zak Annan, you'll like him, and after a bit he brought us a story. He's been a reporter, still writes a little, and runs with the old crowd. Twice in Saigon.'

'I've seen the byline,' Maria said.

'Well, he's with us. Now an L Street guy to the core.'

'And he knew Quincy?'

'Sure. Admired her. And… who knows?'

Maria said, 'OK. Him and how many others?'

'Here's his story,' said Abel. 'He suspected that Quincy had worked him out. Knew he was in touch with us, at least. You saw her at work, the eyes that saw through any mask. But did she drop him, avoid him? No chance. She took it as an invitation, a come-on. Started to feed him useful stuff that never saw the light in a magazine. It checked out, and some of it was golden.'

'She knew where it was ending up?'

'Zak was in no doubt,' Abel said. 'We got him to take it slowly, but eventually he coached her in some methods – transmission, rules of the game – and she used them. Didn't hesitate. Within months, we were certain. Ours.'

Maria said, 'You're going to tell me that your coming to London is part of this.'

'I am,' he said. 'But only a part. She'd got dangerous, and it was worrying.'

Abel said that Maria needed to know something of the pattern of his life in the previous year. 'We have an operation running that's plugged me into Brussels and Berlin. I've been working with people in London – that's why I'm going back – and we were making progress. Not enough, but starting to see a picture. Then Zak Annan warned us that something was going wrong with Quincy, like an affair that was starting to be a bore. She needed more fun. He thought she was on the loose, and confessed his fears. Knew she was sleeping around Paris. She's been writing NATO stories from the French point of view. Teased him as well about people she spoke to in Berlin, Prague. She couldn't resist, and he sounded the alarm.

'I'm posted to London to get a grip of this. And next thing I hear, she's dead, in a cemetery where you tell me she's been servicing a dead letter box that has nothing to do with us. You say they think she's been poisoned, and there's a cigarette lighter that's been stolen from the scene.'

He told her that the previous autumn he'd spent a month at the FBI laboratories at Quantico where they collected as much debris as they could from the other side, and from every scene of trouble, all their agents' gadgets assembled in a ghoulish classroom display. 'I've seen pens and lighters that they've used in Berlin, and in Turkey of all places. This will be one of them. I've seen pictures of the workshop in Rostock where they put them together, and I don't believe in coincidences.'

'What we've got isn't a whodunnit. We know the answer. It's a *why*dunnit.'

'Most of the time they're the same,' she said.

'No. Assume she was killed by the other side. 'This time, "why?" is more difficult than "how?". And as for "who?", if we're right, identity may not matter. We know that whoever he was, he'll be long gone from Paris now.

'Here's my guess. She'd got herself close to some of the people we call the enemy. But she was too good, and liked the game too much. They couldn't trust her – just like us – and there was only one thing they could do. Put an end to her. Because, believe me, this matters.

'The funny thing, Maria, is that we wouldn't want this to come out any more than they would. But what went wrong for them is that, for some reason, when they got rid of Quincy, they left the list behind – that is, if her killer knew it was there.'

Gesturing to him to sit across from her at her low table, she said, 'Now me.' He sat back, flopped out and easy, but his gaze was intense. 'This may help you. Quincy said she was working on a story that was big, even by her lights. It was going to shake us up.'

'About Paris?' he asked.

'No. Will confirmed that.'

'After that last lunch?' Abel said.

'Exactly.'

He gave her time to choose her words. Maria said it was clear to her that Flemyng was interested in Quincy, and a little dazzled. He'd confessed his hope, after it was too late, that they might have got closer. In her view, learning from her brief acquaintanceship, Quincy was able to summon up strong feelings, and excitement, apparently without effort. Her fame and her personality were one; an engine that only ran at full power.

'You felt this yourself,' Abel said, without making it sound like a question.

'I did.'

'And Will fell for her.'

'You could put it like that. Not a crush. He just found her a little irresistible.'

Abel asked if his brother had felt as if he might have been used.

'Ask him, but I'd say no. We're talking about two or three days here.'

'They only had two encounters – at the party, and then the lunch?' Abel asked.

'As far as I know.'

'But she told him something about her story that she didn't tell you. What was it?'

Maria said, 'That it was about the other side. Not the Russians, but their foot soldiers in East Berlin.'

Abel's eyes were black and shining. 'Did she ask him for help?'

Maria said, 'He didn't say that. He was astonished.'

'Why?' Abel pulled himself up and sat forward at the table, leaning towards her.

'His source is East German,' she said. 'The one who sent us back to the cemetery.'

Abel said, 'I have to meet him.'

He looked at Maria with an expression of such sudden intensity that for a moment it was difficult for her to know whether he was going to cry, or laugh at the absurdity of it all.

'And my brother mustn't know.'

TWENTY-THREE

S am had a treasure chest of street stories. He carried them everywhere as a protection against loneliness, and Flemyng knew it.

When they were together in the gardens near Flemyng's apartment, having said goodbye to Maria in the late morning, they spoke first of all about times they had shared, because that was how they always began. Sam called it tuning up. He remembered nights with Freddy Craven in Berlin, they laughed about the time when Bolder was found without a passport at a border crossing where he was supposed to be the link in a secret chain, and they brought old friends to mind. Some of the dead danced for them, and the voices came floating back.

Sam sparkled. For a while they kept Maria out of the conversation and let their memories transport them, a conscious effort to recover their old closeness by stepping away from the here and now. Sam, whose latest marriage had collapsed the previous year, found reassurance and strength in the telling of tales, and by the time they reached the river he was ready for action, as surely as if he had been a runner made eager by a sweaty warm-up. 'I assume you need my help,' he said, as they turned into a narrow street to the restaurant Flemyng had chosen for lunch. 'I'm game.'

'Yes, I do,' Flemyng said. 'Far be it from me to get you drinking again…'

'Perish the thought,' said Sam.

'… but I want you to spend time with some of the boys in London. Vienna, too, when you get back. Let's go in.'

He pushed at the door, and the bell behind the flowered curtain jangled to announce their arrival.

*

Nearly two hours later, they parted in the street. 'I'll be here for the weekend,' Sam said, 'and I'll start the talking around before I get back to my bloody language course. There are some people I can see here, and I'll talk to Vienna.'

He disappeared round the corner, and Flemyng turned towards home. Without knowing it, he passed within a few yards of the alleyway that led to rue de Nevers, where Maria and his brother would meet to plan their own moves. But Flemyng knew nothing of the apartment she kept there, and gave neither of them a thought. Sam was in his mind, and the tasks he had given him were a neat list in his head.

At home, he picked up Abel's telegram, which had arrived at breakfast time. He remembered each word but read it again.

```
Heading your way. Will ring Thursday
late.
```

Flemyng would expect nothing before midnight, so he would have time to prepare.

He spent two hours quietly, making only one phone call. Ringing the embassy, he heard from Janet that Craven was out for the afternoon, and turned to a book for a while. But he was thinking of the street, and decided quickly on an expedition into the Latin Quarter. The radio was broadcasting the news that the authorities had shut down the Nanterre faculty, and he knew that the streets around the Sorbonne would be a gathering place in the evening. Along rue St-Benoît there were already hundreds of students, swarming around Les Deux Magots and crammed in the streets around the church across the way. Afterwards, because it stuck in his mind as the start of everything, he could recall the scene in all its detail – the huddles on every corner, the chants coming from the main gates of the university not far away, the slow burn in the crowd. Then, the deliberate procession of three police vans along the boulevard, each carrying a riot squad and all of them slowing down to watch the crowd through the black windows. As the first one passed, he heard the men inside drumming with their batons on the floor.

The beginning.

Disorder all around. And in the muddle of uncertainties and alarms, there was private anguish for him. Abel's telegram and Freddy's game. His own uncertainties. On the streets, the promise of trouble. He needed a stroke of luck.

It came in Café Tournon.

When he took to the street, he knew it would be a place where he could smell the atmosphere. The crowd made the room uncomfortable, but he wanted to stay. Pressed into a tight corner where it was hard to stand easy, it took him a few minutes to escape for air, squeezing through the throng with a glass of wine held high like a signal of distress.

Then, beside him, he found Edward Abbott. They were both joining the line at a door that opened to reveal a single hole in the floor, with a chipped ceramic rim, that had to serve all the men and women in the establishment. Flemyng made the point that the wall paintings and the café's self-regard for its in-house philosophers made a fine contrast with its plumbing, and Abbott laughed. 'That's why we're enjoying ourselves. The best queue in Paris.' Flemyng, introducing himself, suggested they had a drink together if they could find a space.

'I only know you second-hand, I'm afraid,' Abbott said with a smile when they did sit down. 'We didn't meet in Vienna – I'm right, aren't I? – but we have mutual friends, here and there.'

'I don't doubt it,' said Flemyng. 'And I saw you at the American party the other night.'

Quietly and quickly they made their connection.

Flemyng recalled some of Abbott's columns with an admirer's warmth, and within a few minutes they were like a pair of students, arm in arm on a hike into Middle Europe, talking of bicycles and river barges, fortresses and monasteries on the cliffs, lost days in the antique byways of half a dozen cities along the Danube, and cherishing in their tale-telling the gift they shared, a devotion to curiosity and a nose for trouble.

Abbott was soft-spoken, and his spare frame less alarming at the table than it often seemed when he leaned into a conversation. He seldom raised his voice and his gestures were conservative, so that he didn't show agitation, although he had the appearance of a man who might dominate. His hair was cut short without style, and his complexion sallow, always with the rough shadow of a beard that never seemed to grow. Friends said of him that he was as gentle on the inside as he was fierce outside.

Flemyng didn't mention the embassy, but chose history. That suited them both. For half an hour they swung back and forth between France and the places they knew half a continent away, and Abbott revealed something of his story of the spring.

He'd spent most of March in Prague but was drawn back to Paris by two students, both Germans, he'd met in a bare café behind Wenceslas Square. They'd travelled by slow train through Leipzig, where Abbott said you could feel winds that came from somewhere new. 'They're rounding people up. Everyone's nervous. Even I have friends in prison.' He gave a thin smile.

In Paris, he'd watched the eruptions at Nanterre from the inside, bedding down with new friends. Flemyng recognized a couple of names. Abbott was embarrassed, he said, to have been persuaded to address a meeting there, invited to explain the power of protest. 'They call me the Englishman, because I'm the only one around,' he said. 'It's funny but they rather like someone who looks old-fashioned. The man in the drip-dry shirt. A lot of them are conventional, more than they know.'

Flemyng said he'd like to hear about the speech – 'No, really, I mean it. What did you speak about?'

'Hope, I suppose.' Abbott drank up. 'I wouldn't describe it as a speech. I just joined in, that's all.'

They were both smiling, bright-eyed now, and Abbott entered into the spirit with a few sentences about the excitements of the street, the energy from the angst of war, the giddiness. 'It seems a little overblown,' he said, because he was someone who always drew back from the edge, 'but there's a good deal in it. They've no idea what they're doing, most of them, but that doesn't mean they aren't serious.'

'I know,' Flemyng said. 'Is there a photograph of your oration? I'd promise not to pass it around.' He laughed.

Abbott said he hoped not, then stopped when he saw that Flemyng's expression had changed. Startled, he held up a hand to stop the conversation, turning to look towards a figure framed in the door and trapped by the crowd.

Freddy Craven looked stricken.

The old man had stopped to balance himself on his walking stick, and gazed at the crowd around him with all geniality gone. It was cool outside, but he seemed to have come from the tropics. His face was blotched, wilful spikes of hair sticking from under his tweed hat, and his naval tie badly askew. He was staring across the room with a perplexed expression in which Flemyng, against all his instincts, saw panic. He stood and waved, his own face showing nothing but happiness as he cried out.

'Freddy!'

Craven stood still and looked towards them, as if adjusting his focus before he could identify Flemyng. When he stepped forward, he moved slowly, aware of the dangerous swirl of the crowd around him. They could hear singing from outside. Both Flemyng and Abbott rose as if they wanted to help, but neither wanted to seem alarmed. They let Craven approach them at his own pace. He straightened his tie with one hand, put the other through his hair, and managed a smile for Flemyng. 'I'm sorry, I got a little swept up on the pavement. The tide is running strong tonight.'

Then, with hardly a pause, 'It's Mr Abbott, am I right? Hello. My name is Craven.'

Flemyng gestured to his chair and Craven said as he sat down, 'We work together, you see.'

'Flying the flag,' Abbott said, pouring wine into the glass that Flemyng had taken off the bar. Craven took it from him.

'*Salut!*'

'What have you seen, Freddy?' Flemyng asked, and for a moment Craven looked confused.

Then he smiled. 'Streets full of people. A city on edge.'

Flemyng realized how quickly Craven had recovered his

balance, and with what magic. He looked as if he had been perched comfortably at the table for an hour, and Flemyng and Abbott were attending on him rather than worrying, as they had been a moment earlier, about whether he could steer himself safely through the crowd. His fluency was back, and he drew Abbott's eyes. 'Tell me what you've been hearing. All this' – he waved towards the door – 'really isn't my concern day-to-day, but I'm fascinated by the passion. The speed of it.'

'I've been back for a few days – from the east,' Abbott said. 'Watching the smoke rising from the volcano. Feeling the tremors.'

'You expect an eruption?' Craven said.

'Oh yes. They think nothing can stop that, and they're right.'

Craven smiled. 'Revolution. If we still believe in such things. Your first one, Will.' He turned back to Abbott.

'And what tidings do you bring from points east?'

'Fear,' he said. 'They're as scared as can be.'

Craven said he had been lunching with a friend at the Quai earlier that day – Flemyng suspected it was a useful fib, and loved the brazen moment – who had been amused by the alarm shared across the divide. 'Revolution! Unwelcome in Moscow as it is here. So much better for them if our problem on the streets evaporated and the children went home.'

And, putting the question as if it were a natural follow-up, he said to Abbott, 'You will have known Grace Quincy, I assume.'

Abbott said, 'Sad. We travelled together a few times, obviously. I liked her very much, admired her spirit.'

'And tell me – Edward, if I may – how do you think it was that she came to die?'

Flemyng was startled as much by Craven's speed as by his willingness to give Abbott a glimpse of his real interest.

He knew that their presence together in the café was a chance collision, so his decision must have come after his alarming entrance from the street, dishevelled and half lost, in the few minutes after he sat down. Flemyng wondered why. But if Abbott was thrown, he didn't show it.

'How she came to die?' he said. 'Do you mean the nature of it, or the reason?'

Craven smiled in acknowledgement of the subtle answer.

Flemyng intervened. 'Let's be blunt. You have no doubt, Edward, that she was killed?'

'None,' said Abbott. 'That's why I think you're asking me if I know why.'

Craven said, 'Indeed. I can see that you're surprised – maybe asking what business it is of ours. Why should an embassy functionary like me be playing Maigret, when the unfortunate dead woman was American? It's not as if she was a British subject. I understand your point of view, Edward, but I find that in these tumultuous days we're tied up in each other's affairs more and more.' He clasped his hands together tightly to make the point, as if preparing to pray. Flemyng noticed how bony his fingers had become.

'Don't you find that, too?'

'I do,' Abbott said. 'But, as for Quincy, I've got nothing to offer, except sympathy all round. I really can't help, although I wish I could.'

Craven said, 'If she was killed by an enemy – forgive me, but I'll use that word – you'll realize that it's natural to ask why she was posing a threat. What she knew, or might know. It must have been something important, wouldn't you say, for them – whoever they are – to risk all the fuss that was bound to come with her death? That's what I think, anyway. Do you have any idea what it might have been?'

'Honestly, no,' said Abbott. 'None.'

For the first time, Flemyng saw discomfort, and in an instant the atmosphere changed.

Abbott's languid air was gone. He stood, then reached down for the rough canvas holdall where he kept his notebooks. 'I really must be off. I've arranged to see someone a little later, and the metro may be troublesome this evening. All this.' He looked round at the crowd.

'My apologies to you both.' He was smiling as he told Craven that he had much enjoyed their encounter. 'Please don't misunderstand me when I say that I've heard of you here and there, so I'm delighted we've had a talk. I hope that when I'm here I can ring you at the embassy some day, and perhaps we can take a stroll, have lunch. That kind of thing. May we?'

'I should be delighted,' Craven said. 'Forgive me for not rising, Edward. We old men are a little worn out by the time the evening comes.' He extended a hand, and they all laughed.

Abbott waved at them both, then squeezed through the throng to the door, going out backwards against the tide. The noise seemed to swell as he left.

After a moment, Flemyng asked, 'Why?'

Craven was happier than he had seen him for days, his eyes quick.

'Abbott intrigues me,' he said. 'You, too, I assume.'

'Of course. But Freddy, please, there's more to it than that, I can see.'

'Perhaps.'

Flemyng said, 'Come on, old foxy friend.'

Craven leaned in. It was noisy around them, and no one else could hear his answer.

'He has interesting friends. For example, Sandy Bolder speaks of him often.'

TWENTY-FOUR

Flemyng knew, when he heard Kristof on the phone, that his luck had run out.

It was the first time he had used his number, the first time they had spoken without facing each other alone, and his voice had changed. It was higher and sharper, and had lost the rhythm that Flemyng had come to know. His message was brief, using no names.

'I have to come to you now. This will not be easy. One hour.'

Flemyng said, 'Come', and replaced the receiver. He looked at the clock on the mantelpiece. It would be ten o'clock in a few minutes. He made tea and turned on the radio. The news on the hour reported student demands, police at the Sorbonne, a government appeal for calm. He listened for a few minutes then switched it off to give himself quiet. The room was dark except for the lamp standing behind the chair where he liked to read, and he sat down in the pool of light, pulling the ottoman from the fireplace and putting his feet up. His face was in shadow, and for most of the next hour he appeared not to move, although he was awake. When he got up it was nearly eleven.

Downstairs, he stood inside the front door until it was time, then quietly unlocked it and went into the street. He stood in the darkness of the alleyway for a few minutes and, on the hour, watched Kristof crossing the street at the corner.

As he approached, walking quickly, Flemyng stepped out of the darkness and opened the front door without speaking.

'Thank you,' Kristof said when they were in the apartment. Nothing more.

Flemyng gestured to the chair on the other side of the fireplace from his own, and went into the kitchen. Returning with a bottle of whisky and two crystal glasses he placed them on the low table between them, and said, 'Perhaps we'll need this.'

'I think so,' said Kristof.

Flemyng poured, and lifted his glass in a silent toast. The signal to begin.

Kristof was dressed differently. He was wearing a navy fisherman's jumper and jeans, and hadn't brought a coat. Flemyng was struck by the change, and noticed that his signet ring had gone. Without his worn suit and white shirt he took on a new character, as if his thin trappings of authority had been removed. The face that he had drawn for Freddy Craven was still familiar, but he was looking at a man stripped bare. Kristof couldn't conceal his alarm. He laid his pipe and tobacco on the table.

'I have troubles,' he said.

'Tell me,' said Flemyng.

'I'm in danger. You need not know from where. There is information which may help, and you can get it.'

Flemyng said nothing.

'It is personal, and it may be my lifeline. I have always said the day might come when I needed help. It will be difficult, however.'

His next words were more unexpected than anything Flemyng had experienced in all the wild days since Quincy had arrived in Paris.

'I must see Freddy Craven's diary.'

Flemyng stared at him.

'I know it exists. Never mind how. You are his trusted colleague, and have certain skills. You will be able to find the part I want. It concerns Berlin.'

Flemyng shook his head, but before he could speak Kristof picked up.

'Craven mustn't know, but you have to do this for me.'

Flemyng said, 'I can't', and sipped his drink.

'You must, and I will make you an offer.'

Flemyng watched him pour himself another whisky and light his pipe, and said nothing.

'I can tell you the story that Quincy was hoping to write. As your seafaring friend Mr Craven might say, it will shiver your timbers.'

Flemyng thought again of the mystery Kristof carried with him, his easy English with its sprinkling of antiquated expressions, and the strange comfort he showed in speaking of Craven and his world, without the awkwardness that was characteristic of his kind. Where had he learned it?

'You're asking me to steal from a friend,' he said.

'For a prize,' Kristof said.

'It would be treachery, professional and personal. Unthinkable.'

'I know,' Kristof said, 'and that is why I'm afraid I have to give you no choice.'

'Explain,' said Flemyng.

'It is simple. If you don't help, I shall betray you.'

Flemyng stood up. Stepping away from the lamp light, he became a shadow.

'Are you going to ask me to leave?' Kristof said.

There was silence.

'I am glad. Let me tell you what I would have to do, although I would not enjoy it. Actually hate it. I would let it be known

– this town is full of journalists, as you are aware – who you are and what you do. And your brother. I would blow him to the world, and let out the information I have about him, which would be destructive. The brother spies. A delicious story, with its own mysteries, that would excite everyone in these troubled times, and which would be the end of your career. Out of the dark and into the light. Exposed. You could live quietly somewhere, maybe be a schoolmaster. Marry. Be happy, perhaps. But never be a spy again. And Abel? The end, I think.'

'You bastard,' said Flemyng.

'I am trying to save myself. The instinct we all have. I am sorry, but I must.'

'Are you mad?' Flemyng said.

He turned away and went to the kitchen, where he did nothing but stand at the window. He was breathing fast, and took some moments to calm himself.

When he sat down again, with a drink, he asked his first question of Kristof.

'When you contacted me, was this the purpose?'

'I was serious about your brother. But you know how much has changed in these days. Quincy. Her connections. Her discoveries. We have come to this, and I must ask my favour of you.'

'Blackmail,' Flemyng said.

'No. A deal.'

'Under threat. You can't believe I would accept this, surely?'

'I came here because I had to. What I know is all I have. Therefore I have to use it as best I can.'

Flemyng got up again and spoke.

'There are things you understand that surprise me. Much that you know. So how can you be so stupid? Asking me to let you see a book that's not only private but secret, too. If it even exists. To break every pledge I've ever made, against a threat that you couldn't carry out. Who would believe you?'

'There are people who would be listened to. Storytelling is a powerful business. Quincy knew that.'

Flemyng said, 'How do I know that you have any idea what she was going to write? That you could tell me anything that I don't know already.'

Kristof smiled and poured another whisky. 'It sounds to me as if we're going to make a deal,' he said.

'No.'

'Let me try,' Kristof said. 'I have a story to tell that would be precious to you and your people. Treasure. Quincy had an inkling, but only that. You would be a hero in London, and, I would suggest, in Washington, too. That is the prize. And what do I want in return? Information that is personal to me. That's all.'

He stood and moved to Flemyng's chair, so that the light caught his face and showed his excitement.

'I promise it would not harm your friends. There would be no damage to the interests you are sworn to defend. A diary, no more than that.'

'Prove it,' Flemyng said.

'I can't. Isn't that the trouble with our trade?'

'You mean I have to trust you?' Flemyng said.

'Of course. What else is there but trust, and luck?'

'There's loyalty,' said Flemyng.

'Your loyalty is to your country,' the German said, 'and I can tell you that what I have would let you fulfil that duty.'

He waited for Flemyng, taking a moment to look at the pictures on the wall, getting close to see them in the shadows. Two or three minutes passed, and Flemyng spoke so quietly that it sounded as if he were afraid of being overheard.

'Will you ring me here tomorrow? Late. I have a dinner. And we might arrange to meet at the weekend.'

Kristof said he would be out of Paris for two days. 'We are restricted and I travel with difficulty, as you know. But I have found a way. I will return by Sunday, and I will ring you in the evening.'

'I'll be ready.'

Kristof said, 'I had hoped it would end like this.'

'It hasn't ended, believe me,' Flemyng said.

'But we have begun,' Kristof said, and stretched out his hand.

Flemyng walked him downstairs, staying in the hall as Kristof stepped out. He closed the door quietly without looking into the street and went upstairs, locked the apartment door from the inside and filled his glass before he took his chair. He sat for a long time, as he had done earlier in the evening, and listened to the silence of the night. There were no sirens, almost no traffic in his street, and it was quiet enough to hear the ticking of his clock.

It was just before one when the phone rang, later than he had expected. Abel, as he had promised, wanted to make a date. They exchanged some warm words, said little and arranged to meet at seven. 'Looking forward to seeing you,' Abel said.

'Me too.' They said no more.

He went back to his chair, sitting awake with his mind racing. When it struck two, he got up and put away the whisky. Getting ready for bed, he thought of Abel.

He left the book at his bedside unopened. Switching off the light he said a few words into the darkness and closed his eyes.

Sleep came slowly.

TWENTY-FIVE

B ridger, though he knew so little, got to the heart of it.
'I feel as if I'm in a bloody parlour game where everyone
has been told something that they're obliged to keep to
themselves.'

He had summoned an early meeting in Craven's office
before Friday morning prayers. Wemyss was watching from
the corner. Flemyng and Bolder were facing the desk, alongside Craven, who had surrendered his chair to Bridger. The old
man was smoking, the others drinking tea. Bridger said,
'There will be no note of this conversation. Wemyss is aware.
I must have it out.'

He was interrupted by sirens from the street. Flemyng
counted five vehicles, and heard a posse of motorcycles behind.

'I'm tickled by your parlour game thought,' said Craven.
'Blind man's buff, I'd say.'

Bridger turned red, and picked up without looking at him.
'The ambassador is on his way back from Aix, even now. More
to the point, he dines with us at home tomorrow, and in the
company of my American opposite number, which makes
things very awkward indeed.'

'On the contrary, Pierce,' said Craven. 'We are in luck. I can
provide you with some interesting questions. You – and
Grizelda – have timed your dinner well.'

Flemyng saw that Bridger was working hard to control his temper. When they were young and green, his gusts of rage had been amusing. They would both laugh when the storms passed as quickly as they had come on. But even in his early middle age they had become uglier and more troubling, because time had robbed him of the ability to forget.

He was struggling. 'I do not intend to mince my words.'

More sirens sounded from the window.

'I am aware – how I could I not be?' – he looked at Flemyng – 'that all of you have your own chain of command, and answer to others. We serve in different regiments. But in this embassy I do have certain responsibilities and therefore, to be blunt with you, certain powers. And I am afraid that this morning I am demanding answers. Do I have to spell it out? I am angry.'

Craven interrupted with a coughing fit, and Bolder intervened. 'Pierce, we understand. It is your duty.' The huddled figure who'd sat at the same desk for his dressing down the day before had snapped back to life, his coiffure in place, a crisp handkerchief in his top pocket and his shoes shining. 'I'm sure we all want to help.'

'Very well,' Bridger said. 'Let's begin. Wemyss has something to say.'

They all turned towards him, and the young man took a moment to steady himself.

'I have heard… murmurings. One of my acquaintances among the Americans passed on a concern.'

'A concern,' said Bridger.

Wemyss said that it had seemed to him a helpful piece of information, but also a warning.

Like the other half of a cross-talk act, Bridger said, 'A warning. Do you begin to see the light? Freddy? Will?' He ignored Bolder, cruelly.

'About what, exactly?' said Craven.

Wemyss said, 'The death of Miss Grace Quincy. There's concern that we may be interfering, and… holding things back.'

'Concern,' Bridger repeated.

'This is my office,' said Craven, and they all sensed his anger. He stood up and stepped across the room, a plume of smoke behind him. 'I'm sure that nobody here wants to waste time. I certainly don't. So for God's sake stop meandering. What are we supposed to have done?'

'Wemyss.' Bridger pointed to him.

'I'm afraid they believe someone from this embassy has visited the Père Lachaise cemetery, where she died, on some sort of mission. Poking around was the phrase that was used to me.' Wemyss was uncomfortable, but had to see it through. 'They believe that we are having an investigation of our own, and they don't like it. She was American. They want it stopped.'

'But not before we tell them what we might know,' Craven said.

'Me too!' Bridger slapped the desk. 'I said I wanted co-operation with our friends and allies, not a ruddy competition. And I must know everything.'

Everything. Flemyng's mind slipped back to Abel's phone call. Behind their brief words lay the knowledge that their paths were crossing because of the deeds of others. They hadn't wished their Paris rendezvous on themselves, happy though they might wish it to be. What would it be like when they met, and found themselves trading in secrets again? The thin consolation was that he was certain Abel was feeling some of the emotions that disturbed him. 'I hope we can have some time, despite everything,' his brother had said.

Looking at the scene in Craven's office he wondered what

he would have learned by then, and how much he would have revealed. What he would say to Kristof.

Craven had the floor. 'First of all, there is nothing for which anyone here needs to apologize. As you are aware, Pierce, Will's name and mine turned up in the Quincy notebook. We would have been delinquent if we didn't try to find out why. Do you agree?'

Bridger let him continue.

'That has meant having conversations, of the kind that we have all the time. Except that her name was involved.'

'And the graveyard?' said Bridger.

'I went there,' Flemyng said, and Bridger sighed. Flemyng watched Wemyss, who hadn't learned to conceal embarrassment. He had known.

When Craven had taken his seat, Flemyng gave the version of his story he had devised while he had waited for Kristof the previous evening. Craven's warning that Bridger was summoning the whole station to a meeting in the morning had given him time.

'As Freddy says, we have tried to find out the nature of Quincy's interest in us. I am afraid, Pierce, that we have failed. I did visit Père Lachaise, and I spoke to a superintendent there, because I wanted to know if there had been a rendezvous of any kind, or any activity before her death, that might throw light on her purpose if indeed she was planning to make contact with us.'

No dead letter box and no envelope, and Bridger didn't ask whether or not he had been alone.

'I had come across her on the Saturday evening before she died, as I told you the other day. A journalist called Hoffman was giving a birthday party. Our conversation was fun, but in the context of your question, Pierce, banal. We met only once more.'

But he offered no story from the lunch, and Bridger didn't ask.

'That is what you should tell the Americans. We made a few general inquiries, and got nowhere. If it had been otherwise, we should certainly have told them.'

Craven was smiling.

Bridger swivelled on his axis, as he'd been trained to do, and took the other tack. 'So that's what I'm supposed to report. Failure. My – our – fabled intelligence apparatus can't find out anything? Embarrassing.'

'Would you prefer it if we had a big secret, and were hiding it?' Craven said.

'I tell you what I would prefer, Freddy, and that is not to be in the position of having to mention this wretched business to my American friend in front of our ambassador, and all at my own table. But I shall be asked, and the answer I have been given by you will make us sound foolish.'

Craven told Bridger that he was forgetting something. 'They're jumping around like grasshoppers because this thing is a public event. Her photograph is everywhere. Did you see that someone has written a song about her? Frankly they wouldn't care about interference from us, as long as we could provide them with something new. That's what they're trying to get us to give them, because their cupboard is bare. And we can't, because we don't have anything.'

Bolder offered a thought. 'Don't worry about sounding foolish, Pierce', and Flemyng thought it was certainly the worst thing he could have said.

Bridger ignored him, and said to Craven, 'I want your assessment, Freddy. Everything. Now.'

'Very well. Grace Quincy was celebrated in her trade, and a woman who courted danger. We know that from her travels and her writing, which is powerful. We also know that in recent months she had spent time in Prague, Berlin and Vienna for reasons that are obvious to us all. She followed her instincts in search of stories, and was drawn to the European fault line. This interest, given events in the east, makes her death suspicious. She had decided to swim in dangerous waters. It is our view that for some reason unknown to us she was probably killed by an agent of... another power. The method is one that has been used elsewhere – a poison spray, we think. We can't say why, but I should add that we do not take seriously the theory in some of the American newspapers of a love tangle. We understand the Americans are on the same path. It is the likely explanation, but one for which we have, at the moment, no firm evidence.'

Flemyng liked the 'firm', delicately positioned at the end. Bridger didn't pick Craven up on it.

'So, Pierce, if I were you I would give that to your American counterpart. It has the advantage of being true, confirming their own thoughts, and I expect it will reassure him.'

Turning to Wemyss, he said, 'And I think we can be confident that the murmuring will stop.'

Bridger rose. 'Insubstantial, very insubstantial.'

Opening the door for him, Bolder said, 'But true, Pierce, true. That's what we're here for.'

He left them, Wemyss a step behind.

Craven said, 'Sandy, would you mind? A bit of business with Will.' Bolder closed the door as he left.

'Well?'

'The trouble is that Bridger is right,' said Flemyng.

'Of course,' Craven said. 'We're playing a game and no one's told him the rules.'

But Bridger would have to be kept in the dark. They spoke

about Kristof, Flemyng trying to keep from his mind their conversation in the night. Craven said it was unthinkable that his existence, let alone his identity, such as it was, should be known elsewhere. He hadn't spent a lifetime in embassies defending the territory of his service against the Bridgers of this world – the uniformed branch, he called them – in order to give up now.

Craven turned to the cemetery. Flemyng had been preparing for the question since the previous evening. 'You found something, didn't you?'

'Yes.'

Simply and briefly, Flemyng explained that Craven needed to know that Kristof had pointed him to Père Lachaise for a reason, and that his information had brought them some treasure. 'I was going to take you through it this afternoon, before all this, but I have a better idea. Let's walk to my apartment, where I can show you what I've got, and we can talk on the way. There's so much to say. For a start, I'm seeing Abel tonight. He's here, and we're having dinner, to talk.'

For once, Craven was taken by surprise. But he smiled.

'Well, I shall enjoy this walk. Take it slowly, for my sake, and we can go through everything. I'll tell Sandy we're out of commission until well into the afternoon.'

For the first few minutes, Craven spoke about Altnabuie. 'I felt as if I'd had a blood transfusion. Mungo showed me some of your old walks. We sat by the loch. I wish I could have fished.'

Flemyng talked for a while about the power of memory. 'I've seen so little of the place in the last few years, and I'm at the point in my life where I've spent more time away from home than I ever had there, but the images are as strong as they've ever been. Stronger, perhaps. I see the folds of the hills; hear the birds wheeling over the woods. Smell the air.'

'And watch the orrery?' Craven said.

'Ah.'

'I got it going when I was there. Mungo left me to it. Will, I thought of you as a boy – fiddling with the mechanism, polishing it, watching solar eclipses. Following the moon. It put me in a mood of great calm.'

'I know,' Flemyng said.

'You're lucky with your brothers, despite everything. The Kristof business and so forth. We'll talk about that later. I should tell you that with Mungo I found myself being frank. Freddy, I said to myself, you're being seduced by this place. Watch it. But I came away happy. I haven't slept better on the *Golden Arrow* for years.'

'Did you have my room at the house?'

'Yes. Mungo was kind. You don't mind?'

'Course not,' Flemyng said. 'When I realized you were there – you surprised me – that's what I assumed. Hoped, really. Our closeness is precious. I find I have little enough of it elsewhere.'

It brought them to Abel, as they reached the Left Bank and saw the wide bulk of Les Invalides in front of them, the gold on the dome catching the sun.

'How frank do you think you can be?' Craven asked him.

'I can't decide.'

'If I were you, I'd take my time. Although that will be hard, I can see. Find out why he's here, talk about his London posting.'

He was walking a little too fast for his friend, and felt a hand on his arm. 'Slow down. You forget that I'm not at my best. We're not by the lochside now.'

'Sorry, Freddy.' He took his arm.

From behind them they heard sirens on the bridge, and

they stepped back as a string of police vans, with outriders, sped past them. 'Fun and games today, I expect,' Craven said. They said little more until they reached Flemyng's apartment, a few minutes later.

When they were inside, Flemyng showed his anxiety. He made some coffee quickly, clattering with cups in the pantry, poured a whisky for Craven though not for himself, and went to his bedroom to fetch a small wooden box, with a Celtic knot in delicate inlay on the lid, in which he kept a few precious things.

Without any preliminary explanation, he took a sheet of paper from inside and smoothed it out. Craven read the list of names without touching the paper.

His breathing was heavy and his movements slow. He took time to study the list. 'I feel foreboding,' he said.

'I'll tell you where it came from,' Flemyng said. 'But I want your reaction first.'

'Bad news,' said Craven. He was wheezing softly.

Flemyng said, 'I'm going to ask if any of the names means anything to you.'

'Of course. I understand that.'

'And do they?' Flemyng waited.

Craven sighed heavily, as if in irritation. Flemyng thought he might have lost his train of thought.

'One, and only one, rings a bell from far away,' he said.

TWENTY-SIX

I n their preparations for the evening of 3 May, the day Paris caught fire, Flemyng and Maria took different paths, private to each of them.

He walked alone. She crossed the city to meet Kristof, congratulating herself as she went.

When they had met on the night of Quincy's death, and waited together for Flemyng at his apartment, the surprise lifted her and she settled quickly on one objective. A means of contact. She was confident when she showed the pale-faced German upstairs after his unexpected appearance, introducing herself as a friend of Flemyng's, that he would assume that she was in his business. So she played the brazen reporter in the sure knowledge that he knew her real game. His face brightened at her suggestion that they might be able to talk privately to give her a better impression of how his government was reading the West's intentions, and showed no embarrassment in proposing a clandestine arrangement. 'My people are rather obsessed by rules and regulations, as you will know. Private must mean private,' he said, smiling all the while. Quickly and clearly he described a café where they could meet safely at only two or three hours' notice, if a message were telephoned to Pascal behind the bar. He gave her the number.

'Reporters are used to this kind of thing,' she told him, and they both laughed. Done, and all before Flemyng had returned from the embassy and they talked into the night.

Now it was time to test their system. When she telephoned, a grunting Pascal said nothing except to repeat her message, word for word. She would meet their mutual friend at five.

Walking eastwards from Bastille she wandered into a craftsmen's quarter, where the shopfronts were hung with golden picture frames and plaster mouldings, and every corner was a collecting point for half-upholstered chairs and wardrobe doors. The street smelt of paint and wood shavings. Then she passed from the bustle of the cafés where workmen were on the pavements, drinking into the late afternoon, into territory where the colour of the city seemed to have drained away. The street life quietened and the traffic was thin. There were shuttered shops, and apartment windows painted black. But she found that the front of Kristof's café, at the confluence of three streets, was newly decorated in red, white and blue to make a show of gaiety, and had a shop next door in the same colours with one window revealing a mountain of cheese, against a wall of wine bottles, and another filled with hung meat, pâtés and a pyramid of pigs' trotters. A handwritten notice told her that everything inside came from the Auvergne, '*notre terroir*', and above it the sign read Chez Pascal. She had arrived.

He was behind the semi-circular zinc bar, a bear of a man with short grey hair and a Roman nose. When she opened the swing door he jerked his head towards the back room without saying a word, nor interrupting his card game with two old men at the bar. She guessed that few women came in. Pulling the curtain aside and entering a gloomy space that smelt of sausage and garlic, she found Kristof reading alone in a corner.

He stood quite formally and put out his hand.

'Thank you,' he said, although it was she who had suggested the meeting.

She looked around as if to make the point that their rendezvous could hardly have been more crudely arranged, the stuff of a spy comedy, but only said, 'Kristof.'

'No one comes here,' he said. 'We're alone. My people are elsewhere in the city. And yours? I don't think we'll be troubled by Americans here.' That at least was true. There was little sign at the meeting of streets outside that they were still in the city: no taxi stand to be seen, the traffic thin and a different pace on the pavements. 'Many Algerians live around here,' he said. 'They are poor, like me. Pascal lets me read and write here, and meet some friends. He is quite content, and not at all curious.'

Maria, who believed hardly a word of it, said how much she had appreciated the conversation at Flemyng's apartment. 'You helped us a good deal with our friend Quincy.'

'So you visited the cemetery.' His smile was warm.

'Of course.'

'And?'

'I think you'll understand if I leave it there for now.'

'In that case, how can I help?' he said, and added with emphasis, 'Help you even more, I mean.'

Maria said she had a simple request. She had taken the trouble to leave a message with Pascal and arrange the meeting because he, Kristof, was the only person who could take her on the next stage of her journey. 'When we talked, you spoke of a friend who had been visited by the police because his name – maybe his address or phone number – was found in her notebook, or anyway among her possessions. You told us – Will Flemyng and me – that he was terrified by the knock on his door.'

'It was true.'

'I'm sure it was,' she said. 'I want to know if he is still in Paris.'

Kristof had closed his book when she came in, taking care to keep a bookmark sticking out, and he slid it to one side before leaning closer. 'I can help you. He is away. The police visited my trade mission the day before yesterday to ask after him, for the second time. We told them the truth, once again. That we think he is home in Dresden. We don't know more, except that he left the morning after we spoke and we have heard nothing of him. You will understand if I put it like this – he has officially gone.'

'Within twenty-four hours of Quincy's death.'

'Indeed,' said Kristof.

'And what conclusion do we draw from that?' Maria asked.

'I'm not sure about conclusions. But we can surmise, can we not?'

She answered with a question. 'How long have you known Will Flemyng?'

And he parried. 'Does he know you are here?'

'No,' she said.

'Then why should I tell you?' She had no doubt that he was enjoying himself, his pasty face showing more signs of colour and his eyes on the move. She realized, as Flemyng had on their first meeting, that he was much younger than he first appeared.

'Let's go back to the beginning,' she said. 'You came to his apartment because you knew Quincy was dead.'

'Correct.'

'And it was your friend – the one who was terrified and has gone – who told you, after the police visited him.'

'It was.'

Maria said he would realize that the next question was inevitable, like an expected chess move being played without a pause to take the players to the next stage and a new problem. 'Why should you connect Quincy and Flemyng in the first place?'

She reminded him that in Flemyng's apartment he had told her that they were acquainted, but had not explained how he came to know. 'I am going to be very frank with you. I am sure that Flemyng only met her a few days before she died. He will have known about her, of course, but it was on this last trip of hers to Paris that they spoke for the first time. The same is true of me. So how did you know?'

Kristof asked the obvious question. 'Why should I tell you?'

'Because you and I are helping each other. We pursue different ends, but we've discovered that we need each other.'

Her bluntness brought a pause in their conversation, which had been speeding up. They hadn't bothered with coffee or wine, but they realized that with her statement they had come to an agreement. Kristof said that he'd fetch two glasses of wine, and went through the curtain.

There was nothing on the table except Kristof's book. It was a well-worn edition in dull maroon covers with the spine cracked and nearly gone. She put out a hand, and pulled it quickly across the table, surprised to find that it was not a German text, but *The English Parnassus* of longer poems, collected for schoolchildren. She was amused to see the poem on the page he had bookmarked.

Of man's first disobedience, and the fruit of that forbidden tree…

Hearing him with Pascal in the bar, she realized that he was about to return and just had time to look at the inside cover of the book. She was so startled by what she saw that she had to scramble to replace it before he swung the curtain aside.

*

Flemyng steered Freddy Craven towards rue du Bac, troubled by the tremble in the old man's arm. But their words were warm. Flemyng said that he would take his advice in talking to Abel with care and without sounding an immediate alarm, though it would be difficult to conceal his concern, and his anxiety to tell his brother directly that someone – he knew he wouldn't identify Kristof – was using his name to poison the well. But Craven's advice was more precious to him than ever: the more fragile he became, the more Flemyng felt the weight of his debt to him.

Echoing his thoughts, Craven said, 'I am feeling very close to you on this one, Will. This time may be as important for us – you and me – as anything we'll see on these streets.' He pointed with his umbrella towards the gendarmes who had appeared on the next corner, as they had been doubling up at every road junction along the Left Bank all morning.

Flemyng was moved to silence. He felt the old man gripping him harder as they approached the metro station. Craven turned, and put out his bony hands, laying one on each of Flemyng's shoulders. 'About your brother, try not to be too troubled. But come to me tomorrow, please.' Before Flemyng could think of the right reply, he was gone down the steps, raising an arm in farewell without turning round.

Back at his apartment he picked up pencils and a sketch pad. He was going to make an effort to relax.

Taking a roundabout way to St-Germain-des-Prés – it was a route that he'd often walked with Isabel – he looked for a perch where he could enjoy the late-afternoon sun and draw for a while.

Reaching the junction of two of the main thoroughfares in

the Latin Quarter, he settled down to watch the scene outside the Café de Cluny. Riot squad trucks had come out of the side streets to make their presence more obvious and there were at least a dozen gendarmes at the confluence of the boulevards. The café was crowded, although evening had not yet come, and the noise from inside was carried to the streets. There was a regular wailing of sirens from somewhere not far away, and as he watched a band of students assembled near the café and began to chant some of the slogans familiar to him from Nanterre.

Automatically, he began to draw the place with a thick black pencil, producing a dark sketch as if he had been using charcoal – the café astride the meeting place of two roads that were now filling with crowds, the police motorcycles lined up alongside, the flags that someone had planted in the flowerbeds across the street, flapping in the afternoon breeze. They were red and black, and among them the Viet Cong standard with its yellow star. The place was alive with movement, and uncertainty. As the crowd grew, the police approached and then retreated when the point had been made. He saw one student being pulled aside, then released. From inside the café, the noise grew louder and the place was so full that three harassed waiters were standing guard at the door to repel the crowd.

Someone began to sing, and for a few moments there was a ragged chorus.

Flemyng was absorbed. Two students stopped beside him and looked over his shoulder as he drew, his pencil tracing the pattern of the ironwork on the dome above the café. Only when he paused did they speak to him. They wanted to tell of arrests at the Sorbonne, and the closing of the gates: everyone should know, they said. It was getting rough, and the riot police were beginning to enjoy themselves. Friends had been taken away. 'What next?' he asked them.

'Occupation.'

He folded his drawing book away, and crossed the street. Looking through the glass in the side door of the café he saw a few faces he recognized from Nanterre. The staff behind the bar seemed to have given up – some students were using the space to lay out posters on which they splashed slogans with paint. Flemyng was amused, but not surprised, to see Edward Abbott in the throng, managing to hold a coffee cup steady. As he watched, Edward turned and saw his face through the glass. He smiled, and lifted his cup. Flemyng saluted in return.

A student behind him said that there was a fight down the street. The police had charged, and stones were being thrown. As he set a course for his apartment, aware that he would meet Abel in less than two hours, a phalanx of police cars sped along the boulevard and turned off towards the university, with a tail of motorcycles behind them that left a ribbon of black smoke in the street.

*

Kristof raised his wine, and said, 'To our co-operation.' Maria clinked her glass against his, saying nothing.

'You went to the hiding place in the cemetery? And did you find anything there?'

'We each realize that there are some things that can't be shared between us,' she said. 'We both know why.'

'The proprieties of our lives,' he said. 'But let me say this. You will know that I pointed you towards that place because I knew you might discover something. It is therefore not a surprising piece of news, is it? Nor a secret.'

'There are boundaries that it's right for us both to respect,' she said. 'Still.'

'Because it makes us feel better?' he said, and she caught a change on his face. The lightness disappeared as if a shade had been drawn down. 'Let me tell you that I lost that feeling a long time ago.'

She said nothing, in the hope that he would say more, and pricked by a feeling that she had glimpsed something new. But it was enough for him. Taking a drink, his happy face reappeared, and she realized how much effort it must always have taken to hide what lay behind.

'I'll speak for us both, then,' he said. 'Whatever you found, it will tell you that there was contact between Miss Quincy and some friends of mine. I know that, but I do not know who started the... correspondence, let's call it that... nor the detail of what it involved. You know how it is. But your interest lies in what I know of the relationship between her and Flemyng.'

Kristof said that it should come as no surprise. 'She told my friend – the Terrified One.'

'Why?' said Maria, insisting that he continue.

'She wanted to tell him how much she knew. It's a way they all have, as you will know – those who stumble into our world.'

Maria said, 'And it was a mistake.'

'Yes, of course. It is why she died.'

TWENTY-SEVEN

A city divided.

Across the river from the Latin Quarter, in the warmth of early evening, the weekend calm was seeping in. At Benoit, where Maria had dined with Quincy, the lamps were lit and the room sparkled. Everything laid out in place, glasses ringing like bells, the chatter rising. In a score of dining rooms on either side of the rue de Rivoli an evening pace was set like a stately dance and the ritual established. Oysters lay in heaps outside on their mounds of ice with lobster tanks behind, and from every kitchen there was a spurt of steam and a blast of noise when a chef opened the back door for a smoke in the street. A rich scent hung on the air, with whispers of jazz underneath. Two cocktail parties had assembled in Freddy Craven's apartment building. At the American embassy round the corner, they were partying for a ballerina.

Flemyng, only a mile away on the other side of the Seine, was in another world, where there were signals of distress against a shadow of the unknown. The embers of a fire that had been started on a corner of rue de Tournon, two buckled lamp posts in the next street with their lights hanging off, rough slogans on the walls with the paint still wet, and outside the locked gates of the Sorbonne the lingering sting of tear gas and the remains of a crude barricade – the first – that had been pulled apart by police.

As Flemyng walked to his dinner with Abel, all his senses responded to the change. The cafés were noisier, the crowds round the doors quivering at the prospect of action that they couldn't predict, but that excited them. Their voices rose. On nearly every corner stood two or three gendarmes who on any other Friday would have been raising a glass to the weekend together, their kepis piled up on a bar.

The edginess reflected Flemyng's mood, which refused to let him settle. He felt welcome flashes of lightness – Abel was in town – but then darkness rolled back in, despite his hope of dispelling it. No escape.

Craven's advice was right. They should talk, share some secrets, but he would leave aside the horror of Kristof's accusation. There would be time.

Yet he was still drawn to another course. To warn his brother, clear the air and wipe away the stain.

Anything else would be betrayal, and there had been enough of that.

But he thought of Freddy Craven, and his pleading eyes. Taking time would be painful, but he owed it to the old man.

He arrived at La Coupole within a few minutes of the appointed hour for the drink before dinner that Abel wanted, and before he opened the door he looked through the window under the wide scarlet awning, trying with both hands to blot out the last of the sun. His brother was already there, as Flemyng had known he would be. Abel was leaning against one of the green marbled columns, with a painted art deco nymph seeming to dance on his head, and through the flowing reflections on the thick glass Flemyng could see that he had a cocktail on the bar. He was a picture of contentment.

Pausing outside to collect himself, Flemyng pushed open the door and gave his best smile.

Abel saw him at the door, ducked through the tables and put his arms out. He was in white shirt and blue jeans. Slim, brown and full of health.

They hugged. Flemyng whispered his thanks for Abel's presence and they stood close, basking for a few moments in the colours and the light, and surfing together on the warmth of the crowd.

'You look good,' he said, and Abel smiled.

'Not at all bad, and this town makes me happy. I need that. Difficult times.'

They talked easily for a few minutes and intimacy flowed back naturally, the lines on Flemyng's cheeks softening a little and his face less drawn. He ruffled his black hair in a show of relaxation. Abel described dark days at home, spoke about the war, and they played a little with the uncertainties on the horizons of their world. Neither mentioned Quincy. Flemyng cast off his thin tie and got out of his jacket, hanging it over Abel's on a brass hook at the bar, then opened two buttons on his shirt. He gestured towards the windows, and a wailing police car passing along the Boulevard de Montparnasse. 'There's a current running. A surge. You can feel it.'

Abel said, 'I've been with Maria.'

'Leave that for now,' Flemyng said. 'Family first.' He knew his nervousness must be obvious to his brother, but Mungo was important. 'You've spoken?'

'On the phone, twice. He sounds fine but he's concerned about you. I know because he's sounding more fatherly.'

Flemyng was smiling. 'I was going to say the same about you and him. You know how he likes things to be settled, predictable. He feels a little out of it. Hardly surprising.'

Their limbering up was taking them into territory that both knew was not right for La Coupole, where dinner was a theatrical experience under the painted dome, every table catching some light and a waiter always in earshot. The wrong place. When they had dealt with Mungo it was time to move away.

Flemyng had chosen a small restaurant a short walk from the boulevard in the direction of Saint-Sulpice, where he cherished a particular table near the back window, occupying a corner with an elaborate wooden and glass screen to make it private. The proprietor loved the table, because it gave him power. Flemyng had found it soon after arriving in the city, and he and Craven had often broken bread there.

'So we're in the snug,' said Abel as they arrived.

'Alone,' Flemyng said.

They pleased the waiter by accepting his suggestions, ordering quickly. He opened a bottle, laying the cork in front of Flemyng like a trophy.

'Let me pick up on Mungo, before we start,' Abel said, making the point that there was business to be done afterwards. 'You're right about him being nervous. That's hardly new. But with you, there's something else. Why's he alarmed?'

They were cocooned in their corner, neither overlooked nor overheard. Through the glass they could see the churning dining room – families, well-fed men sitting alone and shrouded in napkins, at least one noisy party of students – and it made their privacy more precious. The low ceiling above them had a yellowed portrait of Venus, long stained by smoke and almost lost in the gloom.

Alone, without a crowd, they began to loosen up. 'You can imagine how the embassy feels,' Flemyng said, looking up with his head back. 'Jumpy as hell, and I'm probably letting it show. Did I tell you that Pierce Bridger's turned up in our midst? Just what we need.'

'Never mind him,' Abel said. 'We need to talk about Quincy. Maria showed me what you and she found in the cemetery.'

'Showed you?' said Flemyng, straightening in his chair.

Their waiter appeared, and they paused for breath. They had begun to eat when the conversation resumed.

'Come on,' Abel said, digging his fork into his steak tartare. He was speaking quietly, which made it sound more urgent.

The darkness that could easily bring a shadow to Flemyng's face had come down. 'What did she tell you?' he said.

'Enough.'

'In that case you'll realize how much we don't know.'

Abel said, 'Like whether Quincy was meant to pick it up, or whether she was the delivery boy.'

'Exactly.'

Flemyng said they still had to accept that Quincy was in touch with the other side, whatever the story of the list turned out to be. 'The envelope was used before. It wasn't her first time.'

'Do her connections bother you?' Abel asked.

'I've seen it before, but... yes.'

'Disappointed?' his brother asked him.

'I'm afraid so,' said Flemyng.

'Writer, spy or both. I wonder if she knew,' said Abel.

They ate for a minute or two without speaking. Abel picked up.

'I should say that these names mean nothing to me. They're going through our system, but nothing yet. New to your people?'

'As far as I know, yes.'

Flemyng said, 'Thanks. We're agreed, then, about Quincy.' A statement not a question. If he was waiting for something else, he didn't show it.

They held another natural pause. The waiter filled their glasses and they spoke of Paris for a few minutes.

'How long will you be here?' he asked Abel.

'Hard to say. Calls at the embassy. People to see. You know.' He gave his brother the name of his hotel. 'A week, maybe.'

'That long?' As he spoke, Flemyng put a hand inside his open shirt and began to massage his scar.

'And then?' he added.

'It looks like London for a while. A spell.' Picking up his brother's discomfort, he said quietly, 'Did you know?'

'A little bird…'

'Who?' said Abel.

'Freddy Craven.'

'Ah. The old bird himself. Did he tell you how?'

'No. He just heard something along the way.'

'That's all?' Abel's eyes were wide and his gaze was insistent. Flemyng, still running his fingers along the scar, had lost some of his poise. The younger brother was in command.

'There was nothing else, I promise.'

'Promise? That word isn't necessary, Will.'

Abel took up his glass, allowing a pause to take hold. He offered no explanation for his summons to London, and turned the conversation back to his brother. When he'd taken a drink, he said, 'I'm going to say this, and it's a probably a good thing. Mungo's right. What the hell is wrong?'

Flemyng buttoned up his shirt as if he'd been caught undressing, and picked up his own glass. 'Nothing you don't know about.'

Abel waited.

'The Quincy business is awful. Bridger's terrible. It's haywire. I've got a colleague who drives us mad.'

'That'll be Bolder,' Abel said. Flemyng didn't respond.

'But that's you at your best, Will. And Paris like this.' He waved to the outside world. 'Irresistible. Think of what you can write for London.'

Flemyng rallied. 'I know, and it's only beginning. But…'

'Whatever it is, say,' Abel said. 'Brother, I care.'

Flemyng smiled – with an effort that Abel noticed – and stretched a hand across the table. 'I don't know what Maria said about Quincy and me. But I'd hoped for something. Maybe it hit me harder than I knew.'

'And?' said Abel.

'It's not usually a friend who dies.'

'You're sure that's all?' Abel wasn't letting go.

'There's the question of loyalty.'

'What she was doing, you mean?' Abel said.

'Of course.'

'And what do you think?'

Flemyng said, 'I'm trying to believe.'

'That she was mostly still the reporter, working at her trade?' Abel gave no hint about what he might think.

'She told me she was on to something. A story.'

'What do you believe?' Abel said.

'I don't know,' said Flemyng, quietly. His eyes were closed.

The warmth of La Coupole was far behind them. The lines on his face were dark and deep again, and one hand lay against a shoulder, as if he wanted to go back to work on his scar. Abel leaned across to touch him lightly. 'You can tell me anything, you know.'

'Can I?' Flemyng said, looking directly into his eyes. He pushed his glass aside. 'We both have secrets. We'll never know everything.'

Abel said, 'Sure.'

'*Can't* know,' Flemyng said. 'Too dangerous.'

'We have to keep some things to ourselves,' Abel said. 'We've always known that.'

'The deal.' Flemyng said it as if it were a full stop.

But Abel went on. 'Without that, we wouldn't be who we are.'

'You still think we're lucky?' Flemyng said.

'Of course. You too.'

'Most of the time,' said Flemyng.

'And the rest?'

'I suppose that's what troubles Mungo.'

To make the break, he stood up. 'Excuse me for a minute or two.' Abel watched him speak to the waiter, then swing downstairs to the lavatory.

When he came back, the table had been cleared and coffee was poured.

Flemyng began. 'You're right about the streets. I've been telling London for weeks. This place is trembling. They're scared – old men who can't believe it. Won't.'

Abel said that Flemyng had always had an attraction to chaos. 'So long as it's not in here,' he said, putting a finger to his temple.

'Not chaos. The unexpected.'

'The same applies,' Abel said. 'Not in your head.'

'I've never liked the feeling that I'm losing my bearings. Whereas you…'

Abel started to laugh.

'… never seem to mind. You'll fly blind into a storm.'

'I suppose that's true,' his brother said. His laughing stopped, and when he caught his brother's eye he looked as serious as Flemyng.

*

Maria had decided to spend the evening alone, but called first at the bureau on the way back to her apartment. A colleague would file about the troubles on the Left Bank, and stay late to update his story for the morning. He was talking to the police on the phone when she walked in, trying to establish a figure for the numbers they had on the streets for whatever the evening might bring, and whether more riot squads were coming, scribbling on a long yellow pad as he listened. She would be lead correspondent on Saturday, and had a word with Jacques, who would keep the office open through the weekend and, unusually, remain at his post. He had established a makeshift larder in the back room, as if for a siege, with four bottles of wine, a bunch of long sausages and salami dangling from a coat hook in a string bag, and a round of ripe cheese, which was already making its presence known. He was reading from a chattering teleprinter with a glass in his hand and a cloud of smoke above him. Blowing another plume, he told Maria without turning that a back-up reporter was on his way from New York. They were ready for whatever the city might deliver.

She walked away. Kristof was in her mind until she reached home. By the time she climbed to the first floor, Quincy had taken over.

Opening the door, she put her bag on the settee in the bedroom and, as if preparing for the arrival of a guest, checked each room so that she could settle happily for the night with everything in its place. Nothing seemed wrong. She had learned that, for her, a calm state of mind came from her surroundings. Outside, she was drawn to confusion, but at home there should be order and familiarity. That comfort sustained her. When she had arranged a nest of cushions on the sofa she opened the deep bottom drawer of the desk with a key from her pocket, and took out the brown leather-covered case that Kristof, unwittingly, had brought back to her mind: Quincy's portable Smith-Corona.

No one had mentioned its absence and nor had she. Neither Flemyng nor Abel knew it was there, and the police had no reason to suppose that Quincy had visited the apartment in the days before she died. It was hers alone.

The secret made Maria light-headed.

Placing the portable on the centre of the desk – she lined it up neatly as if it had to occupy a space that had been prepared for it – she ran a hand over the leather, enjoying the smoothness and then finding the little blemishes and torn corners that spoke of the Smith-Corona's adventures on the road. The brass zip was strong, and she could see where it had been sewn and repaired to prolong its life and keep everything safe inside. Pulling the zip gently round the sides of the case, she lifted back the upper part to reveal the homely machine, stone-grey with dark-green keys, with only one deep scratch to be seen and a taut ribbon threaded between the spools. On the roller there was an indistinct jumble of inky letters, traces of the last stories Quincy had written, and Maria was visited by a cloud of melancholy.

She touched the top row of keys, running a finger from *q* to *p*. Pushing the silver return lever with her left hand, she slid the carriage easily to the right until the bell rang. The mechanism was smooth, and she could see that Quincy had cared for her machine. The type hammers had been oiled, and a few keys had been replaced. Maria placed her hands on the sides, holding it firmly and feeling its weight as she lifted it an inch or two from the desk.

As she did so, the typewriter came away from its cocooning case and, by the luck of the light, she saw that in the black lining underneath there was another zip, a thin one that was easy to miss because it was the same colour as the cloth. She stood quite still.

The lining was attached firmly to the case – it seemed to have been recently sewn in – and she had to fold back a tiny flap on the left-hand side to find the tag for the zip. But when she pulled, it slipped across easily and made an opening. Before pulling the zip all the way, she undid the two clips behind the typewriter and detached the machine from the case, placing it at the back of the desk.

The giddiness that she had felt on touching the keys had gone. She was conscious of nothing but the empty leather-bound case in front of her and when she pressed her hand on the lining she felt the outline of something inside. She knew that it was a thin sheaf of paper, lodged neatly in the pocket of the lining. When the case was closed there was no sign that it contained anything but a sapphire-grey Smith-Corona Super-5, manufactured in Groton, NY, robust companion to a generation of reporters, with a scuffed label underneath that marked it as the property of Grace Quincy, giving the phone number of the magazine where she kept a desk in New York. Maria began to move with a slowness that gave weight to every one of the few seconds it took her to open the pocket she had found.

Pulling the zip fastener carefully as far as it would go to the right, she slid her hand inside. The sheets were rough, like the copy paper piled up around her own office that rolled out of the wire-service teleprinters. Using both hands she eased out the pages that were inside the case. Trying not to look at them too soon, she turned away from the desk and took a few steps towards the low table and her nest of cushions. There was no scramble, no rush. She was in slow-motion.

The room was quiet. The Friday-night traffic seemed to have melted away. She could hear the clock in the hall, and little else.

Taking the cache of paper, she separated the sheets with care, laying them in sequence on the table. There were ten.

With deliberation, she rose, went to the kitchen and poured herself a glass of white wine. She locked the front door of her apartment and removed the key. Returning to the table, she looked at what lay before her – some typed paragraphs and lists, and pages of pencilled notes in Quincy's handwriting. There were a number of French names, notes of arrangements for meetings, and she saw from the three pages written in German that Quincy must have been a fluent speaker, which Maria wasn't. One sheet consisted of a drawing – a pencil caricature of Quincy - which she put to one side.

She closed her eyes.

Then, forcing herself to take it slowly, Maria began to read.

TWENTY-EIGHT

'I hope you remember that Will Flemyng and I have history.' Freddy Craven raised his champagne glass. 'Certainly, Pierce.'

'A good one, broadly speaking,' said Bridger. 'Boy Scouts together, as it were. It compounds my distress.'

They were alone on Bridger's terrace, Craven leaning on the balustrade and looking into the sun. It was just after one o'clock, the Sunday traffic building up beneath them and the surface of the river in the distance alive with streams of light. The skyline was sharp and bright. Craven wore a white jacket with a yellow handkerchief in his breast pocket, a spotted blue cravat that tumbled out of his shirt, and rumpled trousers that didn't match, but he had shoes well polished enough to suggest that he might still be a man about town. 'Will has often spoken about you,' he said. 'We've knocked around a little, as you know.'

'Vienna, Berlin and so forth,' Bridger said.

'World's end,' Craven replied.

But Bridger was in head of chancery mode and, although just back from church with the ambassador and with a glass in his hand, not willing to let the conversation float away. 'It's where we are now that concerns me.'

'Me too,' Craven said, as if he wanted to be helpful.

'This is an affair with no shape, a pudding without a theme. Except that our embassy is under threat.'

'Steady on, Pierce. Strange goings-on, a background noise from the streets. But threat?'

'I chose the word with care,' Bridger said. 'First of all, there is a murder investigation in which you and Flemyng have turned up, God knows why. And secondly, your number two has unleashed the dogs in London with his talk of leaks and shadowy networks. Freddy, we're being watched.'

'By our own side, so you think that's worse,' Craven said.

'I am commanded to keep this place shipshape and that is what I shall do.'

Perhaps because he realized that he might start an argument with the old man, and in his own sitting room, Bridger stayed quiet for a moment and dropped his voice.

'Freddy, can you help?'

'I doubt it,' Craven said.

Bridger counted out his problems on his fingers. 'We have the business of Grace Quincy and the unfortunate connection with the embassy, however loose it may be. Bolder's rumour-mongering has frightened the horses, I can tell you, and, just to add spice, we have our lords' and masters' belated interest in the bloody streets of Paris. They're looking our way. In normal times, I would cry hallelujah, because we're at the centre of things. But we're swimming in uncertainty. There is no pattern I can see, and I hate it. I sense a crisis but can't describe it. Murder, Freddy, is not my business.'

Craven watched a man struggling for handholds in a storm.

'I am in the same position,' he said.

He kept an arm attached to the iron rail as he turned around, conscious of his frailty, and made a point of meeting the gaze of Bridger, who was turned out for parade and hadn't loosened his tie or cast his jacket since morning service. Craven acknowledged to himself that he played the part well. His blond hair was turning gold at the right time, and he looked fit in his tall frame. His smooth-skinned face retained its charm, his blue eyes full of life, and the cut of his jaw was sharp. His voice was musical, never sounding off-key, and he moved with grace despite his bulk. If I went to Harrods and asked for an ambassador, Craven thought, they might well come up with Pierce Bridger.

'I share your discomfort,' he said, to begin.

'A crisis usually unfolds piece by piece. Snakes and ladders, really. You jump ahead, then slide back down, but you have to press on. This is different, because there's no path to follow. And we have a tumult out there, around us, that makes it even more difficult. We can't know whether we're dealing with a difficulty of our own making, inside ourselves – have we missed something, taken a wrong turning? – or if this wildness in the streets has thrown everyone off balance. Priority telegrams from every embassy you can name, telling the same story. Everyone's confused. So we tell stories to make sense of the world. It's what men always do. And we have to remind ourselves that they may not be true.'

Bridger said that, as the younger man, he was affected by Craven's observation. 'My problem is, Freddy, that I have to know what the embassy faces. Danger? A leak? Something in the papers? A murder inquiry that comes to our door? I know a crisis when I feel one.'

Craven stepped away from the rail. He could sense the tension in the man. 'You've summed it up rather well, my boy, if I may say so. All I'm trying to do is to walk through all this trouble, pick up such information as I can along the way and discard all that is irrelevant or wrong. What's left will lead us to the truth.'

Bridger drained his glass. 'Ariadne and her bloody thread.'

'Maybe,' said Craven. 'I'm holding on like billy-o.'

He thought back to the arrival of Bridger's invitation late the previous day, delivered by Wemyss, who explained unnecessarily that Craven's apartment was on his route home. He had spent Saturday morning with the ambassador concocting an assessment of the troubles, and had been assigned by Bridger to be messenger. 'We must talk,' the handwritten note had said. 'Grizelda will conjure up lunch, but she will let us have time to ourselves.' Wemyss said he would pass on the reply, and Craven said he would be with the Bridgers, on time, by one.

He had risen earlier than usual on Sunday, lifted by the flow of events that seemed to him to be moving towards a climax, however mysteriously, and walked along the river for refreshment. There was a cascade of bells on the hour, and he wondered if Flemyng had taken himself to church. Craven never did, except on embassy parade, but he had always had a touch of envy for Flemyng's easy Catholicism, which seemed to come and go with the seasons but persisted as background music that never quite stopped. 'When I go to church, which isn't terribly often, I never feel on duty,' he had told Craven more than once. 'I'm not under orders, just tuning in.' Craven suspected this might be one of his Sundays.

He had taken time over his coffee and the newspapers at the café where he had a regular table, piecing together the story that Bridger would try to get out of him.

Now, at the Bridger home, a sharp note had been sounded from the beginning. 'Freddy,' he had said as he poured the first glass, 'we are on different sides of the shop. No one understands that better than I do. But on this one there is a need for frankness.'

Having raised his shared history with Flemyng, making it

sound like a guarantee of propriety, he said he realized Flemyng had been shaken by Quincy's death. 'And I may tell you, that event is the cause of considerable agitation in London, personified by Ingleby on the European desk. He's panting like a bitch on heat.'

'And you can't satisfy him?' Craven said.

Bridger smiled. 'That's beyond my capacity, Freddy. I need your help.'

Turning inside again, he led Craven by the arm to one of two deep sofas facing each other in front of the fireplace. They sat across a shiny lacquered table on which Grizelda had placed another bottle in a silver ice bucket, and could see each other's reflection against its painted forests of bamboo. She waved from the door as they came in, then disappeared, closing it quietly behind her.

'The reason for the disturbance is that London is aware of our connection with this murder. Remote, as we hope, but a link nonetheless. They know, of course, that Flemyng had lunch with her the day before her death – when he told me, you can imagine how I felt. Concerned. You will appreciate that I simply had to dictate the note I copied to you. I couldn't let it lie. I hope you agree that it was written in a way that would limit interest in London.'

Craven said nothing, and Bridger ploughed on.

'I had to admit that the police had found reason to inquire about him, and about you, because your names had been found in her things. Naturally, that has caused concern because of your positions here, which has no doubt found its way to high places. Unfortunate all round, because her death is also a matter of comment in the public prints. They get excited about one of their own. If the embassy were mentioned, there would be all hell to pay. Edward Abbott – whom I've known for some years, I should say, and who has some standing – wrote about her death last week. Responsibly, I must say.'

'And again today,' said Craven, who had read an airmail edition of one of the London papers at the café.

'My point exactly,' Bridger said. 'Keeps the pot boiling.'

'He had nothing new to say, you'll be pleased to know,' Craven said.

But Bridger had reached his cruising speed, and wasn't slowing down. 'On its own, the fact that we're part of a murder investigation might be manageable, even with Flemyng wandering around cemeteries, at the dead of night for all I know. But I've also got the residue of Bolder's mess to clean up. Why didn't he stay south of the river in that ghastly new tower block of yours instead of blundering around? They ask me if he's right that there's a network feeding material to the Russians that we know nothing about, which is what he seems to be hinting, or if he's just blethering. How do I choose? And let me tell you where it leaves us.

'I have an embassy in which two members of this station are on police files in a murder inquiry, and the other is peddling stories without anything to back them up, and may be a fantasist. Stirring up a potential hornets' nest with the French, just when they've got themselves in a terrible stew, and all our energy is required to keep up with politics here, a contagion that is spreading to London. God save us, Freddy.'

'Calm down, Pierce, please. You're wittering.'

Craven said the febrile first days of May might be casting a spell of confusion. 'Forget the noise, and listen.'

He began by noting that neither he nor Flemyng had been approached by the police since the first contact with the embassy. 'In normal circumstances that would be odd. I don't think so this time. I have no doubt that her notebooks contained many names, ours among them, and that M. Maigret, or whoever he is, is working his way through them patiently. We are not important to them. Meanwhile, this city is preparing for trouble and I imagine their minds are concentrated on the streets, not the cemetery of Père Lachaise and a dead foreigner. The Americans have done a good job with the authorities and the legal processes are going to be strung out.

'My approach is the opposite one. Will is watching the streets – I should say that he reports to me that we can expect fireworks this evening – and I am thinking of what brought about the death of this woman. I suspect it's less a question of who than why. Tell me more, before I continue, of what London is saying about the Sandy Bolder episode. Your people, not mine. He angered me, I should say, and I tore a strip off him.'

'Naval language used, I'm sure, and bully for you,' Bridger said. 'You certainly spoke for me. He broke every commandment. Vague talk about leaks, no minute with proper *detail*, a journey to London of which the rest of the embassy was unaware, and – frankly – a thespian performance in my office that left people cursing him to high heaven.'

'I suppose it would have been worse if they had laughed,' Craven said.

Bridger took a drink.

Craven asked, 'What substance remains?'

'We all read your splendid warning, Freddy. Treat with *exceptional caution*. Appreciated by me, and circulated as widely as possible. I thought you might have mentioned Bolder by name – he deserved it – but there we are. There is still kindness in your heart, Freddy.'

'Substance?' Craven repeated.

'Ingleby is sounding every alarm bell at his disposal and making a noise. Frankly, that is his nature, but he's right. At a time of maximum sensitivity – you've seen the Moscow tele-grams about Prague – this kind of rumour-mongering about leaks is the worst thing. The very worst. Try as we might, no one can find a shred of evidence to back it up – and even asking the question of the French would be an insult. That's the point, Freddy. Substance, nil. Damage – a great deal.'

'And what does Ingleby propose to do about it?' asked Craven. 'Apart from asking my people.'

'He doesn't know, which is giving him the collywobbles.'

Conscious that he was repeating himself and had therefore lost command, Bridger poured a drink and said, 'Please continue.'

'Very well,' Craven began. 'As I told you when we gathered in your room, we believe it likely that she was killed by an agent, unknown, of another power. The Americans, I am told, are of the same view.'

'That I can confirm,' said Bridger, emphatically.

'And then we had Will's cemetery visit.'

Bridger dived in. 'And you will remember that on that matter I had to deal with the American number two last night. I warned you. As it turned out – we were in this very room – he was charm itself. My fears about interference, and Wemyss's alarm, were somewhat relieved. Somewhat.' Craven could see that his admission was tinged with disappointment. 'Anyway, with some effort I was able to steer us through without mishap.'

Craven saw his opening. 'Did he complain that we had interfered with his embassy's inquiry?'

'Not in so many words, but…'

'I see,' said Craven. 'I assume Will's name was not mentioned.'

'Of course not. Out of the question.'

'Thank you,' Craven said. 'I indicated the other day that Will's inquiries didn't help us identify a culprit, and that remains true. However there are other developments.'

Bridger said, 'Good.'

'I'm not sure that they are entirely good,' Craven said.

Carefully, with no reference to times or places, he introduced Bridger to the possibility that an East German operation might have been mounted in Paris and elsewhere, and that the embassy – no doubt one among several – could have been a target. Kristof played no part in his story.

'This is vague, Pierce. But, unlike Bolder's story, it has some substance. At this stage I can go no further. You and I must respect our boundaries. My feeling is that what has been going on is probably rather workaday – the usual prowling around. But Quincy makes a difference. I cannot believe that these indications are unconnected with her death.'

It had the effect he intended.

'Good Lord,' Bridger said, and, displaying some of his quickness at last, added, 'Had she found out?'

'Well, she'd found out *something*.'

Bridger stood up, as if he had to. 'I must ask you this, Freddy, without wishing to sound too formal. Has anyone here been compromised?'

'No.'

'You are sure?'

'Yes.'

'Not Bolder?' Bridger asked.

'This does not come from his rumour mill, I repeat. And although you may have turned against him, Pierce, I have no doubt about his loyalty. None. Nor, for most of the time, his competence.'

'Judgement is another matter,' said Bridger.

'Perhaps. But Sandy does have instinct. It has been his passport.'

'Flemyng?' Bridger said. 'Let's get back to our Will.'

Craven said that he was right to be concerned about Flemyng, because he shared a feeling for him. 'There is family business that I believe may be difficult. I learned something of that in Scotland. And you'll know that he has taken some time to get over Isabel, the girl who left just after you arrived here.'

'He should certainly settle down,' Bridger said. 'He'll be forty the year after next, like me. I'm so relieved to have Grizelda.' He turned to the door as if she might appear.

'But he is so valuable,' Craven said.

'Just so. I hope he isn't entangled in this affair, whatever it is.'

'He is his own man, as you know, Pierce. He avoids entanglements when he can.'

About Abel and Kristof, Maria and Flemyng's confessions about Quincy, Craven said not a word.

But when he took his leave an hour later, after a simple lunch of soup and cold fish with Grizelda, who sparkled briefly and who kissed him enthusiastically on both cheeks at the front door, his mind was on everything he hadn't said.

He walked to Place des Ternes to find a taxi and asked it to wait for him at his apartment building while he fetched his bag. Locking up, and checking that he had packed his hip flask, a heavy tiredness flooded in. He reminded the driver that he was going to Orly, and fell asleep.

Sam Malachy, soon afterwards, was on the metro, taking his own bag to Gare du Nord and the Brussels train. Craven's instructions, delivered in his apartment the previous evening while Flemyng and Abel were dining, were specific, but they also allowed some play time for Sam. 'Make a social appointment with Jonny Hinckley before you go. Old Vienna friends, and so on. I am going to give you some names, and I want you to show them to him. Don't warn him. Just ask if they mean anything, and please don't say that they came from me. As far as he should be concerned they may have dropped on your doorstep in Vienna. This must seem informal, Sam. Please.'

He had produced a list from his inside pocket. They were German names, three of them from Craven's imagination and one from an obscure opera, just for fun. The three others were remembered from Flemyng's list, including the one that had triggered a memory. On the previous night he had spent two hours in the darkness before he slept, listening to jazz and smoking hard, playing with the consequences.

'I can't tell you where these come from, and they may prove to have no significance,' he told Sam. 'But worth a try. I shall come to Brussels on Tuesday morning, off the night train from London. Breakfast? Only if you're in a decent hotel, mind you.' He smiled. 'Try the Amigo.'

Sam had arranged his lunch with Hinckley for the next day, well away from his office in the NATO mission, and had phoned a German friend in Brussels to propose a Sunday night out. 'Get your drinking boots on,' he told Sam.

The third journey on Sunday night began at almost the same time as Flemyng returned to the Café Tournon, to find police at the door and a heaving crowd inside that was eager to spend a night in the streets.

*

Far away, in the cool of a Highland evening, with the warmth of the day spent and a breeze sending a shiver through the ranks of spruce and larch along the lochside, Mungo Flemyng prepared to leave home.

He and Babble had walked that afternoon over the high hill behind Altnabuie, on the zigzag path that made the climb

288

easier, into the mouth of the next glen. They looked north-west across a panorama of hills and high tops that drew the eye to the mountains beyond, on a landscape lit by spring sunshine where the brown moorland was beginning to lose the drabness of the cold months, and new colours were painting the scene with brightness that matched the freshness in the air. There were streaks of yellow on the slopes and patches of greenery in the gullies where the water ran.

They carried wooden staffs, prepared for a long tramp, and spent two hours on a high circuit that took them back through the woods running down to the house and Mungo's garden. They watched deer and found a carcass they thought a wildcat had left behind, spent a while on a slope where they could watch a pair of buzzards hunting, and for an hour followed the course of a burn that worked its way between the hills to join the waters that poured at the last into their own loch.

As usual when they were together outside, they enjoyed long periods when they said nothing. Both knew the land well, and watched for signs of life and death with the eyes of countrymen who felt a rhythm in the landscape as clearly as if it had been music in their ears. Each long walk was an adventure and a restoration. Babble watched for young trout in the burn; Mungo looked for new nests on the edge of the wood. When they spoke seriously, as they finished with the steepest part of the path and paused for breath, it was about Flemyng.

'I assume that the reason Freddy Craven sent his message asking me to go to London tonight is that he has news of Will,' Mungo said. 'Or questions.'

'A telegram is usually bad news,' said Babble.

Mungo asked what he had concluded from Craven's brief visit ten days before.

'I think it was a mighty effort to make. He's not a well man.'

Speaking as if his mind had been elsewhere, Mungo said, 'He said something troubling to me when he was here. That he knew Will wasn't telling him the truth. What do you make of that?'

Babble, whose loyalty to his three boys was absolute, said that it might have involved girlfriends. 'A reasonable excuse.'

'He wouldn't come all this way for that,' Mungo said. 'I'm wondering if there may be a new job in the offing. A move. But I don't see how I can be told. He asked me to look through the boys' letters from the last two years before going down to London, and I have. He knows I keep them in date order. But they are about family things, nothing more.'

'That was nosey. Why did you say yes?'

'He's a good man,' Mungo said, 'and Will thinks of him as a father figure. So I have no qualms.'

'Here's what I think,' Babble said. 'He'll be talking about something that's perplexing him. He needs to settle it.'

They fell silent again as they took the last path home, winding round the lochside to the boathouse from where they could see the herons working on their jumbled nests in tree-tops that were still bare. Returning up the slope to the house, they caught the smells of fresh growth and saw a black cloud of bees at Mungo's hives. 'I'll be ready in ten minutes,' he said. 'Is the car filled up?'

They drove quickly to Pitlochry, Babble letting himself go, and they pulled into the station car park half an hour before the train from Inverness was due. Mungo checked his sleeper ticket, and Babble suggested a glass of beer.

Mungo's nervousness had come to the surface, and he returned to his puzzlement about Craven's purpose. 'I hope I can help, without betraying anything. Will is so precious, and I hope it is good news, not bad.'

Babble put his glass on the table where they sat and they watched the sun drop behind the hills. 'I've been turning it over in my mind, like yourself, since we were on our walk.'

'And?'

'I've got a strong feeling. A conclusion.'

Mungo waited for him.

'I'm a cheery soul, like you.'

'Indeed you are,' Mungo said.

'But not tonight.'

'Tell me,' Mungo said and reached across the table to his old friend.

'This must be bad for the boys. For one of them, at least.'

TWENTY-NINE

Kristof rang late in the evening. 'This time, you come to me.' Flemyng said, 'I will,' and nothing else, wrote down the address of Pascal's bar on a pad beside the phone and replaced the receiver. He found the street in his red book that mapped the city *par arrondissement* and studied the surroundings. He sat in his chair for a while, thinking about Kristof's voice – had it relaxed? – and arranging his thoughts in order. He made some preparations, and a few minutes later he was in a taxi heading east. They skirted the Latin Quarter where he could see streets blocked off by police barricades that were strung with flashing lights. As they turned to cross the river, Flemyng rolled his window all the way down and heard a chorus of sirens rising in the dusk, then falling away as the taxi left them behind. Looking back he saw smoke and a flicker of flame. A convoy of police vans sped past them, going the other way.

A few minutes later they were rattling over the cobblestones at Bastille, and Flemyng felt dampness in the air. He leaned back and turned his face and allowed the light, cleansing rain to fall on his cheeks. Refreshment. The driver knew the turnings, and worked his way through a warren of streets, sometimes turning back. Flemyng said nothing. On one corner, he glimpsed a sign pointing up the street they didn't take – *Cimetière du Père Lachaise*. He brought to mind the lugubrious figure of M. Lebosquet, and remembered the warmth that was revealed underneath. The driver told him they were nearly there, and he looked out at the passing street names that Quincy must have known.

He had given the driver an address on a corner about two hundred yards from Pascal's bar. After paying him off he took a coffee in a run-down café on a roundabout where there was no conversation and he could watch the street without interruption. Traffic was thin and the rain that now fell steadily was clearing the pavements. A few people stood in doorways for shelter, and it was quiet. When he walked towards Pascal's on the next corner, down a narrow street with its shops closed up and a hotel that seemed to be closed for business, though the red-lettered sign above the door was blinking hopefully, he saw that there were only a few cars parked near the bar. Each was empty. He paused a few yards away at the door of the hotel, as if he wanted to see what had happened to it, and looked around him for a minute or two. If the bar was being watched, they were good. He saw nothing.

Two old men came out and stood together on the pavement, putting on hats. They raised arms in farewell and left in different directions, pulling their coats around them. Flemyng walked quickly to the corner with his head down against the rain, pausing outside the bar to look inside. There were five men, two sitting alone and three talking to the man he took for Pascal, red-faced and fierce, who was in full flow. No Kristof, but he could see the ragged red curtain and the back room beyond.

Walking in, he nodded towards the corner, and Pascal waved him through without a word, giving a rough smile. Flemyng pulled the curtain back behind him and walked to the table where Kristof sat alone.

'Thank you, Will. You don't mind me being familiar?' He didn't stand up.

Taking his seat at a scarred wooden table, Flemyng looked dark in the dim room. He was wearing a black polo neck and a navy jacket, the shoulders damp with rain. He smoothed down his hair, wiping his hands on his jacket lining and throwing it over the back of his chair. Without smiling, he said, 'I've come.'

'That tells me something,' Kristof said.

'Does it?' Flemyng came closer.

'Yes. We can talk.'

Flemyng was prepared, and was thinking of Craven, who had helped him without knowing it. 'Not in the way you want, I think. I have news. Freddy Craven's in London.'

'No whisky tonight,' Kristof said, pouring wine from a carafe into two glasses. Flemyng expected it to be quick, without small talk. 'That's very good. When the cat's away...'

'No, you've got it wrong. I've told you I'm not going to go behind his back,' Flemyng said. Thinking of the keyring locked in the box in his apartment, he said, 'How can I find the diary without his help?'

Kristof said, 'He mustn't know.'

'Why not?'

'That's the deal,' said Kristof.

'The threat, you mean.' Flemyng added, 'Kristof.' His voice hadn't altered, the tone was neutral, and the dark furrows made his face look longer. But the atmosphere between them changed with the one word.

The German said, 'Friends at last.' He was drenched in relief.

'I can hardly call you a friend when you're blackmailing me.'

Kristof was smiling, bright-eyed and alive, as if a light had been switched on. His emotions were on the move, fear and exhilaration struggling with each other, and Flemyng recognized a man on the edge.

'But, Will, we're talking and we're together. This wouldn't happen if we were enemies. All I am doing is saying that if you can't get what I want, I may be destroyed.'

'Rubbish,' Flemyng said. 'Exposing me wouldn't help you. It would damage me, that's all. And my brother.'

Kristof shook his head. 'You don't understand my position. There is something I need to know. It is everything to me.'

Flemyng said, 'And as for my brother? You say your people know him as a friend, which I don't believe any more now than when you first said it, so what could you tell them that they don't know?'

'Who his friends are,' Kristof said. 'Maria for one.'

Flemyng concealed his alarm. After a moment's pause, having seen it laid out, he put the threat to one side and returned to Craven. He could see Kristof's surprise. There was nothing threatening in his tone, and he displayed none of the anger that had come out when they spoke in his apartment. Instead, he was encouraging.

'Why is it so important that Freddy Craven knows nothing? Perhaps he can help.' He was watching Kristof's eyes and saw the surprise come immediately.

'No.'

Flemyng was in command. 'You say he has information that you need. Let me ask him.'

'I said no.'

'In that case, you'll have to explain why.' Taking the carafe, Flemyng poured the drinks. Raising his glass, he said, 'I think that's fair. Don't you?'

'I can't explain. We all have secrets.'

'Very weak, Kristof.' Flemyng's face had softened. 'There's a connection here that I'm missing. With Freddy.'

'I am in danger,' said the German. 'That's all.'

'Who from?' Flemyng said.

Kristof shook his head, and Flemyng sensed a change, as if the question unsettled him.

'You say you want a deal,' he went on. 'I'm negotiating. Isn't that what you want?'

Kristof gave no indication that he was going to answer. The darkness that had clung to Flemyng when he arrived seemed to have been transferred to him. He was wearing a black shirt, buttoned up to the collar, and his face had lost its life as quickly as he had experienced his rush of excitement. His eyes were half closed, and Flemyng identified the fearfulness that he had tried to sketch after their first meeting.

Turning the screw, he said, 'Where were you this weekend?'

Kristof shook his head. 'You know how difficult it is. I am supposed to be followed if I leave Paris.'

'And were you?'

'I thought so,' Kristof said. 'I noticed someone near me in Brussels, on the street. Twice in one day.'

'Brussels?'

'I have friends there.'

Flemyng said, 'All of us have.' He sipped his wine, and said, 'What are you telling me?'

'I'm trying to answer your questions.'

Flemyng pulled back, aware of his display of weakness and a nervousness that he had been able to conceal at first. He clasped his hands behind his neck, then stretched like a man who had been cooped up for too long. 'OK. Let's talk about other things for a little. Tell me, where do you think you belong?'

Kristof took a moment to gather himself.

'Why?'

'Berlin?'

'Where else?' Kristof looked away.

Flemyng waited, and the German began to talk, because silence seemed to upset him. He spoke about the difficulties of his life – the restrictions in Paris, colleagues who watched him, the rules of his life – and said that Flemyng would be unlikely to understand that he still felt loyalty to those he served. 'I have my apartment in Berlin that waits for me, and a few friends there. But there are troubles. They come to us all one day.'

'Family?' Flemyng asked.

Kristof shook his head. He spoke about a life under orders, but said nothing that told of his origins, his travels, the staging posts in his life.

Flemyng listened, and then said, 'Why did you come for me?'

'I told you. Your brother.'

'I don't think so,' Flemyng said.

There was nothing more. Kristof was sullen, drawn into himself.

'What's your mystery?' Flemyng said, to make it worse for him.

He shook his head.

Flemyng said, 'I'm familiar with your story, you know. I've seen it before. A loyalty that's threatened. You know what you're like? A believer who loses his faith, then finds that he can't quite let go.'

'How would I know?' Kristof said.

Flemyng waited, but there was no more.

'Perhaps I can help you,' he said.

Kristof's face was questioning, but filled with longing. He said nothing.

'Without threats,' Flemyng said. 'I will try to get the information, in my own way, and then I shall decide what to do with it.' For a moment he sounded formal, a man giving orders.

'Try?' Kristof.

'Certainly. But first I need something more from you. The prize. Entice me.'

Kristof looked defeated.

Flemyng said, 'I need to see the colour of your money. Quincy's, rather. That's better for you than nothing. I'm asking you to trust me, that's all. It's what you said when we first met. Remember?'

'I do. How soon will you want it?'

'I will let you know,' Flemyng said. Kristof said he should ring Pascal, and gave the number.

'So?'

Kristof said that he would be able to reveal Quincy to him.

'What does that mean?' Flemyng said.

'Work it out for yourself.' Against Flemyng's expectations, the German had rallied. His voice had recovered its force and the sharpness in his face had returned.

'And remember, I could bring your whole house down.'

'How?' Flemyng said.

Kristof smiled, a man in control again.

Flemyng reached behind and took the folded sheet of paper from his jacket pocket. Opening it out, he laid it on the table and pushed it towards Kristof.

'With this?' But Flemyng's command had gone.

Kristof shook his head and said, 'No. That isn't my gun, it's my olive branch. The question is, will you be able to believe it?'

He stood up, took his coat and left the room without another word.

THIRTY

Mungo Flemyng was shocked at Freddy Craven's appearance. Since his visit to Altnabuie, less than two weeks before, the years had pulled him down. His jowls hung heavy and his grey hair had lost its spring, heavy with sweat even in the early morning. Mungo saw that he was thinner, and the tremor in his hands could no longer be concealed. An ugly blotch ran down his neck. Only his eyes were full of life.

They met at Craven's club, in a cavernous room where they were alone except for a grumpy waiter who was irritated at the summons to serve an early breakfast before the start of his day. They sat at the end of a long table and he took a chair in the far corner, immobile and gazing towards them while they ate their eggs, like a frozen figure from one of the portraits looking down on him. Mungo had arrived in a cab straight from King's Cross and the night train, enjoying the gentle bustle of the waking city, and Craven showed him to the sinks downstairs where he could spruce up. When he came to the table he was smart and spry, with a fresh shirt and tie from his bag, beaming and smelling of soap. Putting a good face on it, he said, 'It's good to see you. Refreshing. You're well, I hope.'

'I'm not, Mungo. The old frame is shaky.'

'I'm sorry.'

'No need. Life catches up with all of us in the end. I'm seeing the doc today, as it happens, so I'll get the latest bulletin from the front.'

The intimacy startled Mungo, and the effect of Craven's openness was to remove any need for preliminaries. He was able to say, without apology, that he had been alarmed by the telegram asking him to come south for Monday morning. He had been pleased at the chance to meet again, but confessed that he had passed a sleepless night on the train. 'Happy, but rather dreading this breakfast, too,' he said. 'I've been having some bad days.'

'I understand that,' Craven said, 'and I'm sorry for the drama, but certain events are moving fast.'

Craven waved to the waiter, who cleared their places and brought a fresh pot of tea. 'You can leave us alone now, thank you. I'm most grateful.' He closed the door heavily behind him and the room was quiet again. A faint noise of the first rush hour traffic from Pall Mall through the raised window, and nothing else.

He told Mungo first that although he understood that there was still much he couldn't say – names, secret histories, the very shape of his brother's life – he had tried to give him a glimpse of the difficulties with which Flemyng lived every day. 'You warn your students of the fog of war. Well, I know it to be real. I breathe the fumes. The complication is that we enjoy it, need it, even. I never wanted a life where I could clear my office desk at the end of each day, then start again in the morning. I want the game that doesn't end, the riddle that can't be solved.'

Mungo let him talk.

Craven spoke of the atmosphere in Paris, the eruptions of the weekend and the panic in high places. The Americans were caught in the coils of their own despair – 'I've never known them so full of doubt' – and with the world watching

Prague, there was panic in Moscow. They were turning in on themselves as they always did, and when they peered out, over the battlements, they were scared. 'When an elephantine regime starts heaving, everyone runs for cover.' At every point of the compass there was distrust and misunderstanding, he said. It was why disparate events, springing from different sources and with no obvious connection, had woven themselves into a web that trapped them all. In his experience, Craven said, these were the circumstances in which mistakes were made. A time when secret servants, charged with guarding the settled order, found that all their careful schemes could unravel. Instead of holding in place the weird balance across the divide that consumed their lives and both sides understood, they became the cause of its destruction.

'Sorry to sound apocalyptic,' he said.

Mungo poured tea and let him continue, without a word.

'We've had a glimpse in Paris, in my embassy, of how this might happen. I'm afraid I may be talking obscurely for a few minutes, but think of the death of the American journalist – Quincy – the events in the streets, which a country made by revolution well understands as you know, and the nervousness in the citadels of the great powers. Your brothers – both of them, I should say – are caught up in this. I can't explain how, but they are threatened, just as I feared. I'm sure of that. In danger, I'm afraid. Mungo, I'm sorry. I am trying to work out why, and to stop it. I am also aware that the consequence of all this could be devastating for some of those whom Will serves, and who walk with him.

'I have spent my life believing that with a mixture of cunning and bravery we can hold the line, keep the balance. For some reasons that I know, and some that I don't, I have been losing that faith in recent weeks. That's why I need you.'

Mungo was serious. 'What can I do? I'm disturbed about the boys. I understand the picture you're painting, I think, but I know almost nothing. Freddy, I don't even have an idea what Will *does* all day.'

'Nor should you,' Craven said, and smiled. 'And you never will.'

It was the historian's insight he wanted, and the feelings of a man who felt close to both his brothers. He asked if Mungo had reread the boys' letters, as he'd asked him to, and whether anything had helped him to explain Will's alarm over the phone call from Abel the previous month, the little episode that had caused disproportionate disturbance.

'I had that in mind as I looked through the letters, of course. Carefully. They're in date order, as I told you, so they tell a story, month by month. But I'm afraid the answer is no.'

Craven said, as if the thought had just occurred to him, that there was something else. 'You mentioned an observation of Abel's when we were walking at Altnabuie. I thought about it afterwards. He said something about secrets, and why we want them.'

'Yes, indeed,' Mungo said, because it was clear in his mind. 'He remembered what I'd once written about a Roman battle, the strategic deceptions and so on, in the days when that was my preferred territory. I said history taught us that everyone needed secrets. We have to believe in them, perhaps even when they don't exist, because they are necessary to us. We need the reassurance of having illicit knowledge.'

'How did he put it?' Craven said. 'Can you remember?'

'Oh, yes. He said he was amused that people would believe something just because they thought it was secret, and would be much more suspicious if it weren't. He thought that was proof of the power of the unknown. He also said it was useful.'

Craven was smiling. 'I understand. After all, secrets are my currency – I trade in them, and they make my world go round. I got the feeling from you that he said this in a letter.'

'Exactly, and I read it again – on your instruction – the other day.'

'Being the historian,' Craven said, 'you'll remember the date.'

'I do. Almost exactly two years ago.' He gave the month.

'When Will was in Vienna with me,' Craven said.

Mungo said nothing, because the door at the end of the room opened and the waiter's head appeared round it like a puppet's. He retreated without speaking, leaving them alone.

Craven spoke quietly, making it sound like a polite after-thought. 'Where did that letter come from?'

'Berlin. That wasn't a surprise. He's a traveller, as you know. Hotel notepaper. He said he was there for a spell.'

'And did it mention Will?'

'Not directly,' Mungo said. 'The boys always allude to each other in their letters, as I told you, but seldom by name. It's our way. Of course, I'd never pass on Abel's whereabouts to anyone, even Will, and vice versa. An unwritten rule. But Abel did say in this one that he wanted to confide in me alone. Underlined the point. Reading it again the other day, I was moved by its tone. Almost passionate. With my historian's hat, I'd have singled it out from a pile of correspondence. It was written in the usual easy way – obviously, they never use words like "security" and don't give any hint about what they are… up to. Never. I understand the walls around you all, so I got the message and waited for a telephone call when he got home. It never came.'

Craven said, 'Naturally, you'd be concerned. Thank you. You have been of assistance, as I knew you would.'

The morning sun was streaming in, and they spent the next quarter of an hour talking about Altnabuie, and a paper Mungo was writing on one of his new enthusiasms, General Wade and his roads across the Highlands. Then, for a few minutes, they returned to Paris. Craven spoke about the streets, the unknown, and they wondered whether some of old France might have passed away after the battles subsided. Mungo said he wanted to visit his brother and him, when the trouble had gone.

Looking at his watch, Craven suggested a walk in the park, and as they passed the porter's lodge, the waiter, who was doubling up at the front door until the club came properly to life, handed them *The Times*. It told the story of street fighting around the Sorbonne, hundreds of arrests, a hailstorm of cobblestones, and tear gas. 'What will the French do?' Mungo said.

'They haven't the faintest idea,' said Craven as they passed into the street.

Half an hour later, they had circumnavigated the lake and were having a smoke on a bench under the trees, watching a nest of moorhens near the willows that touched the water and, moving in the breeze, sent ripples across the surface.

'I hesitate,' Mungo said, 'but this must have been important to you. Have I really helped?'

'You have, my friend. I noticed at Altnabuie that you do the crossword.'

'A day late,' Mungo said. '*The Times* doesn't reach us until the late afternoon.'

'Well, I spend my life telling myself that you have to let your mind take you in different directions. Seeing things from odd angles to find the answer. You know what I mean – waiting for a shaft of light that makes everything look different, and then, for a brief moment, you can see clearly.'

'I know,' Mungo said.

'Sometimes,' Craven said, 'I don't solve the clues, I write them. Even more fun.'

Mungo pulled on his pipe, and waited for Craven.

'I'm afraid that you will never know how you have helped me,' he said. 'You can't. Does that distress you?'

'A little,' Mungo said. 'But it's the price of keeping my brothers happy.'

'And safe,' Craven said.

They stood, and prepared to part. 'May I ask you, Freddy, do you believe they'll come through this?'

Craven was taking his time in straightening up, leaning on the stick he'd taken from the lobby in the club, and he pulled his coat around him as if it was colder than it was. 'I hope so, Mungo. That's all I can say. I'm sorry.'

They walked together towards a gate on the west side of the park, and Craven continued. 'Anyone who loves history is attracted by uncertainty. You and I love the knowledge that we can never understand it all. It may be painful in life, but, as Abel said to you, we need to feel the touch of the unknown to excite us. That's why we press on.'

They shook hands, old friends from only a few encounters, and Mungo wished him good health. 'Please take some rest,' he said. 'Come to me any time. There will always be a room for you.'

Craven thanked him, and took his hand.

'I shall,' he said as he turned away with a wave and set off across the park, slowly, to another gate.

*

In Paris, Maria and Abel were together in the rue de Nevers with Quincy's papers in front of them.

'Will's a target,' Abel said.

Maria said, 'So it seems.'

He shuffled the papers again, reading a few of them once more. 'What we've got here is her storeroom, her travelling attic. Everything gets here in the end. Fragments from a lunch, little portraits of contacts, a couple of conversations that are like transcripts. Random names. What do we learn? That she's got sources that are better than mine, and in more than one country. It will take some deciphering.'

'All men,' Maria said.

He smiled.

'And this.'

He held up a sketch of Quincy, eyes dancing, hair swinging wide and a wicked smile. 'It gets her.'

Maria said Flemyng must have dropped it at her hotel after Hoffman's party.

'Has he drawn you?' Abel asked.

'Not yet, as far as I know.'

They were sitting together on the sofa, and Maria had laid out the sheets in what she believed to be date order, putting the sketch to one side. They were just as she had seen them first, when she extracted them from the pocket hidden in the case of Quincy's Smith-Corona. Some were typed, some hand-written, and they were a mixture of notes and well-formed paragraphs. There were skeleton stories that had little interest for Maria, but there were cryptic jumbles of names she had been studying. And Quincy's thoughts, jotted down on the run. Abel held one sheet in his hand.

'WF at Hoffman's party. Knows something.'

There was a scribbled date before the typed entry, the Saturday morning after the party on the night before.

'I left Hoffman's apartment with her,' Maria said.

'And what did she say about Will?' he said, not asking why they'd been together.

'That he was attractive at first meeting, and interesting. That was her style. But there was more. Friends of hers knew him, she said. If you're right about her game, that message isn't about Will and her, but someone else.'

'I am right,' Abel said.

Maria said she had no doubt about it, but assumed he had a question.

'I do. Who?' he asked. 'When we looked at the list from the cemetery, you told me about a source of Will's. The one who pointed you towards Père Lachaise. We talked about Quincy, and I told you everything I know. All the twists. It's time for the same from you.'

So Maria introduced Kristof to him for the first time, and painted a picture.

Beginning with his appearance, she told Abel that he sometimes looked young and sometimes much older. She'd noticed his signet ring, the way he dressed, his liking for a black hat, his courtesy. 'Remember, though, I've only met him twice.' She described his visit to Flemyng's apartment on the night of Quincy's death, and their talk before he returned from the embassy. 'He's scared, of course. Same as the rest of them.'

Abel said, 'How long have he and Will known each other?'

'I asked him. He said they'd spoken a few times.'

'Is Will running him?' Abel asked. 'You described him as a source.'

'I'd say not. I'd guess the contact is recent. He talked to me about his unhappiness, and I think he's a guy who doesn't know his own mind. Offered me nothing, I should say. Just wanted to talk, because he knew Quincy was dead.'

'But he sent you to the cemetery,' said Abel.

'He did, and he didn't mention what he knew about the dead letter box until Will was there,' said Maria. 'It was for us both and we were like schoolkids when we went there. But I'll say this about Will. He seemed a little scared of Kristof, even in his own home.'

Abel got up. 'Well, we got the list. Great.' He poured himself water, and took a glass back for Maria and sat down. 'Do you know why?'

He spent a minute or two patrolling the room, with Maria silent, to try to answer his own question.

'What do you think of these names? A Godsend?'

Maria said they couldn't know. 'What if...'

'Exactly,' Abel said.

'... it's a trick to screw us. Get us to start our own little witch hunt.'

Abel said, 'Our biggest fear. Did you make any arrangements with him?'

'Yeah,' she said. 'I got a number. Will didn't know. I wanted to ask about Quincy and his friends.'

Abel said, 'I need to know something else. Did he mention me?'

'By name?' Maria said, showing her surprise.

'Or by reference to Will. A brother, maybe. Anything.'

'Not a word,' she said. 'At the apartment, neither to me, nor to Will when he came home. Why?'

Abel said that he'd swum in waters that Kristof may have known, and it was important that he knew if a connection had been made. 'You said you saw him twice. The second time?'

'I went to see him on my own. Will's still unaware.'

Abel was erect and alert, a sprinter in the blocks. 'When? What did he want?'

'Friday. He said the reason they killed Quincy was because

she knew too much. About his people. Must have charmed one of them.' Smiling, she said, 'She was good at that.'

Abel said it was the old story. Zak Annan had recruited Quincy to help, and she didn't see why she shouldn't play around in the same way with the other side. Had no discipline. Deep down, a reporter who wanted excitement, and that was all.

'They couldn't trust her any more than we could,' he said. 'Her own woman. Admirable, but fatal.'

Maria said, 'I've been through these papers a dozen times. Meetings all over the place. Bolder. Abbott – I'm fascinated by him, you should know. A plan to lunch with Freddy Craven – she doesn't say contact was made, though. Including the one, for all we know, who finished her off. Thoughts about Prague – people we can get the boys on to. All the stuff with our boy Zak. I think she half loved him, you know.

'Kristof. They met. He told us that. She was more fascinated by him than I expected. Wanted more of him. On the story she boasted about to Will, though, not a dicky bird. Zilch.'

'Quite true,' said Abel. 'You must have expected so much from the papers. She was careful.'

Maria watched him get up and walk to her window.

'Don't worry,' he said over his shoulder, standing with his back to her. 'I know exactly what she was getting ready to write. It would have been a catastrophe.'

*

Craven's doctor worked from a basement flat in a scruffy Georgian terrace south of the river. He had more spacious quarters than seemed likely from the street, and there was a steady flow of people, mostly old, who had trusted him for a long time, and who spread the word to friends. But he kept that list short, explaining to some prospective patients that there was only so much he could manage alone, and they might do better elsewhere. He had one secretary who sat upstairs, in a cheery room of her own with a view to the street and travel posters on the walls. Craven knew her from the days when she had arrived in the office typing pool, and he had helped her arrange a speedy escape to the twelfth floor and even more sensitive duties, before Dr O'Casey's summons had come three years ago. His secretary had gone to the country with her dogs, and he needed a new girl who knew the ropes. Marjorie was transferred, and she managed the daily passage of old friends to his rooms below her simple office, making sure that many personal files were taken by messenger at the end of every week to the safe in her former lair where they could lie untouched until there was a panic, or a death.

Craven was a welcome visitor. They took tea together. 'I saw Sam Malachy the other day,' Craven said. 'In fine shape.' Marjorie reported on one of his boys who'd come through from Washington, to get the all-clear for Saigon, and she let Craven know of all the talk below stairs in the office, not far away. 'And you?'

'I've been padding some corridors today. You know me.'

The buzzer rang on her desk. 'Down you go. Mind the stair.'

'Declan.'

'My dear Freddy. How are you bearing up?' He was in loose tweed trousers and blue striped shirt, his tie rolled up on the bookcase behind, and his jacket on the floor. His stethoscope was dangling over the lampshade on his desk, and he waved it at Craven like a gardening hose.

'Weary, weary,' Craven said. 'But that's no surprise.'

'I'm going to get you up on that couch if it kills me,' said O'Casey. He helped Craven to loosen his shirt and heave himself up with a wobbly step on the footstool. When he lay down, the doctor gave him time to get his breath. Craven's public face gave way to the picture of a tired old man, as if an air bag had emptied. 'I've been pushed a lot in recent days,' he said.

'Quiet yourself,' O'Casey said. 'I'll judge.'

He listened to the old man's chest.

'Don't talk for a little bit, if you don't mind.' He felt for a pulse, blew up the rubber ring on his arm, then found a spatula to press on his tongue, and took a flashlight from his desk. He peered into Craven's eyes. Rubbing the blotch on his neck – Craven was reminded of Flemyng and his scar – he then spent some minutes examining patches on his face and his chest, tapping on his ribcage. Taking his stethoscope up again, he spent some time listening. Then he rolled Craven over and lifted his shirt to examine his back, felt his pulse again.

'Waterworks?'

'Fine,' Craven said.

'Well, that's something.'

He put away his implements. 'Pain?' he said as he turned back, patting his chest.

'None. I'm grateful,' Craven said.

'Let's get you dressed.'

They sat across the desk, and O'Casey said, 'You know that it's been downhill for a while now. And that hasn't changed. The stuff, whatever it was, that they took out a couple of years ago – well, some of it is still there I'm sure, eating away. You know that. I'm surprised there's no pain yet. But there's something else.'

Craven smiled. 'I was expecting this.'

'Why?' O'Casey said.

'Because there's a tiredness I haven't known before.'

'I'm not surprised. More ticker trouble, old boy.'

'Don't hold back,' Craven said.

'A wee heart thingummy. I think you've had one, without knowing.'

'When do you think?' Craven said.

'Oh, I couldn't say. Days, not weeks.'

'Declan, tell me everything.'

'I'm never definite about anything. Part of the job. But it tells me that you're weakening, that's all. A harbinger, maybe.'

'You're sending me to a hospital?'

O'Casey shook his head.

'No point, you mean?'

'I didn't say that,' said the doctor.

Craven smiled. 'If anything happens in Paris, I'll get them to call for you. I know they'll do that for me.'

'Of course I'll come. But don't worry. I won't be packing my bags tonight.'

'A last word,' said Craven. 'Don't tell them. Please.'

'I won't. Let's get you out of here.' He rang for Marjorie.

Five minutes later he was on his way. There was time for some supper before the night train to Brussels. He told the driver to take him straight to the White Tower in Percy Street, which meant that he missed Flemyng's phone call to his club.

THIRTY-ONE

Flemyng tried again later. The night porter told the story he'd already been given. There had been no sign of Mr Craven since mid-afternoon, when he picked up the things he had left at breakfast time, having gone for a walk in the park with another gentleman, not a member. His room had been reserved for one night only, and he had said nothing about where he might be found. Of course, if he returned they would find him a bed. He was always welcome.

'Don't worry,' Flemyng said. 'I shall probably be able to track him down.'

Sitting with the curtains drawn shut and his reading light on, he went through his conversation with Kristof, worrying at it like a dog with a bone. Conscious that events in the streets were stoking his sense of crisis, and trying to resist, he persuaded himself that if he promised to be true to Freddy Craven on his return, there was no shame in looking at the diary. Didn't he have the key, from the old man's hand? It was in his box of special objects that he had taken from the bureau and sat on his knee. He fingered the carved Celtic knot on the lid like a talisman.

He had confessed to Craven after looking at the diary ten days before, and the old man had laughed. He said it was the kind of thing he'd done himself, more than once. So where was the harm? Another confession would be required, but there would be a result to change the game with Kristof. No one would lose, and the danger of exposure – the threat to Abel – would be gone. Craven wouldn't want him to do anything else.

Surely.

Kristof's churning emotions told him that he was capable of anything. The Flemyngs were both in danger.

Half an hour, and a long, slow whisky later, he was persuaded.

He rang Janet, at home. 'I'm sorry to ring you late in the evening,' he said, surprised to see the clock at nearly eleven. 'Two things. I may have to drop by the office. Is Sandy working late?' She reassured him. He was out of town.

'That's fine. I'll let myself in.'

Janet said she would come if necessary, but he said no.

Then he said, 'Freddy's away, I know. Have you made any arrangements for him tonight? He's not at his club.'

He listened to her answer. 'Brussels? Thank you.'

His mind was made up. Putting on a hat and coat against the rain that had returned, he took Craven's keys from the box, strung them on the same ring as his embassy set, and walked to the corner to find a taxi.

There was a police cordon across rue du Faubourg St-Honoré, and he had to speak to a guard outside the Élysée to reach the embassy, a hundred yards away. For the first time in his experience he had to show identity papers in the street. At the gate, two Royal Engineers were at George's post. They knew him, and in less than five minutes he was turning on the lights in Freddy Craven's office, having closed the curtains first. Anyone could see a glow from the courtyard, but he didn't want the place to look like a lighthouse.

Where was Craven on his train? Looking at his watch, he reckoned that he would be approaching Dover and the ferry. A rough crossing wouldn't bother the old sailor, but manoeuvring the train off the ship, and the parting of the carriages to send some to Brussels and the rest to Paris, was always a noisy, bumpy business and he had never been able to sleep through it. He looked around the office, so familiar to him. Freddy Craven was there with him, he persuaded himself. He would approve.

Quietly, as if he might be disturbed despite the locked door, he sat in the old man's chair and opened the bottom drawer. The second key opened the deep box inside and he saw the diaries for a second time.

He had promised himself at home that he would resist the temptation to work backwards from the latest entry. That was respectful. He would only do what was necessary for the good of the station.

Bolstered by his reasoning, but conscious of his nerves and a desire to work quickly, he lifted out a bundle of cloth-covered black books, each small enough to slip into a coat pocket. There were four from Vienna, and he had to repeat in his head all the promises he'd made to himself not to read the stories in which he played a part. What was said about the night he got his scar? What had Freddy Craven told London? The answers would be inside. But moving in a deliberate way, he placed the books back in their box. Forbidden fruit. It gave him a feeling of relief, and some pride, that prepared him for the next step.

There were three diaries marked *Berlin*.

He took them in turn.

He switched on Craven's desk lamp and turned off the office lights. Going to the window, he pulled the curtain back. There was a patter of rain on the glass, and looking into the courtyard outside the residence he saw the light catching the water on the stone. The only lamp lit was in the gatehouse, and over the wall he saw the glow from the police cars parked across the street further down. It was well past midnight, and there was no sound.

Sliding Craven's tobacco tin and pipe to the side of his desk, beside his paperweight and a pewter mug full of pencils, he laid the Berlin books in front of him. His first surprise was Craven's style. The contemporary entries which he had seen ten days before were cryptic. The crude code – more like a set of abbreviations – was easily broken, and he had known that Craven left it in a state where any of his colleagues could easily interpret what was there.

But years before, Flemyng could see, it had been different. A storyteller was at work.

He was moved as he read Craven's flowing hand, with its long loops, and enjoyed his descriptions. He saw immediately that sensitive names were either disguised or omitted. He was writing around events. Flicking across the first twenty pages, he could see nothing that could be an operation codename, and no colleague was identified directly. The discipline was meticulous. But the old man was weaving a story and, like a schoolboy under the bedclothes, he took it slowly, to enjoy every chapter. Craven threaded the narrative with references to favourite writers, and poems, giving the diary the flavour of a commonplace book.

Craven's time in his lair in the old Olympic Stadium was written up as an adventure. BRIXMIS they called the mission – a troupe of soldiers, engineers and full-time spies that were hard to tell apart, with rights to cross the city in the name of liaison with the East Germans, and, more to the point, their Soviet opposite numbers. In turn, the other side had the same fishing permit in the west. It was a strange, gentlemanly business. Everyone knew there was plane-spotting and tank-spotting going on, and Craven had mapmakers collating the observations and photographs that came back every day to work out how the land lay beyond East Berlin. But the arrangement was held to be above skulduggery. It had been approved, negotiated.

Craven briefed those who were going into the eastern sector, and for the rest of his time he trained up those who were to spy on the Russians who came west, under the same disposition, to play the game the other way round.

He enjoyed the absurdity.

They had to rescue drunks from beer halls in Potsdam, find a camera that someone had left in a brothel, apologize for boys who had bent the rules and, once, pick up one of the official cars with its painted identification numbers that had crashed where it shouldn't have been. But there was always a Russian who could be shamed in turn. There were moments of strange co-operation. They once provided a lorryload of medicines that weren't available in the east, concluding that they were required for the wife of someone powerful, probably a Russian. In gratitude, a helpful report came back with the record of a conversation at the opera by one of the old spies marooned in Moscow: he had let slip a name. And Craven's account of the Queen's birthday celebration in the Somerset Arms, their purpose-built pub in the mission grounds, was a comic masterpiece. All the invited Russians had come in uniform, and the toasts went on into the night. It was arranged that they could stay in one of the barracks, under a guard that Craven said was so light that it couldn't deal with a case of bed-wetting, quite probable after the party, let alone a breakout by a phalanx of Russians determined to find secrets.

Happy days. But after half an hour, Flemyng had found nothing that suggested any connection with Kristof. Not a clue. Craven gave no detail of what had been learned about the other side.

He turned to the second, later volume, and the tone changed. It dealt with Freddy's efforts to establish his own network in the east, and the narrative gave way to entries that were more like puzzles deliberately contrived to confuse. He used initials and numbers, and occasionally geometric drawings of which Flemyng could make nothing.

For an hour he went back and forth through the book, and the third, in search of a pattern. A name.

Nothing.

He considered what Kristof had said. The secret lay in Berlin, and might be known to Craven.

The three diaries lay in front of him, and he looked at the dates on the covers. He had missed something.

But Kristof hadn't mentioned dates. Why had Flemyng thought that he was most likely to find the link in the days when Craven was in charge in Berlin? Stupid. An assumption without reason. Craven had visited Berlin many times since, and was in touch with Duncan Gilfeather, now in charge of the station, who was one of his boys. Why delve into history when he could look at the here and now?

He was convinced, and felt a prickle of excitement. It was closer than he had thought. Forget the Berlin years. Look at Paris, and work backwards from the latest volume.

He picked up the book he had seen the week before, with pages of Craven's abbreviations.

Within a few minutes, he became fluent in the style that the old man had developed over the years. It had little of the narrative flow that gave the earlier diaries their flavour, and had turned into a shorthand that gave an outline of his days and little more. His style was spare, the descriptions shrinking like Craven himself. But Flemyng noticed immediately that the story was punctuated with sketchy anecdotes and fragments of gossip, and his poetic references had started to return. Craven was making sure that as he got older he wouldn't let such scraps of information slip from his mind. The disciplines of his trade were still obvious – no codenames, nothing to give an outsider a pathway into the work of the station. But hints, and, to Flemyng, the picture was clear.

There were initials that he could recognize, and slowly he began to piece together the account of the year that included his own arrival in Paris. '*W piped aboard*.'

In the silence, with his mind cleared of any other thoughts, he looked at the latest entries and worked backwards, month by month.

December, and Bridger's arrival. A rumour, which came to nothing, that Bolder was getting a promotion in London. Craven's travels – by boat train to London once or twice a month, three flights to Vienna – and, in the high heat of the previous July, two days in Berlin.

He read the entries for June, pricked by a memory at the back of his mind. A dinner on the Left Bank, and an evening of recollection. The dates in his head were right. Gilfeather had visited Paris for two days. The diary made it clear that he had stayed with Craven.

Flemyng recalled the dinner they had together at the Balzar. Gilfeather, freckled and carrot-haired, retained a boyish presence and Flemyng had always enjoyed his good humour. Although they could have been taken for contemporaries, he was Flemyng's senior by eight years. They had overlapped twice in London, and he had taken his place in

Vienna, picking up the contacts and agents that he played, as Craven put it, like an old violin.

Gilfeather and Flemyng liked each other. Their bookishness led them on to shared territory, and Flemyng enjoyed the blend of innocence and cunning that Gilfeather had perfected. Even when he was scheming, cranking the machine in Berlin, he never lost his sense of wonder. Like Craven, he relaxed with naval history and sea stories, and half the dinner involved picking apart Villeneuve's tactics before Trafalgar. Flemyng remembered some Berlin tale-telling, gossip about the latest shuffle of station chiefs, but no revelation. In his notes, Craven gave the date of the dinner.

Turning the page to look at the next day, Flemyng found an entry that held his attention, because he couldn't explain it.

Craven had written, '*DG*' – Gilfeather – '*saw C lst nt.*'

'*C*' could only refer to the chief of the service, seldom known by any other title. Flemyng was puzzled.

He had been at the dinner with Gilfeather and Craven on that date, and they had sat down at eight. Gilfeather could not have been in London, and if C had been in Paris, Craven would have told him. The chief's visits were never secret from his own men, and it would have been odd for him to pass through without the station being aware.

There was a second mystery. Nowhere else in the diary had Craven mentioned C. Flemyng checked. He remembered a visit from the chief's predecessor to Vienna, soon after his own stabbing, and found the diary for that month. Nothing. He looked up several references to Craven's visits to London, when he would usually have seen the chief. Again, nothing.

For several minutes he turned pages at random, and confirmed his suspicion. C was nowhere. He didn't exist in the diary.

Going forward, from June to July, he followed Craven to Berlin.

He met Gilfeather, had a night out with the station – Flemyng recognized the initials of the boys – and paid a visit to the Olympic Stadium and the Somerset Arms. The next morning, he saw the ambassador and the rest of the day seemed to have been spent with Gilfeather, in the office and on a walk in the woods. As usual with Craven, there were no details of their conversation.

Except one, and when he saw it Flemyng knew he was on the way.

'Paris message safely home.'

And a little further down the page, *'C is for cunning.'*

The next day, Craven had visited the American embassy, and flew out that evening.

Back in Paris, he made the last entry of the day.

'The sea is calm tonight.'

Flemyng remembered the end of the poem, and the darkling plain where ignorant armies clashed by night. Ignorant is right, he said to himself. He put the book aside. Opening the last notebook, which he had opened the previous week, he turned the pages to find Friday, 19 April, the day it all began in a café on rue Pigalle, with Kristof.

In his last entry for the day, Craven had written, *'Patience its own reward.'*

In his excitement, he felt a touch of shame. Craven's life lay open before him. But he placed his guilt against his discovery, and found a balance that calmed him. Betrayals by two friends cancelled each other out. Surely.

He heard a clock chiming two as he locked the box containing the diaries in Craven's drawer. He left the desk laid out precisely as he had found it, and checked that he was leaving nothing behind. He switched off the desk lamp, and opened the curtains. Looking out from the darkened room, he saw the soldiers smoking at the gatehouse. Two police cars drove slowly past the front gate to join the others parked outside the Élysée. In the distance he heard a siren, sounding lonely after the cacophony of Sunday night.

He double-locked the security door that separated the station's rooms from the rest of the embassy, and took the stairs slowly in the soft glow of the one bulb on the ceiling that burned all night but did little to lighten the darkness. From the window on the landing he saw the shadowy outline of the garden, the black bulk of the trees and the seat where he liked to be alone. In the thin moonlight he could see a light curtain of rain and he stopped for a minute or two to watch, and think.

He decided to leave a message for Kristof in the morning, on the assumption that he could find Craven in Brussels and talk to him for approval.

He tried to think of the right words for either of them, and failed.

THIRTY-TWO

'A three-breakfast problem,' Craven said in the lobby of the Amigo.

'You've given up your pipe?' Sam said.

'Not quite.' They laughed together, and Sam helped him to the restaurant. Craven was unsteady on his feet, a sailor who'd been too long at sea, and they did a slow waltz towards their table. 'Forgive me,' said the old man as they settled down in a quiet corner, with no one near. 'Not too good, I'm afraid.'

Sam didn't try to laugh it off. The truth was obvious. 'Let's take this slowly. Am I putting you on a train later?'

'Do you think we might travel back together? I'd like that.' Sam thought that age was bringing back his West Country burr, and he felt a warmth.

'Of course, Freddy. I'll see you all the way home.' The old man smiled.

'Now,' said Craven, underlining the feeling that time was short. 'The news from Hinckley.'

'I gather that Sandy Bolder is unlikely to be godfather to his new baby,' Sam said.

Craven said, 'I imagine Jonny's been given the third degree, poor boy. Not his fault.'

Sam described picking him up at NATO. 'I'd forgotten how big the bloody place is getting. Not for me.' He said they got well away, beyond the city, walked in the woods for nearly an hour, and found an open glade where they had privacy but enough space to know if they were being seen or overheard. Sam said he was Craven's emissary, to get that straight from the start, and Hinckley relaxed in the knowledge that he could give a full report without the caution that came in a cable that might find its way anywhere. He and Sam had been in Prague together, and preserved the trust of warriors in the field.

'We had a long talk. Freddy, it's bad.'

'A headline, please.'

'Hinckley says Bolder should stay away from this town, or he mightn't get home alive. I don't pretend to understand it all yet, but here's what he said.' They were still alone, but Sam whispered.

'The trouble with Bolder isn't that he's wrong, but that he's half right. Worse.'

'I feel light breaking in,' Craven said.

Sam said that with luck they might find an empty compartment on the train and they would have three hours to talk. 'I've got fragments in my head, but no picture that makes sense.' In spite of his privileged position at the crossroads in Vienna, where he saw material that bypassed Paris, even Craven's own desk, on this one he felt he was in the dark. 'Can you help, Freddy? Are you in on this?'

Craven shook his head. 'Officially, no. But I have a history. That's the thing about old men – memory.'

Without uttering an operational codename, nor turning one into a joke as Bolder liked to do when he was obliged to have conversations in public places, Craven described the problem that had preoccupied him when he patrolled the eastern front and which had never gone away. In their island of quiet in the restaurant, he could speak quite plainly. 'All the time, we worry about leaks. But sometimes there are things we need them to know. You and I know this. The problem is – how.'

'Hinckley's point exactly,' said Sam.

Craven picked up his frothing coffee cup with both hands and put it to his lips, drinking like a thirsty man who'd been handed a water bowl at the fountain.

After a minute he said, 'Sometimes the most dangerous thing in an enemy is ignorance.'

*

Flemyng rang Pascal's bar at ten and said he would see Mr Kristof at noon, without leaving a name. He couldn't tell if the message got home. He would turn up, and hope.

His second call was to Hinckley's office. 'Freddy's in town, I gather.'

'Malachy's here, or was, on Freddy's behalf. That's the best I can do, Will. I saw him yesterday. I got the feeling that he'll be back in Paris by tonight.'

Flemyng rang the station to say he would be out all morning, and Bolder answered.

'You were right,' he said. 'Fifty thousand at the Arc yesterday, so they say. There isn't an empty cell in Paris. I'm going to take a turn in the streets today. With Freddy away, I shall write it up.'

'Take your tin hat, Sandy.'

The day was fine, and Flemyng wanted to walk. Along the Boul' St-Germain the debris of the night was smouldering. There was a leaning tower of loose cobblestones on one corner, and across the road two smashed cars pulled together to make a barricade. Two of the cafés he knew best were boarded up, and you could find your way to Odéon by following the trail of broken glass. He spoke to some students at Le Rouquet, squashed into the red leatherette banquettes and high on the prospect of battle. When he took to the street again he felt the sour aftertaste of tear gas and, as he cut away on rue Danton towards the river, he could hear the crowd that had survived the night outside the Sorbonne, where the riot police watched them across their barricades. The chanting followed him until he crossed the bridge into the deep streets of Île de la Cité and away.

He had an hour, and wanted to let the time bring him some calm.

Bolder was in Bridger's office, trying to make up lost ground.

'Everything takes second place now. Everything,' he said.

Bridger, who hadn't yet lost the fingertip feeling for events that had served him so well, said he had spent the evening in the streets. 'There's wind in their sails. General strike next week, they say. In our time, Sandy, we haven't known a city in this state – in Europe, anyway. They've occupied Sciences Po. I saw fires in the Luxembourg Gardens. God.'

'I heard something interesting,' Bolder said. 'Digging up the first cobblestone is difficult, but when it's out, the rest are easy.' He spoke as if he had been taking lessons.

They made their plans for the day. Bridger wanted a council of war at five, with Craven in his place, and Flemyng if he could be found. 'We have had a rocky fortnight, I don't need to tell you. If we acquit ourselves well in the days ahead, it may revive the fortunes of this embassy.'

At that moment, Flemyng was troubled.

Far from calming him, the walk which had already taken him east of Bastille had given him time to think, and he was unable to come to a decision about how much to tell Kristof.

In his mind, he replayed the images from the pages of Craven's diary.

Gilfeather had visited Paris, and had made contact with 'C'. Three weeks later Craven was in Berlin celebrating the arrival of a message that had come the other way, from Paris. On his return he confided to his diary that he was playing a waiting game.

If it was the message that Kristof had wanted him to find – and nothing else in the diary seemed to fit – he could see no explanation for how it might help him. Therefore, why should he confide details of Freddy's notes to a man full of threats and whose emotions, he well knew, were veering from exuberance to despair and back again without warning. Yet he couldn't get to the next stage – come closer to the heart of the puzzle – without giving Kristof something. He was hungry and must be fed.

As he came close to Pascal's bar, he was nervous and gloomy. He felt only the faintest tremor of the excitement that usually welled up at such moments. An agent, a meeting, a game. This time there was little but apprehension.

His watch said it was nearly noon.

Pushing open the door, he saw Pascal alone behind the bar. To Flemyng's surprise he laughed, and flapped a long napkin towards the back room like a flag.

Flemyng muttered a thank you and stepped through the curtained doorway.

Kristof was at his table.

Maria and Abel were facing him.

*

Before they went to the south station in Brussels, Sam took Craven to his hotel so that he could bathe and change his clothes.

Leaving him in his room, he took the opportunity to ring London from the lobby. A few minutes later the phone in the wooden kiosk in the corner rang, and Sam was waiting.

'Dr O'Casey – Declan. This is kind of you. I'm worried about Freddy. Alarmed. I know you've seen him.'

He listened. 'Thank you,' Sam said. 'I do think you're right.'

Craven came down a few minutes later, and Sam paid the bill. They took a taxi to the station and set off on a long hike to the end of the platform in search of privacy. Sam found a first-class compartment and spread a few scraps of clothing on the seats, positioning himself at the door to repel intruders. When the train moved away they were alone, and Sam pulled down the blinds so that they couldn't be seen from the corridor.

Craven said they might as well be lovers, lost in each other.

They rolled south, and Sam produced some ham and cheese from his bag. He broke a long baguette in two, and Craven watched him dig around to find the bottle of red wine he had stowed away. 'Picnic time. Splendid.'

Craven said he would help Sam to make sense of the fragments of the story. 'You'll realize that it's for my benefit, too. This business is in need of order.' Watching him eat, and pour some wine into the water glasses they took from their metal rings at the window, Sam realized how his tempo had slowed. Freddy Craven the quick fox was no more. He was a man weighed down by time.

'What Hinckley said was true. When Bolder rang you, then scampered off to London with his tales about leaks, he had half a story. But only half. Let's go through it.

'We know they have some sources, but we think they're low-level. Bolder's convinced there's a network, but he doesn't have the slightest evidence. He's picked it up somewhere and can't give it provenance. We assume they know quite a bit – all about you and me, let's say, and I dare say they talk about the pecking order in London as much as we do, probably with the same amusement – but on the military side, things have been secure, so I'm told. Targeting, dispositions, the plans that would kick in at a time of emergency. What we'd do if they rolled across the plain. However, it's not as simple as that.

'Ignorance is a bit of a problem in the present climate. D'you see?'

Sam, his mouth full of bread, waved a hand. Carry on.

'What they don't know, they make up,' Craven said. 'And they exaggerate, of course. They imagine we have plans that, frankly, don't exist. First strike against them, and so on. And when they panic – with every bit of trouble in Prague or Warsaw – they become even more convinced that we're willing and ready to have a go. Which, as we know, we're not.'

Sam poured the wine. 'I'm beginning to enjoy this.'

Craven said that it had been realized a long way back, when he was in Berlin, that to prepare for a time of trouble a way had to be found to convince the other side. Ministers were no good. They were assumed to speak with forked tongue: what Soviet could believe otherwise? And as for Ingleby's merry men, the harder they tried to persuade the eastern embassies in London, or the negotiators who clustered in Vienna, the less likely they were to be believed.

'Only one thing convinces them,' he said. 'A secret.'

He had been involved at the start, getting the other side to believe that they had got to the truth by their own efforts. It was important that they didn't learn too much, and that had been the trick. Targets, missile placements, warheads – off limits, absolutely. But strategy? They were to be given a glimpse, in a way that persuaded them that they had penetrated some of the most secret places.

'I was aware of something. It had the name of a bird,' Sam said. 'Osprey?'

'Could be. No details, I hope.'

'Me?' Sam said, 'I'm the boy who knows nothing, Freddy.'

'Even now, I can't tell you the whole thing,' Craven said. 'You know that, and in any case there's much I don't know these days. Duncan Gilfeather's the man. We worked a ploy that fed some bits and pieces – rubbish, some of it – to the other side. Just enough. Letting them think they'd got inside. Duncan's so good. And when Prague started to kick off, and Moscow started to panic, the thing got more urgent. They've got to understand Sam, what we *won't* do. The plan for attack that we *don't* have.

'Otherwise, they might do anything.'

The two men fell quiet. Sam crumbled the last of the bread and pulled apart the ham with his fingers.

They spoke little as they watched the flat landscape, noting the moment they crossed the border. Sam waited until Craven was ready.

'I happen to know now, from conversations in London, that Will Flemyng's brother is at the heart of this operation from the American side. I didn't know. So you see, Bolder was tramping about on a minefield. It's a dangerous time. The other side feels threatened, and the last thing we want is for them to be frightened into doing something stupid. So it's not the moment to be shouting about leaks, because some of them are our own. And to stir up a panic about penetration by their spies? The worst moment.'

Having dealt with Bolder, Craven said that he might be unhelpful, but there were others who were positively dangerous.

'Who?' said Sam.

'A woman called Quincy, whom you knew, and a man called Kristof, of whom you've certainly never heard.'

In Pascal's bar, Abel spoke first. Kristof, bemused, was quiet.

'Let's have a party.'

Maria stood up and touched cheeks with Flemyng, which surprised him. She had noticed that he needed steadying. Abel was in suit and tie, and Flemyng wondered if he had been at the embassy. Kristof was in the navy jumper he had worn at Flemyng's apartment and, far from enjoying his popularity, looked as if he was facing an inquisition. His eyes were darting around the room, and he was smoothing down his hair, anxious to smarten himself up in the absence of his white shirt and jacket. He said nothing, took out his pipe and began to stuff it with tobacco from a tin.

Flemyng, all his plans overturned, shook hands with his brother. 'This is slightly absurd,' he said.

'But useful,' said Maria.

'Chance has come along,' Abel said.

'What about me?' said Kristof.

'You're going to talk,' Flemyng said, and as he sat down the atmosphere changed.

The German seemed ready to panic. He'd put down his pipe, unlit, and his hands were pressed on the table, marble-white. He had staring eyes – Flemyng remembered his own sketch – and he gave the impression of a man trapped. Abel went to the curtain and stood bodyguard to listen for activity on the other side, in the bar. The scene came to resemble an interrogation, with the prisoner at a table in his cell.

Maria came to his rescue, voice low and her words carrying no hint of threat.

'You will realize that each of us knows something about you – different things, I'd guess – and I want you to believe that we haven't shared everything. You know that's not the way it works.'

For the first time since Flemyng had arrived, Kristof looked hopeful.

Maria said, 'But we've all been thrown together by Quincy's death. You told me that she knew too much, and that's why she died. So there was a threat to your people. But also – you have to realize this – to us. She said as much. What was she going to reveal?'

From the curtain, Abel said, 'We've all seen the list of names.'

'So you say. That's only the start,' Kristof said.

'Stick with the list. We don't recognize them.'

Kristof said that wasn't surprising. 'They've changed names. Wouldn't you?'

Abel took the list from his pocket, but before he could speak he was interrupted by his brother.

In contrast to Maria, Flemyng adopted the tone of an official rather than an acquaintance. Maria realized that Abel had never seen him in the role – was he anxious, nervous? She couldn't tell, because Abel stood with his head cupped in his hand and half turned away, in shadow. In the other hand he had the list. He was quite still.

'OK,' said Flemyng. 'Tell us what else she had.'

They recognized that the man before them was on the verge of collapse. His hands shook, and he was sweating.

Neither Maria nor Abel interrupted Flemyng when he pressed on.

'You've threatened me directly. I can do the same to you. We can blow you to smithereens, and you'll be on a plane back to some grey barracks where, I have no doubt, your life would come to an end. Not too quickly, and painfully. You've been playing with us. Your friends won't like that.'

He pushed the box of matches towards Kristof, and he lit his pipe at last.

Flemyng said through the first cloud of smoke, 'Co-operate, or you're finished. I promise.'

Quietly, the fight gone out of him for the moment, Kristof began to speak. 'There are many names. She got them from all over, she told me, but they are people of ours who are in the west. Unknown. There are more than you know. One or two here in Paris, and in Bonn, of course. But especially in Brussels. London, who knows?' He tried a smile.

'At NATO,' Abel said.

'Of course,' Kristof said. 'Their loyalty lies elsewhere.'

'How many?' Flemyng said.

'Who can say?' said Kristof. 'Not I. But they are deep inside. Waiting.'

'We know she was in touch with your people,' Abel said. 'Playing games. I'll be honest. It's time for that, at last. She was doing the same for us.'

Kristof stared. 'She was yours?'

'Yes. For some time.'

Kristof put his hands to his face, which had whitened. 'What did you learn?' he said.

'A good deal,' Abel replied, looking at his brother, who was unable to hide his shock.

Maria resumed her role as friendly persuader, keeping the conversation on the move so that as each revelation took hold another was in the making. 'So you see, Kristof, she had gathered information from all over the shop. This is my question. Who would have been the beneficiary of the story she was trying to write? Our side, who'd be revealed as weak, vulnerable to all the people you say have burrowed into the system. Penetrated. Or yours, who would have a secret network exposed. Tell us. Where do you think her interest lay?'

'How can I say?' He had recovered some strength, and managed to smile. 'But it does mean that we both had an interest in stopping her, doesn't it?'

The room was quiet.

Abel came back to the table. He leaned on his hands, his arms stretched and straight, and spoke with the same authority as his brother had shown a few minutes earlier. He was angry.

'Let me tell you something. We don't kill our own citizens with poison sprays. I've seen your gadgets. My friends don't walk around with guns hidden in cigarette lighters, waiting to murder anyone who might make life difficult.'

Kristof looked at Maria and Flemyng to catch their eyes, and said, 'Really?' Then he added, 'But wouldn't you let someone do the dirty deed for you?'

Into the silence, Flemyng said, 'I have another question. Tell us who you really are. I still don't know.'

THIRTY-THREE

When they arrived in Paris, Sam Malachy and Freddy Craven looked like a pair of old comrades rolling home from an outing to the seaside. Perhaps a racetrack. They made a defiant splash of colour. Sam was in a striped jacket that marked him out as a good-time boy, and Craven wore his old white suit, stained and threadbare in places, broadcasting the message that he made his own rules. Sam carried both their bags across the concourse at Nord, and they made their way gradually to the line of taxis outside.

Their appearance belied Craven's weakness. He was slow – Sam took him to a bench to sit down before they stepped into the street – and mopped his face with a dark blue handkerchief. They didn't get up until Sam had asked him if he felt ready, and he had to be helped into the car.

As they drove away, Sam said, 'Freddy, I have to tell you something.' He was holding on to the old man's arm. 'I spoke to London. Sorry, but Declan O'Casey's coming tonight. He didn't need much persuading.'

Craven said he probably fancied a good dinner, that was all, and laughed. Then he put his hand on Sam's. 'Don't worry, you're right. I'm done in.'

At the apartment, Sam said, 'I'm putting you to bed, old boy.' Craven said they should have a drink first. After all, it was nearly five o'clock. They sat for a while, and Sam went through the story Craven had told on the train, to make sure he had it straight.

'We've held the balance. All we can do,' Craven said.

Sam poured him a whisky, and they had a cigarette. The room filled with smoke, and they spoke for a while about Vienna in days when Craven's station was the best in town. 'I miss Will,' said Sam, and added carefully, 'Has he settled here? I find it hard to tell.'

Craven's wise eyes turned on him, 'Yes, Sam. He's had worries – and you know that the Quincy business has disturbed the whole place. But that will soon be over, and you've helped.'

A few minutes later, when Sam had persuaded him to take to his bed, Craven said as they stood at the door, 'There's one more piece to fall into place. Then Will and everyone will see clearly.'

They said goodnight. Sam went to his hotel, and rang Flemyng.

Two hours later they were a quartet, together in his apartment.

'Cards on the table,' said Maria as if they were going to have a bridge evening. Flemyng had given them a picture of Sam before he arrived. 'We're both Freddy's boys, and that's what you need to know. He's been with the old man in Brussels today. Trusted. Nothing should be hidden.' Abel smiled at his brother when he said that. 'Nothing? You mean it?'

With Sam in his place among them, Maria said they should begin with their experience in the afternoon. Kristof and his state of mind.

'He's close to collapse,' Flemyng said. 'I first met him nearly three weeks ago and the man I saw in the bar this afternoon had lost all his bearings.'

'Which makes him more dangerous,' Abel said.

'This is where you'll have to indulge me,' Sam interrupted. 'I know from Freddy that he's been threatening you, maybe in different ways. I want to know how, exactly.'

Flemyng was expressionless. He was in his favourite chair, his drink balanced on a pile of poetry books on his little table. The lighting in the room was low, and he got a special glow from the lamp behind his chair. It meant that the familiar shadows on his face were emphasized, the two creases deep and dark. He didn't respond immediately to Sam.

Abel spoke instead.

'Come on, Will.' He smiled at his brother. 'What do you have for me?'

After it was all over, Maria recalled the moment as a test of Flemyng's resolve. She had been clear from the start that he had carried a burden through the days since Quincy's death that pulled him down. They had shared a great deal, found the list and explored some of Quincy's mysteries, but she knew there was more.

She spoke. 'I do think, after this afternoon, that we need to lay it out. You said nothing would be hidden, Will.'

'I did,' he said softly, regretting it.

'Maybe I can help,' said Abel, who seemed, by contrast, to have discovered a source of energy. He was standing, back in his jeans, with a loose summer shirt, and he looked more like a figure from the Paris streets than a man in his brother's business. Flemyng still wore his office shirt, the trousers of his dark suit, and shoes that were polished high.

'I'll tell you what Kristof said before you found us with him today, Will. He was as plain as can be. He knew I was watching his people and knew some of them by name. He pushed as far as he could go. Nearly accused me of treachery, though I guess something stopped him from going that far.'

Released from his torment, Flemyng said, 'He did with me.'

'Ah,' said Abel. 'I'm not surprised.'

Sam, hearing the brothers' story for the first time, said that he was beginning to realize why the embassy – and the Americans in theirs, camped round the corner in Avenue Gabriel – had been on the boil.

Abel stepped away from the others and stood by the fireplace. None of them said a word. They waited for Flemyng, and when he spoke he took them back to the beginning.

'He approached me on the metro. No warning. We met again three days later.'

He took time with detail, describing Kristof's appearance and the sketch he had made, recalling the atmosphere in the café where they had their first conversation. 'At first I thought he was older than me. I was surprised when I realized that he was younger. He was grey, trailing a cloud of smoke. Tired.'

Flemyng was speaking softly, his eyes down. To the others it seemed as if he was speaking to himself.

'Out of the blue, he accused you.' He looked up at Abel. 'It was mad. Should I have walked away? Well, I couldn't pass up the chance that he might be offering himself as a source, or wanting to come over. I had to let him talk, whatever he said.'

'Of course you did,' Abel said. 'I'd have done the same.'

Flemyng still wore the most sombre expression of the four.

'Come on, Will,' Maria said, 'the guy was saying the worst thing he could think of, to hook you. Desperate to excite you.'

'As Freddy said, was he buying or selling?' Flemyng said. 'How was I to know?'

Sam asked if he had asked for evidence, to call Kristof's bluff.

Abel intervened before Flemyng could answer. Stepping to the table and sitting alongside Maria, he spoke directly at his brother. 'Are you saying you need my assurance, now, that it isn't true?'

To Sam, Flemyng looked ill.

He held his brother's gaze. 'Yes.'

Maria broke the tension. 'For God's sake, Will. What's got into you?'

Sam joined in. 'Come on, old friend.'

And Abel, whose face had darkened like his brother's, said, 'The trouble is that we're never going to forget this moment, are we? Never.'

Maria thought they had never looked more alike.

'You're right,' Flemyng said, 'and that's painful.'

'But you know it's not true,' Maria said, taking Abel's hand in hers.

He said, 'Will needs to hear it from me. So let me explain what I've been doing.'

His story was an echo of Freddy Craven's conversation on the train with Sam.

'I have a friend in bomb disposal,' he began, 'and he's just like me. He sits with his box of tools, a surgeon with scalpels. Where does the first cut go, and what's underneath? Where's the artery you have to avoid? He's slow, prodding and scraping and living on his nerves until he makes the thing safe – waiting all the time for the explosion. That's been my life these last two years or so.'

The problem, he said, was in finding a way of getting some information to the other side, without setting off the big bang. They had to know the truth, but only part of it.

'We know we're not going to attack them unless they move first, but they don't believe us. I've been trying to find a way to convince them. So I had to make them trust me.'

Flemyng was watching Sam, and saw no sign of surprise. His friend knew what was coming next.

Abel said, 'I had to get as close as I could.'

Maria interrupted him to say, for the benefit of Flemyng and Sam, that she had known nothing. 'This was buried deep.' When she saw Sam's smile, she signalled to Abel to hold back.

And Sam said, 'Just like our side.'

Flemyng appeared the unhappiest of the four as Abel resumed. He sipped a drink, his head moving out of the pool of light from his standing lamp so that for a moment they couldn't see the expression on his face. 'You first,' he said to his brother, and his tone was sharper. 'All of it.'

'I was Mr Ambiguity,' Abel said. 'I used a contact of ours in East Berlin, somebody from their trade mission here in Paris, and a Russian in Brussels who seemed promising. And, Sam, a talkative friend on the other side in Vienna. Did you know?'

Sam was smiling. 'Carry on.'

Abel said he had never suggested that he might be selling secrets, nor thinking of going over. 'It was more difficult than that, in a way. I was the guy who could see their point of view, might even help them from time to time, but was never going to go all the way. The tempter. I was never going to betray, but I might be willing to deal. A trader in no man's land.'

He described four trips to Berlin – 'I wrote a letter to Mungo from there, probably shouldn't have' – and time in Brussels. 'Your friend Jonny Hinckley, Will, was helpful.' As for Vienna, he'd been attached for three months to the mission and had made contact with a Pole who was subsequently posted to Paris. 'I found I had a little network of my own. I wasn't buying secrets, and neither were they. But we were exchanging thoughts.'

'Did we know?' Flemyng asked, and looked at Sam.

His time come, Sam said that it was clear that he should say something about Freddy Craven. 'I'll tell you all now that I was able to help him a little when this whole business started.

When Sandy Bolder started stomping around, he rang me in Vienna. Then Freddy was on the trail, wanted help, and I sniffed around. And, Abel, I picked up your tracks. Your Pole – well, he was a friend of mine, too. A bit of a tart, I'm afraid – everybody had a piece of him. Freddy wondered if you'd been seen around town, and I could say that you had. So suddenly, I was just about the most popular man on the circuit.

'Freddy was the person on our side who'd started this whole operation. But it passed out of his hands when he left Berlin, and I guess that these days there's a little group of people in London who're on board with you, Abel, and keeping this show on the road. Am I right?'

Abel and Flemyng were contrasts. From his chair, Flemyng seemed to Maria to be glowering. Abel was evidently happy, and told Sam that he was bang on the money.

'I can say no more.' Laughing.

Maria raised her glass. 'Allies.'

Flemyng rose for the first time since the conversation had started. 'I've learned a lot. Thank you. But where does it get us with Quincy?'

'I'd rather start with your friend Kristof,' Abel said, 'because he's going to lead us to her.'

His three listeners settled down, Flemyng back in his chair, his expression sullen. Abel was sprightly, speaking without hesitation and turning the story into a drama. His hands were mobile and his eyes alive. Before he started, he stood up and they all recognized that he was going to give a performance.

'Before you arrived at the bar this afternoon, Will, I showed a picture of Quincy to the grumpy guy who runs the place.'

Flemyng said, 'Pascal.'

'The same. He recognized her, said she'd been there at least twice in the last month. To meet our friend, obviously. They were in touch. Who started it, we've no way of knowing. But she wasn't going to that bar to have fun. She was getting something, because that was her business. The only one she knew. Kristof was helping her, must have been. She told both of you' – he looked at Maria and then his brother – 'that she had a big story about the East Germans, and she had.

'The trouble is, it was too big. She was better than any of them thought. After all, she was the kind of person that's completely foreign to them. Star reporter, glamour-puss, clever as can be and just as ruthless. Over time, she'd picked up stuff on both sides of the wall, in Vienna, here in Paris and in Brussels. Kristof, maybe a little bit dazzled like all of us, had helped a little. But it had all gotten out of control, and someone panicked.'

Sam asked him to explain what convinced Abel that she knew too much.

'In the end, the list. It was hers, of course. They weren't passing it to her. She was telling them what she knew. Must have had someone who had offered to confirm it.'

Flemyng stood up. 'The most dangerous game of them all.'

Abel said, 'Sure. It's why I said I'd start with Kristof. She thought he'd turned against his own people, and suspected he just might stand up her information. Certainly she thought he wouldn't betray her, so there was nothing to be lost. She would have told him already that she had a list of names, but he hadn't got far enough down the road to play that game. He may have fooled around with her, but he wasn't ready for that stuff to come out. Both of them had swum out of their depth. She was revealing how much she knew; he was consorting with a woman who he probably suspected was in touch with us too. We confirmed that to him in the bar today, and we all saw his reaction. It wasn't shock, it was the sight of a nightmare come true. She didn't know how much danger they were in. He did.

'Quincy had excited them – probably passing some stuff she'd learned in her dealings with our man Zak Annan. Anything for a story. Zak was sure she'd wandered off the reservation, and was trading information. Name by name, she put together that list. People that have some significance, for reasons we don't yet know. When Kristof and his lot realized that the point of all her coming and going between us and them was to write it up in a magazine, they had to stop her. Simple as that.'

Flemyng was still. Speaking softly, so that Maria had to come closer to hear him, he said that Abel's story pointed to one conclusion. 'Kristof was responsible for her death.'

'I think so,' his brother said. 'I don't know whether it was him, or whether he caused someone else to do it, but the decision was his.'

They watched Flemyng get up again, this time without the hint of anger that had marked him since they started. He was alert, excited, and his voice had risen. 'You realize what this means?' he said.

'I think I do,' said Maria.

She went on. 'He will have known, when she was killed, that she had left the list in the dead letter box. But they'd never leave it nearby – the very information that they killed her to protect.'

'Exactly,' Abel said.

Flemyng was standing beside Maria. 'And we remember what happened on the night of Quincy's death. Kristof told us where to find the dead letter box.'

'And the list,' she said.

'I love it,' said Sam.

'Oh yes,' Abel said. 'He wanted you to have it. I've been practising ambiguity this last year or two. Your friend Kristof is a past master at the same game.'

'Which means,' said Flemyng, 'that we can't know if these names are a gift…'

'… or siren voices luring us to the rocks,' said Maria.

THIRTY-FOUR

When Flemyng rang Craven's apartment early the next morning, Declan O'Casey answered the phone.

'Will Flemyng, a pleasure.'

Flemyng said, 'You answered Sam's summons. Be honest with me about Freddy.'

'It's not good, but even a garrulous old medic like me prefers not to talk about such things on the phone. Freddy's having a wee snooze. You know the café on his corner, I take it. Half an hour?'

And from the doctor who had listened to his own heart and taken some of his blood only a month before in his annual check-up, he learned that the previous evening O'Casey had decided to go to the flat soon after he arrived from Orly, and found the old man in a daze. He'd gone into a deep sleep soon afterwards and the first time O'Casey had rung in the morning there was no reply. At the second attempt he got through, and found Craven lucid, but weary and slow.

'I've examined him as best I can. He won't hear of hospital, although I tried. Says it's been a busy time, too much travelling, and he's exhausted.'

Flemyng didn't interrupt, knowing there was more.

'I'll tell you alone, Will. Be sure that I won't go to the embassy – Freddy forbids it – and I'll leave you boys to deal with London. I told him two days ago that I thought he'd had what you'd call

345

a heart attack. Small, but telling, and not for the first time. You know that with everything he's got inside – or hasn't, I should say – he's weaker than he was. There's been a decline. And overnight... well, I think something else has happened. I'll let him get up, but if he doesn't stay put in that bloody chair I'll have him in hospital, whatever he says. I'd like to be straight with him and avoid the embassy. Who's chancery now?'

'Pierce Bridger.'

'Oh God.'

'Can I ask,' Flemyng said, 'whether I can come round? There's an urgent matter we should talk through. I'll try not to tire him. He'd be surprised if I didn't want to see him, I'm sure.'

'I'd prefer to be there,' O'Casey said.

'Not in the room, I'm afraid. You understand why.'

'Sure. But not far away. Come at noon.'

Flemyng took to the streets. He told Janet that he was going to look at the latest damage in the Latin Quarter, and would ring in the afternoon. She said that Sandy was beetling about, and all would be well. 'Mr Bridger was disappointed that neither you nor Mr Craven could come round yesterday afternoon. I think he'll want to reconvene. Mr Bolder was agitated, I'm afraid.'

'Let him stew, Janet,' Flemyng said and put down the phone. Feeling the guilt, he knew that Janet, who understood his moods, would play his hand for him.

He walked along the river. The spring sunshine brought home to mind. Mungo loved the moments at Altnabuie when one season turned into the next, and the slow coming of spring was one of the thrills of the Highlands that he savoured every year. Flemyng remembered long walks up the glen, where the broom and the hawthorn were coming into flower and carpeting the hillside with colour. The burn swollen with spring rain, and the woods fresh with new growth. There was always a mild wind in early May; the last April storms were gone, and the light on the hills began to wash the landscape in colours that foretold the summer months. He longed for it.

Craven had spoken of his exhilaration when he come back from his trip to see Mungo, but Flemyng had caught the valedictory tone. He didn't expect to see Scotland again.

Then he forced himself to abandon the meditation. Craven was tired, and even if O'Casey suspected an episode he would be ready to receive him at noon. Until then, he would walk.

But Kristof was in his mind, and Abel. The pain of the evening conversation had stayed with him through the night. In the early hours, he'd risen and, sitting in the chair, wondered whether he could have avoided the question; let Abel tell it in his own way. No. They knew the rules, and they were bound to follow them. Maybe condemned. There was never an escape from that.

At about eleven he was in rue de Tournon, a battleground. Someone had tried, and failed, to uproot a lamp post that now jutted into the street like a piece of field artillery. There was a barricade near the café which had reached a height of about four feet, with rocks and scrap metal and, he was astonished to see, a tree trunk. Two trucks with riot police were parked end to end at the corner, and a student shouted at them as he passed. Slogans covered the walls.

'*Sous les pavés, la plage*' on a hoarding above a stockpile of cobblestones, ready for the fight that everyone said was coming tomorrow. At one corner the police had hung a green canvas over a barricade, to conceal it, and he saw a message splashed across it in white paint that made him laugh for the first time that morning, '*Je suis Marxiste, tendance Groucho.*'

A familiar figure was sitting at a table outside a café in the parallel street. Edward Abbott was writing, as usual, his head down. Flemyng took a seat beside him.

'On patrol?'

Flemyng said, 'What do you hear?'

'The same as you, no doubt. Strike tomorrow. A march. They've occupied a factory in Toulouse, apparently, and they think that's the start of something. We were in flames in these parts last night. Remarkable. Maria Cooney was here.'

'Really?' Flemyng said. 'Quite an operator.'

'Yes, talking about Grace Quincy again.'

'And?' said Flemyng.

'I think she's got a story about her. I'd like to get it first.'

'If I can help, I'll ring.' Flemyng said he had an appointment and waved goodbye.

He got away from the battle zone and found a taxi. A few minutes later he was at Craven's building.

The old man came to the apartment door. He was dressed in his Paisley pattern dressing gown, and Flemyng could see O'Casey behind. He shook hands with the doctor, who said he'd be in the kitchen if he was needed for anything.

As they sat down, Craven in his high easy chair and Flemyng on the sofa, he noticed that he had lost his interest in pretence. 'I'm fading, Will. Declan talks about "episodes". I know what that means. I'm running out of steam, and quickly.'

Flemyng said, 'I don't want to tire you, but we must talk.'

'I agree.'

Flemyng explained how the four of them had come to meet on the previous day, and how Sam had been introduced to some of the events that together had troubled them.

'Quincy?'

'He knows everything, and much more than I knew until last night. Did you know she was playing on both sides of the street, after a fashion?'

Craven said, 'When we realized she was sending and

receiving envelopes at the cemetery I thought to myself that it was unlikely she was first taught how to do that by a Russian, far less an East Berliner. Not her style. So I thought it was a good old American boy who got her involved in the first place. Sam was able to help. There were whispers about her in Vienna – stay clear. She was somebody's, but whose nobody knew. That kind always come unstuck in the end.'

'Time and fate,' Flemyng said. 'The agent's lot.'

Craven was tiring, but Flemyng had to press him.

'Despite all that's happened, we're still trying to understand Kristof's threat, the beginning of this whole affair. If we're going to know what he might do next that's the first step. But I still don't understand why. I know you can help.'

'Know?'

'Suspect, then.'

'That's better, my boy. I certainly can.'

His old friend rose. It took an effort for him to cross the room but he wanted to look in charge, captain of the ship, and not a shaky figure curled up in a chair.

'From the start, you've wondered about his history. His travels, his origins. The story that he carries on his back, like all of us, because he gave you nothing. You were right to be puzzled. I can help.'

Flemyng's senses were sharp. He felt ready to spring, his energy about to be released.

'You were intrigued by his language and his style. His ease with our ways, and his understanding of them.'

'I couldn't place him.'

'The explanation is easy,' Craven said, smiling in a way that caught Flemyng's heart. 'The simplest one of all.

'Kristof is as English as I am.'

THIRTY-FIVE

B erlin, city of secrets.

Flemyng's closeness to Craven was rooted in their first forays in its streets, where he had learned his trade and the joys of observation. They laughed together, sometimes schemed, Flemyng absorbing the satisfaction of an older man who saw reflected in a young friend the pattern of his own life, the thrills and the sadness. In the hours that followed the unmasking of Kristof, that commitment in Flemyng was renewed. It would never be broken.

Craven enjoyed the first shock on his face.

He was sparkling for a moment, calling through the kitchen door for some tea from O'Casey, and settling Flemyng down for a piece of vintage storytelling. 'I wish we could raise a glass. He won't let me.'

Kristof.

'I had no idea,' Flemyng said. 'Why didn't I think of it?'

'Everything pointed the other way,' said Craven. 'How he behaved, and the look of him. The threats. You thought his English had been taught, and that's our old failing. We think they are rather better at it than they are. I don't care, by the way. I'm lighting up.'

O'Casey brought the coffee and found Craven laughing in a plume of smoke.

'No point now, Declan. Let it go.' The doctor left the room, closing the door behind him.

'I have a confession to make to you,' Craven said. 'And you to me, no doubt.'

Flemyng acknowledged that it was true.

'I'll go first,' Craven said. 'I don't think it would have changed the course of events, but I could have told you that I knew who Kristof was. But it had to play out… naturally, if you follow me. I didn't want you putting on an act. You're good, Will, but he'd have spotted it.'

He took him back to Berlin, and their expeditions together when Flemyng was young and easy. Craven was looking for recruits on the other side, lines he could run into the eastern sector. A policeman, a nurse, a student – no matter, any link had promise. One day he heard a story – 'it was Tommy Critchley, before your time and long gone from us, who picked up a whisper. There was a young Englishman who'd left home after school, ran away. Good family and so on. They had a letter from him, from Berlin of all places, but the wrong side of the city. He'd had a conversion, religious-style, but with him it was politics. They couldn't believe it – burned the letter, of course – but it was true.

'Critchley knew one of the uncles, who had dealings with us in Hong Kong after the war. Whole thing hushed up. You can understand it, embarrassment beyond measure.

'So he was lost to the world, and not spoken of again. Word went out that he'd been travelling and had an accident. Terrible for the family, sadness all round, but time moved on. They guarded their secret guilt. The parents are dead now, but there are brothers and sisters. One, at least, in the public eye.

'So Tommy Critchley gave me the fact of this boy as a parting present. He was off to his Dorset village to squirrel himself away for the last time. He was sure – this came from the family – that the prodigal son was still on the other side. If not, he'd have come home. Apparently, he was that kind of boy, despite everything. This is important – he was fond of the family. You told me he wears a signet ring. I'm not surprised. His father's, I'd bet. Funny how loyalty works, isn't it? That was his nature.

'Anyway, I kept an ear to the ground. No trace. Every now and then I'd get the BRIXMIS boys in Berlin to nose around in the eastern sector, see if they'd heard talk of a young Englishman. No name, of course. I didn't want it advertised. Very occasional questions. I didn't know if he was in the apparatus, but I thought it likely. You'd hardly jump across at his age to work as a farmer, would you?

'Time passed. Nothing. He came to mind from time to time but we had other business on hand, and it never seemed urgent. A long game at best.

'Then, many moons after I'd left Berlin, Duncan Gilfeather got a sniff. A word in the ether. We had somebody who came over, across the bridge, low-level but helpful. Gilfeather was in on the questioning, and he picked up a hint. You know how sharp he is. I had told him about Critchley, and he always had an ear cocked, just in case. This defector, an old man, remembered a security building where he'd worked and an English boy who was there. Stood out, obviously. He heard people around him speaking of Paris. We wondered if he was bound for the trade mission. So we watched. The Americans keep an eye on the list here, from one of their sources, and we spotted him only a few weeks after he arrived.'

Flemyng broke in. 'I don't want to interrupt, Freddy, but I think I know the date. This is a confession. It was when Gilfeather had dinner with us here.'

Craven was enjoying himself, and lighting another cigarette. He stood up, with difficulty, and took a few steps. 'You've been in the diaries again. I'm glad.'

Flemyng felt an overwhelming humility, and a rush of relief that took him back to a time before the crisis began.

'Thank you. I've worried.'

Craven waved him away. 'To continue. We wanted to entice him. Gilfeather and I had a plan. We'd find a way to getting contact – something simple, trade delegation to Paris, that kind of thing – and ask for help in passing on a message. Something that might be useful to his people.

'And remember this, Will. Nothing was going to alarm him. There would be no indication – none at all – that we knew of his background. He'd be just another East German, alone in the west. But we knew.

'The information we passed would be harmless. Some trade nonsense. Maybe in time, a tiny piece of gossip about the tabs we're keeping on their people in London. But not at first. I was keeping out of it. Too much risk of me being spotted around the place by some of his people – one or two of them are rather good. Gilfeather, on the other hand, is completely unknown here. So we put him up as a businessman. Ran into Kristof, accidentally on purpose as it were, and they met for a second time on the night we all had dinner together at the Balzar. Gilfeather passed him a message that might be interesting to them, to set himself up as a source. Tantalising for your friend. We waited. And, lo and behold, it got back to Berlin. So we had a conduit, and one who was ignorant of what we knew about him.'

'Neat,' said Flemyng.

He said he remembered reading '*message arrived home*' in the diary.

'Just so,' said Craven. 'One of our sources let us know that our titbit had arrived safely in Berlin. Gilfeather passed one more message after a few months, then we would wait until he was needed. We were keeping him for store. Because we knew his secret, and that gave us power.'

'And then?' said Flemyng.

'And then your friend Grace Quincy blundered in, and got interested in the people around Kristof. Met him. My bet is that he worried that she had worked him out and guessed his origins. I'm told she was always asking questions.'

'She was,' Flemyng said. 'And those eyes.'

Craven said that, like so many others, Kristof would have fallen under her spell.

'And he panicked. Was she on to him? He hadn't given up on his commitments back in the east, though they pained him. He was beginning to lose his faith. The problem for him was that she had bigger games to play, at the wrong moment. Couldn't make up her mind if she wanted stories for the papers, or the thrill of the underworld. Decided on both, and it killed her.'

Flemyng said that he felt as if he were high on the hills at home, lifted by the air that comes after a storm. He was tingling. 'I'm so sorry, Freddy, for the stupidities in this business. My worries about Abel, my dissembling. The diaries, for God's sake.'

Craven said that helped him to make his own apology. 'When he picked you up, I was excited, you know. We looked at those pictures in the archive. I've always made sure he's not in that file. There was no one you recognized, so I was convinced it was him. He'd come back to life, as I knew he would some day. And with you of all people. I wondered if the doubts were kicking in at last. Do you understand?

'I trusted you, of course, and it was better to let you go in blind, and play it your way. When you told me about Abel, I worried. But the game was on, and I let it run. I think, funnily enough, that it's turned out for the best. We've learned something about Kristof, have we not? That he's a little more important than any of us imagined. From what you say, by your reasoning he had enough clout to order – or at least advise – that Quincy should be killed.'

'I know that now,' Flemyng said.

'I see myself in you,' Craven went on. 'Forgive this comparison, under the circumstances – but we're brothers.'

He spoke about Sandy Bolder. 'Loyal as they come, of course, but you can't depend on him. All that smartness, the perfect look, is rubbish. He's wild. I got him to admit that he'd got the first hint of the famous list from Edward Abbott. Just a whiff, but enough. A journalist peddling the rumour of the moment. And, even worse, *he'd* got it from Max Anderson at lunch, whose rather large nose was out of joint because Quincy had fetched up here. He'd got it from New York that she had some agents' names, so he spread the tale. Best way for a rival to draw her sting. And Sandy, hearing it second-hand from Abbott, got himself into a state of excitement and started to dig.'

'Except,' said Flemyng, 'that he was right, more or less.'

Craven gave a laugh.

'Well, if he was right about a network in NATO and elsewhere – London, who can say? – it's something that we would never want to see the light of day. How strange it is, Will, that the more tense things get across the great divide, the more important it is not to try to embarrass them. The more danger there is, the kinder we are to each other. We're funny people, aren't we?'

It took a little time for Craven to build up his strength again. He was still smoking, and asked Flemyng to pour him a drink.

'Your brother understood that. I learned from Sam, and indirectly from Mungo, what he was doing. The old game that I'd started in Berlin. Helping to manage the knowledge of the other side, shall we say. The nightmare was that Quincy would upset everything with a spy story.' He took a drink. 'Never mind dear Declan. He knows.'

Holding his glass in both hands like a little trophy, he said, 'Will, let me put it as simply as I can. She was promising a scandal. Penetration. Military secrets leaking. The worst stuff. Look at Europe. Neither side would want such a thing.' After a pause for a drink, he said, 'Odd, isn't it? Not the way things are supposed to be.'

Flemyng was quiet for a while. Then he said, 'There's still a risk from Kristof. I saw him yesterday. There a wildness loose inside him. He could do anything – try to blow Abel and me sky high.'

Craven sat down, because the talking had taken its toll. He was breathing heavily and he fumbled when he tried to get at another cigarette. Flemyng lit it for him.

'I have an idea,' Craven said.

'Tell me,' Flemyng said. 'We need something clever.'

'Do you doubt me?'

'Never,' said Flemyng.

'The talented Mr Abbott is still in Paris, I take it.'

'I've seen him this very afternoon,' Flemyng said.

'Well,' said Craven, 'Edward has the same drive as the late Miss Quincy, although I think that, all round, he is not prone to her love of expeditions into the dark.'

Flemyng said he was sure that was true.

Craven was ready. 'Abbott, as you can tell, went to a good school. By chance, the same one as Mr Kristof. They're of an age. So our Edward has an inkling of the story. Heard it years ago from a younger brother, behind the bike sheds you might say. And, you may not be surprised to know, I have made it my business to make sure that he has a little more. Only a little. Not enough to write a story, mind, but enough to keep him on the trail. He has no idea that Kristof is in Paris. If he had... well I think he would put two and two together and his newspaper would think it one of the stories of the year. Even in this year. Don't you? A big splash. And Kristof would be finished, before he had time to flee for the hills. Kaput.' He managed to snap his fingers. 'We have an opportunity.'

'You mean...?' Flemyng said. He thought of Craven's cleverness, and his own devotion to the man.

'I do.'

He drew on his cigarette and smiled through the clouds.

'The blackmail of a blackmailer is good for the soul.'

*

In the afternoon, Flemyng found that he responded with vigour to the excitement of the streets. He wandered. Au Petit Suisse had employed extra staff to control the crowd at the doors, and the place was alive with talk of the march on the Sorbonne planned for the next day. There were broadsheets proclaiming revolution on sale at the door, factions with their own slogans, and he noticed English accents in the crowd. One student told him of a drama in the street earlier, when there appeared at the door one of the academic attendants from the Sorbonne – men in formal dress with chains round their necks who still announced the arrival of a professor for a lecture, like red-coated servants at the Élysée. This one had wandered unawares into the lions' den. There was a moment of alarm, but the crowd took pity on him. He was carted off to Le Basile on rue de Grenelle and stripped of his uniform, then plied with his favourite pastis. The uniform was burned on a pyre outside, and by the time he left in jeans and an old T-shirt he was making promises of fealty to the revolution. Flemyng was smiling more than he had for days, tieless with his shirt open, and drinking in the mad spirit of the day. It wouldn't last. Like the crowd, he didn't care.

At four, he rang Maria.

'We need to talk.'

She told him, for the first time, about the flat on rue de Nevers, a gift that he knew was a reward. They met there an hour later. Briefly, without a hint of deception, he told her Craven's story. 'He meant it for us all. We're together in this.'

'It makes sense of something I saw,' she told him. 'I wondered about it. When I met Kristof at the bar, he went to the men's room and left his book of poems on the table. A schoolbook. He'd been reading *Paradise Lost*, of all things. I opened it.'

'Of course.' Flemyng said.

'Naturally. I turned to the title page. I should have realized sooner what it meant.'

'What did you see?'

'The book was inscribed to "*Christopher*". He'd scored that out and written "*Kristof*".'

Flemyng thought of Craven's diary and 'C'. The jigsaw was almost complete. He realized why Kristof wanted sight of Craven's diary. Not because of danger from his own side, but because he feared – Quincy's questioning must have scared him – that his name might be known at the embassy, and in

London, which might be a prelude to disaster for him. If Craven had spread the word, he was on borrowed time.

And all the while, as they'd agreed the previous night, he was willing for them to see Quincy's list. A man sunk in confusion, and fear.

Flemyng had mistaken the source of the threat to Kristof. It wasn't from some grey figure in Berlin, but from the very thought of exposure.

'I'm going to see him,' he said. 'I'll leave a message for a meeting tomorrow morning. I'll make it clear – he gets out of Paris, or Edward Abbott gets his story. All of it. Freddy says Kristof's loyal to his family. He wouldn't be able to take it, and he knows that his people wouldn't forgive him. A lamb for the slaughter.

'And I'm afraid I'll tell him that if he tries to undermine any of us in the future, the same rule applies. Abbott will get his story.'

'And then you'll give him a hug?' Maria said.

'Maybe.'

He left in the same high spirits. With Craven away, he should go to the embassy, where Sandy would be complaining. He didn't mind.

Bolder was predictably agitated, although he wanted Flemyng to read the telegram he'd composed the previous evening with an account of the battle in the streets and his predictions for the coming weekend. He also showed him the message of congratulations he'd received from London in response, of which he was even prouder.

'Quite a stirring moment,' he said.

Flemyng took himself to his own room, and Janet delivered some telegrams for him to read.

He was lost to the world for a while.

At half past six – he noted the time precisely – Janet returned. Unhappy.

'I apologize, Will, that I have to disturb you with very bad news. I have had Dr O'Casey on the telephone. Freddy has been taken ill, I'm very sorry to say. He wants you to go imme-diately. I'll clear up for you.'

He raced to the corner for a taxi, and banged a shopfront in frustration at the empty rank. It was five minutes before he saw a green light moving down the hill, and he had the door open before the car had properly stopped. When he got to Craven's apartment, there was another resident of the building unlocking the front door and he pushed past and jumped to the lift.

O'Casey came to Craven's door, opening it quietly.

'This is bad, Will. I'm afraid he won't last. There has been a big episode. He's forbidden me to get him to hospital, or even to tell the ambassador. He knows that even if he gets through this one, it won't be long, and he's reconciled. That happens. He asked for you. I'll leave you alone. Call me if you're concerned. I'll wait outside the door.'

The bedroom wasn't dark. Craven wanted the lights on, and the curtains open to catch the evening sun. The window was raised a little, and they heard the sounds of sirens outside. Craven was in his red striped pyjamas, his hair combed back as if he was going out, and, although he didn't raise a hand when Flemyng came in, his face broke into a smile.

'I'm glad. You know something's happened.'

'Freddy. I'm so sorry.'

'Don't be. You'll be sad, of course, but don't feel bad for me. I've had my time and it's been good, from start to finish. I have loved my boys, you most of all. You do know that?'

'I do.'

The old man sighed. He closed his eyes. 'I'm glad I had the chance to tell you about our German friend who isn't,' he said, still smiling. 'And it seems that in a cack-handed way – typical when a man starts to doubt himself – he wanted to find you. Help him, Will. There's something else that you need to know – only you – about that list of names. You know I said that one of them rang a bell?'

'I do.'

Craven said, 'We're supposed to believe these are the names of sleepers, the traitors in the nest, waiting for their moment. Germans who we think are ours, but are really theirs. Correct? An East German operation that's rather cleverer than we've expected from them. You'll have realized the difficulty, however.'

'It could be the greatest deception of them all,' Flemyng said, 'that turns us inside out, looking for spies who aren't there.'

'A nightmare we've seen before,' said Craven, who bore the scars. 'That will be for others to judge, over time, but I have a particular problem for you. One name.'

Flemyng knew, before Craven said anything more, that the moment was a prelude. His life would be shaped, in some way he couldn't tell, by what Craven said next.

'The name,' Craven said quietly, 'is one that no one here will recognize, except me. Almost no one, I should say. The reason I remember her is that she was investigated before, very thoroughly and distressingly, under another name, because there was a whisper and nobody could be sure of the back-ground in Germany. But she came out as clean as a whistle. That's important for you to know.'

He looked at Flemyng in silence. 'You'll have to decide whether this list means the whole thing will have to be done again. It will be painful.'

Flemyng, his heartbeat quickening, asked why.

'I'm afraid you know her as Grizelda Bridger.'

Flemyng stared. He thought of his friend and rival, Bridger's pride, and everything he attached to his career. His love for Grizelda. Another vetting, more questions? The black spot.

Craven raised a hand. 'I can imagine how you feel.'

Flemyng, by habit, concealed most of his emotion, and said, 'I'll decide what to do, for the best.'

'I know.'

Flemyng felt Craven's eyes on him, even as his power ebbed away.

He had slipped down the pile of pillows, and Flemyng tucked them in to let him lie more naturally, helping to ease him on to his side.

'Dear boy. Do stay near.'

The effort had been too much. His eyes closed and Craven slept.

Flemyng sat still beside the bed for nearly an hour. O'Casey didn't disturb them. The clock in the next room struck nine. Flemyng went to the door, and spoke to the doctor. 'He's drifted away. I'm not going to leave. Can you sit with him for a while?'

'Surely. I'll come right out if you're needed.'

Flemyng took Craven's chair in the sitting room, for the first time. He was engulfed by sadness. Would he speak to the old man again? His near-euphoria from the afternoon had passed. Grizelda. He knew that if there had been any shadow, Bridger would not be in Paris. But even if she were cleared again, the fact would be known.

Bridger's rise would be over.

It compounded his sadness. Their history was difficult, but shouldn't be corrupted by this.

His mind wandered, and it fixed suddenly on the strange

question Quincy had asked Maria. Could she meet Craven's wife? He didn't have one, Flemyng had told Maria. Never had.

She had got the wrong man, that was all. If she had lived, she would have been on Bridger's trail. Was there a hidden reference, concealed in the notes Maria had found? Would he have to tell her?

Poor Pierce. He didn't deserve this.

Distracted, consumed by the guilt of an old rivalry, and agonized by Craven's decline, his mind raced until, exhausted, he slid into sleep.

He woke an hour later. O'Casey was shaking his shoulder. 'Will, please come.'

Craven's breathing was uneven and guttural. Flemyng came close and took his hand, leaning down to whisper, 'Freddy, it's me.'

His hand was squeezed. Craven said nothing.

Flemyng sat on the bed and held the hand, feeling a trembling that had almost gone. After a few minutes he brushed the hair back from where it had fallen on the old man's forehead, and kissed him on the brow. Another squeeze on his hand, softer this time.

O'Casey stood at the side of the room. He said nothing, and made no move to interfere.

Craven's breathing was lighter, and the roughness passed. Flemyng felt his hand losing its grip and slipping away.

Putting his head down, he heard the last breath.

Flemyng wept.

He smoothed his old friend's hair, ran his hand with a gentle touch across his face, remembered happy times once again, and felt the beat of his own heart. He stayed for a few minutes, holding his hand as it began to get cold.

As he got up, words came back to him from childhood, lines that he knew Freddy Craven had loved:

> Under the wide and starry sky,
> Dig the grave and let me lie:
> Glad did I live and gladly die,
> And I laid me down with a will.

> This be the verse you 'grave for me:

> *Here he lies where he long'd to be;*
> *Home is the sailor, home from sea,*
> *And the hunter home from the hill.*

THIRTY-SIX

In the chill of the early morning, Flemyng felt a bleakness in Paris he had never known. A hurricane might have passed along the Left Bank, leaving lifeless streets and ruination. The excitement that had moved him in previous days had ebbed away, and when he steered round the barricades at the end of his own street and saw smoke rising from the encampments near the Sorbonne, he found himself succumbing, for the first time in a month of exhilaration, to a feeling of creeping melancholy. The thrill was gone, the city's colours turned grey.

He was taking a walk soon after dawn, because he was crushed by the intimacy of his apartment and its memories. One of Craven's pipes was on the kitchen table. He hoped for escape in the streets. Only a day before, the need to plunge into events, and run with the crowd, had spurred him on. But on Friday morning, even as he saw signs of the battles to come, he felt removed from it all.

Freddy Craven was gone and his life changed.

By habit, he took refuge in home thoughts. He would talk to Mungo, because he knew his brother would need comfort, and first he transported himself to the landscape where he knew every rise and fall in the land, the sound of a river and the quiet of the woods. The dogs would soon be on the hill, and in his head he could hear the water in the burn splashing over the rocks that had been his stepping stones into the trees and away. Standing near a burned-out car on the Boul' Mich where a hundred kids had set up a pretend commune behind their barricades, he took himself to a different world, where nothing seemed to change and the seasons followed their settled patterns, predictable as the mechanism of the orrery at Altnabuie.

But as he walked, Flemyng shook himself, disturbed by his own mood.

Sadness couldn't save him. He had to see Kristof.

Putting the danger aside, he decided to walk to Pascal's bar. He could make use of the time. And as he walked out, eastwards along the *quai*, he prepared for the encounter that would decide how the crisis ended.

At the embassy, he knew, Bridger had taken charge. The mourning machinery was in motion, and, with Bolder drafting the station's cables, that part of the world that knew Freddy Craven was informed of his death, the shock of his friends and comrades, and assured that before too long, after his private burial in the West Country in the family plot on a hillside overlooking the sea, there would be a gathering of all who had known him and who owed him their loyalty. Bridger had summoned the entire embassy to a brief memorial that afternoon in the ambassador's residence, and there would be prayers in church on Sunday. All were expected to be there.

Flemyng wanted something else. Not far from Bastille he found a small church that was open, even as the city was still waking, because two old women were washing the steps before early mass and had pulled back the doors to get at their buckets. He didn't want a priest, only quiet, and took a seat alone in the side chapel, relieved that he was the only occupant of the building.

He closed his eyes and thought of the old man. A prayer came into his head, but he made no formal devotions. It was a small, dark place where some incense always hung on the air because there was never a breeze to take it away, and he felt light-headed. Softly, his face lit by a rack of flickering candles, he spoke to Freddy Craven. Made promises.

After a quarter of an hour, he was outside as two priests arrived for their morning duties. He avoided them, preferring to give no explanation, and hurried on.

He was at Pascal's bar before nine. The street was deserted, but inside a woman was wiping down the tables. He asked for Pascal, and she pointed him towards a café on the corner diagonally over the crossroads. There was little traffic so he walked straight over, and found him with a coffee and cognac beside him.

Little had to be said. Pascal recognized him, and he explained in a few words that it was an emergency.

With no sign of surprise, Kristof's friend went to the kiosk beside the bar and dropped some coins in the box. He came back to Flemyng and pointed across the street to his own café. One hour.

He spent it preparing himself for a conversation that had taken shape in his mind through the long night. Taking coffee at a table near the window, he refused the offer of a newspaper and took no part in the conversations that filled the café as the morning regulars came and went. The high emotions that kept him awake through the early hours had subsided, and sitting still and quiet at his table, scarcely changing position until he rose to leave, he was a man bent on business. No one disturbed him.

In Pascal's bar, their positions were reversed. It was Flemyng who sat inside and Kristof who had to pull aside the curtain to see the man who waited for him. He was dressed as Flemyng had first seen him, but with a fresh white shirt and his hair neatly combed, having clearly taken trouble to prepare after the summons. When he sat down, Flemyng noticed that the quick, darting eyes of the day before were focused again. He was under control.

'Why?' Kristof said, without any greeting.

'I can answer the question you asked me,' said Flemyng. 'I've read the diary – the diary of a dead man.'

If Kristof was shaken, he gave no sign.

'Craven?'

'Yes. Last night.'

'How?'

'Exactly what I expected you to ask,' Flemyng said. He paused. 'His heart.'

'You must be very sad. You have my sympathy.'

'Thank you,' Flemyng said. 'I believe you.'

'Men like him inspire great loyalty. I wish I had met him.'

They faced each other across the table, both sitting upright. Neither smiled, and each seemed to take strength from the other. There would be no more tears.

'I can help you,' said Flemyng. 'I'll tell you what I know.'

Kristof spoke calmly. 'About me?'

'Of course. Are you surprised?'

Kristof's expression didn't change. He was at rest.

'I know your history,' said Flemyng, 'and if you'll allow me I want to give you my account of what happened. I think you were scared, because of Quincy's intimacy with you and others in her visits here over many months. You thought she had worked out your secret, too, and that drove you to despair. Probably for the first time, you wondered if Craven knew, and others like me. You had to find out, and that's why you used my brother as a lever to force yourself into my life. Our families make us vulnerable as well as strong, don't they?

'Well, I can tell you that Freddy did know. And one other, too, whom you met here in Paris. What name he used when you met him as a businessman I don't know, but he is a friend of mine in Berlin.' He thought of patient Duncan Gilfeather, lifting his skirts for Kristof on Freddy Craven's orders. 'They were both aware of your story, as I am now. But I think it very unlikely that anyone else does. You're safe.'

Kristof had lowered his head. The morning sun was coming through the window, and where Flemyng had expected shock, perhaps the reappearance of fear, there was calm.

'They knew all along?'

'Yes.'

Flemyng, aware of his own effort in preparing for their conversation and the struggle with his emotions, wondered how much Kristof's control was costing him.

'Perhaps you are relieved,' he said.

There was no reply. Kristof's face gave no sign of his feelings. His eyes were still. Without a word, he waited for Flemyng to continue.

'I can't know how and when you decided to tell us about the hiding place in the cemetery, but here's what I think,' he said. 'You knew that Maria Cooney and I would find a list of names in the dead letter box, put there by Quincy, probably on the day she was killed, although it could have been earlier. Whoever killed her left the envelope untouched because he was ordered to. That instruction came, I think, from you. You arranged Quincy's death – or, at the very least, encouraged it – and at the same time you wanted us to see the names. That was puzzling to me, and still is. Whose side are you on?'

He paused. 'Christopher.'

Kristof's face seemed to have lost all its weariness. His defences fell away, and he looked at Flemyng with an innocence that moved him.

The question was repeated. 'Why did you want us to get that list?'

Kristof began quietly, his voice calm.

'I had learned enough about Quincy to know that she couldn't keep a secret for long, and she'd boasted to me about everyone she knew. She had helped my people – we knew she had been doing the same for the Americans – and so she learned things. That was her way. In time, she had worked out what our organization was putting in place in the west, our grand scheme, and she had worked out some names. It was typical of her to want to pass on the list – and to see my reaction. For her, there were no rules. I should tell you that I saw the names, in their hiding place, before I decided to leave them for you.'

Flemyng's response was a statement, not a question. 'Very soon after she died.'

'Yes, very soon.'

Flemyng didn't question him, and Kristof resumed. 'I was sure that some names would soon be doing the rounds, because she was trying to identify characters who would make her story come to life. She didn't mind that her researches would become the talk of the town in certain secret places, because her story would be all the bigger when it broke. The tension would rise among those in the know, she would time her revelation skilfully and the truth of it would be known by people like you. Her sensation would be all the greater. She told me, you know, that your Sandy Bolder had picked up the scent and was beginning to spin his own tales as a result.

'That terrified me, but it excited her.'

'And her excitement was a death sentence,' Flemyng said.

Kristof's expression didn't change. 'I realized the secret wasn't going to be a secret for long. So I pointed you towards it because I wanted to help you, Will. You.'

Aware of the power they had both employed to control their feelings, Flemyng replied with only one word. 'Why?'

'Because I think you are vulnerable in the same way as I am. You're supposed to be hard, trained to be tough, but your emotions run strong, and never far under the surface. They lead you on. I knew it from the first time we met, and it moves me.'

There was silence for a while. Kristof's hands were clasped, and his eyes were fixed on Flemyng. He was a man at peace, his energy spent.

Flemyng would always remember the moment of peacefulness they shared.

But he had to finish. It was a difficult day for him, he said. Freddy Craven wasn't yet in his grave. 'After everything you've said, what I'm going to say now may seem unkind, even cruel. But I think you will understand why it's necessary for us both.

'You will leave Paris, Kristof. How you do that is a matter for you, but you will forget your threats to my brother and me and leave this town. If you don't, I promise that your own story will be told to the world. It will be as good as if Grace Quincy had written it herself.'

The expression on Kristof's white face didn't change. He fingered his signet ring.

'I do feel for you,' Flemyng said. 'Believe me. But this isn't a moral question, and I'm not taking sides. It is simply practical. This chapter of our story is over.'

Kristof bowed his head to make his request. 'I will need time.'

'Yes, you can have some time,' Flemyng said. 'A little. But we will be watching you. When you leave, you will be safe. I promise.'

He added a question, feeling its cruelty as he did so. 'Tell me, are you happy?'

For the first time, Kristof managed a weak smile. 'What do you think?'

He asked if they could walk outside.

Flemyng rose without speaking, and they went through the curtain together, waving to Pascal at the bar as they pulled the door open and went into the street.

'I need some air,' Kristof said.

Flemyng said he understood. He had been walking all morning, and felt the better for it. 'My head is clear. You'll be fine.'

Kristof said they should walk together.

'Quincy did scare me,' he said quietly. 'She seemed to know everything. Whether or not she did, we'll never be sure. But I thought she might have my own story. And there were the names. I know some of them were correct. About others, I don't know. I am a small cog in a heavy machine. But you are right. This chapter is over.'

'And a new one opens,' Flemyng said.

He looked straight ahead as he spoke. 'You and I have reached a balance in the last half-hour, haven't we? You can continue with your chosen life, somewhere else. My brother and I with ours. We'll work on those names, of course. But none of us will be destroyed by this and our wounds will heal. Freddy would say that was a kind of victory. What good is blood?'

Kristof asked if he could be sure that his story would never be known.

'It's impossible to be sure, but I think so.' Flemyng let a few beats pass before he went on. 'And there is something I can do for you.'

Kristof stopped in the street and turned to him. He was ready.

Speaking quietly and quite slowly, Flemyng said. 'I can destroy Freddy's diary.'

'Will you?'

'Difficult, but I can. I think Freddy would approve, under certain circumstances.'

Turning away, Kristof began to walk again and Flemyng strode out to catch up.

'You know what those circumstances are, don't you?' he said from behind, unable to see Kristof's face.

'Yes.'

'That we meet again,' Flemyng said as he came alongside. 'On my terms.'

And it was done.

*

When they sat down to lunch together at Benoit, Maria told Abel and Flemyng of her dinner there with Quincy. 'It was happy. Can you believe that now? She was high. Had no idea of the danger she'd stoked up.'

They began with a toast to Freddy Craven, and Flemyng told them of the night when the old man washed his wound in Vienna. 'I thought I was dead. It was Freddy's operation that had gone wrong, so he tended me as if I were his son.'

'A dark day, but a time for thanks,' Maria said, and she spoke of Quincy and her own infatuation. Abel watched Flemyng. Had his brother known? Yes.

That wasn't a mistake, Flemyng told her, only a hazard of their lives. They were humans, still.

'Which means there's always going to be pain,' Abel said, 'even when things turn out right.'

They turned to Abel's London posting, and Flemyng said they should plan a visit home. They needed time in the hills. 'Mungo doesn't know about Freddy yet. I'll ring today. I think they became close in this business, and they were both grateful for that.'

'Imagine home this weekend,' Abel said. 'I want to walk in the woods, get to the high tops. Take the dogs on the long loop round the loch. I can see it in my mind. You?'

'I felt this morning, even here, that I could feel the air. Sometimes I think you can smell the water,' Flemyng said.

'You brothers are lucky,' said Maria.

'In some ways,' Flemyng said, and Abel laughed at him.

'The noncommittal Mr Flemyng.'

Abel went on, 'We'll work on this. The names and everything. We've been thrown together and we'll see it through. A long road. We know that. But we've begun.'

'It's weird that we have Quincy to thank for it,' Maria said.

'We lead the strangest lives,' said Abel.

After an hour, they parted. Flemyng put an arm round each of them, and promised that they would talk over the weekend. Abel would leave for London on Monday, and the following week Flemyng would take a break in Scotland where the three brothers could be together and follow each other on their favourite walks. 'After Freddy's funeral,' Flemyng said.

'I'll envy you from here,' Maria said.

Flemyng smiled. 'At least you'll have a revolution to write about.'

He walked a mile and a half along rue St-Honoré to the embassy. George at the gate spoke about Craven, and Flemyng noticed that someone had drawn down the blind on the window in his office. He caught his breath when he saw it.

Sandy Bolder was a man off balance. His efforts to turn himself out smartly for Bridger's memorial had failed. His hair was refusing to behave and he'd put on the wrong shoes. Flemyng gripped his hand, and for a moment both felt unable to speak. 'Sandy, I'm sorry for us both. We loved him.'

He saw tears in Bolder's eyes, and they said no more, turning away to their desks. Bolder sat down and put his head in his hands, the man who'd been half right by accident and would never be believed.

Bridger presided gracefully when they gathered together in the salon of the residence to remember Craven. He read from scripture, and gave a tribute which surprised everyone by its tasteful brevity. Asking Flemyng if he wanted to say anything, he repeated Stevenson's lines that had come to mind in the minutes after the old man's death. Bowing his head, he said no more and took his place between Janet and Bolder, looking through the high windows to the garden and the place where he liked to be alone.

'Freddy Craven made better people of us all,' he heard Bridger say. 'We shall remember him at St Michael's on Sunday, and I should say that anyone who wishes to attend his funeral should have a word with me. Despite the events around us in Paris, I shall be sympathetic to all requests.'

He caught Flemyng's eye, and a look of understanding passed between them.

When it was over, Flemyng went to his corner in the garden. He could see Bridger standing at his window, with a book in his hand. He thought of Quincy's list, the pursuit that he and Abel were bound to endure, his own commitments and the weight of the duty he feared. Grizelda.

Freddy Craven's game was over. Against the tide of sadness, Flemyng's life drew him on.

His old rival was still at the window when he left the garden and looked towards him, into the sun. Bridger raised an arm, almost in salute. As he closed the gate, Flemyng waved back and found himself, unbidden, putting a hand on his heart in a signal of fellow-feeling.

He crossed the courtyard and found that the street beyond was closed by a police blockade. He spoke to the gendarmes near the embassy gate. That night, one of them said, he might see the battle for Paris.

'Only the beginning,' said Flemyng, and turned for home.

After the Story

In the days after Freddy Craven's death, Paris erupted. Dozens of barricades went up on the Left Bank, and hundreds were arrested in a storm of tear gas and flying cobblestones that continued for many nights. The Sorbonne was occupied, then dozens of factories across the country, and two-thirds of the French workforce joined a general strike. But by the end of the month the Communist Party and its client unions had drawn back from the streets in exchange for government concessions on wages, having had enough of the student radicals. President de Gaulle announced elections for June, and won a dramatic political reprieve. Elsewhere, the turmoil of 1968 deepened. Robert F. Kennedy was assassinated in Los Angeles on 6 June, and a few weeks later the Democratic Convention in Chicago turned into a running fight between anti-war protestors and Mayor Daley's police. The Czech government failed to persuade Moscow of the case for reform, and on the night of 20 August more than half a million Soviet-led Warsaw Pact troops crossed the border to crush dissent. The Cold War, roughly halfway through its life, was in a notably frosty and brittle state.

The story of *Paris Spring* is fiction, but the background is real. BRIXMIS operated across the Berlin divide for more than fifty years from 1946, unknown to almost everyone in

Britain – and its personnel did have their own pub, The Somerset Arms. Likewise I have tried to describe faithfully the byways of Paris, especially its restaurants. Inside the British Embassy, however, I have taken liberties. The building has been reconfigured to suit Flemyng and his colleagues, and no one who knows the place will recognise it in these pages, let alone its imaginary inhabitants and their adventures.

I am grateful to friends who knew Paris in 1968 for their memories, and above all to my editor at Head of Zeus, Rosie de Courcy, for her golden insights and all the fun. Ellie, as ever, and Flora, Catherine and Andrew, have my love and thanks, and I am dedicating this story to everyone on the Today programme, past and present, who are such fine and lasting friends.